FIRED UP

G. P. Putnam's Sons

New York

FIRED UP

Jayne Ann Krentz

PUTNAM

G. P. PUTNAM'S SONS   •
Publishers Since 1838
Published by the Penguin Group
Penguin Group (USA) Inc., 375 Hudson Street, New York, New York 10014, USA • Penguin Group (Canada),
90 Eglinton Avenue East, Suite 700, Toronto, Ontario M4P 2Y3, Canada (a division of Pearson Penguin Canada Inc.) •
Penguin Books Ltd, 80 Strand, London WC2R 0RL, England • Penguin Ireland, 25 St Stephen's Green, Dublin 2,
Ireland (a division of Penguin Books Ltd) • Penguin Group (Australia), 250 Camberwell Road, Camberwell,
Victoria 3124, Australia (a division of Pearson Australia Group Pty Ltd) • Penguin Books India Pvt Ltd,
11 Community Centre, Panchsheel Park, New Delhi–110 017, India • Penguin Group (NZ), 67 Apollo Drive,
Rosedale, North Shore 0632, New Zealand (a division of Pearson New Zealand Ltd) • Penguin Books
(South Africa) (Pty) Ltd, 24 Sturdee Avenue, Rosebank, Johannesburg 2196, South Africa

Penguin Books Ltd, Registered Offices: 80 Strand, London WC2R 0RL, England

Library of Congress Cataloging-in-Publication Data
Krentz, Jayne Ann.
Fired up / Jayne Ann Krentz.
p.   cm.
ISBN 978-0-399-15596-3
I. Title.
PS3561.R44F53   2009   2009023796
813'.54—dc22

Printed in the United States of America
1   3   5   7   9   10   8   6   4   2

Book design by Meighan Cavanaugh

This is a work of fiction. Names, characters, places, and incidents either are the product
of the author's imagination or are used fictitiously, and any resemblance to actual persons,
living or dead, businesses, companies, events, or locales is entirely coincidental.

While the author has made every effort to provide accurate telephone numbers and Internet addresses
at the time of publication, neither the publisher nor the author assumes any responsibility for errors,
or for changes that occur after publication. Further, the publisher does not have any control
over and does not assume any responsibility for author or third-party websites or their content.

For my brother, Steve Castle:

with love and thanks for the

insider's tour of Vegas

THE DREAMLIGHT TRILOGY

Dear Reader:

The Arcane Society was founded on secrets. Few of those secrets are more dangerous than those kept by the descendants of the alchemist Nicholas Winters, fierce rival of Sylvester Jones.

The legend of the Burning Lamp goes back to the earliest days of the Society. Nicholas Winters and Sylvester Jones started out as friends and eventually became deadly adversaries. Each sought the same goal: a way to enhance psychic talents. Sylvester chose the path of chemistry and plunged into illicit experiments with strange herbs and plants. Ultimately he concocted the flawed formula that bedevils the Society to this day.

Nicholas took the engineering approach and forged the Burning Lamp, a device with unknown powers. Radiation from the lamp produced a twist in his DNA, creating a psychic genetic "curse" destined to be passed down through the males of his bloodline.

The Winters Curse strikes very rarely, but when it does the Arcane Society has good reason for grave concern. It is said that the Winters man who inherits Nicholas's genetically altered talent is destined to become a Cerberus—Arcane slang for an insane psychic who possesses multiple lethal abilities. Jones & Jones and the Governing Council are convinced that such human monsters must be hunted down and terminated as swiftly as possible.

There is only one hope for the men of the Burning Lamp. Each must find the artifact and a woman who can work the dreamlight energy that the device produces in order to reverse the changes brought on by the curse.

In the Dreamlight Trilogy you will meet the three men—past, present and future—of the Burning Lamp, all passionate descendants of Nicholas Winters. Each will discover some of the deadly secrets of the lamp. Each will encounter the woman with the power to shape his destiny.

And ultimately, far in the future, in a world called Harmony, one of them will unravel the lamp's final and most dangerous mystery, the secret of the Midnight Crystal.

I hope you will enjoy the trilogy.

Sincerely,
Jayne

I shall not long survive, but I will have my revenge, if not in this generation, then in some future time and place. For I am certain now that the three talents are locked into the blood and will descend down through my line.

Each talent comes at a great price. It is ever thus with power.

The first talent fills the mind with a rising tide of restlessness that cannot be assuaged by endless hours in the laboratory or soothed with strong drink or the milk of the poppy.

The second talent is accompanied by dark dreams and terrible visions.

The third talent is the most powerful and the most dangerous. If the key is not turned properly in the lock, this last psychical ability will prove lethal, bringing on first insanity and then death.

Grave risk attends the onset of the third and final power. Those of my line who would survive must find the Burning Lamp and a woman who can work dreamlight energy. Only she can turn the key in the lock that opens the door to the last talent. Only such a female can halt or reverse the transformation once it has begun.

But beware, women of power can prove treacherous. I know this now, to my great cost.

FROM THE JOURNAL OF NICHOLAS WINTERS, APRIL 17, 1694 . . .

It is done. My last and greatest creation, the Midnight Crystal, is finished. I have set it into the lamp together with the other crystals. It is a most astonishing stone. I have sealed great forces within it, but even I, who forged it, cannot begin to guess at all of its properties, nor do I know how its light can be unleashed. That discovery must be left to one of the heirs of my blood.

But of this much I am certain: The one who controls the light of the Midnight Crystal will be the agent of my revenge. For I have infused the stone with a psychical command stronger than any act of magic or sorcery. The radiation of the crystal will compel the man who wields its power to destroy the descendants of Sylvester Jones.

Vengeance will be mine.

PROLOGUE

Capitol Hill neighborhood, Seattle . . .

The two-block walk from the bus stop on Broadway to her apartment was a terrifying ordeal late at night. Reluctantly she left the small island of light cast by the streetlamp and started the treacherous journey into the darkness. At least it had stopped raining. She clamped her purse tightly to her side and clutched her keys the way she had been taught in the two-hour self-defense class the hospital had offered to its staff. The small jagged bits of metal protruded between her fingers like claws.

Should never have agreed to take the night shift, she thought. But the extra pay had been too tantalizing to resist. Six months from now she would have enough saved up to buy a used car. No more lonely late-night rides on the bus.

She was a block and a half from her apartment house when she heard the footsteps behind her. She thought her heart would stop. She fought her instincts and forced herself to turn around and look. A man emerged from a nearly empty parking lot. For a few seconds the streetlight gleamed on his shaved head. He had the bulky frame of a bodybuilder on steroids. She relaxed a little. She did not know him, but she knew where he was going.

The big man disappeared through the glass doors of the gym. The small neon sign in the window announced that it was open twenty-four hours a day. It was the only establishment on the street that was still illuminated. The bookstore, with its window full of occult books and Goth jewelry, the pawnshop, the tiny hair salon and the payday loan operation had been closed for hours.

The gym was not one of those upscale fitness clubs that catered to the spandex-and-yoga crowd; it was the kind of facility frequented by dedicated bodybuilders. The beefy men who came and went from the premises did not know it, but she sometimes thought of them as her guardian angels. If anything ever happened to her on the long walk home, her only hope was that someone inside the gym would hear her scream and come to help.

She was almost at the intersection when she caught the shift of shadows in a doorway across the street. A man waited there. Was he watching her? Something about the way he moved told her that he was not one of the men from the gym. He wasn't pumped up on steroids and weights. There was, instead, a lean, sleek, almost predatory air about him.

Her pulse, already beating much too quickly, started to pound as the fight-or-flight response kicked in. There was a terrible prickling on the nape of her neck. The urge to run was almost overwhelming, but she could hardly breathe now. In any event, she had no hope of outrunning a man. The only refuge was the gym, but the dark silhouette on the other side of the street stood between her and the entrance. Maybe she should scream. But what if her imagination had gotten the better of her? The man across the street did not seem to be paying any attention to her. He was intent on the entrance of the gym.

She froze, unable to make a decision. She watched the figure on the other side of the street the way a baby rabbit watches a snake.

She never heard the killer come out of the shadows behind her. A sweaty, masculine hand clamped across her mouth. A sharp blade pricked her throat. She heard a clatter of metal on the sidewalk and realized that she had just dropped her only weapon, the keys.

"Quiet or you die now," a hoarse voice muttered in her ear. "Be a shame if we didn't have time to play."

She was going to die, anyway, she thought. She had nothing to lose. She dropped her purse and tried to struggle but it was useless. The man had an arm around her throat. He dragged her into the alley, choking her. She reached up and managed to rake her fingernails across the back of his hand. She would not survive the night but she could damn well collect some of the bastard's DNA for the cops.

"I warned you, bitch. I'm really going to take my time with you. I want to hear you beg."

She could not breathe, and the hand across her mouth made it impossible to scream. To think that her fallback plan had always been to yell for help from the gym.

The alley was drenched in night, but there was another kind of darkness enveloping her. With luck she would suffocate from the pressure of his arm on her throat before he could use the knife, she thought. She'd worked in the trauma center at Harborview. She knew what knives could do.

A figure loomed at the entrance of the alley, silhouetted by the weak streetlight behind him. She knew it was the man she had seen in the doorway across the street. Two killers working as a team? She was so sunk into panic and despair that she wondered if she was hallucinating.

"Let her go," the newcomer said, coming down the alley. His voice promised death as clearly as the knife at her throat.

Her captor stopped. "Get out of here or I'll slit her throat. I swear I will."

"Too late." The stranger walked forward. He was not rushing in, but there was something lethal and relentless about his approach, a predator who knows the prey is trapped. "You're already dead."

She felt something then, something she could not explain. It was as if she was caught in the center of an electrical storm. Currents of energy flooded her senses.

"No," her captor shouted. "She's mine."

And then he was screaming, horror and shock mingling in a nerve-shattering shriek.

"Get away from me," he shouted.

Suddenly she was free-falling. She landed with a jolt on the damp pavement. The man with the knife reeled back and fetched up against the alley wall.

The unnerving energy evaporated as swiftly and mysteriously as it had appeared.

The killer came away from the wall as though he had been released from a cage.

"No," he hissed, madness and rage vibrating in the single word.

He lurched toward the other man. Light glinted on the knife he still clutched.

More energy shivered in a heavy wave through the alley.

The killer screamed again, a shrill, sharp screech that ended with stunning abruptness. He dropped the knife, clutched at his chest and dropped to the pavement.

The dark figure loomed over the killer for a moment. She saw him lean down and realized that he was checking for a pulse. She knew that he would not find one. She recognized death when she saw it.

The man straightened and turned toward her. Fear held her immobile. There was something wrong with his face. It was too dark to make out his features, but she thought she could see a smoldering energy in the dark spheres where his eyes should have been.

Another wave of panic slammed through her, bringing with it a fresh dose of adrenaline. She scrambled to her feet and fled toward the street, knowing, even as she ran, that it was hopeless. The creature with the burning eyes would cut her down as easily as he had the killer with the knife.

But the monster did not pursue her. A block away she finally stopped to catch her breath. When she looked back she saw nothing. The street was empty.

She had always hoped that if the worst happened on the way home she might get some help from the men in the gym. But in the end it was a demon that had saved her.

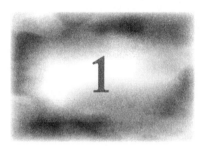

1

DREAMLIGHT GLOWED FAINTLY ON THE SMALL STATUE OF THE Egyptian queen. The prints were murky and thickly layered. A lot of people had handled the object over the decades, but none of the prints went back any farther than the late eighteen hundreds, Chloe Harper concluded. Certainly none dated from the Eighteenth Dynasty.

"I'm afraid it's a fake." She lowered her senses, turned away from the small statue and looked at Bernard Paddon. "A very fine fake, but a fake, nonetheless."

"Damn it, are you absolutely certain?" Paddon's bushy silver brows scrunched together. His face reddened in annoyance and disbelief. "I bought it from Crofton. He's always been reliable."

The Paddon collection of antiquities put a lot of big city museums to shame, but it was not open to the public. Paddon was a secretive, obsessive collector who hoarded his treasures in a vault like some cranky troll guarding his gold. He dealt almost exclusively in the notoriously gray world of the underground antiquities market, preferring to avoid the troublesome paperwork, customs requirements and other assorted legal authorizations required to buy and sell in the aboveground, more legitimate end of the trade.

He was, in fact, just the sort of client that Harper Investigations liked to cultivate, the kind that paid the bills. She did not relish having to tell him that his statue was a fake. On the other hand, the client she was representing in this deal would no doubt be suitably grateful.

Paddon had inherited a large number of the Egyptian, Roman and Greek artifacts in the vault from his father, a wealthy industrialist who had built the family fortune in a very different era. Bernard was now in his seventies. Sadly, while he had continued the family traditions of collecting, he had not done such a great job when it came to investing. The result was that these days he was reduced to selling items from his collection in order to finance new acquisitions. He had been counting on the sale of the statue to pay for some other relic he craved.

Chloe was very careful never to get involved with the actual financial end of the transactions. That was an excellent way to draw the attention not only of the police and Interpol but, in her case, the extremely irritating self-appointed psychic cops from Jones & Jones.

Her job, as she saw it, was to track down items of interest and then put buyers and sellers in touch with each other. She collected a fee for her service and then she got the heck out of Dodge, as Aunt Phyllis put it.

She glanced over her shoulder at the statue. "Nineteenth century, I'd say. Victorian era. It was a period of remarkably brilliant fakes."

"Stop calling it a fake," Paddon sputtered. "I know fakes when I see them."

"Don't feel bad, sir. A lot of major institutions like the British Museum and the Met, not to mention a host of serious collectors such as yourself, have been deceived by fakes and forgeries from that era."

"*Don't feel bad?* I paid a fortune for that statue. The provenance is pristine."

"I'm sure Crofton will refund your money. As you say, he has a very good reputation. He was no doubt taken in as well. It's safe to say that piece has been floating around undetected since the eighteen eighties." Actually she was sure of it. "But under the circumstances, I really can't advise my client to buy it."

Paddon's expression would have been better suited to a bulldog. "Just look at those exquisite hieroglyphs."

"Yes, they are very well done."

"Because they were done in the Eighteenth Dynasty," Paddon gritted. "I'm going to get a second opinion."

"Of course. If you'll excuse me, I'll be on my way." She picked up her black leather satchel. "No need to show me out."

She went briskly toward the door.

"Hold on, here." Paddon rushed after her. "Are you going to tell your client about this?"

"Well, he is paying me for my expert opinion."

"I can come up with any number of experts who will give him a different opinion, including Crofton."

"I'm sure you can." She did not doubt that. The little statue had passed for the real thing since it had been created. Along the way any number of experts had probably declared it to be an original.

"This is your way of negotiating for an additional fee from me, isn't it, Miss Harper?" Paddon snorted. "I have no problem with that. What number did you have in mind? If it's reasonable I'm sure we can come to some agreement."

"I'm sorry, Mr. Paddon. I don't work that way. That sort of arrangement would be very damaging to my professional reputation."

"You call yourself a professional? You're nothing but a two-bit private investigator who happens to dabble in the antiquities market. If I'd known that you were so unknowledgeable I would never have agreed to let you examine the piece. Furthermore, you can bet I'll never hire you to consult for me."

"I'm sorry you feel that way, of course, but maybe you should consider one thing."

"What's that?" he called after her.

She paused in the doorway and looked back at him. "If you ever did hire me you could rest assured that you would be getting an honest appraisal. You would know for certain that I could not be bought."

She did not wait for a response. She walked out of the gallery and went down the hall to the foyer of the large house. A woman in a housekeeper's uniform handed her the still-damp trench coat and floppy-brimmed hat.

Chloe put on the coat. The trench was a gift from her Aunt Phyllis. Phyllis had spent her working years in Hollywood. She claimed she knew how private investigators were supposed to dress because she'd known so many stars who played those kinds of roles. Chloe wasn't so sure about the style statement, but she liked the convenience of the numerous pockets in the coat.

Outside on the front steps she paused to pull the hat down low over her eyes. It was raining again, and although it was only a quarter to five, it was almost full dark. This was the Pacific Northwest, and it was early December. Darkness and rain came with the territory at this time of year. Some people considered it atmospheric. They didn't mind the short days because they knew that a kind of karmic balance would kick in come summer when there would be daylight until nearly ten o'clock at night.

Those who weren't into the yin-yang thing went out and bought special light boxes designed to treat the depressive condition known as SAD, seasonal affective disorder.

She was okay with darkness and rain. But maybe that was because of her talent for reading dreamlight. Dreams and darkness went together.

She went down the steps and crossed the vast, circular drive to where her small, nondescript car was parked. The dog sitting patiently in the passenger seat watched her intently as she came toward him. She knew that he had been fixated on the front door of the house, waiting for her to reappear since she had vanished inside forty minutes ago. The dog's name was Hector, and he had abandonment issues.

When she opened the car door he got excited, just as if she had been gone for a week. She rubbed his ears and let him lick her hand.

"Mr. Paddon is not a happy man, Hector." The greeting ritual finished, she put the satchel on the backseat and got behind the wheel. "I don't think we'll be seeing him as a client of Harper Investigations anytime soon."

Hector was not interested in clients. Satisfied that she was back, he resumed his customary position, riding shotgun in the passenger seat.

She fired up the engine. She had told Paddon the truth about the little Egyptian queen. It was a fake, and it had been floating around in the private market since the Victorian period. She was certain of that for three reasons, none of which she could explain to Paddon. The first was that her talent allowed her to date objects quite accurately. Reason number two was that she came from a long line of art and antiquities experts. She had been raised in the business.

Reason number three was also straightforward. She had recognized the workmanship and the telltale dreamlight the moment she saw the statue.

"You can't rat out your own several times great grandfather, Hector, even if he has been dead since the first quarter of the twentieth century. Family is family."

Norwood Harper had been a master. His work was on display in some of the finest museums in the Western world, albeit not under his own name. And now one of his most charmingly brilliant fakes was sitting in Paddon's private collection.

It wasn't the first time she had stumbled onto a Harper fake. Her extensive family tree boasted a number of branches that specialized in fakes, forgeries and assorted art frauds. Other limbs featured individuals with a remarkable talent for deception, illusion and sleight-of-hand. Her relatives all had what could only be described as a true talent for less-than-legal activities.

Her own paranormal ability had taken a different and far less marketable form. She had inherited the ability to read dreamlight from her Aunt Phyllis's side of the tree. There were few practical applications—although Phyllis had managed to make it pay very well—and one really huge downside. Because of that downside, the odds were overwhelming that she would never marry.

Sex wasn't the problem. But over the course of the past year or two she had begun to lose interest in it. Perhaps that was because she had finally accepted that she would never have a relationship that lasted longer than a few months. Somehow, that realization had removed what little pleasure was left in short-term affairs. In the wake of the fiasco with Fletcher Monroe a few months ago she had settled into celibacy with a sense of enormous relief.

"There is a kind of freedom in the celibate lifestyle," she explained to Hector.

Hector twitched his ears but otherwise showed no interest in the subject.

She left the street of elegant homes on Queen Anne Hill and drove back downtown through the rain, heading toward her office and apartment in Pioneer Square.

2

JACK WINTERS WAS TRACKING DARKLY IRIDESCENT DREAM-
light all over the hardwood floor of her office.

"Please sit down, Mr. Winters," Chloe said.

Clients came in an endless variety of guises, but you did not last long
in the investigation business unless you learned to distinguish between
two broad groups: safe and dangerous. Jack Winters was clearly in the
second category.

Hector got up to greet the newcomer. He usually gave clients a brief,
assessing once-over and then proceeded to ignore them. But he was treat-
ing Jack Winters with what looked like a canine version of polite respect.

In spite of the icy control and sense of determination that radiated
from Winters in an almost visible aura, he surprised her by taking a
moment to acknowledge her dog. Most clients lost interest in Hector
once they had been assured that he was not likely to bite. Hector was
not cute or fluffy. Then again, neither was Jack Winters. Maybe that
allowed for some male bonding.

Winters had been cool about Rose, her secretary, as well. The elaborate tattoos and piercings sometimes made clients nervous. Then again, she decided that it would probably take a lot more than some extensive body art and unusually placed jewelry to make Winters uneasy. Hand the man a flaming sword, and you would have a warrior-priest or maybe an avenging angel, she thought. It wasn't just the stern, ascetic features or the lean, hard body. It was the cold, *knowing* look in his green eyes. It was as if he sensed all your weaknesses and wouldn't hesitate to use them against you.

Satisfied, Hector retreated to his bed in the corner of the room and settled down. But he did not go back to sleep. Instead, he continued to watch Jack with an expression of rapt attention.

It occurred to her that, in her own, hopefully more subtle, way she was doing pretty much the same thing; watching Jack Winters closely. She was torn between fascination and profound wariness. The energy stirring in the room disturbed her in new and unsettling ways. She probably should be a lot more worried, she thought. Instead she was intrigued.

Winters ignored her invitation to sit. He walked across the hardwood floor to the windows overlooking First Avenue and the rain-drenched scene of Pioneer Square. Her senses still heightened, she took another quick look at his footprints. No question about it, Winters was a powerful talent.

On general principle, she was always deeply suspicious of strong talents. It was not just that high-level sensitives were rare and potentially dangerous. The more serious issue was that there was always the possibility that they were affiliated with the Arcane Society. Avoiding contact with Arcane was a Harper family motto.

Most of her regular clients came to her through referral. Someone who knew someone who needed her services arranged for an introduction. Jack had not been referred. Harper Investigations was not in the phone book. Her online presence was extremely discreet and so was her upstairs office. She rarely got walk-ins. Yet somehow Winters had discovered her. Intuition told her that it was not random chance that had brought him to her. Common sense dictated that she be wary.

"What can I do for you, Mr. Winters?" she heard herself say instead.

"I want to hire you to find an old family heirloom." Jack did not turn around. Instead, he concentrated on the view outside the window, as if the sight of the late-nineteenth-century brick and stone buildings in the city's oldest neighborhood was riveting. "I understand you're good at that kind of thing."

In the Northwest it was never smart to judge a man's financial status by his clothes because a lot of wealthy people, especially the new-money folks who had made their fortunes in high-tech businesses, bought their jackets, running shoes and pants from the same outdoor gear stores as everyone else. Nevertheless, there were always subtle clues and signs. She was sure that whatever Jack Winters did, he was very, very good at it and therefore successful.

"Yes, as a matter of fact, I am very good at finding things," she said. "What, exactly are you looking for, Mr. Winters?"

"A lamp."

She folded her hands together on top of the desk and thought about that for a moment. For some reason the name *Winters* and the word *lamp* in the same sentence rang a very distant bell, an *alarm* bell. But she could not put it together. She made a note to call her grandfather later. Harry Harper was the family historian.

"Perhaps you could describe this lamp, Mr. Winters," she said.

"It's old," he said. He finally turned around to look at her. "Late seventeenth century."

"I see. You're a collector, I assume?"

"No. But I do want this particular lamp. Like I said, it's a family heirloom."

"When did it go missing?"

"Thirty-six years ago."

"Stolen?"

"Possibly." He shrugged. "Or maybe just lost. All I know is that it disappeared during the course of a cross-country move the same year that I was born. Not the first time it's gone missing."

"I beg your pardon?"

His mouth kicked up at one corner, but there was no humor in the smile. "It has a habit of getting lost."

She frowned. "I don't understand."

"It's complicated."

"Can you tell me a little more about the lamp?"

"I've never seen it, but my parents told me that it isn't particularly attractive or even interesting. Not the kind of thing you put on display in the living room. It's about eighteen inches high and made of some kind of gold colored metal."

"Real gold?"

"No," Jack said. "Not real gold. It's not a real lamp, either. It was never meant to hold oil and a wick. I'm told that it looks more like a tall vase." He used both hands to illustrate.

"It's narrower at the bottom and flares out at the top. There's a ring of stones or crystals set in the rim."

"Why is it called a lamp?"

"Because, according to the legend, it can be made to give off powerful rays of light."

She pulled a pad of paper toward her across the desk, picked up a pen and started to make notes.

"When was it last seen?" she asked.

"My parents stored it in the basement of their Chicago home. After they moved to California, they didn't even notice that it was gone until

I got curious about it and started asking questions. That would have been when I was in my teens."

She tried to pay close attention to the description, but it was hard to ignore the shivery little thrills of awareness that were lifting the hair on the nape of her neck. She'd dated her share of men. Some would say more than her share. It wasn't her looks or body that drew them. She strongly suspected that she qualified as merely okay in both departments. There was a certain type, however, who was attracted to her because of her profession. That kind found it intriguing to date a lady PI; always wanted to know if she carried a gun and seemed disappointed when she said no.

Others responded unconsciously to her aura. She possessed a very high level of talent, and psi power could be seductive, especially to a man who was endowed with some degree of sensitivity of his own, even if he wasn't consciously aware of his own psychic nature.

And then there were always those like Fletcher Monroe who were initially ecstatic about the prospect of dating a woman who made no demands when it came to long-term commitment. To them she was a fantasy come true. At least for a while.

But although she liked men and she'd had some experience with the species, she could not recall the last time any man had aroused this fizzy sensation of sensual awareness and anticipation in her.

It was as if something inside her recognized Jack Winters in ways she could not explain. Maybe she was simply responding to his own very high level of talent, she thought. Or perhaps it was the darkly fascinating dreamlight she saw in his footprints. Whatever the case, she was fairly certain she'd caught a flash of sexual heat in his eyes when he'd come through the door. She could not be absolutely positive, however, because he'd concealed his reaction so quickly.

There is a certain kind of freedom in celibacy, she reminded herself.

"There is something else you should know about this case," Jack said.

"What is that?"

"It's critical that the lamp is found as soon as possible."

More tiny alarm bells went off.

"You just told me that it was lost thirty-six years ago," she said. "Why the rush to find it now?"

He raised his brows a little. "I'm the client, Miss Harper. That means I decide if the matter is urgent. If you're too busy to take the case, please tell me now and save us both some time."

She returned his smile, icicle for icicle. "You're bluffing. You're here because you need me, or, at least, you think you need me to get this job done."

"What makes you say that?"

"Let's review. You are a very successful man. You've got money. Enough to hire any of the best investigation firms in the city. I'm a one-person office and I am very, very low-profile. I work by referral only. Yet you found me. That means you had to come looking."

He nodded once, silently approving. "Okay, you sound like a competent investigator."

"Gosh, thanks. Now, let's clear up a few things before we go any farther."

"Such as?"

"Are you a cop of some kind, Mr. Winters? FBI? Interpol, maybe? If so, I want to see your identification now."

"Trust me, this isn't a police matter," Jack said. "You have my word on it."

She took another look at his footprints and decided she believed him. It wasn't that the dreamlight told her whether or not he was lying. What it indicated very strongly was that he was hiding secrets as dark as any in the Harper family.

"If this isn't about a crime and you're not here in an official capacity, why the rush to find a missing lamp?" she asked. "Is someone else after it?"

"Not as far as I know."

She tapped the tip of her pen on the desktop. "You're a dealer, aren't you? And you're under a deadline. Either you produce the lamp within a short period of time or you don't collect your fee."

"No." He walked to the desk and stood looking down at her. "I'm a businessman, Miss Harper. I'm not interested in the art and antiquities world. I run a venture capital firm. Winters Investments. I doubt that you've heard of it. I keep a very low profile, too."

She smiled, oddly pleased that her intuition had hit the nail on the head, even if it was in a rather indirect way.

"So you are an angel," she said.

His eyes tightened a little at the corners. "What are you talking about?"

"Isn't that what they call people who provide the start-up money for small companies and businesses? Angels?"

"I've been called a lot of things in my time but none of my clients or competitors has ever called me an angel. At least, not after they found out that I would be taking a seat on their board of directors and a controlling interest in their business."

"I see." She cleared her throat. "Moving right along, are you going to tell me how you found me?"

He studied her for a moment. She was almost positive she could feel currents of energy shifting in the atmosphere. Over on his bed Hector moved restlessly. Jack had cranked up his senses, she thought. Well, it wasn't as if she wasn't employing her own talent.

After a few seconds, Jack inclined his head again. This time she knew that he had decided to accept the terms of the deal.

"If I don't tell you how I came up with your name you won't take my case, will you?" he said.

"No, Mr. Winters. I have some rules here at Harper Investigations. I need to know how you found me."

He waited a beat, and then he smiled slightly. "I found you in a computer database," he said.

She froze, anxiety and a wholly irrational disappointment coiling deep inside her. She pulled on everything she had in the way of willpower to keep her expression calm and controlled.

"Oh, damn," she said. "I was afraid of that."

"Afraid of what?"

"You're from Jones & Jones, aren't you?" She shook her head, disgusted. "Really, I should have guessed. Well, if you think for one moment that you can blackmail me into helping you find your lamp, you can think again. I have done nothing wrong, and I refuse to allow anyone connected to that dipsquat investigation agency to try to manipulate me."

Something in his expression told her that she had managed to catch him off guard. She got the feeling that the accusation was the last thing he had expected. He recovered swiftly and even seemed to relax a little.

"Take it easy, Chloe," he said. He flattened his palms on the top of her desk, leaning in a little to emphasize his point. "I give you my word, I am not from J&J. Believe me, I've got an even better reason than you do for wanting to avoid drawing the agency's attention. The fact that we share a similar attitude toward that outfit is one of the reasons I'm here."

"That's not exactly the most reassuring thing you could have said. If you're not from J&J, how, exactly, did you find me?"

"I told you, in the agency's files."

She got to her feet and faced him across the desk. "Let's back up here for a moment. I'm not officially registered with Arcane. I've suspected for a long time that J&J probably had a file on my family, but I would have thought that only one of their agents could access it. How did you get into it?"

"The usual way." He straightened, taking his hands off the desk. "I hacked into it."

"Oh, great. So you're not only ducking J&J, you've invaded their files. And you think this information is going to encourage me to help you? I should throw you out of my office as fast as I can."

"If you do, there's a good chance you will be signing my death warrant."

She raised her eyes to the ceiling. "I'm really not in the mood for this kind of drama. Especially if it involves J&J. I've got enough excitement in my life, trust me."

"Here's the bottom line, Chloe Harper. If you don't help me there's a strong possibility that at some point in the next few weeks or months J&J will hire someone to take me out. The only thing that can change my future is finding that damned lamp."

She stared at him, appalled. "You're serious."

"Oh, yeah."

She drew a sharp breath. "Now you're going way too fast for me. Slow down. Why does the name Winters sound ever so faintly familiar?"

"You and your family have been dodging J&J for years. That means you probably know something about the Arcane Society."

"Unfortunately, yes."

"Does the name Nicholas Winters mean anything to you?" he asked softly.

"Good grief." She sank slowly back down onto her chair, stunned. "Are you saying you're related to that Winters? The alchemist who turned himself into a double-talent, went mad and tried to murder Sylvester Jones?"

"I'm Winters's direct descendant."

"Good grief," she repeated. She could not think of anything to add to that, so she shut up.

"And here's the really bad news," Jack said. "I'm the first man since Griffin Winters back in the late Victorian era to inherit the family curse."

She almost stopped breathing. "But it's all a myth," she whispered. "Heaven knows, Arcane thrives on myths and legends. But most of them involve Sylvester Jones and his descendants."

"And those that don't involve the Joneses usually involved the Winterses. Unfortunately, the legends about my family aren't nearly as entertaining as those that are based on the Joneses."

"Yes, well, that's probably because the Winterses' legend ended badly," she said without stopping to think. She winced when she heard her own words. "Sorry."

He gave her another thin, ice-and-lava smile. "No need to apologize. You're right. There have always been those who say that the Winters family tree is the dark side of Arcane."

"But the thing is, the stories are all myths," she insisted. "Don't tell me you really believe you're going to turn into some kind of psychic monster."

He just looked at her, not speaking.

"You *do* believe it," she said finally.

He remained silent.

She spread her hands. "But that's ridiculous. If you had some genetic abnormality that involved your para-senses it would have manifested itself by now. Talent of any kind, abnormal or otherwise, always shows up in the teens and early twenties. No offense, but you don't look like a teenager."

"I'm thirty-six. According to the stories I managed to turn up, that's the age Nicholas Winters was when he became a double-talent."

A chill fluttered through her. "You're not going to stand there and tell me that you actually believe that you are a monster, are you?"

"I don't know what I am, Chloe, or what I'm becoming. But I do know that historically J&J has a shoot, shovel and shut-up policy when it comes to dangerously unstable multi-talents."

"Oh, I really don't think—"

"Not much else you can do with a Cerberus."

"*Cerberus?*" Horrified, she stared at him. "For heaven's sake, you aren't some sort of mythical, three-headed dog guarding the gate of hell."

"Find my lamp, Miss Harper. I don't care what it costs. Name your price."

3

Scargill Cove, California

Fallon Jones looked out the window of his second-story office. There were no three-story offices in the small town, no buildings higher than his own, not even the tiny six-room inn at the far end of the street.

It was afternoon but the sky was leaden. Down below the cliffs the vast expanse of the Pacific Ocean was the color of steel. Another storm was moving in from the sea.

The tiny village clinging to the Northern California coast was a throwback to another era, with its craft and crystal shops, seaweed harvesting business and New Age bookstore. The terminally green, fiercely no-growth town council had long ago outlawed paper and plastic along with chain restaurants and condos. Not that any restaurant chains or condo developers had ever shown any interest in Scargill Cove. The community was, for all intents and purposes, lost in its own private time warp. It was the ideal setting for a psychic detective agency.

From his window he had an excellent view of the Sunshine Café. Earlier that morning he had watched Isabella open the small coffee shop at six-thirty. Right on time, as usual. She had arrived wearing her gleaming yellow raincoat. As usual. He had watched her turn over the Closed sign in the window as usual, and then, as usual, she had looked up at his office window and given him a cheery wave and a bright smile. He had lifted his hand in response. As usual.

The silent, distant acknowledgment of each other's presence had become a ritual for both of them. It was repeated every afternoon at five-thirty, when Isabella closed the café. He found himself looking forward to it every day. That was probably not a good sign.

She always seemed to know when he was there, at the window, watching.

Well, she probably *did* know, he thought, feeling like an idiot. He was certain that Isabella Valdez was a high-level sensitive, most likely an intuitive talent, although he wasn't sure whether or not she was aware of her psychic nature. He could feel her energy. It thrilled his senses in ways he could not explain.

She was definitely not Arcane. He had checked the files himself two weeks earlier when she had moved into town and taken the job at the Sunshine. When he'd found no record of any Isabella Valdez that matched her age and description in the Society's database, he had immediately expanded the background check, pulling in all the considerable resources at his disposal.

Nothing personal, he told himself, just a reasonable precaution. A powerful talent moves into the same small, undiscovered dot on the map where the headquarters of the West Coast branch of the Society's investigation agency just happens to be located? Yeah, sure. What were the odds?

His first thought was that she had to be a Nightshade operative. But he'd called in two of his best aura-talents, Grace and Luther Malone. They had flown in from Hawaii yesterday, landing in San Francisco. After they had picked up a car, they had driven up the coast to Scargill Cove.

From his window he had watched them park in front of his office and cross the street to the Sunshine Café, looking for all the world like a couple of tourists in search of a cup of coffee. Twenty minutes later they had climbed the single flight of stairs to his office.

"She's clean, Mr. Jones," Grace said. "There are no signs of the drug in her aura."

Grace always called him Mr. Jones. He liked that. So few of his agents showed him the sort of respect that one expected from an employee. Most had an attitude.

Technically speaking his agents were independent consultants who worked under contract to J&J. In addition to possessing psychic talents of one kind or another, they were smart, resourceful and capable of thinking for themselves in the field. The combination made for good, reliable investigators but, unfortunately, was usually coupled with the attitude problem.

Grace was different. She was unfailingly polite and respectful. More important, however, was her ability to detect indications of the effects of a certain dangerous drug that had the capability of greatly enhancing the psychic senses. Luther possessed the same talent. Their abilities had given J&J another weapon to use in their struggle with the shadowy organization known as Nightshade.

Nightshade was a threat not just to Arcane but to the whole country. Fallon and everyone else at the top of the Society knew that they were on their own in the underground struggle against a ruthless opponent. Regular law enforcement, the intelligence community and government officials had their hands full dealing with standard-issue bad actors like criminals and terrorists. No one wanted to hear about a bunch of psychic mobsters who had re-created an ancient alchemical formula that gave the users powerful paranormal talents. Hell, no one would even give credence to such a wild conspiracy theory.

"Okay, no signs of the drug in her aura," Fallon said, not wanting to let Grace and Luther know that he felt as if a mountain had just been lifted from his shoulders. "But it's possible Nightshade has started using operatives who aren't yet taking the formula."

Grace smiled. "Your paranoia is showing, sir."

"I don't like coincidences."

"Neither do I," Luther said. He went to stand at the window and looked down at the café. "But sometimes a waitress is just a waitress."

It struck Fallon that there was something weird about Luther. He still looked like the battered ex-cop that he was, right down to the bum leg and the cane. But there was a sense of positive energy around him that felt odd. The same kind of strange energy was coming off of Grace, too. What was up with this pair?

"I ran my own check of the genealogy files," Grace said. "But I didn't find anything. Evidently none of Miss Valdez's ancestors was ever affiliated with the Society."

"Wouldn't be the first time Nightshade hacked into our database and altered records," Fallon reminded her grimly.

She shook her head, very certain. "I think she's exactly what she appears to be: a woman with a strong talent who found herself alone in the world. I didn't turn up any immediate family or close relatives. Looks like she grew up outside Arcane, so there would have been no one to help her understand and accept the psychic side of her nature. I think she came here because she's lonely, Mr. Jones. She was looking for a place to call home. Trust me, I know the feeling."

Fallon contemplated that for a moment. "Valdez feels different all of her life, so she ends up here, where ninety-nine point nine percent of the town's population could be labeled misfits. Is that what you're saying?"

"Yes," Grace said. "That's what I'm saying."

Luther looked back over his shoulder. "Only ninety-nine point nine percent of the locals are misfits? Who's your token normal?"

Fallon frowned, mystified by the question.

"Me," he said.

Luther grinned. "Right. Well, now that we've assured you that the new coffee shop waitress is not a Nightshade operative sent here to spy on you, Grace and I are going to be on our way."

"What's the rush?" Fallon asked. He didn't get a lot of visitors. For the most part he didn't like visitors, at least not for long. Visitors were a distraction. High maintenance. But for some reason he was reluctant to see Luther and Grace leave.

"Figured as long as we had to come over here to the mainland on J&J business, we might as well visit a friend in Eclipse Bay before we fly home to the Islands," Luther said. "It's called padding the expense account."

"Who's the friend?" Fallon asked, ignoring the unsubtle dig.

Grace smiled. "Her name is Arizona Snow."

"Snow." Fallon searched his memory. "The name sounds familiar."

"She used to be my landlady," Grace explained.

"Something else." Fallon frowned, trying to remember where he had come across the name.

Luther gave him a knowing look. "She's a senior citizen, the town eccentric. She's harmless, but years ago she used to work for a classified government agency."

"Got it," Fallon snapped his fingers. "I came across the data in a file when you moved to Eclipse Bay, Grace. I remember checking into it. Snow was some kind of high-level talent at one time. Never registered with the Society, so there's no record of exactly what type of ability she had. Somewhere along the line she self-destructed. Went over the edge and got lost in her own crazy conspiracy theories. Harmless, but definitely a total whack job."

Grace and Luther exchanged looks. Fallon got the feeling he was missing something. But, then, that happened a lot when he was around other people.

Belatedly, the meaning of the glance that had passed between Grace and Luther hit him. He exhaled heavily.

"You think I've got a few things in common with Arizona Snow, don't you?" he asked. He suddenly felt inexpressibly weary. "You think that I'm a conspiracy nut, too."

"No, of course not," Grace said quickly. "It's just that your talent is so unusual. This thing you do, your ability to see connections between seemingly random bits of information, it's quite rare."

"No, it's not," Fallon said flatly. "People do it all the time. Check out the Internet if you want to see real conspiracy buffs."

"Here's the big difference between you and most of the other conspiracy-theory folks," Luther said. "Ninety-five percent of the time you're right."

"Actually, it's more like ninety-six point two percent," Fallon corrected absently. "It used to be higher, but I had to recalculate after the Hawaii case. Regardless, it leaves a small but very real margin for error. You two found that out the hard way."

"Well, you wouldn't be human if you didn't make a few mistakes," Grace said generously. "Have you given my suggestion any thought, Mr. Jones?"

"What suggestion?"

"I told you that you needed an assistant." Grace looked around the office. "You're getting buried in paperwork and computers here. You need someone to organize this place."

He surveyed the office. "I know where everything is."

"Maybe, but that doesn't mean that things are organized efficiently," Grace said. "We talked about this. The burden of commanding the fight against Nightshade falls mostly on your shoulders. You're the man in charge, but you have to face the fact that you can't do it all. You need someone who can take over the day-to-day administrative tasks so that you will be able to focus on more important priorities."

"She's right," Luther said. "Might help if you got more sleep, too. No offense, but you look like you've been hit by a truck. When was the last time you got a full night's rest?"

For some reason he felt the need to defend himself. "I don't need a lot of sleep," he muttered.

"Yes, you do," Grace said. "Hire an assistant, Mr. Jones. And soon."

"And on that note, we're out of here," Luther said. He smiled at Grace. "Ready, honey?"

"Yes." She glanced at her watch as she walked toward the door. "Oh, wow, look at the time. We definitely need to be on our way north."

Luther nodded at Fallon. "Later, Fallon."

"One thing before you leave," Fallon said. He looked at Grace. "None of my business, but are you okay?"

She blinked, startled. Then she laughed. "Never better, Mr. Jones. I'm pregnant. I'm surprised you noticed, though. I'm just a little over two months along."

Fallon felt himself redden. "Congratulations. Guess it's true what they say about the glow, huh?" He switched his attention to Luther. "But that doesn't explain why I'm picking up the same energy around you, Malone."

Grace smiled. "We're happy, Mr. Jones. You should try it some-time."

She went out onto the landing. Luther followed her, closing the door behind him. A few minutes later Fallon watched them drive away, and he was alone again.

He used to like being alone. He needed to be alone. Most of the time.

He pulled his thoughts back to the present and contemplated the cheery light of the Sunshine Café. He'd called in Grace and Luther to give Isabella Valdez their seal of approval because for some bizarre reason he did not trust his own judgment. The uncertainty was not like him. He was usually confident in his own powers of logic and observation.

Grace and Luther might have cleared Isabella, but his own intuition was warning him that there were mysteries swirling around her.

After a while he went back to his desk, sat down and took another look at the newspaper article displayed on the computer. He routinely scanned the online editions of nearly two dozen West Coast dailies every morning, hoping for subtle indications of Nightshade activity. The organization was sophisticated and operated under deep cover. It did not engage in the kind of overt criminal activity that would be likely to draw the attention of the authorities.

But for some reason it was a routine crime story that had caught his attention recently. The piece had first appeared several days ago, but every morning he reread it. Something in the report sent tiny currents of awareness whispering through him. No matter how often he read it, though, he could not figure out what it was that triggered his senses.

SUSPECT IN KILLINGS FOUND DEAD.
LAST VICTIM SURVIVES ATTACK.

Seattle: A man identified as Aaron Paul Hanney, believed to have been responsible for the rape and murder of at least two women, was found dead in an alley in the Capitol Hill neighborhood last night. A third woman, Sharon Billings, told police that she escaped Hanney thanks to the intervention of a passerby who confronted her attacker. Hanney collapsed and died at the scene. An autopsy has been ordered, but authorities said the cause of death appears to have been a heart attack.

Miss Billings gave a statement to the police. In it she said that she was unable to identify the man who came to her rescue due to the fact that the lighting was so poor.

Authorities are asking the man who went to the aid of Sharon Billings to contact the police immediately.

There was something important here, Fallon thought. But he did not have time to pursue it this afternoon. He closed the heavily encrypted laptop, rose, grabbed a leather jacket off the coatrack, and left the office.

He kept plenty of high-test coffee on hand. It was his drug of choice these days. But lately he'd gotten into the habit of going across the street to drink a couple of cups of coffee at the Sunshine while he made notes and organized his thoughts.

Outside on Scargill's twisty little main street the air was chill and damp. He went toward the Sunshine, drawn by the aura of warmth and light.

Like a stupid moth to a flame, he thought.

4

THIS WAS NOT GOING WELL, JACK MUSED. CHLOE HARPER HAD concluded that he was delusional. He could see it in her eyes. He'd been called a variety of names, including ruthless, demanding and driven—Shannon had come up with all three descriptors just before she filed for divorce—but he was pretty sure that until now no one had considered him full-on crazy. Of course, until today he hadn't told anyone that he was becoming a psychic monster, either.

Shouldn't have tried to explain that I was Old Nick's descendant. Why had he done that? He hadn't intended to mention his ancestral connection to the lamp. That had been uncharacteristically stupid.

Shouldn't have told her to name her price, either. That had been a serious mistake. She might well be the shady operator that the J&J files indicated but simple, straightforward greed was not her chief weakness. Her vulnerable spot lay in another direction altogether. He knew that for certain, because his talent had picked up the vibes two minutes after walking into her office.

Chloe Harper was a natural-born rescuer. She probably took on all sorts of deadbeat clients who never paid their bills. She was the type who fell for a good sob story. The tattooed receptionist had the old-beyond-her-years eyes of a young woman who had spent a lot of time living on the streets. The rangy mongrel sprawled in the corner had probably come from a shelter or the nearest alley.

The rescuer thing wasn't what he had expected, but he could work with it. He felt a small twinge of guilt because he was preparing to manipulate her, but he knew he'd get over it. Besides, it wasn't like he was here under false pretenses. He really did need rescuing. All he had to do was convince her of the truth, and he would regain control of the situation. He'd have her in the palm of his hand.

"I've got nowhere else to turn," he said quietly. "You're my only hope."

"Really?"

Looking spectacularly unconvinced, she got up and walked around to the front of her desk. A trickle of unease sparked across his senses. Her change of position in the room had been very casual, maybe a little too smooth. He wondered if she was getting ready to sic the dog on him while she made a run for the door. Maybe he was scaring her. Not that she looked frightened, he thought. If anything, she appeared interested, maybe curious. Intrigued.

Interested, curious and *intrigued* didn't begin to describe his reaction to her. Until he had walked into her office all he had known about her was what he'd lifted from the J&J files. Her entire family had an extensive and wide-ranging history with Arcane, very little of it reputable. He'd figured that was a plus for him. According to the files, she was ideal for his purposes, a strong dreamlight reader who had connections in the gray world of the underground collectors' market. And she lived in Seattle. Talk about convenient. The other dreamlight talents he'd located on the West Coast were down in California.

Chloe was perfect.

What he hadn't anticipated was the heat lightning of sexual aware-ness that had crackled through him when he saw her sitting there, prim and composed, behind her desk. It was as if some elemental force deep inside him was stirring. That was not good. What with the blackouts, the nightmares, the hallucinations and the very real possibility that he might have to go on the run for the rest of his weird life, he had enough to deal with. He definitely should not be thinking about sleeping with the private investigator he was trying to hire.

He sure as hell shouldn't be wasting time trying to figure out what it was that attracted him to her, either. On the surface she looked like a stern, uptight school mistress. Not his type at all. Sharp, insightful intelligence animated vivid blue-green eyes and a face that otherwise would not have stood out in a crowd. Her sunset red hair was pulled back into a tight twist at the nape of her neck.

She was dressed in a businesslike black pantsuit with a white silk shell and a pair of black, high-heeled boots. Her jewelry was limited to a couple of small gold studs in her ears and a gold wristwatch with a black leather band. He estimated her to be in her early thirties, but there was no sign of a wedding band.

What had kicked him in the gut when he came through the door was the aura of energy about her. It translated directly into power, and power was always compelling, especially when it came in an unex-pected package like Chloe Harper. He realized then that if he had sim-ply passed her on the street, not knowing who she was, he would have looked twice. Make that three times. Turned around maybe. Followed her? Tried to introduce himself?

Oh, shit. This was not good. He did not need this kind of distrac-tion. Not now. He should be concentrating on staying alive. There were priorities here.

Chloe lounged against the front edge of her desk, crossed one booted foot over the other and reached back very casually to brace her hands on the desktop behind her.

"About the old Winters legend," she began.

She stiffened abruptly, gasped and snatched her hands off the desktop. Eyes widening a little, she turned to look at the place on the desk where one of his palms had been resting a moment ago.

Acting like she had just touched a red-hot stove, he thought. What was going on?

"Are you okay?" he asked.

"Yes, fine." She sounded a little breathless. She slanted him a long, impossible-to-read look. "Very well, Mr. Winters," she said briskly. "Tell me your story. But without the drama if you don't mind."

"Sure." He glanced at the desktop. "But would you mind telling me what gave you that shock just now?"

She frowned. "I'm a dreamlight reader."

"I know. It's in the J&J files. Your talent is one of the reasons I want to hire you. According to the old legends, it takes a woman who can read dreamlight to find the lamp and work it. Something about your kind of talent having an affinity for dream psi."

"And just what do the agency's files say about me and my talent?"

He shrugged. "According to what I dug up, the analysts estimate you to be a Level Seven or Eight."

Her mouth twisted in a derisive little smile. "If I were you, Mr. Winters, I would not rely too heavily on the information in Arcane's files. Not when it comes to me and my family."

A chill went through him. "*Are* you a dreamlight reader?"

"Yes. But the talent is rare and not well understood, especially at the higher end of the scale. Arcane hasn't had an opportunity to do much research on people like me. For obvious reasons I've never volunteered to be tested."

"The Society has a few other dreamlight readers registered. I counted at least four on staff at various Arcane museums."

"Yes, I know." She gave him a cool, politely smug look. "But none of those four can see more than a limited portion of the ultralight spectrum from which dream psi emanates. I'm sure they do well enough when it comes to detecting fake artifacts and such. But I doubt if any of them can read the kind of details in dreamlight prints that I can read. It's that ability that makes me a successful investigator, Mr. Winters."

He smiled, amused by her air of confidence. "You're good, is that what you're telling me?"

"I'm very good. Not only can I see a wide range of dreamprints, but I also can tell you a great deal about the individual who left the prints. To quote an old saying, *Ye shall know them by their dreams.*"

"Who said that?"

"My aunt Phyllis."

"Is that right? So tell me, how does the ability to read dreamlight make you a good investigator?"

She raised one shoulder in a dainty shrug. "Dreams create an energy field that is part of a person's aura, but the wavelengths can only be seen by someone with my kind of talent. My intuition is linked to my ability. It interprets dreamlight in a very precise way. Intuition is what makes a good investigator."

"How strong are you?" he asked.

"Everyone in my family thinks I'm probably off the charts."

"How does this talent of yours work?"

She glanced down at the desk and drew a fingertip across the spot where his hand had been. This time she caught her breath a little, but she did not flinch.

"You know as well as I do that every living thing emits some psi," she said. "People, even those at the bottom of the Jones Scale, the ones who think they have no talent at all, give off a considerable amount of energy even when they are in a calm state of mind."

"Auras," he said, a little impatient with the lecture.

"Yes. Strong aura-talents can read the energy emitted during the waking state. But humans also emit a lot of energy in the dreamstate. Even if we aren't aware that we are dreaming and even if we forget our dreams the energy is nevertheless produced. We leave traces of it wherever we go and on whatever we touch."

"And you can perceive that energy?"

"I see it in the form of psi prints, sort of like fingerprints and handprints. They give off various hues of ultralight."

He looked at the place on the desk where he had flattened his hand earlier. "Learn anything interesting about me?"

"Yes, Mr. Winters, I did." She took her fingertip off the desk and regarded him with bright curiosity. "Who or what did you kill recently?"

5

IF SHE HAD NOT BEEN WATCHING HIM CLOSELY, SHE WOULD never have noticed the small indications that told her just how much she had managed to stun him. The physical signs were minimal: a faint hardening of his jaw and some tightening around the mouth. For a second or two she could have sworn that his eyes heated up a little, and not with sexual interest this time. It seemed to her they actually became a darker, hotter shade of green, as if he was running a fever. She could have sworn she felt a soul-chilling whisper of energy at that moment. It raised the hair on the nape of her neck.

Hector whined softly. That made it official, she thought. They were both a little unnerved. Not frightened, not yet, at any rate, just tense and aware. Cautious, the way any sensible person and dog ought to be when they found themselves in the same room with a large beast of prey. Together she and Hector watched Jack.

The strange energy dissipated. Jack's eyes were no longer feverish.

"What are you talking about?" he asked. His tone implied he had begun to suspect that he was conversing with someone who was out of the asylum on a day pass.

She braced herself for the jolt she knew was coming and brushed her fingertips across the desktop again. Hot, acid-hued ultralight splashed through her senses, the colors of violence. But there were other hues glowing fierce and bright, as well. And it was those shades of light and dark that reassured her. Jack could be scary, she knew, but he was in full control.

"You confronted something monstrous," she said, working her way through it. "And you destroyed it." She hesitated, processing a little more light. "I think you were protecting someone else. Is he or she okay?"

Jack did not move. "You're making this up."

"The remnants of the violence are still simmering inside you. That kind of energy takes a while to cool down. It never entirely dissipates. It just recedes into the dream wavelengths. Ten, twenty, fifty years from now someone with my kind of talent will be able to pick up your prints in this office. And you'll still dream about whatever happened from time to time."

"If you really believe what you're saying, I'm surprised you aren't running from this room, yelling for the cops."

"I'm not running because I know that, whatever occurred, you were trying to defend someone else. What happened? Were you and your date attacked?"

"No."

"You fought him off, didn't you? And you killed him." She touched the desktop again and watched the light show with her other senses, picking up more nuances. "You killed him with your *talent*."

"I'm a strat," he said without inflection.

She frowned. "Being a strat would make you very good at plotting someone's death, if that was your goal. But you couldn't actually kill with your kind of talent. At least, I've never heard of any strat-sensitive who could do that."

Another couple of heartbeats passed. Then, to her surprise, Jack nodded once, as though he had made a decision.

"I did mention the Winters family curse," he said. "I am a strat. A strong one. It was my talent that helped me find you. But thanks to Nicholas Winters and his damned alchemical experiments with dream-light radiation, I'm becoming something else as well."

She frowned. "Everyone knows that people can't develop two equally powerful talents, at least not at the higher ranges. Something about the human mind's inability to handle so much psi stimulation. It's hard enough to control a single very high level talent."

"Trust me; I've done the research on this. There have been a few cases of two strong talents occurring naturally in a single individual, but they show up together at an early age and invariably the result is insanity. In the handful of cases that I was able to find in J&J's files the victims were all dead by their late teens or mid-twenties."

"No offense, but I'm guessing you are not in your twenties."

"I'm thirty-six."

"And you're telling me that this new talent of yours just started showing up?"

"The symptoms that something was going on started about a month ago."

"What kind of symptoms?"

"Hallucinations. Nightmares." He started to pace the office. "Serious nightmares. The kind that leave me shaking in a cold sweat. But they were starting to dissipate, or at least I was telling myself that they were getting less intense, less frequent. But then something else happened."

"Stop." She held up a hand, palm out. "Tell me about the hallucinations and the nightmares first."

He shrugged. "Not much to tell. The nightmares were bad but nothing I couldn't handle. It was the hallucinations that really worried me. They can hit at any time. I'll be walking down the street or sitting in a bar, and suddenly I'll see things that aren't there."

"Things you *know* aren't there?" she asked.

"Right. Images in mirrors. Scenes from the nightmares sometimes."

"But you're always aware that you are hallucinating?" she clarified. "You don't mistake those images and scenes for reality?"

He frowned. "No. But the fact that I know I'm seeing things doesn't make it any better, believe me."

"Maybe not, but it's an important detail. Okay, go on."

"Like I said, I had convinced myself that the visions and the dreams were starting to become less intense or, at least less frequent. But then I had the first blackout. It lasted a full twenty-four hours, although I'll admit that my memory is a little fuzzy on both sides of that time frame."

She folded her arms, thinking. "Sounds like some sort of short-term amnesia. There is a technical name for it: transient global amnesia. It's rare, but it's well documented."

He stopped and turned back to look at her. "All I know is that about a week ago I lost about twenty-four hours of my life. I have no idea where I went or what I did during that time."

"What's your last memory before the episode?"

"I was walking home after having a couple of beers with a friend. I blanked out at First and Blanchard, not far from my condo."

"And where were you when you came out of it?"

"In my condo." He walked back to the window and stood looking out at the gray skies. "I was in a raging fever. Thought I had the flu."

She relaxed a little. "If you were ill, that explains a lot. A high fever can play all sorts of tricks. Among other things, it can trigger hallucinations and nightmares."

"No." He shook his head once. "I was somewhere else during that twenty-four-hour period but I don't know where."

"What makes you so sure of that?"

He looked back at her. "I *know* it. What's more, I've had three more blackouts since then. All at night. The first two times I went to bed as usual. When I woke up I was back in bed, but I was fully dressed. My clothes were wet from the rain, and my shoes had fresh dirt on them."

"Sleepwalking. It's not that uncommon."

"The last time I came to after one of the episodes, I was standing in an alley on Capitol Hill," he said evenly. "There was a dead man at my feet and a woman was running for her life." He paused a beat to let the meaning sink in. "Her name is Susan Billings. The dead man's name was Aaron Paul Hanney."

A strange sensation twisted through her, as if she were looking into a very, very deep well. "The guy they think killed those two women? The one they found dead in . . . Oh, geez." She took a deep breath in an attempt to settle her rattled senses. "The one they found dead of a heart attack in an alley on Capitol Hill."

"Evidently I went out for a late-night walk and killed a man."

She frowned. "He was going to murder that nurse."

"I'm not saying I have a problem with the fact that he's dead. The problem is that I don't know what the hell I was doing in that alley in the first place. The problem is that I killed him with my talent, my new, *second* talent."

"What makes you think that you killed him? The papers said he died of a heart attack. Maybe you just happened on the scene."

"Trust me," he said. "I killed him. Without a trace."

"But how? You're a strat."

"I'm not absolutely sure." He rubbed the back of his neck in a weary gesture. "But I think I scared him to death. Literally. I think that is my new talent."

She went back behind her desk and more or less collapsed into her chair. She said nothing for a moment, trying to wrap her brain around what he had just told her. He watched her intently.

"You think I'm crazy," he said at last.

"No." She drummed her fingers on the desk blotter. "I know what crazy looks like because it shows up very clearly in dream psi. Whatever else you are, Mr. Winters, you are not crazy."

Some of the hard tension in him eased a little. "I guess that's a start."

"I think," she said slowly, "that you had better tell me a little more about what you call the family curse."

"The short version is that Nicholas Winters's DNA evidently got fried the first time he used what he called his Burning Lamp. The genetic change was locked into the male bloodline of my family. The mutation doesn't show up very often. According to family legend and Arcane rumors, it has only appeared one other time. That was in the late eighteen hundreds."

"What, exactly, happens to those who get this so-called curse?"

"I don't know." He gave her a chilling smile. "No one does because there's just not enough hard information to go on. But the theory is that I'll become a psycho and start trying to murder anyone with the last name of Jones along with anyone else who gets in my way."

She exhaled slowly. "I see. Is that what happened to your ancestor? The one who lived in the eighteen hundreds?"

"No. Evidently Griffin Winters managed to find the Burning Lamp and a woman who could work it. Family legend holds that Adelaide Pyne was able to reverse the process. She kept Griffin Winters from becoming a triple-talent. The Arcane records agree with that version of history."

"*Hmm.*"

"I have developed a second talent. As far as J&J is concerned, I've already become a Cerberus."

"Cerberus had three heads, not two," she said absently.

"Unfortunately, the distinction isn't going to matter much to J&J. The agency will hunt me down and take me out."

"You're sure of that?"

He smiled a very cold smile. "If I were Fallon Jones, it's what I'd do."

He was telling the truth, she realized. In Fallon Jones's shoes, he would do what he thought had to be done.

She exhaled deeply while she pondered that.

"All right, assuming that you actually are turning into a multi-talent—and for the record, I am not convinced that is what is happening—do you really think the lamp can help you?"

"It's a long shot but it's all I've got," he said simply. "Will you take my case?"

She had made her decision the moment he walked into her office. But there was no need to tell him that.

"Yes," she said.

"Thank you." He sounded like he meant it.

She cleared her throat. "There are a couple of things we need to go over. Have you considered the possibility that the Winters lamp has been destroyed?"

The cold fire leaped in his eyes and just as quickly faded. "It would take a hell of a lot to do that. According to the legend, Old Nick forged the metal and the crystals of what he called his Burning Lamp using his own alchemical secrets. Even Sylvester Jones admitted that when it came to furnace work, Nicholas Winters had no equal."

"Few things are indestructible. It could have wound up in an auto-wrecking yard."

"I'm not sure that even a car compactor could destroy an object created by Old Nick. In any event, the legend says that the lamp reeks of energy. You know how it is with paranormal artifacts. They tend to survive."

"That's true," she admitted. "People, even folks with no real talent, are usually fascinated by them. Para-energy is always intriguing to the senses, whether you're consciously aware of it or not." She reached for a pad of paper.

"What else?" he asked.

"*Hmm?*" She did not look up from the notes she was making.

"You said there were a couple of things you wanted to talk about."

"Oh, right." She glanced again at the glowing palm print on her desk. "What kind of medication are you taking?"

He did not respond immediately. She put the pen down and waited.

"What makes you think I'm taking medication?" he asked finally.

"I can see the effects in your dream psi. Whatever it is, it's heavy-duty stuff, and it's disturbing the energy at that end of the spectrum." She paused delicately. "Are you by any chance taking some kind of sleeping medication?"

His ascetic features hardened. "I started using the meds after I woke up in that alley. Got them from my doctor. I told him I was having some problems sleeping. They seem to work. They knock me out. I haven't had any sleepwalking episodes since I began taking them."

She clicked her tongue against her teeth, making a tut-tutting sound.

"You must realize that any kind of strong psychotropic medication can be problematic for a strong talent like you."

"It's not like I had a lot of choice, Chloe."

"The meds may knock you out, as you say, but it's obvious that you are not sleeping properly. You aren't getting the deep rest that you need and that your psychic senses require. The result is that you're walking around on the verge of exhaustion."

Cold amusement flickered in his expression. "Do I look like I'm about to fall asleep?"

"No, but that's because you're using a low level of psi to overcome the effects of sleep deprivation. That trick will work for a while, but eventually it's all going to catch up with you. Sooner or later you're going to crash, and when you do, you'll crash hard."

"I'll worry about getting some sleep after you find my lamp."

She sighed. "Why is it that no one ever takes my good advice when I have so much of it to give? That's why I became a private investigator instead of a dream therapist, you know."

"Yeah?"

"When I was younger I planned to get a degree in psychology and go into dream therapy work. But I found out soon enough that it would be terribly frustrating. Oh, sure, people are willing to pay for good advice, but they won't follow it."

"I hope you're a better PI than you are a therapist."

That hurt, but she refused to let it show. She straightened a little and picked up the pen again. "I told you, I'm good at what I do. Give me your contact information. I've got another case that I'll be winding up tonight, but I'll start the search for your lamp immediately. I'll be in touch within a couple of days."

"You sound very confident."

"Are you kidding?" She gave what she hoped was a ladylike sniff. "A paranormal artifact created by the alchemist Nicholas Winters? If I can't locate it within forty-eight hours or find out what happened to it, I'll go back to school and get that degree in psychology."

6

AT SEVEN O'CLOCK THAT EVENING ROSE STALKED INTO THE
office, a pizza box in her hands. Raindrops glittered like ebony diamonds on her long, black raincoat. Rose always stalked rather than
walked. Chloe thought it probably had something to do with the
two-inch platform soles of the steel-buckled, black leather boots
she wore.

"Dinner time," Rose declared. "You've been at that computer or on
the phone ever since Mr. Winters left. All you've had is a few cups of
tea. Got to keep up your energy, boss."

"Thanks." Chloe studied the e-mail that had just arrived in her in-
box. "I am feeling a little hungry, now that I think about it."

Hector trotted across the room to greet Rose. He sat down directly
in front of her, blocking her path, and gazed at the pizza box with an
expression that, in a human, would have indicated that the carton contained a winning lottery ticket.

"Don't worry—there's enough for three," Rose told him. She set the box on Chloe's desk and took off her raincoat. "How's the investigation going?"

"Let's just say it's been interesting." Chloe swiveled around in her chair. "And getting more interesting by the minute."

Rose hung up the raincoat and sat down in the client chair. "Find the lamp yet?"

"I think so. Got a solid lead on it hours ago from Aunt Beatrice."

"Your relative who runs that antiques shop in Los Angeles? The one that specializes in old movie star memorabilia?"

"Right."

Beatrice Harper did a thriving business in original movie posters signed by famous stars, rare film footage, and other artifacts associated with Hollywood's golden era. From long-lost outtakes of Marlene Dietrich, Cary Grant or Joan Crawford to one-of-a-kind Art Deco cigarette lighters guaranteed to have been used by Humphrey Bogart, Beatrice could find it for you.

Mostly Beatrice found such valuables in a certain workshop located in Redondo Beach. The shop was operated by Clive and Evelyn Harper. The pair had a talent for "discovering" vintage original film clips that had been lost since the 1930s. Their daughters, Rhonda and Alison, were true artists: Rhonda produced an unlimited number of "original" posters; Alison forged the stars' signatures.

Beatrice went to others in the family for the cigarette lighters or the odd piece of furniture that had belonged to William Holden or Gloria Swanson. The reproductions were so good they could pass for the real thing. So that's what Beatrice did. The arrangement worked well for everyone concerned.

Chloe studied her notes. "The last probable owner of the lamp is Drake Stone. All indications are that he still owns it."

"You're kidding." Rose opened the pizza box. "Are you talking about that old rocker Drake Stone?"

"Right."

Rose removed a slice of the vegetarian pizza and gave it to Hector. "I didn't realize he was still alive."

"There may be some room for debate on the subject." Chloe helped herself to a slice from the box. "After all, he lives in Las Vegas. Still performs six nights a week, two shows a night. You know what they say, old stars never die; they just go to Vegas."

"Huh." Rose slid a slice of pizza onto a napkin. Her blue eyes, heavily outlined in black, seemed to soften. "I remember my Mom used to like Drake Stone. There was this one song she loved. Played it over and over when I was a kid."

Chloe tried to conceal her surprise. Rose rarely talked about her childhood, which had come to a shattering end the night her parents were murdered. She had been fifteen, and she was the one who had found the bodies. She had gone to live with her aunt, a divorced mother already struggling with two kids. The aunt had tried to do what she saw as her duty, but a third mouth, especially one that belonged to a traumatized teenager, had not been welcome. There had not been enough love and affection to go around, let alone money.

Rose had bailed a few months later, having concluded that the streets were friendlier than her aunt's home. She had managed to survive nearly six months out in the cold, relying on shelters and her natural intuitive talents, before she fetched up at Harper Investigations. Chloe had found her in the same place she later discovered Hector: scrounging out of the garbage containers in the alley.

"By any chance was the name of your mother's favorite song 'Blue Champagne'?" Chloe asked.

"Yeah, that's it." Rose brightened. She hummed a few bars. "How did you know?"

Chloe tapped the computer screen. "According to my research it was Stone's first and only real megahit. That was over thirty years ago. But it was enough to make him famous. It's his signature song. He still does it at every performance. Evidently the women in the audience still line up for a kiss after the show."

Rose rolled her raccoon eyes. "I'll bet he's really sick of singing it."

"Probably. At any rate, I just talked to Uncle Edward in Vegas. He confirmed that he thinks Stone has an old lamp matching the rather vague description Winters gave me, or at least he did at one time. I'm going to consult with Aunt Phyllis tomorrow."

"Your uncle in Vegas is the one who sells the high-end antique furniture, right?"

"Uncle Edward is the go-to dealer for antiques in Vegas and the whole Southwest. He supplied a lot of the furnishings that Drake Stone's interior designer used in Stone's mansion. When Stone acquired the lamp last year he evidently asked Edward to take a look at it to verify its authenticity. But my uncle told me that he never got the chance to inspect it."

Rose fed another bite of pizza to Hector. "Why not?"

"Because Stone changed his mind. He told Uncle Edward that after he received the lamp he could see right away that it was a modern piece. But Uncle Edward isn't so sure. Harper intuition. At any rate, he told me that if anyone could arrange for me to meet with Stone, it would be Aunt Phyllis."

"Bet your new client is thrilled with the news that you've located his lamp."

"I haven't informed Mr. Winters of my progress yet," Chloe said. She took a bite of the pizza.

"I thought he was in a big rush to find that lamp."

"He is. But I want to be sure it's the real deal. I hate to say it, but when you're dealing with a legendary artifact you have to consider the possibility that you've got a fake."

Rose grinned. "You mean there's actually an outside chance that someone made a copy of some old lamp and sold it to Drake Stone?"

"Heaven forbid," Chloe said.

Rose's black brows spiked a couple of times. "I seem to recall some-one telling me that faithful copies and exact reproductions of works of art or antiquities are not considered fakes or forgeries."

"Except when they're represented and sold as originals," Chloe con-cluded drily. "I know. Hard to believe that could happen. I'm going to need an intro to get to Stone. Aunt Phyllis knows everyone in the show-business world, at least the stars in Drake Stone's age group. I'll talk to her tomorrow morning and see if she can help me contact him. Then I'll make a quick trip to Vegas to check out the lamp. If it's the real thing I'll call Mr. Winters and tell him to go ahead with the deal."

"I love Vegas. Can I go with you?"

"No, you cannot," Chloe said firmly. "You're my administrative as-sistant, remember? Your job is to look after things here and take care of Hector. You know he can't be left alone for long."

They both looked at Hector. He thumped his tail once or twice and waited to see if he was going to get any more pizza.

"Bummer," Rose said. "I really love Vegas."

"I seem to recall that you have a psych test coming up this week," Chloe said before taking the next bite.

Rose was in her first year at a local community college. Her goal was to become a partner in Harper Investigations. Chloe assumed that her assistant would change her mind a million times before she found the career she really wanted, but Rose was showing no such uncertainty.

"Promise me you'll ask Drake Stone for an autographed picture," Rose said.

"I'll do that."

Rose frowned. "Just thought of something. What if Stone doesn't want to sell the lamp?"

"I'll worry about that after I've verified that it's the right lamp. One step at a time, as we in the investigation business like to say."

"Mostly what you say is that the client is a pain in the ass."

"That, too."

"Mr. Winters is different, though, isn't he?"

"What makes you say that?"

Rose studied her with a thoughtful expression. "You think he's hot. Weird, but hot."

"Jack Winters? Hot?" Chloe sputtered on the pizza. She finally managed to swallow. "He's a client, Rose."

"Doesn't mean he can't be hot." Rose grinned. "I saw your face when he left the office. You're attracted to him, aren't you? Admit it."

"You know Rule Number One here at Harper Investigations."

"*Never sleep with a client.* Sure. But what about when the case is closed?"

"Rose—"

"You never looked at Fletcher Monroe the way you looked at Mr. Winters."

Chloe narrowed her eyes in warning. "Speaking of Fletcher Monroe."

"Right. This is the night, isn't it?"

"Yes." Chloe glanced at her watch. "But not until midnight, at the earliest. I'd better make a pot of coffee."

"You don't like coffee. You drink tea."

"I'll need the caffeine to stay awake. Meanwhile I've still got time for a little more research on the Burning Lamp. You want to give me a hand?"

Rose's eyes glinted with enthusiasm. "Absolutely. I really love these woo-woo cases."

Chloe looked at her. "I haven't told you anything except that I'm looking for an old lamp. What makes you think this is one of the woo-woo cases?"

Rose reached for the last slice of pizza. "I always know."

7

CHLOE EASED THE CAR TO THE CURB AND TURNED OFF THE engine. She studied the small house through the windshield and felt the hair stir on the nape of her neck.

The shades and curtains were closed upstairs and down. Only the faint glow of a television screen showed at the edge of the living room window. The rest of the lights were off.

"That's not right," she said to Hector. "All of the lights and the television were supposed to be off by midnight. I swear if Fletcher decided to bring a date back here tonight, I'm off the case. I'm not about to go through all this trouble again."

Hector was sitting upright in the passenger seat. He turned his head briefly at the sound of her voice but otherwise showed no great interest in the matter. He was just content to be with her.

She sat for a while behind the wheel. Most of the other houses on the quiet street in the North Seattle neighborhood were shrouded in darkness, save for the lights above the front doors and the occasional glow from an upstairs window.

"You see, this is one of the reasons I ended my relationship with Fletcher," she said to Hector. "He's unreliable. He can't help himself. He makes a commitment, and then he can't follow through on it."

Her satchel was on the floor in front of Hector. She fumbled briefly with the straps, reached inside and found her phone. Fletcher was still on her list of contacts under Personal.

"Should have moved him to Business," she told Hector.

She punched in the number. Four rings later she was dumped into voice mail. She did not leave a message.

"To be fair, I suppose it's possible that he's not actually having sex with a new girlfriend," she said. "Highly unlikely but possible. Maybe he just fell asleep in front of the TV. Guys do that."

Hector looked at her, patient as always. She did not do a lot of stakeout work. With the advent of the Internet it had become increasingly unnecessary. If you wanted to verify that a person who was filing a medical disability claim with his insurance company didn't really have to wear a neck brace all you had to do was check out his home page at one of the social networking sites or find his blog. Invariably the claimant had posted numerous photos of his recent skiing vacation or hiking trip together with a chatty little comment about how much fun he'd had and how he planned to spend the money he would get when the insurance company settled his claim. And she never did divorce work, period. It was one of her rules.

She almost never took cases like the one she was on tonight, either. They were always messy. But she'd made the fatal mistake of letting herself feel sorry for Fletcher.

"I admit I have a soft spot for him," she said to Hector. "That's because for a few brief, shining moments I was convinced that he was

Mr. Perfect. I was actually thinking of giving up celibacy for him. It's not his fault it turned out that I was wrong."

She sat quietly for a few more minutes, contemplating the almost-dark house. Invisible energy feathered her senses.

"There's something screwy with this picture, Hector."

Hector yawned.

She tried Fletcher's number again. Still no answer. She closed the phone.

"Okay, that's it, we're going to wake him up," she announced. "I don't care if he is having great sex. It will serve him right if we interrupt his postcoital glow."

She plucked the leash from the dashboard and attached it to Hector's collar. They got out of the car. She took a minute to transfer the tiny camera and her phone to the pocket of her trench coat.

She stashed the satchel in the trunk and picked up the end of Hector's leash. Together they crossed the street in the middle of the block and went up the front walk to the door of Fletcher's house.

The flickering glow of the television set showed at the cracks in the curtains. The bluish light appeared eerie for some inexplicable reason. Once again, she felt the hair stir on the nape of her neck. Instinctively she ramped up her senses a little and looked around. There were several layers of psi prints on the steps and the doorknob but none of the dreamlight looked fresh or dangerous. Most of the residue had been left by Fletcher.

"Nerves," she said to Hector. "Probably shouldn't have had that second cup of coffee."

She leaned on the bell for a while and listened to the muffled sound of the chimes inside. There was no response. Her skin prickled. She looked down at Hector. He appeared monumentally unconcerned.

"Well, you never did like Fletcher," she said. "If he actually was in trouble in there you'd probably just lift a leg and pee on him."

She tried the door, expecting to find it locked. It was. Fletcher had become very security conscious recently.

She glanced back down at Hector. He was idly sniffing the ceramic planter on the front step. As she watched, he marked the territory, but she could tell his heart wasn't in it. Nothing about Fletcher interested Hector.

"But he's a client now," she explained. "We can't just ignore this."

Hector looked bored.

She dug into another pocket of her trench coat and found the high-tech tool that her cousin Abe had given her as a birthday gift. *"Any respectable PI should be able to pick a lock,"* he'd explained. *"This little gadget will open just about any standard-issue door lock. Think of me whenever you use it."*

She thought about Abe now. He had a talent for locks and related technology. But, then, his branch of the family tree boasted a number of what Arcane liked to call crypto-talents. In previous eras they had been known by less politically correct labels: cat burglars and safe-crackers. Cryptos came in many iterations and permutations, but they all had one thing in common: they had a preternatural ability to get through locked doors, including the cyberspace variety. Like her, Abe made his living in a fairly respectable fashion: he designed computer security systems.

She pushed the door open, cranked her senses a little higher, and looked into the darkened foyer. She could hear the television clearly now. The fast, sparkling dialogue of a vintage film blared. Fletcher was not a fan of old movies. That meant he probably was asleep on the sofa.

"Fletcher?"

There was no response.

Another wave of jitters swept through her, but she could see no reason for it. Not only was Hector quiet, but her other vision revealed nothing alarming. There were no dangerously hot footsteps on the foyer tiles.

Hector gazed intently into the small, shadowed entry. He was showing some interest now, but no more than he would have upon entering any new environment, she decided. Of course, given his profound disdain for Fletcher, it would not bother him at all if Fletcher was lying dead or ill on the floor of the living room.

Dead or ill. Her stomach knotted with acute anxiety.

Fletcher was in his early thirties. He worked out three times a week, and he watched his diet. But it was not unheard of for an otherwise healthy man to collapse from an undiagnosed heart condition or an aneurism.

Another wave of unease swept over her. She moved into the foyer and groped for the wall switch. The dim light from the sconce illuminated the entry and a small portion of the living room. She could make out a man's legs on the floor. The rest of the figure was concealed by the sofa.

"Oh, my God, *Fletcher.*"

She dropped the leash and rushed forward, simultaneously plunging her hand into her pocket for her cell phone.

She fell to her knees beside Fletcher's too-still form and fumbled for a pulse. Relief surged through her when she found the slow but steady beat at his throat. The hall light and the glow of the television revealed no signs of blood. She wondered if he'd had a seizure of some kind. She punched in the emergency number on her phone.

Hector whined. She glanced up and saw that he was standing at the foot of the stairs, gazing intently up into the darkness of the second floor.

For the first time she got a look at the steps and the banister. She froze at the sight of the violent, black and purple dreamprints glowing ominously in the shadows.

Hector growled. He did not take his attention off the top of the stairs.

The 911 operator came on the line. *"What is the nature of your emergency?"*

"Intruder in the house," Chloe whispered.

"Does he have a gun?"

"I don't know. He's upstairs."

"Get out of the house immediately, ma'am."

"Someone has been hurt. He's unconscious."

"Get out of the house. Now."

8

HE WAS ON THE COMPUTER, TRYING NOT TO THINK ABOUT THE night of doped-up sleep and bad dreams that awaited him when the jolt of awareness struck. It hit like a body blow. He was out of the chair and on his feet, searching for nameless enemies in the shadows of his office before he realized what had happened.

Take it easy. Just another hallucination. They rarely lasted more than a few minutes at most. But invariably he *knew* that what he was seeing was not real. It was as if his para-senses short-circuited for a brief period and his brain tried to make sense of the resulting confusion.

But what was happening to him now was different. It wasn't a disorienting moment of visual disturbance when the real world blurred and took on the surreal quality of a dreamscape. It wasn't an auditory hallucination, either. His first thought was that it was yet another aspect of his new talent. But for some reason the deep, intense awareness and alarm he was experiencing seemed focused on Chloe Harper.

His unease was not irrational, he thought. After all, he had a hell of a lot riding on Chloe. If she could not locate the lamp he was going to find himself right up against a very hard wall. He'd been thinking about her constantly since he had left her office, the strat side of his nature trying to plot ways to stay in control of what was fast becoming an out-of-control situation.

But logic went only so far. He could not escape the feeling that something really bad was going down and that Chloe was in the middle of it.

He took out his phone and punched in the number of Harper Investigations. Goth Girl answered on the third or fourth ring. He heard the sound of music playing in the background. Opera, of all things.

"Is your boss there?" he asked.

"She's out on a case," Rose said.

"It's after midnight."

"Stakeout. Her sort-of ex thinks one of his students is stalking him."

"Where is she?"

"That kind of information is supposed to be confidential at a detective agency," Rose said.

"She's in trouble—I can feel it." He did not bother to put the energy of his new talent into words. He wanted to scare her a little, but the laws of para-physics being what they were, psi waves did not travel through cell phones, cyberspace or any other kind of high-tech device. But he was still a strat. He had picked up on the close bond between Rose and Chloe that afternoon. You didn't have to have a lot of talent to know how to work an angle like that.

"You really think so?" Rose asked, dubious, but concerned.

"Look, you know your boss is psychic, don't you?"

"Well, yeah, sure."

It was a relief to be dealing with someone who actually believed in the paranormal.

"So am I," he said. "Trust me on this. Chloe is in danger."

"Okay, this is really weird. I've been getting a little nervous, myself, for the past few minutes. Chloe says I've got good intuition. Hang on, I'll give her a call."

He left his office and went out into the living room. The sight of his newly decorated condo with its cold, polished concrete floor and sleek steel-and-glass design did nothing to ease his prowling tension. He went to the wall of windows and looked out at the view of the black expanse of Elliott Bay and the lights of West Seattle while he waited. Another storm was coming in. He could feel it.

Rose came back a moment later. She sounded seriously worried now.

"She's not answering her phone," Rose said. "You're right, something's wrong. I *knew* that weasel was using the Mad Cheerleader to manipulate her."

He headed for the door, fishing his keys out of his pocket. "Give me an address."

"What are you going to do?" Rose asked.

"Find her."

"Pick me up first. I'm coming with you."

"Waste of time."

"Please. I don't have a car of my own. I need to get to her."

The rising anxiety in Rose's voice cut deep. She was starting to panic.

"Where are you?" he asked.

"I have an apartment across the hall from Chloe's. Right above the office. I'll meet you downstairs on the sidewalk."

9

THE SMELL OF KEROSENE WAFTED DOWN THE STAIRCASE. HEC-
tor growled again. There was a sudden, terrifying *whoosh*. The top of
the stairs was abruptly illuminated with a hellish glow.

"Oh, shit," Chloe whispered.

"Ma'am? Are you out of the house?" the 911 operator demanded.

The smoke detectors kicked in. The screech drowned out Hector,
who was now barking furiously. Upstairs the fire roared like a freight
train as it gathered energy.

"Trust me, I'm getting out of here as fast as I can," Chloe said.

She closed the phone, dropped it into her pocket and jumped to her
feet. Hooking her hands under Fletcher's shoulders she heaved with
all of her strength. His head lolled. His body moved only a couple of
inches on the carpet. He weighed a ton.

So much for the famous adrenaline rush that was supposed to give a
woman abnormal strength in an emergency, she thought. It dawned on
her that she had to get Fletcher off the carpet and onto the hardwood

floor where there would be less friction. She dropped his shoulders, knelt beside him and started to roll him toward the entrance.

To her amazement, the technique worked. Fletcher's head flopped on the rug a few times in the process. He would probably have some bruises in the morning, she thought, but at least he would be alive. Maybe. Always assuming she could haul him out the door before the house burned down around them.

Hector was in a frenzy now. He trotted back and forth between the open door and the foot of the staircase, howling.

"*Outside*," she ordered. It was the word she always used when she announced that they were going for a walk.

Hector obeyed. He charged out onto the front step, leash flapping behind him.

She got Fletcher onto the floor and scrambled to her feet again. Smoke was billowing down the stairs now. She started to cough. This time when she seized Fletcher's arms and hauled he slid forward a good foot and a half.

A shriek of rage came from halfway down the staircase.

"*Let him go.*" A slender woman dressed in a trendy black hooded track suit appeared at the foot of the stairs. Viewed through the pall of smoke she looked like the ghost of a crazed cheerleader. The glow of firelight from above danced on her blond ponytail and sparked off the gun in her hand. Her face was the only thing about her that was not impossibly cute. Her pretty features were twisted with rage.

"You can't have him," she screamed. "Fletcher is mine. We belong together. Leave him alone."

Chloe recognized her immediately from Fletcher's description. Madeline Gibson. Fresh splashes of wild energy burned on the treads of the staircase behind her. Demented obsession always produced a lot of raw psi.

"We all have to get out of here," Chloe shouted, trying to pitch her voice above the shriek of the alarm. She managed to drag Fletcher a little closer to the door. "Don't worry—you can have him as soon as we're safe. Believe me, I don't want him."

"I told you to leave him alone." Madeline aimed the gun at her. "He's mine."

"Come with us, Madeline," she urged. "You can have Fletcher as soon as we get him outside, I promise."

"No, he stays here with me. You can't have him." Madeline's voice rose to a shrill screech. "No one else can have him. I told him that, but he didn't believe me."

Chloe sensed rather than heard the rush of movement behind her. Belatedly she realized that Hector was no longer barking. He slammed through the door, going straight past her. He was moving low and fast, heading straight for Madeline.

"Hector, *no*," Chloe yelled.

But it was too late. Madeline, probably reacting more on instinct than intent, swung the barrel of the gun toward Hector. There was a deafening explosion when she pulled the trigger. Hector tumbled to the floor.

Stunned, Chloe looked down at the dog.

"Hector," she whispered.

Madeline switched the barrel of the gun toward Fletcher, her face now terrifyingly calm and composed as she prepared to pull the trigger a second time.

"Wait," Chloe said tightly. She dropped Fletcher and went slowly toward Madeline. She was forced to step across Hector's still form to reach her. "Not yet. Fletcher is unconscious. If you shoot him now he'll die without ever understanding that he was supposed to be with you. You want him to understand that, don't you?"

"Yes." Madeline's face crumpled with confusion. "He has to understand."

Above the noise of the smoke detector Chloe was remotely aware of the sound of a car slamming to a halt in front of the house. She did not take her attention off Madeline Gibson.

"Right," she said. "We have to wake him up so that you can explain everything to him. Why is he asleep?"

"The cookies," Madeline said. "I ground up the pills and put them into the cookies. Left them on the back doorstep. I signed the note with *her* name. He should never have eaten them. It was a test, you see."

"A test," Chloe repeated.

"To see if he understood that she was all wrong for him. If he threw the cookies into the garbage I would know that he realized she was all wrong for him. But the bastard ate the cookies."

"Got it." She was very close to Madeline now, almost within touching distance. "That explains everything."

"You shouldn't be here," Madeline said.

"Don't worry, I'm just leaving."

She touched Madeline's shoulder. Madeline did not seem to notice.

Jack loomed in the open doorway. Simultaneously, energy surged through the hall. Chloe sensed that the hot currents of psi were directed at Madeline, but she still had her hand on the young woman's shoulder when the storm of nightmares struck.

It was like touching a live electrical wire. The physical contact with Madeline ensured that she took much of the shock, too. Horrors from the primordial darkness buried in the deepest regions of her psyche twisted through her. Phantoms and specters and things that go bump in the night rode the raging waves of energy that cascaded through the small space. Terrifying things flickered at the edge of her vision and slithered at her feet.

She heard a scream, the high, keening wail of a woman staring into hell. *Not her*, she thought. *Madeline*. With a gasp, she jerked her hand away from Madeline's shoulder, breaking the connection. The nightmares receded immediately. Breathless, heart pounding, she reeled back against the wall.

Madeline finally stopped screaming. She went rigid, shuddered and collapsed. The gun clattered on the tile floor of the hall.

Jack Winters was giving orders.

"Rose, help her with this guy," he said, moving past Chloe. "I'll get the woman."

Rose grabbed one of Fletcher's arms. Chloe grabbed the other. Together they hauled him out onto the front step and down onto the lawn. Chloe looked back into the burning house and saw Jack emerge with Madeline slung over one shoulder. Hector's limp body was tucked under his arm. He paused long enough to kick an object out the door. It landed on the grass near Rose.

"Oh, shit," Rose said. "She had a *gun?*"

"Don't touch it," Chloe said. "It will be covered with her fingerprints. Evidence."

She was still shivering in reaction to the icy sea of nightmares that had lapped at her senses for those few seconds. As bad as it was, she knew that she had not gotten the full blast. She could not begin to imagine what the experience had been like for Madeline.

She watched Jack come toward them, a dark and powerful figure carrying the unconscious woman and Hector from the burning house.

Avenging angel.

10

HE STOOD A LITTLE DISTANCE FROM CHLOE WHILE SHE talked to the police officer. Hector was alive. One of the medics at the scene had taken a look at him and bandaged the wound in the dog's head and offered the reassuring assessment that Hector would probably live. A kindhearted neighbor had volunteered to take Hector to the nearest emergency veterinary clinic.

Rose pressed close to Chloe in silent support. Jack realized that he wanted to stand close, too, but that wasn't his job. He was not part of her inner circle. He was just the client, the client who had burned her badly with a psychic blast of nightmares. It was a wonder she had not collapsed like Madeline. Probably a tribute to her own strong talent.

Fletcher Monroe and Madeline Gibson had been taken away in ambulances. An officer had accompanied Madeline, who was still unconscious when she was loaded into the vehicle. Monroe had begun to stir when he was secured to the stretcher. Jack had overheard him say something about cookies.

The firemen had beaten back the worst of the flames, but the house was still smoldering. There was a tangle of hoses on the lawn, a lot of flashing lights from the emergency vehicles and a great deal of water in the street. The neighbors had emerged and now stood around in small groups, watching the action.

"CSI will test the cookies, but it looks like Gibson was telling you the truth when she said she put some sleeping meds in them," the officer said to Chloe. He checked his notes. "She waited until midnight and then came back to burn the house down around him." He looked up. "Think she was intending suicide as well as murdering Monroe?"

"She wasn't thinking clearly at all." Chloe folded her arms tightly beneath her breasts. "But, no, I don't think she intended to die in the fire. She just wanted to make sure that no other woman would ever get Fletcher, I mean, Mr. Monroe."

"You say she's a student in one of his classes?"

"She *was* a student. Last quarter, I think. They dated, but when the quarter ended, so did the relationship. Then she started stalking Mr. Monroe. She got into a pattern of showing up here at midnight and leaving little presents on the front steps."

The officer nodded. "Enough to give any man the creeps. Did Monroe get a restraining order?"

"No. He was hoping to avoid that because of the scandal it would cause at the college. I was supposed to get some incriminating pictures. He intended to use them to confront her. I told him it probably wouldn't work, but he was convinced he could handle the situation if I got him the photos."

"What made him think he could deal with her in a rational way?" the officer asked with a quizzical expression.

"Mr. Monroe is a psychologist."

The officer grimaced. "Got it. Well, thanks very much, Miss Harper.

Someone will be in touch about getting a statement. I'll need your contact information."

"I've got a card." Chloe looked down as though she expected to find a card in one of the pockets of her trench coat. A confused expression crossed her face. "My cards are in my satchel. It's in the trunk of my car."

"I'll get it," Rose said. "Give me your keys, Chloe."

"Keys." Chloe reached into a pocket, withdrew a key chain and handed it to Rose.

Rose hurried off toward the small vehicle parked halfway down the street.

The officer examined Chloe with a thoughtful expression. "I recognize your name, Miss Harper. You consulted on the Anderson Point murders a year ago, didn't you?"

Chloe glanced over her shoulder as if checking to see if Rose had found her car.

"I gave Detective Takahashi some information," she said quietly. "He was able to use it to identify a suspect."

"I know. That one was as cold as it gets. They say Takahashi worked it night and day. Kept the file under his desk, but it stayed cold until he caught a break with the information you gave him. I remember the hostage situation at the end. It was a real squeaker."

"Yes." Chloe's voice was tight.

"They sent the crazy bastard to Winter Cove hospital. Luckily for everyone involved he found a way to hang himself. Saved the state a lot of money."

Rose returned with a card. "You sure you're okay, boss?" She examined Chloe from head to foot again. "You didn't get singed or anything?"

"I'm fine," Chloe said. She handed the card to the officer and waited until he had moved off to talk to some people who were getting out of a CSI van. She looked first at Rose and then at Jack. "Don't get me wrong, I'm really glad to see you both, but what are you two doing here, anyway?"

"You heard what Mr. Winters told the cop," Rose said. "He was worried about you being out here alone on a stakeout."

"I know what you told the officer, Mr. Winters." Chloe's frown darkened. "But how did you find out that I was working tonight?"

"I called Rose with some questions," Jack said. "She told me you were out here on your own."

"You called my office in the middle of the night?" Disbelief tightened her soot-streaked face. "And the two of you just decided to come racing over here to see if I was okay?"

"Chloe," Rose said quietly. "Mr. Winters had a feeling, okay? So did I. How often have you told me to pay attention to intuition?"

"Sorry." Chloe rubbed her forehead. "I'm not complaining. I just don't understand what made you think that something was wrong."

"I've got a lot invested in you." Jack took her arm. "You're starting to shiver."

"It's cold out here."

"It's the adrenaline," he said. "Makes you jittery. You need to sit down."

"Actually, I think I need a drink," Chloe said.

"That, too. I'll drive you home."

"I've got my car," Chloe said.

She probably didn't even want to be in the same car with him now, not after the way he had burned her.

Rose snorted. "Like you're in any condition to drive, boss. You've had one heck of a close call. Mr. Winters is right. Let him drive you back to the office. I'll take care of your car."

Chloe looked mutinous for a few seconds, but she finally abandoned the battle.

"Okay," she said.

He bundled her into the front seat, then went around to the driver's side. He peeled off his leather jacket, which now smelled of smoke, and tossed it onto the floor of the backseat. He got in beside her.

When he closed the door the small space was suddenly infused with a startling sense of intense intimacy. He was very conscious of Chloe sitting so close. She smelled of smoke and woman and the aftereffects of adrenaline. She had been in the red zone, running wide open, when he went through the doorway. He had sensed it immediately. He, too, had been cranked to the max. Now they were both enveloped in the rush of the after-burn. He realized he was fully aroused, every muscle in his body hard and tight.

He'd heard rumors about the erotic heat that could be generated by two strong talents who were sexually attracted to each other. He'd encountered more than one powerful female talent over the years and felt a certain pleasant stirring of his senses. But he'd never been slammed into overdrive like this. *Get a grip, man.*

They sat quietly for a couple of minutes, watching the activity in the front yard of the burning house.

"You saved my dog," Chloe said after a while. "And probably Fletcher and me as well. Thank you."

"Sure."

She pushed some hair out of her eyes. "Hector went for Madeline. Trying to protect me. I've never seen him do anything like that before. I think that in another life he must have had some guard dog training."

"Maybe. Or maybe he was just acting on instinct. He's a tough dog. The medic seemed pretty sure he'll make it."

"Thanks to you. But I need to get him home from the vet as soon as possible." Anxiety laced her voice. "He's got abandonment issues. If he wakes up in strange surroundings—"

"The vet will know how to deal with him."

"Yes, I suppose so." She exhaled slowly. "Sorry, I'm a little rattled."

"Understandable."

She looked around as if seeing the interior of the car for the first time.

"Nice ride," she said.

"Thanks."

"But it's going to smell like smoke after I get out." She fumbled with her seat belt. "Probably cost you a fortune to get the interior cleaned."

"I can afford it. And you're not the only one who picked up some smoke and soot tonight."

She glanced over her shoulder into the backseat, where he had tossed his jacket. "No, I guess not."

He watched her take a couple more stabs at the belt buckle, missing each time. He reached over and buckled it for her. She exhaled, rested her head against the back of the seat and closed her eyes.

"I'm sorry," he said finally. He couldn't think of anything else to add to that. What did you say to a woman after you had hit her with a wave of nightmares?

"That is one heck of a talent you've got," she said. Her voice was absolutely neutral. "The second one, I take it? The one you think means you've been hit with the Winters Curse?"

He watched the smoking house. "I'm still learning to control it. For obvious reasons I haven't been able to run a lot of experiments."

"Yeah, I can see the problem there."

He had literally terrified her tonight. She'd probably have nightmares about him for weeks. Not the best way to impress a woman on a first date.

"Are you okay?" he asked.

"Sure. Just a little jittery, that's all. The adrenaline, like you said."

He almost smiled. His very own gutsy, hard-boiled private eye.

"I'm sorry," he repeated.

"Forget it. Under the circumstances, I'm more than happy to cut you a little slack."

He got the car started. "So, do you do this kind of thing a lot?"

She opened her eyes and looked straight ahead through the windshield. "Almost never. I hate this kind of work; it's always messy."

"Rose said something about Monroe being your sort of ex."

"Ex-*boyfriend*, not ex-husband. We stopped seeing each other several months ago. Last quarter he dated Madeline Gibson. When he tried to end it, she started stalking him. Madeline didn't understand Fletcher. She didn't realize that he has a very predictable pattern."

"What kind of pattern?"

"Every quarter he picks out a new female student in one of his classes and fires up a relationship. Said relationship always comes to an end when the quarter is over. For Fletcher, a new quarter always means a new girlfriend. He is the quintessential serial monogamist."

"Madeline did not take it well when he explained the rules?"

"No. She became increasingly intense. She was always there, waiting outside his classroom. She showed up at his gym while he was working out. The little gifts began to appear on his front step. Flowers. Fresh coffee and doughnuts. She always came around after midnight. Fletcher tried to talk to her, but she just laughed and said she was teasing him."

"So he contacted you?"

"We had stopped seeing each other, but we were still friends. He knew what I did for a living, of course. And he was desperate to keep the problem under wraps."

"You told the cop that Monroe was worried about the fallout at the college."

"Fletcher's dating pattern has started to cause talk. There have been complaints from other members of the faculty and some nasty gossip.

At the college level it's certainly not unheard of for instructors to date their students. But when it happens over and over again, people do tend to notice. And not everyone approves."

"In other words, Monroe was looking at the possibility of losing his job."

She turned her head and looked at him. "You appear to have grasped the big picture here, Mr. Winters."

"My other talent is for strategy, remember? I get big pictures and bottom lines."

"Yes, Fletcher was afraid that he would lose his position if he made an accusation. He wanted to deal with it privately."

"So he came to you to get proof."

"I turned up a lot of stuff on the Internet, of course. It's amazing what people will write in their blogs and on their personal websites. They treat cyberspace as if it were a private diary. Madeline chatted at length about the affair. Her obsession was clear, but she did not implicate herself in the stalking. She just wrote that she had given Fletcher a few presents and that he had not appreciated them. He wanted photographic proof of what was going on."

"You took the case because you felt sorry for him."

"And because we're still friends," she said. "I could tell that he was very nervous. Fletcher is a nice guy. Intelligent. Fun to be with. Even-tempered. Great sense of humor. What can I say? I like him."

"You didn't mind that he terminated your relationship at the end of the quarter?"

"Well, actually, I was the one who ended it," she said.

"Because you found out about his serial monogamy?"

"No, of course not." She sounded genuinely surprised. "His dating pattern was one of his two best features as far as I was concerned."

"What was the second one?"

"His commitment phobia. The problem was that once Fletcher discovered that I also have commitment issues he kept trying to fix me. Probably some form of misguided projection."

"Misguided projection." He realized that he was still grappling with the serial monogamy thing and the commitment issues. Somehow, he hadn't seen either coming.

"Things got even more awkward between us when I told Fletcher that I have some talent. At that point I think that I became a patient to him."

"Let me take a wild guess here. Monroe doesn't believe in the paranormal."

"He's got a Ph.D. in psychology. Of course he doesn't believe in it." She sighed. "All in all, I had no choice but to end things after only a few dates. We never even made it as far as the bedroom. Rose thinks that still bothers Fletcher, but I have a hard time buying it."

"Why?"

"Because he moved on immediately. Started dating someone else right away. Fell right back into his usual pattern. It wasn't like he couldn't let go. I think he just sees me as a professional failure, that's all."

"Because he couldn't fix your issues."

"Right," Chloe said.

"How did you meet him?"

"I took one of his classes. I thought it would be useful in my work."

"What, exactly, does he teach?"

"Criminal psychology."

"Learn anything?"

"Mostly what I learned is that psychologists look for explanations and motives. Me, I'm just a PI. I look for bad psi."

He took the on-ramp onto I-5, heading toward downtown. The freeway was nearly empty at this hour. The lights of the city's high-rise buildings, including the one in which he lived, glittered in the night.

"You really thought that Monroe's serial monogamy habit and his commitment issues were good features?" he asked after a while.

"Are you kidding? I was almost convinced that he was Mr. Perfect. When I gave him The Talk, he looked downright thrilled. Then, again, men often seem happy enough at first. I've never been able to figure out why they change their minds. Aunt Phyllis says it's just the way men are."

"I'm probably going to regret asking this, but what is The Talk?"

"That's when I explain about my commitment issues. I make it clear that any relationship I enter into is likely to be short-term and that there are no strings attached. I make sure that the other person knows that he is free to dump me on a moment's notice without feeling any guilt." She frowned a little. "But for some reason I'm usually the one who ends up doing the dumping."

"You're a real romantic, aren't you?" he said flatly.

"I can't afford to be a romantic, Mr. Winters. Not with my talent."

He shot her a quick, searching look. "What does your talent have to do with it?"

"It's hard to explain," she said. She leaned her head against the back of the seat, folded her arms. "It doesn't matter now, anyway."

"Why not?"

"The serial monogamy thing got old. I moved into a new phase about a year ago. I admit that I toyed with the idea of going back to serial monogamy for a time with Fletcher, but I finally realized it just wouldn't work."

"And what comes after serial monogamy?"

"Celibacy."

He felt blindsided again. "Celibacy?"

"There's a kind of freedom in the celibate lifestyle."

"Yeah? I hadn't heard that."

11

HE PARKED ON THE STREET IN FRONT OF THE BUILDING THAT housed Harper Investigations. Chloe got out before he could open the door. Energy crackled in the air around her. It kept his senses aroused and on edge.

She reached into one of the trench coat pockets and pulled out her keys. An odd looking gadget came out with the keys and fell to the sidewalk. There was a muffled clank of metal. He picked up the small high-tech device and held it to the streetlight.

"I'm not even going to ask," he said, handing it back to her, "because it looks like a very fancy lock pick and is probably highly illegal."

"It was a birthday gift."

"Another ex-boyfriend?"

"No, my cousin Abe."

"Your family gives interesting gifts."

She opened the door and stepped into the tiny lobby. He followed her inside and shut the door. Together they started up the stairs. Chloe gripped the banister tightly, half hauling herself up the steps. When he took her other arm she did not protest.

He knew immediately that the physical contact was a mistake. It intensified the sexual urgency that was heating his blood, stirring things deep inside him. He got a sudden vision of taking her right there on the stairs. Not a hallucination, he realized, more like an almost overpowering need.

They paused on the second floor so that she could rest.

"This is embarrassing," she muttered. "Didn't realize I was so out of shape."

"You're exhausted," he said. "Monroe is a big man. How far did you drag him?"

"He was in the living room when I arrived."

He'd seen enough of the house to know that she'd exerted a lot of effort to get Monroe all the way into the front hall. And then there was the business of having a gun pointed in her face, her dog getting shot and her being hit with a blast of nightmares.

"You've had a rough night," he said.

"You know, now that you mention it—"

Rose appeared on the third-floor landing.

"I just talked to the vet hospital," she said. "Hector is okay, but they knocked him out to stitch him up and he's still sleeping. They said we can pick him up in the morning. Are you all right, Chloe? You look like you're going to crash right there."

"Not," Chloe said, hauling herself up another step, "before I get that drink. And a shower. I definitely need a shower first."

Jack took her arm again and more or less levitated her up the stairs to the third floor. Rose opened a door.

"Home, sweet home," Chloe muttered. "You'll have to excuse me. I can't stand the smell of smoke a minute longer."

She vanished through the doorway. Rose followed. Jack considered for a moment and concluded that no one had told him to leave or bothered to shut the door in his face. That amounted to something of an invitation. He walked into the apartment and closed the door behind him.

The room was very non-Seattle. It was drenched in the rich, warm colors of the Mediterranean Coast. The walls that weren't red brick were painted in deep shades of amber and ochre. The carpet was patterned with an abstract design done in saffron and rust-red. The honey-colored sofa was covered with a rainbow of throw pillows. Lush green plants in red ceramic pots stood near the windows.

Rose returned with a pile of clothing that smelled strongly of smoke.

"Chloe likes color," she explained. "Lots of it."

"I can see that," he said.

He thought about his own cold, steel-and-concrete condo. Everyone said it suited him. He had a feeling it was not necessarily a compliment.

"You can clean up in the kitchen," Rose said. She motioned him toward the sink. "I'm going to put these in the washing machine."

"Thanks." What he really needed was a shower, but he didn't want to go home just yet. He wanted to stay here near Chloe until she kicked him out.

There is a certain kind of freedom in celibacy.

Like hell.

He rolled up his sleeves and ran the water in the sink. Rose disappeared into a tiny laundry room. He heard the washer start. When she returned a moment later she opened a cupboard and took down a bottle of red wine.

"I thought private investigators always drank whiskey," he said.

"Chloe tried that. Unfortunately, it turned out she didn't like whiskey." Rose reached into a cupboard for a glass. "Want some?"

"No, thanks."

"Whatever." Rose set the bottle and the glass on the table. Concern darkened her expression. "She's okay, isn't she?"

"Chloe? She seems fine. A little shaken, that's all. Why?"

"It's just that she looked like she'd been through hell when she came out of that house. I haven't seen her like that since—"

Rose stopped abruptly.

"Since when, Rose?" he prompted.

"Since she closed the Anderson Point case for the cops."

"She told me that she rarely did the kind of work she was doing tonight," he said.

"That's true. She doesn't like what she calls the messy stuff. She says her real talent is for finding lost things like your lamp."

"She's really good at that, huh?"

"She's brilliant. Like you said, she's psychic."

He lowered himself into a chair. "You wouldn't happen to know if she's made any progress on my case, would you?"

"Didn't she tell you?" Rose poured half a glass of wine. "She found your lamp in Vegas this afternoon."

"*What?*"

"Well, she thinks it's the right lamp but she's going to arrange an intro to the owner tomorrow. If all goes well, she'll fly down to Vegas the day after to make sure it isn't a fake or replica. She says she can't be sure until she gets into the same room with it. The woo-woo factor, you know."

He stared at Rose's back, disbelief splashing through him. "I spent years on and off trying to find that damn lamp. This past month I've been looking for it full time and I'm a strat-talent. Are you saying that she located it in one afternoon?"

Chloe appeared in the doorway. "Told you I was good."

He looked at her and felt everything inside him clench. She was muffled in a white spa robe. Her hair was wrapped in a towel. She looked flushed and warm, but he could see the strain in her eyes.

"Yes," he said. "You did tell me that."

"I don't know for sure that the lamp I've got a lead on is the genuine artifact yet." She sat down at the table, picked up the glass and took a healthy swallow of the wine. "I'm hoping to verify it in person as soon as possible."

"I'm coming with you."

"No. Absolutely not." She waved one hand and drank some more wine. "Dealing with collectors, especially the kind who acquire paranormal objects, can be an extremely delicate matter. In my experience, it's never good to have the client in the same room. This sort of thing is always best handled by a third party, trust me."

"Damn it—"

"If Mr. Stone wants to sell the lamp, I'll let you know. You can then transfer the funds into his account. I will pick up the lamp and bring it back here to you. That's how it works."

"Let's get something straight," he said. "Given what almost happened tonight, you're not going anywhere very far without me."

"Oh, for crying out loud." She made a face. "What happened tonight had nothing to do with your case."

"That's not the point. The point is you're not going to take any more chances until that lamp is in my hands."

She looked at Rose. "You see? This is always the problem with clients. They hire me to fix a problem, and then they try to tell me how to do my job."

12

HE WALKED BACK INTO HIS CONDO AN HOUR LATER AND POW-
ered up his laptop. The newspaper accounts he was searching for
popped up almost immediately. The long-delayed arrest in the Anderson Point murders had received a fair amount of coverage because of
the drama at the end. He hadn't paid much attention because at the
time he'd been out of town putting together a deal with a start-up in
Southern California.

The killer had managed to evade the police sent to arrest him long
enough to grab a hostage. He had barricaded himself in his house with
the girl and threatened to kill her.

> The suspect, Richard Sawyer, told negotiators that he had been
> framed by a private investigator, Chloe Harper, who was work-
> ing on behalf of the teenager he had taken hostage. The young
> woman was the daughter of the murdered couple, John and
> Elaine Tranner.

Sawyer offered to exchange his captive for Miss Harper. Police were reluctant, but in the end, amidst some confusion at the scene, Harper walked into the house.

What happened next is unclear. Shortly after entering the residence, Harper and the hostage emerged, unharmed. When police entered the house they found Sawyer on the floor, unconscious, having apparently suffered a seizure.

A few months later a follow-up story appeared:

> . . . The thirty-one-year-old suspect in the murders of an Anderson Point couple confessed to the killings but was found incompetent to stand trial. He was ordered committed to Winter Cove Psychiatric Hospital, where he likely will spend the rest of his life.

Three weeks later there was one last piece. It was a small one:

> Richard Sawyer, the confessed killer of an Anderson Point couple was found dead in his room at Winter Cove Psychiatric Hospital, the victim of an apparent suicide . . .

It took a little more digging to turn up the name of the murdered couple's daughter. There was a photo of her leaving the courtroom with Chloe. Most of the tattoos were discreetly covered by a coat, and the makeup had been toned down, but he recognized her easily. Rose.

He closed the computer and went to stand at the window, looking out into the night. He thought about the rush of psi he had sensed when he went through the door of the burning house. The energy had come from Chloe. She had just reached out to touch Madeline Gibson's shoulder.

"Well, now, Chloe Harper," he said aloud. The words echoed in the silence of the cold steel-and-concrete space. "What would have happened if I hadn't arrived when I did tonight? Would Madeline Gibson have suffered a mysterious bout of unconsciousness like Richard Sawyer? And here I thought the only thing a dreamlight reader could do was read a little dream psi. What secrets are you hiding?"

He stood contemplating the darkness for a while longer. Eventually he went into the bedroom and took out the bottle of sleeping meds.

13

A seething darkness filled the abyss. She looked into it and knew that no light could ever penetrate the depths. This hunger that was tearing her apart could never be satisfied.

It was his fault. He was responsible for arousing this insatiable need. But he was walking away from her. Telling her that he did not want her; that she could never have him.

If that was true then no one else would have him either.

THIS WAS ALL WRONG. NOT HER ENERGY. NOT HER DREAM.

Chloe came awake with a start. Her heart was pounding and her nightgown was damp with sweat. Instinctively she reached for Hector, but his warm, heavy weight was missing from the bed. Belatedly she remembered that he was still at the hospital.

She took a few more deep breaths. Gradually her pulse calmed.

What had happened tonight was just bad luck and bad timing, she thought. She'd been running wide open when she'd touched Madeline Gibson. At that very instant, thanks to Jack, Madeline just happened to be plunging into a terrible dreamscape.

There was no such thing as telepathy—no way she could actually dream another person's dream. But the currents of dreamlight given off by an individual when he or she dreamed were much stronger than when the person was awake. In the active dreamstate the dream psi was not only deposited on everything the individual touched, it saturated the atmosphere around the dreamer.

Ever since she'd come into her talent in her teenage years she had been uncomfortable just being near someone who was dreaming. Physical contact with the person made it a thousand times worse.

Tonight when Jack had directed that blast of energy at Madeline he had, in effect, forced Gibson into a full-blown nightmare. And Chloe had been touching her at the time. The shock had been as bad as the one she had gotten last year from Richard Sawyer when she'd put the bastard to sleep.

Bad luck and bad timing, that's all. Stuff happened when you were in her line of work.

But the experience had given her a firsthand look at Jack's emerging talent for generating nightmares.

Interesting.

14

"MORE TEA?" PHYLLIS ASKED.

"Yes, thanks." Chloe held out her cup and saucer.

At home in her apartment she drank her tea out of an oversized mug, but here in her great-aunt's elegant old mansion on Queen Anne Hill, delicate china, fine crystal and polished silver were the rule. Of course, it helped that Phyllis could afford to pay a full-time housekeeper to maintain her luxurious lifestyle.

Hector sprawled in front of the window overlooking the garden, which, in turn, overlooked Elliott Bay and downtown Seattle. He appeared oblivious to the refined things that surrounded him. He wore a dashing bandage that covered a portion of his head and one ear. The cone-shaped gadget on his neck that prevented him from scratching at the bandage detracted somewhat from the warrior image, but he was alpha enough to handle the indignity. Phyllis had given him a new chew toy when he had arrived. Worked for him.

For decades, Phyllis Harper had been known as the Psychic to the

Stars. She had been the favorite confidante of celebrities, producers, media moguls and others who reigned in Hollywood. In addition she had also consulted for various politicians, CEOs and assorted underworld figures. The pink velvet–flocked walls of her living room were hung with framed photographs of her with famous people. The house had been paid for by her long series of lovers.

Following her official announcement of retirement she had moved back to her hometown of Seattle. She no longer accepted new clients, but she still took phone calls from those who had sought her advice over the years and the occasional old lover.

Chloe had always felt a special connection with her aunt. Phyllis was the only one in the family who truly understood her talent. That was because Phyllis possessed a very similar ability. Although Chloe was the more powerful talent of the two, they had both been stuck with the downside that accompanied the sensitivity to dreamlight.

Phyllis picked up the pot with a hand that sparkled with diamonds and other assorted stones. She winked.

"Your prints are positively glowing today," she said. "What's his name?"

"He's a client, Aunt Phyllis."

"Yes, I know all about your silly rule. You know I don't approve. I had affairs with any number of clients over the years, and no harm ever came of it."

"You lived in Hollywood. I live in Seattle."

"I don't see why that should matter." Phyllis tilted the pot to pour the tea. "I don't believe I've ever seen that particular kind of energy in your prints." She set the pot down. "He must be very interesting."

"He is, but that doesn't change the fact that he is still a client," Chloe said. "Besides, I told you that I've entered a new phase in my life."

"The celibacy thing. Ridiculous decision." Phyllis clucked disapprovingly. "I'm sure it will pass. But I can see that you're here on business. What can I do for you?"

"My new client hired me to find an old family heirloom. Aunt Beatrice and Uncle Edward helped me track it down. Looks like it's currently in the hands of Drake Stone. He's still doing shows in Vegas."

Phyllis beamed. "I know Drake. Charming man. I remember how concerned he was when the news broke that he was gay. But I was able to assure him that the publicity could be managed in a way that would actually boost his career."

"I thought there was a good chance that you would be acquainted with him. Can I talk you into making a phone call to arrange an introduction? It's a little hard for a small-time PI like me to get through to a famous star like Stone."

"Certainly, dear. What shall I tell him?"

"That I have a client who would very much like to purchase a certain antique lamp from him."

"Not a problem. That's all?" Phyllis managed a tiny frown. It could not have been easy given the amount of cosmetic surgery she'd had over the years. "Why do I have the feeling that things might be somewhat more complicated than you're letting on?"

"My client's name is Jack Winters. And the family heirloom is the Burning Lamp. Ring any bells?"

"Oh, my," Phyllis murmured. The vivacious energy that had animated her a moment ago dimmed abruptly. Her heavily made-up eyes narrowed with shrewd intelligence. "That definitely complicates the picture. Do you think he actually is a Winters? A true descendant of Nicholas Winters, I mean? The name is not that uncommon after all."

Chloe thought about the nightmare energy that had slammed through her last night. "I'm pretty sure he's the real deal."

"Why does he want the lamp?"

"He believes that he'll turn into some sort of psychic monster if he doesn't find it."

"But surely he realizes those old tales about Nicholas and the Burning Lamp are just myths and legends."

"He's convinced they're real," Chloe said.

Phyllis sniffed. "Then he must have a few loose screws."

"If I refused to accept every client who had a loose screw I'd go out of business in a week."

"How did he find you?"

"He admitted that he hacked into the Arcane files to find a strong dreamlight reader."

"And he came up with you? But you aren't registered with the Society. No Harper is."

"Evidently Arcane has kept tabs on the family over the years," Chloe said.

"Supercilious bastards." Phyllis bristled. "I'd like to know who granted them the right to set down rules for the rest of us who also happen to possess a modicum of talent. If I had a nickel for every time someone from J&J had the nerve to warn a member of our family that he or she was engaged in some enterprise that, as Arcane likes to put it, *gives psychics a bad name*, I would be a wealthy woman."

Chloe grinned. "You are a wealthy woman."

"That's not the point, and you know it."

Chloe nodded and sipped her tea. There was no need to go into detail. Everyone in the family understood that Arcane and J&J were to be avoided whenever and wherever possible.

"Trust me, under the circumstances Mr. Winters has no more desire to draw the attention of the Society than I do," she said.

"*Hmm.* That certainly gives the two of you something in common, doesn't it?"

"Are you trying to play matchmaker, Aunt Phyllis?"

Phyllis sighed. "I'm sorry, dear. I didn't mean to tease you. But I do worry about you and this new celibacy phase of yours. Just because a traditional marriage is not an option for you doesn't mean you can't have a little fun."

"I'm tired of having The Talk with men. It always goes the same way: Initially they jump at the offer of a no-strings-attached affair. They think it's the perfect setup."

"A male fantasy come true."

"But when they find out that I really am serious about not making a long-term commitment, they get mad and go all self-righteous on me. It only works if I let them dump me first. But who has the patience to sit around waiting for that to happen?"

"I know, dear," Phyllis said, her tone soothing. "You must learn how to finesse things."

"I try, Aunt Phyllis, but I always end up having to waste a lot of time and energy maneuvering seemingly intelligent men into thinking that they're the ones who are ready to move on." She was warming to her topic now. The frustration of it all spilled out of her. "It's not only tedious, it's stressful."

"It's tricky, I admit. In my younger days I assumed that the arrangement would work best with married men," Phyllis said. "They had every incentive to want a discreet arrangement with a woman who would never demand a commitment from them. But oddly enough the married ones always got just as upset as the single men did when I tried to end things. Something to do with the masculine ego, I suppose."

"You know I don't do married men," Chloe reminded her.

"I know, dear, another one of your rules. I really don't know how you manage with so many of them. I have always found that rules tended to take all the fun and spontaneity out of life."

"And then there's the problem of sleepovers," Chloe continued, ignoring the interruption. "Sooner or later men always want to go away with you for a romantic weekend. Heck, sooner or later I want to get away for a few days in Hawaii, too. But when they find out that they'll have to book two rooms they get irate, even when I make it clear that I'll pay for the second room."

Phyllis nodded solemnly. "I think it's the sense of knowing that they can never really possess you. So many men always seem to want what they can't have."

"The fiasco with that psych instructor a few months ago was the last straw. For Pete's sake, Fletcher Monroe seemed absolutely perfect for me. How could I have been so wrong?"

"Well, I did tell you that it is never a good idea to get involved with people involved in the field of psychology. They always try to fix you."

"I admit that was a mistake."

"But you really mustn't give up on love and a normal or at least seminormal sex life," Phyllis said firmly. "You're young and healthy. Your hormones are humming. There's always the possibility that you'll find that special person, a man who will accept a relationship on your terms."

"A man who will be okay with a committed relationship with a woman who won't sleep with him? Hah. What are the odds?"

"You know, in previous centuries it was not unusual for husbands and wives to have separate bedrooms."

"I think that was mainly an upper-class phenomenon." Chloe frowned. "Probably because the upper classes were the only ones who could afford a second bedroom and because marriages at that level of society were contracted for reasons other than love."

"I suppose that's true," Phyllis agreed. "But, still, there is a precedent for that approach to marriage."

Chloe looked at her. "You could afford a second bedroom. You could afford a dozen bedrooms. But you never married."

Phyllis expelled a surprisingly wistful sigh. "Yes, well, let's just say I never found the right man, either."

"Face it, marriage is not in the cards for women like us, Aunt Phyllis."

"Perhaps not, but that does not mean one cannot enjoy life and men. Think of yourself as a honeybee flitting from flower to flower."

Chloe tried to envision Jack Winters as a delicate blossom in a field of daisies. And failed.

"Somehow I don't think that imagery applies to Mr. Winters," she said. "There really is a kind of freedom in celibacy, you know."

"Is that so, dear?" Phyllis paused, her cup halfway to her lips. "I never noticed."

Phyllis called her on her cell phone an hour later.

"I got in touch with Drake. The dear man remembers me, bless his heart. He says he'll be happy to let you view his lamp. He suggests tomorrow afternoon."

"That's great," Chloe said. "Thanks so much. I could get to Vegas in the morning if that would be more convenient for him."

"Drake is in show business, dear. He doesn't do mornings."

15

SHE TOOK HECTOR FOR HIS CUSTOMARY WALK EARLY THE NEXT
morning. It was still dark, and it was raining, a classic Seattle mist. She
wore her trench coat and a hat pulled down low over her eyes. Umbrel-
las were for tourists.

Hector had established his territory early on after moving in with
her and Rose. Daily he patrolled the perimeter, which consisted of a
few blocks of Pioneer Square, marking trees and the corners of various buildings. Along the route they greeted the men and women who
emerged from the shelters, doorways, alleys and cribs under the viaduct
where they had spent the night.

Some of the street people had gotten into the habit of stopping to
chat with Hector. They knew he made no judgments. In addition,
he served as a conduit through which they could communicate with
Chloe. She considered them her Irregular Clients.

The one she thought of as Mountain Man because of his scraggly
beard leaned down to pat Hector's side.

"Hey, there, Big Guy," he mumbled. "What's with the funny collar and that bandage? You get hurt?"

"Hector says to tell you that he got shot trying to protect me," Chloe said.

"Shot, huh? Bummer. Been there, done that. You gonna be okay, Big Guy?"

"He'll be fine," Chloe said. "He wants to know how you're doing?"

"Doin' okay," Mountain Man said to Hector. "Had another bad dream last night, though. Can't seem to shake it. Keep seein' it in my head, y'know?"

"Hector wants to know if you want him to help you forget the dream," Chloe said.

"I'd appreciate that," Mountain Man said. He continued to pat Hector.

Chloe opened her senses and put her hand on Hector's back close to where Mountain Man was petting him. She readied herself for the inevitable psychic shock and let her fingers brush against Mountain Man's weathered hand.

A shivering jolt of fear and pain lanced through her. Although she could not actually see another person's dream images, her dream reader's intuition interpreted the energy residue in a very visual and visceral way. Mountain Man's dreamscape was a terrible canvas painted in darkness, blood and body parts. The sounds of explosives, guns and helicopters roared silently in the background. The nightmare was familiar. It was not the first time she had brushed up against it.

She set her teeth and went to work identifying the disturbed currents of dreamlight. Swiftly she pulsed counterpoint psi to dampen the seething patterns. Mountain Man's wavelengths would never be normal, but at least she could provide some relief from the night terrors that haunted his days.

Mountain Man straightened after a while. "Feels better. Thanks, Hector. You two have a good day now."

"We will," Chloe said. "By the way, how's the cough this morning?"

Mountain Man responded with a harsh, rasping hack. Then he thumped his chest. "Better."

"Did you go to the clinic?"

"Not yet."

"Please, go. Hector thinks you should."

"Yeah?" Mountain Man looked down at Hector. "Okay, maybe I'll do that."

"Today," Chloe said gently. "Hector wants you to promise to go today."

"I will," Mountain Man vowed to Hector. "Got my word on it, Big Guy."

He turned and shambled off across the intersection, heading for his day job, panhandling near the Pike Place Market. There was a clinic in the Market designed for people like Mountain Man. She could only hope that he would follow through on his promise this time.

SHE WAS IN THE BEDROOM, throwing a few things into a small carry-on bag on the off chance that she might have to spend the night in Vegas, when Rose shouted from the landing on the second floor.

"Chloe? Fletcher Monroe is here. He'd like to talk to you."

Just what she did not need. She tossed the long-sleeved silk nightgown onto the neatly folded silk travel sheet already in the suitcase and went to the open doorway. Hector, who had been napping on the floor, lumbered to his feet and followed her. Fletcher was already on the stairs that led up to her third-floor apartment. Hector glared at him, turned around and went back into the living room.

Fletcher was dressed in jeans, a button-down shirt with a T-shirt underneath, running shoes and no tie. He had the vaguely rumpled, decidedly un-crisp look that was de rigueur in the academic world. Heaven forbid a Pacific Northwest instructor be mistaken for a denizen of the corporate establishment.

It was annoying that Fletcher still felt he had a right to come up here and invade her private space, Chloe thought. Sure, she'd invited him in for tea and after-dinner drinks a few times and they'd done some good-natured petting on the sofa. But he was a client now.

This was one of the problems that came up when you mixed business and pleasure. Boyfriends who metamorphosed into clients and vice versa never got the rules straight. She was forced to set boundaries, and then guys got mad.

She was about to tell Fletcher that she would meet him downstairs when she noticed the wobbly light of his psi prints. He was giving her his easy, charming smile, acting as if all was normal. But the unsteady, shifting hues of dreamlight told her he was still badly unnerved. He'd had a close brush with death and he knew it. He would be awhile getting over the scare.

"Hey, there, Miss Psychic Private Eye," he said. "I hear you saved my life the other night."

She hated it when he called her Miss Psychic Private Eye. It was his unsubtle way of mocking what he considered her delusional talent.

"I had some help." She surveyed him. "How do you feel?"

He stopped smiling and exhaled heavily. "I've got the mother of all hangovers, thanks to the sleeping meds that bitch put in those cookies, but obviously it could be worse." He halted on the landing and glanced past her into the apartment. "Actually, it is worse. I don't have any place to sleep. I know it's a lot to ask, but would you mind if I stayed here until I can rent an apartment?"

"I'm sorry, Fletcher," she said gently. "That's not possible. You'll have to go to a hotel."

"I lost everything in that damn fire."

He was starting to whine. She hated when clients whined. "You've still got a bank account, right?" she said. "And what about your wallet? Was that in your pants when we dragged you out the door?"

"Well, yeah, but—"

"So you've got your credit cards and access to an ATM. That should be enough to get you a hotel room for a few nights. I'm sure it won't take long to find an apartment. I'm really sorry about the house."

"Why didn't you stop her?" Fletcher demanded. The whining tone got worse. "That's why I hired you."

"You hired me to get some proof that she was stalking you."

"She tried to burn my house down around me."

"I realize that. I was there."

"So why didn't you stop her?"

She sighed. "Things escalated rapidly. I didn't realize what was happening in time to stop her. All I could do was try to save you."

"Evidently you didn't even do that very well. They said your assistant and some stranger came along and helped you drag me out of the house."

"That's true."

"They also said that Madeline Gibson had a psychotic break and collapsed. That's probably the real reason you were able to save me."

"Probably," she agreed. "Look, Fletcher, I'm in a hurry. Got a plane to catch."

"So now you're taking off on vacation?"

"No. It's business."

"If you're going to leave town I don't see why I can't stay here for a couple of nights. It's the least you can do under the circumstances."

"No, Fletcher. I'm afraid that's not possible."

No man stayed overnight in her private space. Not even when she was not around. Dream energy stuck to sheets and bedding like darkness on night. You couldn't wash out that kind of psi. If she allowed Fletcher to sleep in her bed she would have to buy a new mattress, a new set of sheets, a new mattress pad, new pillows and probably a new comforter as well. She could handle strange beds for a few nights if she took the proper precautions, but when it came to her own bed, she liked things pristine.

"What is it with you?" he grumbled. "I thought we were friends."

Before she could answer she heard the muffled sound of the first-floor lobby door opening and closing. A tingle of awareness whispered through her, stirring things deep inside. She did not have to go out onto the landing to see who was coming up the stairs. Hector went past her to greet Jack.

"Sorry, Fletcher," she said. "My client is here. I have to go now."

"What client?" Fletcher turned to look back down the stairs.

"The one who helped me save your life," she said.

Jack arrived on the third-floor landing. He looked at Fletcher with the same lack of interest that Hector displayed.

"Jack Winters," he said.

"Fletcher Monroe." Fletcher frowned. "You're the guy who was at my house last night?"

"Right."

"Why the hell did you save Madeline Gibson?"

Jack looked at Chloe.

She shrugged. "I told you, clients are never satisfied."

16

VICTORIA KNIGHT PICKED UP HER DEEPLY ENCRYPTED PHONE
and punched in a number. There were several rings before her new associate answered.

"What is it?" Humphrey Hulsey whispered. "Do you have some
news?"

"The initial experiment is definitely a success. It's been over a week
now and Winters is alive. He's showing no indications of insanity or
deterioration."

"Then your first theory is correct." Hulsey was exultant.

"Looks like it." She kept her voice cool, refusing to let her own elation show.

"That settles it. You must find the lamp and a dream talent who can
work it as soon as possible so that we can move forward."

"As it happens, we've caught a very lucky break."

"What do you mean?" Hulsey said.

"Winters himself is now searching for the lamp," she said. "In fact, it appears that he has dropped everything else, including his business, to go after it. There's only one reason he would suddenly decide to make such an effort."

"His second talent is emerging."

"It seems that my grandfather was also right about age being a genetic trigger. Jack Winters turned thirty-six a couple of months ago. He is now the same age Griffin Winters was when his second talent emerged."

"Interesting. It makes sense that the genetic change is tied to chronological age. You said Jack Winters is searching for the lamp?"

"He's hired a dreamlight reader to help him find it. Evidently he believes the legends, too."

"Where did he find a high-level dreamlight reader?" Hulsey asked. "It's not a common talent."

"He hired a low-rent private eye who just happens to have that particular ability. Looks like they've had some success already."

"How do you know?" Hulsey demanded.

"They boarded a flight to Las Vegas about twenty minutes ago. I doubt very much that they're going there to gamble."

"Do you think it's possible that they've actually found the lamp already?"

"We'll know soon enough. I've got two people watching them."

The upper echelons of Nightshade were in hushed but seething turmoil at the moment. That was a good thing. Nothing like a temporary power vacuum at the top of an organization to provide cover for a little maneuvering farther down the chain of command.

It had taken the members of the Inner Circle of Nightshade—known officially as the Board of Directors—some time to become convinced that the founder and Master was no longer alive. William Craigmore was a legend, a dangerous one, and such men did not die easily. But the board had finally concluded that he was dead. There was some question as to the cause of death. No one was sure if Arcane had discovered that Craigmore was the founder of Nightshade and terminated him or if he actually had dropped dead of a heart attack. He had been on the formula for decades. There was no knowing what the long-term effects had been on his cardiovascular system. Either way a new director had to be chosen as soon as possible.

Back at the beginning Craigmore had not referred to his organization as Nightshade. He had established it as a legitimate, very low-profile corporation. The melodramatic label had been coined by Fallon Jones as a code for what had become Arcane's twenty-first-century nemesis.

Craigmore had been aware of the J&J code name because of his position on Arcane's Governing Council. Evidently he'd liked the theatrical touch and had adopted it. Probably a legacy of his days as a government agent, Victoria thought. For some reason, spy agencies were very big on exotic code names. Whatever the case, the members of the shadowy conspiracy Craigmore had founded now routinely referred to their organization as Nightshade.

In addition to the recent loss of its founder, Nightshade was also reeling from the shock of J&J's discovery and destruction of several clandestine formula labs. There was no doubt a lot of finger-pointing going on at the top. Victoria suspected that some of those at the highest levels would not survive. Nightshade was nothing if not an exercise in Darwinian theory. It wouldn't be the first time that its corporate politics took a deadly turn.

She did not care what happened in the upper echelons. Not yet. There was little she could do to affect the outcome of the power struggles at this point, anyway. Someday she would control Nightshade, but that time had not yet come.

Her immediate goal was to take charge of one of the three surviving drug labs, specifically the one located in Portland, Oregon.

"Do you think the dream talent Winters found will be strong enough to work the lamp?" Hulsey asked anxiously.

"According to the J&J files she looks like a Level Seven."

"I'm not at all sure that will be enough sensitivity. Most dreamlight readers can see only a limited portion of the dream spectrum. Very few can actually work that kind of energy."

Victoria looked at her computer screen where her notes about the colorful Harper family were displayed. "The seven has a very big asterisk after it. J&J suspects she's probably a lot stronger."

"The agency isn't sure?"

"She has never been officially registered with the Society or tested. No one in her family registers and gets tested. In fact, the Harpers have a long history of going out of their way to avoid Arcane. Probably another reason why Winters chose Chloe Harper. He wouldn't want a dream talent who would pick up the phone and call J&J as soon as she heard his name."

"We can't proceed with the rest of the experiment until Winters locates that lamp," Hulsey stated. "Keep me informed."

"Of course, Doctor."

She broke the connection and spent a few minutes going over the plan yet again. There were always risks involved in a scheme this daring, but she had done a good job of limiting them. She had also provided several escape routes and bolt holes for herself in the event everything went south.

If things went wrong it would not be the first time she'd pulled off a disappearing act. After the Oriana Bay disaster a few months ago she had been obliged to destroy her Niki Plumer identity in a way that had convinced both Nightshade and J&J that she was dead. Being a strong para-hypnotist had its advantages. All in all, however, the new venture was coming together very nicely.

Unlike a lot of people, she took the legends and myths of the Arcane Society seriously. She was, after all, the product of one of those legends.

17

CHLOE LOOKED OUT THE WINDOW OF THE PLANE AND CON-
templated the fantasy landscape that was the Las Vegas Strip. From
the air the sharp divide between the real and the fake was clear. Like
the movie sets on Hollywood's back lots, the exotic, fanciful façades
of the big casino-hotels were only skin deep.

Immediately behind the phony Renaissance palaces, medieval cas-
tles, Roman temples, Egyptian pyramids, waterfalls, rain forests, artifi-
cial islands and pirate ships lay acres of concrete. The massive rooftops
of the resorts were laden with the huge HVAC equipment required to
keep the gaming floors icy cool even when the outside temperatures
soared past 110°F.

Beyond the rooftops lay the big garages, parking lots and RV parks.
Next came streets filled with shabby budget motels and cheap apartment buildings. And sprawling out to the distant circle of mountains
lay vast stretches of desert punctuated by subdivisions, golf courses and
acres of sagebrush.

But when you were down on the ground, in the middle of the Strip, all you could see was the fantasy, Chloe thought.

"I still think this is a really bad idea," she said. "I never take clients along on a verification trip. They always get emotional, regardless of how things turn out."

"You've mentioned that several times," Jack said. "Trust me; I'm not the emotional type."

She believed him. *Control* was clearly his middle name. The man probably lived on a steady diet of ice and glacial melt. But that did not make him any more predictable than the client who was at the mercy of his emotions.

"Remember, I'll do the talking," she said.

"You've already mentioned that at least twelve times." He checked his watch. "How are you feeling?"

"I told you, I'm fine."

"How much sleep did you get the past couple of nights?"

"Enough," she said.

"How bad were they?"

"What?" she asked. But she knew what he was talking about.

"The dreams," he said.

"Don't worry, I didn't wake up screaming. The wine took the edge off. Besides, I'm a dream talent, remember? I can handle a few bad dreams."

"They were brutal, weren't they?"

"Well," she said, "Madeline Gibson is a very disturbed young woman. Stands to reason that her dream energy is also pretty unstable."

He frowned. "What do you mean? Didn't you get hit with my nightmares?"

"No. I got a dose of her energy." She turned in the seat, frowning a little. "What did you think happened?"

"I'm not sure," he said. "I told you, it's not like I've been able to run any controlled experiments with this damn second talent. But I assumed that when I used it, I was generating energy and images from my own dreamscape and that it was those visions that struck the target."

She thought about that and then shook her head. "I admit I've only had the single close encounter, but I think what happens is that when you use your talent, you send out currents of very strong, intensely focused energy from the dark end of your dream spectrum. That energy, however, doesn't carry the images from your dreams and nightmares. It's just energy."

"How does it work, then?"

"I got the impression that you use your talent to trigger the target's own dark dream energy. When you hit Madeline Gibson with that shock of psi she was suddenly plunged into her own nightmares, not yours. It was the ultralight from her dream world that I brushed up against." She shuddered. "Like I said, she's one sick woman."

"So the way this works is, I can force another person into a really bad dream?"

"Even regular, garden-variety nightmares produce strong physiological changes. Heart rate speeds up. Breathing becomes shallow. Blood pressure is elevated. People wake up in a cold sweat. It makes sense that the shock of being plunged into a nightmare while in the waking state would create extreme disorientation and panic or even cause a person to faint like Madeline did."

"Or the heart fails and someone dies," Jack said grimly. "Like that guy in the alley the other night."

"There is that possibility," she allowed.

"Shit," Jack whispered. He stared hard at the seat back in front of him. "My new talent is turning me into everyone's worst nightmare."

She considered that for a few seconds, and then she started to grin. She couldn't help herself. The next thing she knew, the laughter was bubbling up out of her like champagne.

"What the hell is so damn funny?" he demanded.

"I don't know." She managed to get control of her laughter, but she knew her lips were still twitching. "It's just something about the way you said that. For what it's worth, my advice is not to get too worked up about this new talent of yours."

"I'm a double-talent," he said evenly. "That makes me a monster in Arcane's eyes."

"Screw Arcane. According to my aunt Phyllis, they're just a bunch of supercilious bastards who think they have the right to tell other sensitives what to do. Who put the Joneses in charge of making rules for the rest of us? That's what I'd like to know."

A glint of humor came and went in his eyes. "Good question," he agreed judiciously.

"I'll bet the real problem Arcane has with double- or multi-talents is that they haven't had much experience with them. They've made assumptions based on a few anecdotal records of a handful of individuals who exhibited more than one strong talent. But those people were obviously too weak psychically to handle that much power. They self-destructed, so to speak."

"They've also got Nicholas Winters," Jack reminded her.

"Yeah, well, according to the legend, Old Nick tried to murder Sylvester. Stands to reason that the Joneses might have taken a somewhat less than fair and balanced view of the entire situation. Anyhow, the bottom line here is that you are not weak. You've obviously got all the wattage you need to control your second talent."

"For now," he said grimly.

"Mr. Positive Thinker. As far as what happened the night before last, you can stop apologizing. Heck, the sight of Madeline Gibson holding that gun was more than enough to trigger some nasty dreams. Now you know why I hate those kinds of cases."

He looked at her. "I love it when you do that."

"Do what?"

"Play the tough PI." His mouth kicked up a little at the corner. "What makes it so interesting is that you really are tough. How did you end up in a legitimate line of work?"

She went still in the seat. "What are you implying, Mr. Winters?"

He was even more amused by her sudden bristling. "Don't take offense. I'm making no moral or ethical judgments here. I'm just curious. The Harper family has a long history with Arcane and a lot of that history could be considered thorny, to put it mildly."

"Most of my relatives have a talent for art of one sort or another," she said stiffly. "I lacked that kind of ability, so I had to find another way to make a living."

"I'm not buying that, not for a minute."

"I assure you, I have absolutely no artistic talent. I'm good at finding things, that's all."

"But that's not why you went legit."

"It isn't?"

She infused her voice with all the icy reserve she could summon. It didn't seem to faze him.

"No," he said. "You became a PI because you're one of the good guys. You're a natural-born fixer. You want to find answers and fix things for people."

"And just what makes you so sure you know so much about me?"

He shrugged. "Part of my strat talent. I'm good at scoping out weaknesses and vulnerabilities in people. That's why I've been able to make so much money."

"How nice for you."

"The talent has its uses," he agreed neutrally.

The flight attendant's voice came over the PA system, instructing the passengers to prepare for the landing. Chloe straightened in her seat and checked the belt.

"One more thing before we meet with Drake Stone," she said.

"What?"

"Whatever you do, don't try to coerce him into selling you the lamp. Take it from me, that never works."

"I'm a strategy-talent who has made a lot of money putting deals together."

"I know, but—"

"Trust me, everyone really does have a price, Chloe. I'll know Stone's within five minutes of meeting him."

She did not like the sound of that.

"I want your word that you will let me handle this situation," she insisted. "Collectors are an odd bunch."

"I doubt that they are any more weird than some of the folks I've backed."

"Just remember, I'm in charge."

"You're the expert."

Not quite what she had wanted to hear.

18

"THERE ARE DAYS, MISS HARPER, WHEN I THINK THAT IF I HAVE
to sing "Blue Champagne" one more time I'm going to lose it completely and go bonkers right there on stage."

Chloe smiled. "So this probably isn't the time to tell you that my assistant informed me that you were her mother's favorite singer."

They were sitting on a patio overlooking a sparkling turquoise pool
framed by stone columns and twin rows of classical statues. The day
was bright and sunny, but it was, in Chloe's opinion, a tad cool to be
sitting outdoors, even if this was the desert. It was still December, after
all, and sixty-two degrees was still sixty-two degrees; not true patio
weather even if you were from Seattle. They were all quite comfortable,
however, because two towering propane patio heaters cast a warm glow
over the scene.

Here in Vegas, you didn't let a little thing like the weather get in
the way of the ambience. Come high summer, when the temps were
routinely in the low one hundreds, Drake Stone's patio would be just

as comfortable as it was now. The row of misters installed at the edge of the awning would cool the atmosphere with an airy spray of water.

Stone had given them a true Vegas welcome. He had dispatched a stretch limo to pick them up at the airport. The bar in the rear of the vehicle had offered cold beer, chilled champagne and an assortment of soft drinks. She and Jack had sipped sparkling spring water in hushed luxury on the drive out to Warm Springs Road to an exclusive enclave of private estates. Along the way they passed subdivisions and small strip malls interspersed with acres of undeveloped land covered in sagebrush.

High stone walls surrounded Drake Stone's home. The gate was manned by a uniformed guard. Pines and purple plums shaded the grounds. The main house resembled one of the fantasy hotel-casinos on the strip, an over-the-top Mediterranean villa built around the pool and a large, lushly landscaped courtyard.

Stone's interior designer had gone mad with what in Vegas passed for the Renaissance look. The heavily gilded furniture was oversized, covered in rich brocades and trimmed with a lot of gold tassels and velvet pillows. In the vast living room a hand-painted sky complete with fluffy clouds and plump cherubs adorned the ceiling. Tapestries covered the walls.

Stone had proven to be a genial host who was obviously enjoying his guests. He was dressed in a pair of loose, elegantly draped white trousers, a white, long-sleeved shirt, white sandals and designer sunglasses. There were a lot of rings on his hands and some gold chains around his throat. The gemstones and the gold looked real.

Chloe knew that he had to be in his mid-sixties, but there was an ageless quality about him, as if he had been preserved in plastic or maybe embalmed. He had obviously had a lot of work done, and it had all been of the highest quality. His jaw line was amazingly firm, his teeth were brilliantly white and the sprayed-on tan was just the right shade. His hair was as dark and thick as that of any nineteen-year-old, although the average nineteen-year-old probably would not have gone with the blow-dried pompadour.

It would have been easy to assume that Drake Stone was a caricature of an aging Vegas lounge crooner, but that would have been a serious mistake, Chloe thought. She knew, because Phyllis had explained often enough that it took intelligence, pragmatism, luck and sheer grit to keep a career in show business going as long as Stone had. That was especially true when that career was founded on a single hit song. It also took a lot of financial savvy and connections to amass the kind of fortune that could re-create a Roman villa in the Las Vegas desert.

There was something else about Drake Stone that caught her attention, a faint but discernable aura of energy. She could see it in his psi prints. She was willing to bet that he was a low-level sensitive, maybe a two on the Jones Scale. He was probably unaware of his talent. People with above-average intuition usually took the gift for granted. But over the years it would have given him an edge that no doubt accounted for his long-lived success in a cutthroat business.

She took a sip of the tea that Drake's housekeeper had served. The men drank coffee. She was having a good time. Meeting people like Drake Stone was one of the perks of her job. But Jack, seated on the chair next to her, was barely masking his impatience with the pleasantries. Dark glasses shielded his eyes and his face was impassive, but she could feel the cold anticipation in him.

Drake laughed. "Trust me, I'm always thrilled to hear that I'm anyone's favorite singer. But I'll admit I'd have been even more flattered if you had said that I was your *assistant's* favorite singer, not her mother's."

"Her mother was murdered a few years ago," Chloe said gently. "The memory of her mom listening to your music is very important to her."

"Understood," Drake said, going very serious. "Tell her I feel honored."

"I will." She smiled. "Is it true that the ladies in the audience still line up for a kiss after the show?"

"It's true." Drake winked. "But I've been doing my show here for thirty years. Back at the start, the women in the audience were thirty years younger. Hell, so was I. But enough about me. How is Phyllis doing? I miss her wise counsel."

"My aunt is doing great. She still takes calls from old clients. You should give her a ring."

"I'll do that," Drake said. He flicked a look of veiled assessment at Jack and then turned back to her. "I'm curious to know how you found out that I owned the lamp. I bought it last year from an online dealer. You two are the first people who have asked me about it."

"Finding things like the lamp is what I do," Chloe said. "As my aunt explained to you on the phone, Mr. Winters hired me to locate it. He's considering acquiring it for his collection."

Drake looked at Jack. "And what's your interest in it?"

"Family heirloom," Jack said. "It got lost during a cross-country move several years ago."

"You must come from a rather interesting family," Drake said.

"Why do you say that?" Jack asked.

"Call it a hunch based on what you consider a valuable family heirloom," Drake said drily.

"What made you decide to buy it?" Jack asked.

"Beats me." Drake moved one hand in a vague manner. "I was approached online by a dealer shortly after one of the major design magazines did a spread on this place. The guy convinced me that he had a genuine late-seventeenth-century lamp with an interesting history that would look terrific in my house. Claimed it was made out of gold and decorated with a lot of good gemstones. What can I say? I was interested."

"You agreed to buy it sight unseen?" Chloe asked.

"Of course not," Drake said. "I told him I wanted it evaluated by an expert first. I invited him to bring the lamp here to Vegas. I planned to have a local authority I know take a look at it."

Chloe nodded. "Edward Harper. He's one of my uncles."

"That's right. My interior designer used him for a lot of the pieces she put into this place."

"Uncle Edward was the person who told me that you might have the lamp," she said. "But he couldn't confirm it. He said he never actually saw it. Who did you get to examine and appraise the lamp?"

"No one," Drake said. He drank some coffee and leaned back in his chair. "The morning after I informed the online dealer that I had arranged for the evaluation, the crate containing the lamp showed up on my doorstep. There was no invoice, no delivery papers, no records of any kind. I went back online and tried to find the dealer, but he had disappeared. I figured the lamp had been stolen and someone didn't want it traced back to him."

"Why didn't you go ahead and have the lamp appraised?" Chloe asked.

"As soon as I opened the crate, I realized it would be a waste of time. At first glance the metal looks a lot like gold, but it isn't gold. That was obvious immediately. Gold is soft, but you can't even put a dent in that lamp. Believe me, I tried. The thing just has to be made of some kind of modern alloy."

"What about the gemstones?" Chloe asked.

Drake grimaced. "They're just big, cloudy glass rocks. I didn't need Edward Harper to tell me the lamp was definitely not late seventeenth century."

"Hell," Jack said, his tone flat. He looked at Chloe. "Should have known that finding the lamp so quickly was too good to be true."

Disappointment and frustration twisted through her. There was also a lot of embarrassment in the mix. All in all she felt utterly deflated.

"I was so certain," she said. She looked at Drake. "Are you absolutely sure the gemstones are glass?"

"Well, I couldn't put a scratch on them, so I guess it's possible that they may be some high-tech crystals," he admitted. "I ran a couple of experiments with a hammer and then with a drill. Couldn't even chip the stones."

"Let me get this straight," Jack said evenly. "You did your best to destroy the lamp?"

Drake shrugged, unperturbed. "I have to admit it aroused my curiosity. Something about it interested me. But after a while, it started to bother me. Can't really explain it. At first I stuck it on a pedestal in one of the guest bathrooms. As a joke, you know? But my housekeeper told me it bothered her. After a while I realized that I didn't even want it in the house. I put it back in the crate, nailed the crate shut and stashed it where I wouldn't have to look at it on a regular basis."

Chloe cleared her throat. "If you didn't like the lamp, why did you keep it? Why not just chuck it into the trash?"

"Beats me," Drake said. "I thought about doing just that from time to time. But, for whatever reason, I didn't. There's something about it." He looked at Jack. "Every time I considered getting rid of it I got this weird feeling that I should hold on to it." He smiled his stage-lights smile. "Like maybe until the real owner showed up."

There's just something about it. A tiny flicker of hope sparked inside Chloe. Paranormal artifacts exerted their own kind of compelling attraction, especially on those who possessed even a small measure of talent. Maybe Drake Stone had sensed some energy in the object. But the Winters lamp had been forged in the late 1600s. Drake seemed certain the item he had bought online was modern.

Jack was looking interested again. "I'd like to see it, if you don't mind."

"Come with me." Drake put his coffee aside and rose from the lounge chair. "Frankly, I'll be thrilled if you take it off my hands. Hell, I'll pay you to remove it."

He started across the heavily landscaped pool gardens.

Chloe glanced at Jack, but he was already on his feet, moving to follow Drake. She put down her tea and got up to follow the two men. A familiar fizzy sensation was whispering through her. Harper intuition always told her when she was on the right track.

Drake threaded a path through the maze of plantings, statuary and fountains to a low building tucked out of sight behind a high hedge. He stopped, dug out some keys and opened the door.

"Like I said, I kept it in the house for about a week." Drake pushed the door open. "After that I couldn't stand it any longer. The guys from the pool service gave me some static when I stored it in here, but given what I pay them, I figured they could just get over it."

"Why did the pool service people complain?" Jack asked.

"They decided that the crate contained some toxic gardening chemicals or pesticides. They wanted me to get rid of whatever was inside it."

"Bad smell?" Chloe asked.

"No," Drake said. He smiled wryly. "Whatever it is, it seems to affect the nerves."

He reached around the edge of the door, flipped a light switch and stood back.

A tendril of dark, powerful energy wafted out of the opening. It didn't just stir the hair on the nape of Chloe's neck, it prickled the skin on her upper arms and caused her pulse to quicken. An unsettling chill swept through her. She knew Jack sensed the currents, too. He said nothing, but she could tell that he had opened up all of his senses. Energy pulsed invisibly in the atmosphere around him. He stood in the doorway and looked into the shadowy interior of the pool house.

She took a couple of steps closer and peered past him into the crowded space. It took a few seconds for her eyes to adjust to the low light. When they did, all she saw was a lot of gardening equipment, pool chemicals and cleaning devices. She did not see a crate.

"It's all the way at the back," Drake said, as if he'd read her mind. "Under some tarps."

Jack removed his dark glasses, dropped them into his shirt pocket and entered the pool house as if he knew precisely where he was going.

"I'll wait out here," Chloe said. He gave no indication that he had heard her.

Energy spiked higher in the atmosphere, not the stuff that was uncoiling in ominous waves from inside the structure. She slipped into her other vision and looked down. Hot ultralight dream energy burned in Jack's footsteps.

She heard the clang and thud of some gardening tools being shifted about inside the shed. A moment later Jack emerged, a wooden crate under one arm. He used his free hand to put on his dark glasses.

"I'll take it," he said to Drake. "What's your price?"

"You haven't even opened the crate," Drake pointed out.

"That won't be necessary," Jack said. "Whatever is inside this crate belongs to me."

Drake studied him for a long, considering moment and then his neon-bright teeth flashed in the sun. "It's yours, Winters, free and clear. It didn't cost me a damn thing in the first place, and you're saving me the cost of having it carted away by the garbage company. A real deal as far as I'm concerned."

"I can afford to pay for it," Jack said.

"I know that. You're Jack Winters of Winters Investments, right?"

"You did your research."

"Of course. You've got more money than God. But so do I. Take the lamp. It's yours."

Jack studied him for a moment. Chloe felt another little rush of energy. Then Jack nodded once, as though a bargain had been struck.

"I owe you," Jack said. "If there's ever anything you need that I can supply, you've got it."

"Yeah, I can see that," Drake said. He was obviously satisfied with the deal. "Good to know. Money can't buy everything, even in this town. I learned a long time ago that sometimes a favor owed is a hell of a lot more valuable."

He closed the door of the shed.

19

"AREN'T YOU EVEN GOING TO LOOK AT IT BEFORE WE GET ON the plane?" Chloe asked. "Don't you want to make sure that whatever is inside that crate really is the Burning Lamp?"

"Like I told Stone, whatever is inside that crate has got my name on it," Jack said. "And, yes, I intend to examine it before we go back to Seattle. But not here. Not now."

They were standing outside the entrance to McCarran Airport. The long limo had just deposited them and the crate on the sidewalk. The big vehicle was already vanishing into the endless stream of cabs and cars.

She glanced at her watch. "You want to find someplace more private? I understand, but our plane leaves in an hour and a half." She looked around. "I suppose we could take a cab to a nearby hotel, but we'd need to get a room. There's just not enough time."

"A room is exactly what we need," Jack said. He gripped the crate tightly under his arm. He had not let go of it since he had carried it out of the pool house. The case containing his computer was slung over his shoulder. "We'll spend the night here. Figure out how to work the lamp and fly back to Seattle in the morning."

She blinked. "I'm not sure that's a good idea."

"I want to get this done. Tonight."

She sensed the psi burning through him. He was focused one hundred percent on the object inside the crate, obsessed with it. In this condition he was not likely to listen to anything she had to say. But she had to try.

"I realize that you're anxious to see if the lamp can stop what you think is happening to you," she said, "but I'm the one who is supposed to work it, remember? I don't have a clue about how I'm going to do that. I'll need time to study the lamp. Time to do some research online. Time to think."

"What's to study or think about? The lamp emits radiation on the dreamlight end of the spectrum. You're a high-level dreamlight reader. You're supposed to be able to work that radiation to make sure I don't turn into a monster."

"You make it sound so simple."

"It is simple."

"Oh, yeah? And what happens if I screw up my part of this business?"

He looked at her through the dark shield of his sunglasses. "According to the legends, if things go wrong there are two possibilities: You'll either destroy all of my talent or you'll kill me."

"Gee, you know, given those options, I think we might want to allow a little time for study and contemplation here."

For a moment he did not speak. She was beginning to hope that he was starting to see the wisdom of her logic when his jaw tightened.

"There's something else, Chloe," he said finally.

"What?"

"If things go wrong, if you can't get rid of this second talent and stabilize my dreamstate, I will have to disappear."

"Because of J&J, you mean?"

"For all I know they've been watching me for months. Years, maybe."

"For heaven's sake, why?"

"Because that's the way Fallon Jones is when it comes to potential problems that could blow up into major headaches for the Society. As Nicholas Winters's direct male descendant, his *only* male descendant, I fit the profile of a walking time bomb as far as Fallon is concerned."

"Just how do you plan to pull this disappearing act?"

"A year ago I established a second ID for myself. I carry the passport and credit cards with me at all times. If the lamp doesn't work, I'll get on a plane and vanish."

She cleared her throat. "Uh, Jack, does it strike you that you're becoming a trifle paranoid here?"

"Fallon and I talked about it once."

"You and Fallon Jones talked about this human time-bomb thing?" she asked, incredulous.

"The last time we went out together for a beer. Just before he moved to Scargill Cove. We've known each other since childhood. We were friends once upon a time. He knew the history of the lamp, knew what might happen to me if I got hit by the curse. And he made it clear what he would have to do if I turned rogue."

"He actually warned you that he would hunt you down?" She sniffed, disgusted. "Guess that's what you get when you have a Jones for a friend."

"I knew where he was coming from. I told you at the start of this thing that if I were in his place, I'd do the same. The Society has a responsibility in situations like this. It can't allow artificially enhanced psychic rogues to run free."

"Whoa." She put both hands up, palms out. "Back up here. You are not a rogue. I can personally testify to that. I've read your dreamlight. I know the bad guys when I see them. You are not one of them."

"I agree that I haven't gone rogue yet. But who knows how long I've got before some switch gets tripped at the paranormal end of my energy field? Now that I've got the lamp, I can't waste any time. I told you, the damn thing has a habit of disappearing."

She was never going to get him on a plane. That was obvious.

"Okay," she said. "I'll make a deal with you. We'll get a room here in town. I'll take a look at the lamp. If I feel comfortable trying to work it, I'll go for it. But if I don't think I can handle it—"

"You have to work it, Chloe. I told you, the only other dream readers I identified in the Arcane files are employed by the Society. Even if I could take the risk of contacting one of them it wouldn't do any good. None of them are as strong as you."

She exhaled slowly, out of arguments. "Aunt Phyllis always said that someday I'd find a man who didn't have a problem with my talent."

20

THE NEED TO GET THE LAMP OUT OF THE CRATE, TO TOUCH it, to find out if it could save him from whatever was happening to him was a heavy, intensifying pressure. He felt as if he was trying to resist a strong gravitational field. But he would not be ruled by the demands of his senses. He was still in control of the demon inside him, and he was going to stay in control. Even if it killed him.

When they got into the cab he instructed the driver to stop first at the nearest hardware store. He left Chloe sitting in the back, the meter running, while he went inside to pick up a crow bar and a screwdriver. He was back in the car within ten minutes.

"Downtown," he said.

The driver looked at him in the rearview mirror. "Where, downtown?"

"I'll tell you when we get there."

The driver shrugged and headed for the old section of the city. When you drove a cab in Vegas, you didn't ask a lot of questions.

Chloe didn't ask any questions, either. She said nothing when they bypassed the glittering high-rise resorts on the palm-studded Strip and headed for the grittier, seedier downtown. She had probably guessed that he would not give her any answers as long as they were sitting in the backseat of a cab where the driver could overhear.

He was pretty sure he knew what she was thinking. She had concluded that he was now in full-blown paranoid mode. She was right. As the old saying went, even paranoids had enemies, and when one of those enemies might turn out to be J&J, it was only common sense to take precautions. If the agency did come looking for him they would start with the big hotels on the Strip because that was where someone with his kind of money would stay.

Paranoid, for sure.

The cab exited I-15 and plunged into the streets of faded, two-story motels, dingy gentlemen's clubs, storefront casinos and gaudy, drive-through wedding chapels that cluttered what was known as Old Town.

He told the driver to stop on a side street in front of an adult bookstore.

Chloe got out and stood beside him on the sidewalk. She grasped the handle of her carry-on in one hand and her satchel in the other. Together they watched the vehicle speed away, and then Chloe turned to survey the nearby pawnshop and neighboring tattoo parlor.

"The real Vegas," she said drily.

"Nothing's real in Vegas." He adjusted the crate under his arm and gripped the computer case in his other hand. The computer was not the only thing in the case. His overnight kit and a full set of IDs for a man named John Stewart Carter was also inside. He started walking. "Let's go."

She hurried to keep up with him. "Where are we going?"

He contemplated a sun-bleached sign halfway down the street. "What would you say to one hour in a private hot tub at the Tropical Gardens Motel?"

"The word *yuck* comes to mind."

"Okay, be that way. Forget the hot tub. We'll just get a room. But don't say I never take you anywhere."

At the front desk of the Tropical Gardens, there was no need to bother with the Carter ID. He just gave a fake name and paid in cash. The Vegas Way.

The bored clerk handed him a key. "Enjoy your stay, Mr. and Mrs. Rivers."

They went through the small, grimy lobby, past the two senior citizens perched on the stools in front of a pair of slot machines and climbed a flight of stairs to the second floor.

"I can feel it, too, you know," Chloe said quietly.

He knew what she meant. "It's not just that I'm picking up on the energy coming from the lamp. The weird part is that I recognize the vibes. They're familiar. It's like looking into a foggy mirror."

They stopped in front of room twelve. He shoved the key into the lock. She followed him into the shabby room. The tang of stale smoke and bleach greeted them. Chloe wrinkled her nose, but she made no comment.

"That makes sense," she said instead.

He closed the door behind her and locked it. "It makes sense that I would recognize the energy coming from the lamp?"

"Sure." She put down her carry-on and the satchel. "You said the lamp was created by Nicholas Winters and was later used by at least one of his descendants, Griffin Winters."

"Right." He set the crate on the stained, threadbare rug.

"Both men would have left their psi prints on it. You're related to them. It's a genetic thing."

He looked down at the wooden box. "Can you sense the age of whatever is in this crate?"

"I can't be absolutely certain until I see it, but the dreamlight that's leaking out is very strong and, yes, I think that the object inside could date from the late seventeenth century."

"Stone was so sure it came out of a modern lab."

She shook her head, frowning a little in concentration. He felt energy shift in the atmosphere and knew that she had just pushed her senses a couple of notches higher.

"No," she said. "The object in that box is definitely not modern."

He met her eyes. "Is it dangerous?"

"I just sense power, Jack. Energy in and of itself is neutral. You know that."

He studied the crate. "Just raw power?"

"A lot of it. And not all of it is masculine. Some of it is feminine."

He looked up again at that. "Dream energy has a gender?"

"Probably not but people who leave traces of it behind certainly do. I can't always perceive it distinctly because that kind of energy often gets muddled, but in this case some of it is very clear. At least two women of talent have handled that lamp."

He thought about that. "Eleanor Fleming was the woman who worked the lamp for Nicholas. Adelaide Pyne was the one who worked it for Griffin Winters."

Chloe smiled faintly. "They must have been very interesting women."

Like you, he thought. *Not just interesting. Fascinating.*

"According to the records and the legends, they were," he said instead. "It's a fact that Eleanor worked the lamp to give Old Nick his second talent. Later she deliberately fried his para-senses with it. Figured destroying his talent would be the ultimate revenge."

"Why did she want revenge?"

"You don't know the tale?" he asked.

"Hey, until I met you I assumed the Burning Lamp was just another Arcane Society myth. You know, like Sylvester and his talent-enhancing formula."

"Right, the formula. Just another legend. Okay, here's what I know about the curse. Nicholas and Sylvester started out as friends. They were both alchemists, both strong sensitives, and both were convinced that they could not only enhance their talents but also develop additional powers by using the secrets of alchemy."

"I do remember that much of the story," she said. "Sylvester took the chemical approach. He studied herbs and plants looking for a drug that would do the job."

"Nicholas took the engineering approach. Alchemists were notorious for trying to transmute metals with fire."

"Ah, yes," Chloe said. "The ancient dream of turning lead into gold."

"Old Nick took it a step further. His goal was to forge a device that would produce powerful waves of dreamlight that could force open the channels between the dreamstate and the waking state and keep them open. Figured that would allow him to access the additional paranormal energy available along the dream spectrum."

"Bad idea. That way lies madness." She raised her brows. "Or so the Arcane experts believe. Just too much energy and stimulation for the human mind to handle all at once. The dreamstate and the waking state are separate for a reason."

"Yeah, well, Nick was an alchemist. They were all a little mad. He also had an ego problem. He was sure that he was strong enough to handle the additional psi."

"So he constructed the lamp. Then what happened?"

"Even though he was the one who created the lamp, he discovered that his own talent did not allow him to work it in the way required to open his own channels. He concluded that he needed a dreamlight reader."

"Someone like me," Chloe said.

He smiled at that. "I doubt if there is anyone else quite like you,

Chloe Harper. But, yes, he needed someone with your talent and for whatever reason he was convinced the person had to be female. Or maybe he just assumed it would be easier to manipulate a woman. Took him a while, but he finally located a dreamlight reader in a small village outside London. Eleanor Fleming. She agreed to work the lamp for him, but the price was high."

"How high?"

"She demanded marriage. Old Nick agreed to the bargain."

"No wonder the legend had a bad outcome," Chloe said.

"Eleanor worked the lamp. Afterward Nick took her straight to bed."

"Poor Eleanor probably thought it would be okay to sleep with him because he was going to marry her."

"Evidently. Shortly afterward Nick began developing his second talent."

"Was it like yours?"

"The legend is unclear about the specific nature of his talent. No two are exactly the same, anyway. But whatever Nick got, it was definitely dangerous. He recorded in his journal that the initial indications that something was happening to his senses were the nightmares and hallucinations."

"Is there any record that he experienced the blackouts and the sleep-walking episodes that you say you're having?"

"No. But the side effects probably vary with each individual, just as the talent does." He shoved his fingers through his hair. "There just isn't much information to go on because so few in my line have been born with the curse."

She glared. "Stop calling it a curse."

He looked at her. "Got a better word?"

"Never mind. What happened between Nick and Eleanor?"

"By all accounts the affair continued, but Nick was spending most of his time back in his laboratory. That's when the rumors began. The people who worked on his estate reported seeing demons and monsters on the grounds."

"Oh, geez. He was running experiments on them."

"Apparently. The local villagers became terrified of Nick, and the stories just got worse over time."

"That's what happens with a legend," she said.

"Meanwhile, Nick was still plagued with the hallucinations and nightmares. He concluded that Eleanor might be able to fix the problem with the lamp. She was pregnant by then."

"And no doubt busily planning her wedding," Chloe said.

"You guessed it. She worked the lamp energy a second time and managed to stop the nightmares and hallucinations. That was when Nick told her that he had no intention of marrying her."

"Bastard."

"He explained that it was impossible for a man of his rank and station to marry the daughter of a poor tradesman, but he was quite willing to carry on with her as his mistress and to provide for the child."

"Big of him," Chloe muttered.

"Eleanor told him to get lost."

"Good for her."

"He disappeared back into his lab for a few months and started to work on new crystals for the lamp."

Chloe folded her arms and frowned. "Why new crystals?"

"That's another part of the story that is very unclear. The assumption is that he hoped he could use the lamp to develop a third talent."

"Oh, for crying out loud. Idiot."

"Yeah, well, he was a really brilliant idiot. What is known is that he created some new stones in his alchemical furnace and inserted them into the lamp. And then he went back to see Eleanor a third time."

Chloe sighed. "By now she had a son, right?"

"Old Nick did have some interest in the boy. Like Sylvester, he was curious to see if his offspring would inherit his talent. I don't think he ever wanted the encumbrance of a wife, but he had run out of money to finance his experiments. To shore up his finances he had contracted a marriage with the daughter of a wealthy landowner."

"Eleanor knew about the engagement, I assume?"

"Yes. When Nick showed up on her doorstep again it was too much. She agreed to work the lamp for him one more time. And she did. But instead of using it to provide him with a third talent, she took her revenge by frying all of his senses with it."

"What happened?" Chloe asked.

"There was a struggle. Nick survived. Eleanor did not."

Chloe's eyes widened. "He killed her?"

"It's not clear. One theory is that the radiation that Eleanor unleashed affected her as well as Nick. She died at the scene, that much is known. Nick lived, but not long afterward his psychic talents began to fail. He realized what had happened and went crazy with rage. He was convinced that his old friend, Sylvester, had paid Eleanor to erase his new powers."

"So that's why he tried to murder Sylvester," Chloe said.

"Yes. But before the final confrontation he went back into his laboratory one last time. He had enough talent left to finish forging one more stone to insert into the lamp. He called it the Midnight Crystal. He believed it had some extraordinary properties and that somehow it would ensure that one of his descendants would use the lamp to destroy the descendants of Sylvester Jones."

"Then he confronted Jones?"

"Right. He didn't expect to survive the encounter. But he wanted Sylvester to know that he had prepared his revenge and that it was a dish that would be served ice cold. There is no record of exactly what happened that day. All we know is that when the final meeting between the two men was over, Nicholas was dead."

"What about Eleanor's son?" Chloe asked.

"You don't know that part of the story, either?"

"No."

"Sylvester took the boy and gave him to one of his three mistresses to raise."

Chloe looked stunned. "Sylvester *adopted* Nicholas's son?"

"Not formally. He didn't make the boy a Jones. But he saw to it that he was cared for and educated."

"*Hmm.*" Chloe pursed her lips. "Sylvester was never known for being kindhearted."

"I doubt that kindness had anything to do with it. It's possible that he was curious to see if Nicholas's son would inherit his father's first and second talents. More likely he wanted to keep an eye on the boy to make certain he didn't show any signs of becoming the anti-Jones."

"In other words, the Winters boy was just another lab experiment to Sylvester."

"Neither Nicholas nor Sylvester went down in the historical record as good fathers."

21

THE PULL CORD THAT WORKED THE YELLOWED CURTAINS COV-
ering the small window was broken. She used both hands to drag the
tattered fabric across the grimy glass, cutting off the view of the aging
casino and the adjoining café across the street.

"Do you really think that J&J is watching you?" she asked.

"When it comes to Fallon Jones, paranoia is the only intelligent
response," Jack said. He was crouched on the floor beside the crate,
crowbar in hand. "Now that I've got the lamp, I intend to keep the
lowest possible profile until I find out if you can work it."

"And if I can't work it?"

"Then my profile is going to get a hell of a lot lower."

She chilled. "But where will you go?"

"For your own sake, it's better if you don't know anything more
than that."

She sighed. "Well, this place certainly qualifies as low profile. I have a feeling the rooms usually rent by the hour, not the night. No telling when the sheets were last changed."

"Got a hunch you're right."

There was a metallic groan of steel and wood. A couple of nails popped free. She slipped into her other sight and studied the ultra-light wavelengths seeping out of the crate. Dark energy swirled in the atmosphere.

"If things do work out as planned, how are you going to get the lamp back to Seattle?" she asked.

"As a carry-on," Jack said. "How did you think I was going to get it back?"

Two more nails popped free.

"That might not be such a good idea," she said. "The energy leaking out of that thing will probably make the passengers sitting around us a little edgy."

"A lot of people get uneasy when they fly. I'm sure as hell not going to check the lamp and risk having it wind up in St. Louis or Acapulco."

The last nail came free. Jack put down the crowbar. For a few seconds he just looked at the crate. Then he raised the lid, slowly, deliberately. *As if it were a coffin lid*, she thought.

More energy from the dark end of the spectrum swirled into the room. Her senses were still wide open. She could see icy ultrablues, strange purples, eerie greens and countless shades of black. A midnight rainbow from a very dark dream.

The object inside the crate was encased in a sack made of worn black velvet. Jack picked it up, stood and carried it to the small table. Slowly he untied the cord that secured the sack. The psi radiation got stronger, the hues more intense. Fascinated, she moved closer to the lamp.

The velvet bag fell away, revealing the artifact.

"Drake Stone was right," she said. "It's not what anyone would call attractive, but there is something fascinating about it."

The lamp stood about eighteen inches high. It looked very much as Jack had described it. Narrow at the base, it flared out toward the rim. It was fashioned of a strange, gold-toned metal that looked oddly modern, as Drake Stone had said, but ancient alchemical designs were worked into it. Large, murky gray crystals were positioned in a circle just below the rim.

She looked at Jack. He was studying the lamp with rapt attention, an alchemist gazing into his fires. Currents of psi pulsed strongly in the room. The energy was as dark as that of the lamp, but there was a thrilling, disturbingly sensual quality to it. She recognized it immediately: Jack was in the zone. She realized something else as well: Her own senses were responding to his energy, starting to resonate a little.

She folded her arms tightly around herself and concentrated on the lamp. She felt a sudden need to break the crystalline atmosphere that had settled on the room.

"How does it work?" she asked.

Jack did not answer for a few seconds. When he did, she got the impression that he'd had to summon the will to look away from the lamp.

"Damned if I know," he said. "Adelaide Pyne's journal supposedly contained some advice and directions, but it vanished. Without it, all I've got is you. If you can't fix the damage, my options are nonexistent."

She eyed the lamp, uncertainty tingling through her.

"You're absolutely *sure* you've been damaged?" she asked.

His jaw hardened, and his eyes heated. "We've been over this. I'm a double-talent and my second talent is lethal. That is not a good thing. Who knows how long I've got before I start going crazy?"

"Okay, okay," she said soothingly. "It's just that, well, you seem so stable. In control."

"For now."

The grim, haunted look in his eyes told her that he was braced for the worst-case scenario. He was not in a mood to listen to a glass-half-full view of the situation. What did she know about the lamp, anyway? It was his lamp and his curse. He was the expert here, not her.

She walked around the table, studying the lamp from every angle.

"What happened to Adelaide Pyne's journal?" she said.

"The story is that a rare books dealer came to see my grandmother one day while my grandfather was out of town on a business trip. The dealer claimed to be in the market for personal diaries and journals from the Victorian era. She told him that she didn't have any to sell, but she showed him Adelaide's journal. A few weeks later she noticed that it was missing."

"The dealer stole it?"

"That's what Grandmother always believed."

"If the rare books dealer knew about the journal, I wonder why he didn't want to see the lamp, too?"

"She said he asked about old lamps, but at that point she started to feel uneasy. She told him that she didn't have any antique lamps. That much was true. My father was married by then, and she had already given him the lamp. She didn't give him the journal at the same time because she had forgotten about it. In any event my parents moved to California shortly after that. The lamp disappeared along the way."

"Did you ever try to find the rare books dealer?"

"Sure. I spent months trying to locate him. But the trail was completely cold from the start. It's like he never existed."

Chloe took a deep breath and put her fingertips on the rim of the lamp. Dream energy shivered through her. She drew her hand back very quickly.

"I need some time with this thing," she said. "I've got to analyze the latent energy that I'm sensing in it. I've never experienced anything like it. There's a lot of power here. If I screw up . . ." She let the sentence trail off.

"How much time?"

Clients were always in a rush, she thought.

"A few hours should do it," she said. "I should know by then whether I can handle this thing. But before I even begin to study it, I need food. I haven't eaten since breakfast. Something tells me that working the heavy-duty dreamlight in this lamp is going to create a major psi burn. I'll need all my reserves." She paused a beat to make sure she had his attention. "And so will you."

Jack did not look pleased, but he did not protest. He was impatient, desperate, even, but he was not stupid. They were about to mess with some very serious energy. He knew as well as she that it would not be smart to sail into that kind of lightning storm without all their re-sources in good working order.

He went to the window and twitched the curtains aside. "There's a café across the street. The sign says it's open twenty-four hours a day."

"Like most things in Vegas."

He unzipped the duffel bag and stuffed the lamp into it. Then he picked up his computer case. She collected her satchel. They went downstairs, through the lobby and across the cracked, weed-infested parking lot. The early December night had fallen hard on the desert, but the street was brightly lit with aged, sparking and flickering neon.

The windows of the café were as dingy as the one in the motel room. Beer signs offered a cold welcome. The laminated tops of the tables in the booths looked as if they had been wiped with a very old, very dirty sponge. At the small bar, three people sat hunched over their drinks. They were all staring at a ball game on television, but none of them showed any real interest in it.

The waitress looked as hard and weathered as the café, her features ravaged by smoking and bad cosmetic surgery. But her long legs, the artificially enhanced bosom and the underlying bone structure of a once-beautiful face testified to a previous career. *Former showgirl*, Chloe thought.

"This town is like the Bermuda Triangle for beautiful women," she said softly. "Sucks 'em in and drowns them. But still they keep coming here in endless waves. I've never been able to figure out why."

Jack gave her an odd look before glancing at the waitress.

"Do you feel sorry for everyone you meet?" he asked, turning back. "I would think that would be a real handicap in your line of work."

For some obscure reason she felt obliged to defend herself. "I just wondered about the waitress, that's all."

"So you spin a little story about her that probably has no basis in reality, and suddenly you feel sorry for her."

"Take another look, Jack."

"Not necessary. I'll go with the odds. Given that this is Vegas and that a lot of former showgirls end up waiting tables, it's a good bet she's on the same downwardly mobile career path."

They ate their sandwiches and greasy fries in silence. Jack paid for the meal in cash. Chloe glanced at the stack of bills he left on the table. She smiled.

"You overtipped," she said. "I mean, *way* overtipped."

"Everyone overtips in Vegas. Sends the message that you're a winner."

"Hah." She smiled. "You left her the big tip because you felt sorry for her. Admit it."

"I admit nothing. But I'll tell you this much, it was a damn fool thing to do."

"Why?"

"Because people remember big tippers."

22

"I KNOW YOU DON'T WANT TO HEAR THIS," SHE SAID, "BUT I can't concentrate with you pacing the room and pausing to look over my shoulder every five minutes. It's distracting, to put it mildly."

He came to a halt near the tiny bathroom and looked at her across the bed. "Sorry."

"What's more you're still burning psi to overcome your sleep deprivation," she added. "I realize that you want to get this done as fast as possible, but even if by some miracle I get the lamp figured out right away, you're in no shape to take a big dose of paranormal radiation. You're exhausted. Get some sleep."

His eyes tightened ominously at the corners. "You're right. I don't want to hear any of that."

"Listen to me, Jack. You need rest before we tackle this artifact. Whatever happens with this experiment you will require all of your talent to deal with it. If you refuse to get the sleep you need, I won't work the lamp for you."

"Damn it, Chloe, I'm paying you to do a job."

"You're not paying me enough to take the risk of accidentally killing you," she shot back. "Trust me, it would not be good for future business."

He contemplated her with a brooding air. For a moment she thought he was going to refuse. Then he nodded once.

"Maybe you're right," he said. "I'll take the meds. Knock myself out for a few hours."

"No meds," she said sternly. "Not when we're going to be dealing with a lot of powerful dream energy. It's too dangerous. The effects are going to be unpredictable enough as it is. We don't need the complications that sleeping medication might produce."

Wearily he massaged the back of his neck. "When I use the meds I don't sleepwalk."

"The pills may be knocking you out, but you aren't getting the real rest that your senses need. You require sleep, Jack, quality sleep. Trust me on this."

"I'm not taking any chances. When I sleepwalk I lose control."

"I'll be here."

His mouth twisted in a cold smile that she knew was meant to be intimidating. "You're the main reason that I'm not going to take the risk. A few nights ago I killed a man while I was in a fugue state, remember?"

"Only because you were trying to protect someone else. Don't worry—I'll keep an eye on you. If you show signs of weirdness or sleepwalking I'll wake you up."

"Do you really think you could pull me out of one of those episodes?"

"How hard could it be?" she said, trying to lighten the atmosphere.

He looked at her, not speaking.

She sighed. "It's just dream energy. I can handle it."

"But if you can't? I have no way of knowing what I'll do when I'm in that condition."

"Relax. You won't hurt me."

"What makes you so damn sure?"

"I'll admit that the ability to read dreamlight doesn't have a lot of practical applications, but it is very useful when it comes to figuring out whether or not someone is likely to be dangerous." She waved a hand at the carpet behind him. "I can read your prints. You're not a danger to me."

"Not in the waking state."

"And not in the sleeping state. Now, go down to the front desk, book the adjoining room and get some sleep."

He looked at the bed. "I can take a nap here."

"No," she said, keeping her tone very even. "You cannot under any circumstances sleep in this room. I won't be able to work if you do."

He frowned. "Why not? I won't be pacing, and I won't be looking over your shoulder—I'll be asleep."

She had tried to explain the complications of her talent to a few men over the years, but none of them had accepted the explanation, not really. Most, like Fletcher, had simply concluded that she was either deluded or that she had major intimacy problems. But Jack was different, she thought. Not only was he a strong talent, but he also had problems of his own with dream energy. Maybe he would understand.

"When people sleep, they dream, whether they are aware of it or not," she said patiently. "I'm fine around most folks when they're awake. Unless they're mentally or emotionally unbalanced, their dream energy is suppressed. I only notice it if I open my senses and look at their prints. But when they're asleep, they produce a lot of uncontrolled ultralight from the dream spectrum. If they are in close proximity, I have to concentrate hard to tune out the currents, and if I do that, I won't be able to focus my attention on the lamp."

He gave her a considering look. "Must be kind of weird."

"Weird doesn't begin to describe it." A small shudder went through her. "Adult dream energy at full throttle is chaotic and weird and just way too *intimate*. I find it deeply disturbing."

"What about kids' dream energy?"

She shrugged. "I'm okay with that. The ability to dream seems to be something that develops over time. It usually matures along with everything else in the teenage years. The dreamlight of babies and children is generally so pale that I can usually ignore it."

"I'll be damned," Jack said. "You can't sleep with a man."

"Not in the literal sense, no."

"That's why you practice serial monogamy, as you call it. Why your relationships don't last. Why you've never married."

"Why I *used* to practice serial monogamy. I'm celibate now, remember." She managed her best client smile. "But back in the day I was every man's secret fantasy. A woman who doesn't mind having an affair with no strings attached."

He contemplated that for a while. "It's an interesting concept," he agreed without inflection.

For some irrational reason, that hurt. She turned back to the lamp.

"Get the adjoining room, Jack," she said. "I'll make sure you don't wander off."

23

ULTRAVIOLET DREAMLIGHT STIRRED SLOWLY, SLUGGISHLY deep within the lamp. Like some primordial sea beast aroused from hibernation, the faint currents of energy shifted and swirled. She watched the rising glow, excitement and fascination sweeping through her. It was nearly midnight, but she had finally managed to make the artifact heat a little with psi. She was on the right track.

She had turned off the room lights earlier in order to be able to focus more intently. She was sitting in darkness, transfixed by the faint light of the lamp, trying to sort out the currents when the jolt of awareness struck. It came out of nowhere, shattering her concentration in a heartbeat. It took her a few seconds to realize that the disturbing new energy was not coming from the lamp. *Jack.*

She jumped to her feet and whirled to face the entrance of the adjoining bedroom. There was enough light from the cold neon of the casino sign across the street to show her that the door was still closed. She released the air she had not realized she had been holding in her lungs.

Jack was dreaming. But he had been asleep for nearly two hours and until now she had not been bothered by any stray dream vibes. He was in the other room with the door closed between them. She shouldn't even be able to sense him from this distance. The energy that she was picking up not only was very strong but also carried the taint of some kind of heavy sedative.

He had promised her that he wouldn't take any meds.

She crossed the room, made a fist and rapped loudly on the door.

"Jack? Are you okay?"

There was no response. Cautiously she opened the door, expecting to see Jack lying on the bed. But he wasn't there. He was on his feet, looming directly in front of her.

"*Jack*. For Pete's sake, you scared the living daylights out of me."

She glanced behind him and saw that the bed was still fully made. She could see the depression of his body on the bedspread where he had sprawled earlier. He had removed only his shirt and shoes. He was still in his trousers and black crewneck T-shirt. In the sparking neon light his face was an implacable mask, but his eyes burned with psi. So did the footprints on the carpet behind him.

"Jack?"

"I'll keep you safe." The words were spoken in a chilling mono-tone, devoid of all nuance and emotion. It was the voice of a man in a trance.

She braced herself for the shock she knew was coming and touched his shoulder. To her amazement there was no electric crackle across her senses. She couldn't believe it. She was touching a person who was deep in the dreamstate, but her senses were not recoiling from the brush with the energy field.

She badly wanted to think about what it all meant, to try to figure out the implications. But there was no time. She had to deal with Jack's sleepwalking.

He seemed unaware of her fingertips on his shoulder. Cautiously she pulsed a little more energy, searching for the pattern of the sleepwalking currents. She found it quickly.

"Jack, wake up," she said.

"You're in danger."

"Not now. Not tonight. Not from you." She set up a dampening current, trying to interrupt the heavy flow of fugue-state energy. There was no response. That was not good news. By now he should have been fully awake. "Jack, can you hear me?"

He raised a hand and touched her face, his eyes hot in the shadows. "I'm dreaming."

Another kind of energy suddenly infused the atmosphere. It was elemental, fiercely masculine and stunningly sexual. It rattled her senses like the first winds of an oncoming storm striking the closed windows of a well-sealed house. She was suddenly disoriented and, for the first time, seriously alarmed.

But underneath the rising tide of uncertainty and confusion she was aware of the sensual heat shimmering to life inside her. She knew what sexual attraction felt like. Under normal circumstances the pleasant warmth and the sense of arousal were nothing she couldn't suppress or ignore if necessary. But what was happening now could no more be ignored than lightning. And it was probably just as dangerous.

"Yes, you're dreaming," she said. Her voice sounded a little husky to her own ears.

She pulled more energy, struggling to push through the compelling distraction created by the currents of desire so that she could zap Jack with a stronger jolt of dreamlight. She tightened her grip on his shoulder.

Psi flashed across the spectrum. To her heightened senses the energy looked like iridescent snow falling through the beams of a car's headlights. She had no idea how Jack perceived the sparkling, glittering waves of light, but she felt the change in the pattern instantly.

Jack did not simply emerge from the trance—he slammed into the waking state riding shockwaves of energy. The currents of psi roared over her own energy field, swamping the delicate pulses of dreamlight she was generating.

For a few seconds she felt consciousness start to slide away into a very deep hole in the ground. The room spun around her. The neon moonlight outside the window blazed as bright as a spotlight. Instinctively she covered her eyes with her arm, but that offered no protection. When she was using her other senses she perceived light psychically, not with her normal vision.

Instinctively she shoved back at the raging tide with all the energy at her command. She felt like a swimmer trying to stay on the surface of a violent sea while a whirlpool threatened to pull her down into the depths. For an eternity she thought she might actually go under permanently.

Without warning the wavelengths of heavy psi stopped trying to drown her. Instead, they began to resonate with her own currents.

It happened so quickly she had difficulty processing the shift. Between one breath and the next she was no longer trying to block Jack's power. Just the opposite—she was responding to it in ways she had never dreamed were possible. Okay, maybe she had *dreamed* about this kind of experience, she thought, but she had never actually let herself believe it could happen.

Awareness blazed in Jack's eyes. She knew for certain that he was no longer in the fugue state, but he was running hot on intense sexual arousal. He was focused wholly and entirely on her.

"Are you all right?" He closed his hands around her shoulders. "What the hell happened?"

"I'm okay," she managed, fighting not to sound breathless. The feel of his strong hands sent shivers of excitement through her. She wanted him to keep touching her. She wanted to touch him, needed to touch him. "You were in a trance, just like you described. I woke you up. As promised. All part of the service."

His fingers tightened around her. "I could have hurt you."

"No," she said, very certain. She glanced past him, checking out his smoldering footprints. "Never."

"I shouldn't have let you talk me into going to sleep without the meds."

She flattened her palms on his chest. The sleek muscles beneath the T-shirt felt very good. She tried to ignore the sensation.

"Pay attention here, Winters. There is no problem. I was able to bring you out of the fugue, just as I said I would."

He searched her face. "When I came back to my senses I had the feeling that I was crushing you, overwhelming you."

"It was the first time I've ever tried anything like that with someone as powerful as you. First times are always a learning experience." She sank her fingertips a little deeper into the T-shirt. "I had to make a few adjustments, that's all. Like I said, no problem."

Another one of her rules, she thought. *Never let the client think you might just possibly be out of your depth.*

He studied her, clearly awed, for a couple of beats.

"You are one hell of a bad liar," he said finally.

"Hey, I learn fast, and I know what I'm doing now. Look, it's after midnight. Go back to sleep. And whatever you do, don't take any meds."

"And if I sleepwalk again?"

"I'll deal with it. Go back to bed, Jack."

"I don't want to go back to bed." He pulled her closer, not forcing her but making his intent clear. "Not alone."

She tried to think, but the fizzy, giddy elation sweeping through her made thinking difficult.

"I have this rule," she whispered. "About sleeping with clients."

"Chloe," he said.

That was all he said. Just her name. But his voice was rough and urgent. Sensual hunger heated his eyes and his aura. The raw power of his still-hot senses created a dazzling whirlwind in the small space. Her own currents were still resonating strongly with his. Desire burned hot and deep inside her, incinerating the last vestiges of caution. She knew that if she did not seize this moment with this man she would regret it for the rest of her life.

Entranced by the magic and the mystery of the sensation, she raised her fingers to his face.

"Yes," she whispered. "Oh, *yes.*"

24

THE ANTICIPATION THAT HAD BEEN SIMMERING DEEP INSIDE him since the moment he had plucked her name out of J&J's secret files flared into fierce exultation.

He pulled her close, hard and tight against him, and savored the thrill of the kiss. Chloe responded with a red-hot hunger that ignited his senses. She was vibrant, supple, eager; shivering with excitement. Her lips opened for him. Her hands wrapped around his neck.

She returned the kiss with passion but there was an unexpected awkwardness about the embrace. It dawned on him that she was no more accustomed to this kind of intense urgency than he was. They were both headed into unfamiliar territory, taking the leap together.

He was sure that he had experienced his share of good sex. But it was shatteringly clear to him now that he had never been truly, deeply satisfied the way he was going to be tonight. He understood what had been missing in his previous relationships. This sense of bone-deep connection, of elemental recognition, was intoxicating.

He captured her face between his hands and managed to free his mouth for a moment.

"Well, damn," he said softly. "It's all true."

"What's true?" she asked softly. Her lips were wet and full and her eyes a little unfocused.

Like a woman in a trance, he thought. A really good trance.

"The legends and myths, the rumors and whispers that you hear in the Society," he said. "For years I've listened to other talents talk about what it's like when the energy between two strong sensitives is right. I've never really believed it."

"Oh, those rumors." She gave him a slightly dazed smile. "Personally I've never believed those tales, either. Not until now."

He kissed her throat. "Think maybe we've been missing something?"

"I think so." She sank her teeth lightly into his ear and moved her hands up under his T-shirt. "Yes. Definitely."

The feel of her palms on his bare skin sent another rush of need through him. He reached down, seized the bottom edge of her black turtleneck and hauled the top straight up and off. He tossed it across a chair.

The dark purple bra went next. He was breathing harder now, but he had to stop for a moment in order to enjoy the sweet curves of her breasts. By the time he was ready to move on, she had unfastened the waistband of his pants with fumbling fingers.

He picked her up and put her down on the bed. Starving for her, he ripped off his T-shirt and trousers, then lowered himself alongside her. The ancient springs groaned and the worn-out mattress sagged beneath their combined weight, but neither of them paid any attention. He knew that the fever was on both of them, heating their blood and their senses.

He rolled onto his back, taking her with him so that she sprawled on top. The warm, vital weight of her body sent another sizzle of energy through him. The ripe, compelling scent of her arousal was a potent elixir. He was sure he had never been so hard or so far into the zone of his talent.

She scrambled to rain kisses on his shoulders and across his chest. He felt her tongue on his bare skin and almost came apart right then. He got her pants down over her butt and slowed briefly to squeeze the soft, resilient globes. The only thing that stood in his way now was a tiny triangle of purple cotton. He tugged the panties lower and traced the cleft of her rear with one finger all the way down to the source of her damp heat. She gasped and stiffened briefly when he touched the small, tight bundle of nerve endings.

"*Jack.* I can't stand it. It's never been like this."

He put her on her back so that he could get the pants and the purple cotton panties all the way off. She slipped her fingers inside his briefs and found him. He caught his breath, groaning with the effort it took to keep himself from exploding.

He got the briefs off and one knee between her legs. She reached for him, pulling him to her. He could feel her hands on his back, nails sinking in just a little. The smooth skin on the inside of her thighs was as soft and luxurious as warm cream. She was damp and hot and lush.

He wanted to spend hours exploring all her mysteries, but he knew that he could not wait, not this first time. The energy between them was too fierce, too demanding. The need to be inside her, to discover where the heady, intimate sensation would take them was an overriding compulsion.

"*Yes*," she said again. Invitation, command and plea fused into the single word.

He guided himself into her. She drew a sharp little breath when he thrust past the tight, delicate muscles at the entrance, but when he tried to stop, to give her time to adjust, she closed herself around him.

"No," she said. She watched him through half-closed eyes. "I want you inside. I want to find out how it feels."

"So do I," he rasped.

He covered her mouth, kissed her hard and went deep, going all the way. And then he was flying on the hot currents of sensation, and she soared with him.

When her climax swept through her a short time later, he followed her into the burning rain.

25

JACK WAS ASLEEP AND DREAMING. THE ENERGY HE WAS RADI-ating wasn't disturbing her, but there was something not quite right about it. She levered herself up on one elbow and looked down at him. He was lying on his side, facing her, the sheet pushed down to his waist. Energy stirred in the atmosphere, subtle but strong.

He had fallen asleep almost immediately in the aftermath of the profound release. That was good, she thought. The man needed to relax. But what his senses desperately required was some truly deep sleep, and that wasn't what he was getting.

She studied the murky energy seething in the prints on the pillow. The residue of the currents was weaker now than it had been two days ago when he had walked into her office, but it was still detectable. Whatever meds he had been taking to halt the sleepwalking evidently had a long half-life. That wasn't surprising. Traces of some strong psychotropic medications frequently remained in the bloodstream for days. It could take the body a long time to get rid of the last vestiges of particularly strong medicine. In the case of a few really potent sedatives there was occasionally permanent damage to the para-senses. She could see that Jack was recovering, however. He just needed a little more time.

She might be able to help him get the true sleep he required tonight, however.

Gingerly she put her palm on his bare shoulder. He stirred but did not awaken. Jack was into control. She was almost certain that he would not like what she was about to do. On the other hand, if the procedure worked he would get the rest he needed. She could always explain and apologize in the morning.

She opened her senses to the max, cautiously tuning in to the currents of his dream energy. She was braced again for the unpleasant crackle of sensation she always got when she brushed up against someone else's dreamlight, but, again, to her amazement there was no shock. The currents were strong, but they weren't painful.

And then she was into the pattern, getting a fix. The dark taint of the sleeping meds was more obvious now. The stuff was still disturbing a portion of Jack's dream spectrum in an unwholesome way, and it was very powerful. But she might be able to calm the disturbance temporarily, long enough for him to get some real rest. It was the same technique she used to give her Irregular Clients of the street a vacation from their nightmares.

She went to work, pulsing delicate currents of psi into Jack's field.

Energy recoiled across the spectrum like the blowback of a firestorm, stunning her. She lost her focus. Before she could retreat she was caught in a fist of raw power. Like a surfer with bad timing she was sucked under and tumbled along the bottom of the sea. She snatched her hand off Jack's shoulder, heart pounding, fighting for air.

Jack looked at her, hot psi burning in his eyes.

"What the hell are you doing?" His voice was shockingly calm and cold.

She sat up fast and took several breaths in an attempt to pull herself together. "Sorry," she managed. "I was just trying to make sure you got some proper sleep."

"How?"

"Uh, well, it's part of my talent."

"You can put people to sleep?"

She winced. "That doesn't sound good, does it?"

"No. What are you? The sand lady?"

"Sorry," she repeated. "I wouldn't have hurt you. I think you know that. I just wanted to make sure you got a good night's sleep."

"How?" he said again.

She sighed. "Well, if you let me, I can sort of adjust your dreamlight."

"*Sort* of adjust it?"

"Just a smidge, honest. Those meds you took to stop the sleepwalking are still affecting your sleep."

"And you think you can overcome the effects?"

"I think so, yes. Temporarily. Long enough to give you some quality sleep, at least."

He thought about that. "Could you force me to go to sleep?"

"Not now that you're fully awake, no. You're too powerful. You'd have to cooperate. And to do that you'd have to trust me, I mean really trust me."

"Huh."

"Sorry."

"You said that a couple of times already."

"Right. Sorry."

He just looked at her. There was still a little anger in his eyes.

"But you can put some people out, can't you?" he said. "That's what you did to that bastard, Sawyer, who murdered Rose's parents. You went in as a hostage and you put him to sleep."

She hesitated and then nodded. "The minute he touched me it was all over. He went out like a light."

"And when he came to he was crazy."

She stiffened. "He was a killer. He was already crazy."

Jack watched her with his knowing look, the one that said he saw every weakness and vulnerable point. "But not crazy in that way. He wasn't suicidal. Guy like that would have tried to game the system. Probably would have sold his story to the newspapers or maybe to a publisher. He would have gloried in the attention. Instead he hung himself."

She exhaled slowly. "There are many kinds of sleep. Some are deep and often irreversible."

"Like a coma?"

"Yes." She paused. "But there is another stage of sleep that, if you were to get trapped in it for an extended period, would be psychologically devastating."

"What's that?"

"The border between the sleeping state and the waking state. I think of it as the gray zone. We've all been there, but we usually don't spend more than a few seconds or minutes in that place. It is disturbing and disorienting, however. You can't tell whether you're dreaming or awake. Sometimes you are physically paralyzed. You see things that aren't there. With my talent I can put someone into that state."

"Permanently?"

"Probably not," she said quietly. "But in Richard Sawyer's case, long enough to drive him mad. He was already disturbed. What I did to him pushed him over the edge."

Jack was silent for a moment. "To quote a certain private investigator I know, that is one hell of a talent you've got."

"The truth is, I didn't even know for sure I could do what I did until I did it to Richard Sawyer. But when I sent him into the gray zone I did it deliberately. I knew what I was doing."

"Just like I knew what I was doing when I killed that man on Capitol Hill."

"Yes. And we're both going to dream about what we did from time to time for the rest of our lives."

"The price we pay?"

"No matter how well justified, the destruction of another human being exacts a price somewhere on the spectrum."

"I can live with what I did," he said.

She thought of the sense of closure that had come over Rose after Richard Sawyer's death, how the nightmares had finally begun to fade. How Rose had been able to start the healing journey.

"So can I," she said.

"You were about to put Madeline Gibson to sleep the other night, weren't you? That's why you had your hand on her shoulder when I came through the doorway."

"I was just going to put her under, not send her into the gray zone."

"And now you want to put me to sleep."

She smiled, rueful. "After what I just told you, I can understand why you'd be reluctant to let me help you."

"Try it," he said.

She blinked. "You really want me to put you to sleep?"

"You're right; I can't keep running on psi. I need some real sleep. Do your thing. Let's see if it works."

"Like I said, you'd have to cooperate," she said. "You'd have to open your senses and not fight me."

"I trust you."

She took another deep breath. "All right, here goes."

She felt energy whisper in the atmosphere again. She elevated her own senses in response, seeking a gentle, soothing pattern. He watched her for a moment, not resisting, and then he closed his eyes.

He was suddenly, completely asleep, plunging swiftly into the dream-state. But this time the energy felt stable. The disturbance created by the medication had been overcome, at least for now. She did a little more tweaking to ensure that the currents would remain steady for a few hours, and then she carefully withdrew from the pattern.

She waited, but Jack remained sound asleep. Sound asleep and *dreaming*. By rights she should be looking for the nearest exit. But she was okay here with Jack. How was that possible?

She studied him with a growing sense of wonder. The neon-infused moonlight filtering through the thin curtains gleamed on his sleekly muscled shoulder.

Cautiously she opened her senses again, testing. Jack's dreamprints were on the pillow and the sheet, and she could see the dark ultralight aura that enveloped him. He was definitely dreaming. But her own energy patterns remained undisturbed.

It dawned on her that, for the first time in her life, she might actually be able to sleep in the same bed with a man.

But even as the astonishing thought struck she became aware of the irritating, unsettling traces of the old dream psi of previous hotel guests that stained the sheets and bedding. She might be able to sleep with Jack, but there was no way she could sleep in this particular bed without protection.

She pushed aside the sheet, got to her feet and crossed the room to the small carry-on bag she had brought with her. Unzipping the bag, she took out the long-sleeved, high-necked silk nightgown and silk travel sheet. For some reason that she and Phyllis had never under-stood, silk was a barrier of sorts. It did not entirely block old dream psi, but it provided a buffering layer that sometimes—not always—allowed them to sleep on tainted sheets.

She put on the nightgown and unfolded the travel sheet on the bed next to Jack. The sheet was constructed like a sleeping bag with a zippered opening on the side and a large flap at the top that was designed to cover a pillow. Jack did not stir. She crawled inside the silk cocoon, zipped it shut and prepared to conduct the Great Experiment.

She fell asleep before she could contemplate the implications of what it all meant.

26

FOR THE FIRST TIME IN A MONTH HE AWOKE FEELING RESTED and genuinely refreshed. No nightmares. *Almost normal,* he thought. Thanks to Chloe. He reached for her and came up with a handful of silk instead.

"What the hell?"

He sat up and looked down at the crumpled fabric in his hand. It took him a moment to realize that he was holding a silken sheet sewn into the shape of a Chloe-sized sack.

He rolled out of the sagging bed and got to his feet. The door that separated the adjoining rooms stood half open. Chloe was in the other room. She was sitting at the table in front of the computer busily making notes in a small notebook.

There was something very intimate about seeing her like this, first thing in the morning, he thought. She was wearing the pants she'd had on yesterday, but the top was different, a dark green turtleneck this time. It was obvious that she had showered. Her coppery hair was still damp. She had pulled it back behind her ears to dry. The motel's limited assortment of amenities probably didn't extend to hair dryers.

He smiled. She didn't have the soft, warm, inviting air of a lover who had just gotten out of bed after hours of great sex. She looked like a determined investigator who was hard at work. But he was pretty sure he'd never seen a sexier woman in his life.

For a moment he just stood there, absorbing the sight of her, the sensation of her subtle feminine power, and remembering the bone-deep sense of intimacy that had connected them last night. He was aware of a compelling need to keep her close, keep her safe. But the shattering truth was that at the moment he was the biggest threat she faced. A guy who could kill with the energy of pure fear. How could that work? If he ever lost control . . .

She looked up. "Good morning."

"Good morning," he replied.

She gave him a critical head-to-toe survey and nodded once, evidently satisfied. "You look a lot better than you did yesterday or the day before."

He rubbed his jaw, testing the stubble of a beard. "I haven't checked a mirror yet, but I've got a hunch that I look like hell."

Laughter glinted in her eyes. "Don't worry, the slightly unshaved look is still in fashion."

"I've got a shaver in my overnight kit."

"Good thing we both came prepared to spend a night away from home," she said lightly.

He did not return her smile. "I wasn't fully prepared last night," he said quietly. "In fact, you could say I never saw last night coming. I woke up in the middle of a sleepwalking episode and you were there, and then we were in bed. There was no thinking or planning involved."

She didn't get it right away. Then he saw understanding hit. She turned pink and was suddenly very busy with the computer.

"Yes, well, I'm sure there won't be a problem. I mean, it was only the one time. What are the odds?"

"Probably not a good question to ask in Vegas." He folded his arms and propped one shoulder against the door frame. "You're not using anything?"

She cleared her throat. "Well, no. There hasn't been any reason to use anything. I told you, I've moved on. I'm in a new phase."

"Right. The celibate lifestyle thing." He waited. "So how is that working for you?"

She turned very pink, gave him a frosty glare and angled her chin. "We were both flying on a lot of energy last night. There was a bed in the room. We're both mature adults. Sometimes things just happen."

"Even in the middle of a celibate lifestyle?"

"I think it's time that you took a shower so we can go get some breakfast," she said coolly.

"One more thing," he said.

She looked wary. "What?"

He held up the silken sheet. "What's with the little sleeping bag?"

At first he thought she wasn't going to answer. Then she shrugged and turned back to the computer.

"It's hard for me to sleep in bedding that has absorbed the dream psi of other people," she said. "Silk acts as a partial barrier to that kind of energy. I never leave home without that sheet."

"If you can barely stand to sleep in a bed that other people have slept in and if the energy given off by dreamers disturbs you, how did you manage to sleep with me?"

She went very still, staring hard at the computer screen. Her fingers froze in midair.

"I don't know," she said softly. "It was different with you."

He watched her for a long moment. "And if it turns out you're pregnant?"

This time the silence lasted for an eternity. And then her hand fluttered lightly over her slim belly.

"That would be different, too," she said finally. "I've always assumed that I would probably never have children."

"And now?" He didn't know why he was pushing her. She was right. The odds were good that she wasn't pregnant. But for some reason he had to know.

She glanced at the carpet behind him and smiled a little as if whatever she saw there satisfied her. He knew she was looking at his psi prints.

"You would make an excellent father," she stated.

She went back to work on the computer. Keys clicked madly.

He couldn't think of anything to say. He was, according to all the definitions of the Arcane Society, half monster. He carried a genetic twist that would go down through future generations. And she thought he would make a terrific father?

Smiling a little, he went back into the other room and headed for the shower.

27

HE WAS STILL FEELING GOOD TWENTY MINUTES LATER WHEN they went downstairs for breakfast. He carried the lamp in the leather duffel. His computer case was in his other hand. Chloe had stuffed her computer back into her black satchel.

There was a fresh pair of white-haired senior citizens on the stools in front of the slots in the lobby. Neither of them looked up when he and Chloe went past. The front-desk clerk did not come out of his office.

They walked through the weedy parking lot and crossed the street to the small café attached to the casino. The waitress working the morning shift was not the same one who had served them last night, but she looked like she could tell the same hard-luck story.

He and Chloe sat down across from each other in the same booth they had used the previous evening. From his position he had a view into the dark cave of the adjoining casino. It was seven forty-five in the morning, but there were a few intrepid souls feeding the slots. The blackjack and poker tables were quiet. He knew that activity would pick up as the day wore on, growing brisker during the afternoon and evening. By midnight the place would be filled to capacity. The rhythm would be the same tomorrow and the day after and next year. The pattern of casino gaming never changed.

There was always a pattern, Jack thought. Once you identified it you could figure out the strengths and weaknesses. He took some comfort from that. At least he could still think like a strat-talent.

Chloe picked up her fork. "Vegas is always reinventing itself, blowing up old hotels and casinos and building new ones in their place. There's always new computer technology in the gaming machines. New theme-park resorts on the Strip. Newer and more astonishing high-tech shows in the casino theaters. But underneath it all nothing changes. It's as if it exists in another dimension."

Jack shrugged and ate some of his eggs. "That's the appeal. This town is built on sex and sin. Get too far away from your core business, and you lose your customers."

Chloe's fork paused in midair. Her brows rose. "You know, sometimes I forget that you're a coldhearted zillionaire businessman who makes his living investing."

For some reason the *coldhearted* bothered him.

"What's your problem with Vegas?" he asked.

"Who said I had a problem?"

"No offense, but it's obvious."

She sighed. "I'm not a prude, and I have no particular issues involving games of chance. But the energy in a casino bothers me."

"Yeah? How?"

"What do you see when you look into that other room?"

He glanced at the entrance of the casino again. "Rows of slots. Lots of flashing lights. Croupiers waiting for players. A woman in a sexy outfit carrying a tray of drinks."

"At seven forty-five in the morning," Chloe said drily.

He forked up more eggs. "It's a casino. Not as fancy as those on the Strip but, still, a casino. It is what it is."

She glanced over her shoulder and contemplated the dark gaming floor for a moment. He felt energy pulse and knew that she had opened her senses.

"To me it looks like someone splashed hot, radioactive acid all over the place," she said. She turned back to her eggs. "Layers and layers of it. Years, decades of the stuff. There's a reason they call gambling a fever. It's like a drug. It affects dream psi in a major way."

"People with a lot of talent, you and me, for instance, tend to get lucky when we play," he pointed out. "The psychic side of our natures gives us an edge."

She regarded him with stern disapproval. "Do you gamble?"

"All the time." He smiled. "But only when I have enough information to calculate the odds."

Her expression cleared. "You mean your venture-capital business. Obviously that line of work does require that you take risks."

"So does yours."

She brushed that aside. "I meant financial risk."

He drank some coffee and thought about how to get back to the subject that seemed to matter as much as the lamp did this morning.

He put the mug down and looked at her. "About last night."

He could have sworn she flinched a little, but she gave him a dazzling smile.

"You know," she said, "I doubt that in the entire history of civilization there has ever been a good conversation that started with *about last night*."

He got an odd sensation of heat but not the sexual kind. It took him a couple of beats to realize that he was probably turning a dull red.

"You know we need to talk about it," he said.

"Why?"

She was still smiling, but she was starting to get a deer-in-the-headlights look in her eyes. He knew he was pushing into dangerous territory.

"Don't know about you," he said neutrally, "but it's never been like that for me."

She cleared her throat. "I absolutely agree that it was a very unique experience."

"Unique." He drank some more coffee. "Okay, that's one way to describe it."

"But, as you said, there have always been stories about what it's like when two strong talents get together," she added earnestly. "In that way, I mean."

"I've met other strong talents," he said, keeping his voice even. "My ex-wife was a Level Eight. Can't say that it's ever been like that for me. You?"

"Like I said, it was unique," she declared briskly. "Let's just leave it at that. We have other priorities at the moment."

"What are you afraid of?"

She exhaled slowly and put down her fork. "You don't know what it's been like for me all these years. I've never even been able to share a bedroom with anyone, let alone a bed. I'm uncomfortable just being in the same room with someone who is taking a nap in a chair. When I was younger there were no sleepovers with friends. No trips to camp because I couldn't bunk with anyone. In college I had to rent my own apartment because I couldn't deal with a roommate. Since college I've always lived alone."

"And last night?"

"Like I said, last night was different," she said. "That's all I know. Could we please change the subject?"

"Sure."

She slipped instantly back into her competent investigator mode, sharp and resolved once again. "At least we now know that we've got a technique for dealing with your trances."

"Hot sex?" He smiled. "Works for me."

She blushed furiously and fixed him with her steely look. "I was talking about the fact that I was able to bring you out of the sleepwalking state, not what happened afterward."

"Right." He finished the last of his eggs and lounged against the back of the booth. "Why are you so determined to help me? Is it because you feel sorry for me?"

She bristled. "I don't take cases because I feel sorry for people."

"Sure you do."

"Well, that's not why I'm sticking with this case," she insisted.

"Why, then?"

"Because of the challenge, of course. This is the most interesting case I've ever had. You couldn't fire me now if you tried."

I couldn't let you out of my sight now, if I tried, he thought.

"You're an amazing woman, Chloe Harper."

"That's me, Amazing Woman. Remember that when you get my bill." She finished her eggs and took her notebook out of her bag. "Now, then, before you went into your sleepwalking mode last night, I made some notes about the lamp."

"Learn anything?"

"Yes, I think so. The lamp is definitely imbued with a lot of extremely powerful dreamlight that is in a state of suspended animation. I can light the thing, or at least I can stir up enough energy to make it glow, but I can't access its full power. Got a feeling only you or someone with a similar genetic psychic makeup can do that."

"What happens after we get it running at full power?"

"I'm not sure, but I think the lamp requires two people to operate it." She looked up from her notes. "There's just too much power in the thing for any one individual to handle."

"Let's get to the bottom line. Once we get the lamp fired up do you think you can manipulate the light waves in a way that will stop whatever is happening to me?"

She hesitated. "Maybe."

"*Maybe*. Now, there's a word guaranteed to reassure the client."

"I'm sorry, it's just that there are so many unknowns here. All I can tell you at the moment is that I think I can work the energy in some specific ways. Since the lamp is tuned to your psychic frequencies, I can probably use it to affect your talent." She paused. "If you're really sure that's what you want me to do."

"That's the whole point here," he said grimly.

"There's something else you should know."

"What?"

"Like I said, there's a lot of power in that lamp, but I don't think all of it was meant to manipulate your personal talent. There's just too much energy in the thing."

"What does that mean?"

"I don't know." Clearly troubled, she looked back at her notes. "There are some really strange light waves in stasis within the lamp. I sense colors I've never seen before. They're inert at the moment, and, as I said, I think only you can activate them. But once they are revved up we may have a serious problem."

"What kind of problem?"

She closed the notebook. "All I can tell you is that I think the lamp is capable of doing something else besides stabilize your dream psi channels. Are you sure you don't want to take this to the experts at Arcane?"

"If they screw it up and I turn into a Cerberus I'll be a dead man, anyway. I'd rather take my chances with you."

"It's just that the Society's researchers know so much more about the laws of para-physics. I'm working in the dark here. Literally."

He drummed his fingers on the table, thinking. "Old Nick asked Eleanor Fleming to work the lamp three times. The first time the goal was to give him a second talent. The second time he wanted her to get rid of the hallucinations and nightmares brought on by the new talent. But it is unclear what he intended on the third occasion. What if the legends are wrong? What if he wasn't trying to create a third talent? What if he was smart enough to realize that no human being could generate that much psi naturally, let alone control it?"

"So what did he want Eleanor to do with the lamp that last time?"

"I don't know. But what is clear is that before he went back to her the third time, he had created and installed some new crystals in the lamp. Maybe he intended to use it in some way that no one has even considered."

"Such as?"

"Hell if I know."

He stopped speaking because the muffled noise of a cascade of cheerful chimes interrupted him. Chloe started a little and then dove back into her satchel. She came up with her cell phone.

"Rose? Yes, we're still in Vegas. Everything okay on that end? *What?* Are you all right?"

Shock and intense concern flashed across her face. Jack felt a chill of icy intuition crackle across his senses.

"Are you sure you're okay?" Chloe continued. "Yes, fine. Right. No, I agree, it probably won't do any good to call the police, but we should report it, anyway. Hang on, I want to tell Jack what's going on." She took the phone away from her ear.

"What happened?" he asked.

"Rose thinks someone broke into my office and my apartment last night while she was at a class. She had Hector with her."

"She *thinks* someone broke in? She's not sure?"

"She says nothing was stolen and only a couple of small things looked out of place. But she's almost certain that someone went through my trash and my desk."

"And probably your office computer." He was on his feet, fishing out his wallet.

"I don't think there's much danger of anyone accessing any of my files." She slid out of the booth and got to her feet. "My cousin Abe is a high-end crypto talent. He has all of my stuff locked up with some industrial-strength encryption."

"Nothing a J&J crypto couldn't hack into. Let's go."

28

HER EYES WIDENED. "YOU REALLY BELIEVE THAT IT WAS SOME-
one from Jones & Jones who broke in?"

"They're the only folks I can think of who would have an interest in
this case." The adrenaline-charged sense of urgency was riding him hard
now. He picked up the duffel bag and the computer case and went toward the door. "Tell Rose to forget the cops. You and I need to move."

"Okay, okay." She hurried after him. "Rose? Got to run. I'll call you
back later. Meanwhile, hold off notifying the cops. Jack thinks Arcane
is involved, which means it wouldn't do any good to report it, anyway.
There won't be any evidence to find. I'll call you later."

Jack reached the door and opened it for her. She went quickly past
him. He followed her out onto the sidewalk and checked the street.
There were no new cars in the motel parking lot, but that didn't mean
much. They started across the street.

"Jack, what do you think is happening?" Chloe asked.

"I think Fallon Jones somehow tumbled onto the fact that I went looking for a dreamlight talent and figured that there was only one reason I'd do that. He's concluded that I've started to change. He's got people looking for me."

"I can't believe that he would hire someone to murder you just because you might be developing another talent. I'm no fan of J&J, but the agency doesn't go around killing people. Arcane can be very annoying, but it isn't that bad. Besides, murdering a wealthy man who is as well connected as you are would draw a lot of attention. That's the last thing the Society would want."

"We have some time. I know Fallon Jones. He's got his own agenda. He'll want to play this out before he makes his move."

"What do you mean?" she demanded.

"Everyone has a vulnerable point. You know what they say, your greatest weakness is always linked to your greatest strength."

"From what I've heard, Fallon Jones's greatest strength is his ability to see patterns and connections in situations where others see only random facts or coincidences. Something to do with his unique form of intuitive talent."

"Technically, he's some kind of chaos-theory-talent, but that's just a fancy way of saying that he's a world-class conspiracy buff. He could give lessons to the black-helicopter folks and the Area Fifty-one crowd. The problem with Jones is that, unlike other conspiracy buffs, he's usually right."

"You said he has a major weakness." Chloe walked briskly beside him. "What is it?"

"To a true conspiracy theorist nothing is the result of random chance or coincidence. Everything fits into the grand scheme of things. The trick is to figure out what goes where."

"So?"

"That means Jones's greatest weakness is his curiosity. He needs answers the way other people need food and oxygen."

"Got it," Chloe said. "He'll want to know if the lamp actually works and what effect it has."

"Right. And he needs me to run the experiment."

"Think he knows we're in Vegas?"

"If he knows I hired you, then we have to assume he also knows we're here and that we've got the lamp. With luck he hasn't found us yet because we didn't use any ID at the motel. But it won't take him long to track us down. We need to get off the grid altogether."

"*Hmm.*"

"What are you thinking?"

"I'm thinking Uncle Edward," she said.

"Your uncle who specializes in antique furniture here in town? What good can he do us? I'm not in the market for a Louis the Sixteenth commode at the moment."

"Uncle Edward operates a little sideline with his son, Dex, and Dex's wife, Beth. You could call it another traditional family business."

"From what I've heard, the Harper family businesses usually involve fakes and forgeries."

"Turns out one of the things Cousin Dex and Beth have a talent for is producing fake IDs," Chloe said.

"That is very good news. The one I commissioned last year may not be good now. I wouldn't put it past Jones to know about it."

"Assuming you're reading him right," she said.

"I told you I know him, or, at least, I did at one time."

"What went wrong with your friendship?" she asked.

"A few years ago Fallon started showing some quirks. He was never what you'd call a real social kind of guy, but more and more he began to withdraw. He'd disappear into an Arcane lab or one of the Society's museums for weeks at a time. When he took over J&J he pretty much vanished altogether. Went to live in a small town on the Northern

California coast. Lately he's become obsessed with some shadowy conspiracy he calls Nightshade."

"What in the world is Nightshade?" she asked.

"From what I could gather, it's an organization run by a bunch of
psychic bad actors. Apparently they've re-created the founder's formula.
Fallon thinks J&J is the only agency that can stop them."

"Good grief. A group of criminal sensitives hyped up on Sylvester's
drug? Sounds like Fallon Jones has gone over the edge, all right."

"Don't bet on it," he said. "This is Fallon Jones we're talking about.
I told you, he's almost always right when it comes to his conspiracy
theories. But whether or not there is such a thing as Nightshade is not
my problem. All I care about is the lamp."

He urged her through the glass doors of the motel lobby. The desk
clerk leaned around the corner of the office door, gave them a bored
once-over and went back to his centerfold.

There was only one player sitting in front of the slots now, not a
senior citizen this time, but a man in his early twenties who looked
like he spent a lot of time pumping iron and injecting steroids. He was
dressed in jeans, heavy boots and a leather jacket. He didn't pay any
attention when Jack urged Chloe toward the stairs. He punched the
play button.

Wheels of fruit whirled, bells clanged. The bulked-up biker had just
won. Probably all of ten bucks, Jack thought. No telling how much
money the guy had poured into the machine before getting the pay-
off. But it would probably be enough to make him hit *play* again. He
would feed all ten dollars back into the slot. That was how gambling
worked. You only had to win occasionally to keep you coming back for
more: the theory of intermittent reinforcement in action.

On the landing, he brought Chloe to a halt and looked back down
into the lobby. Instead of hitting *play* again, the heavily muscled man

in leather and denim was collecting his winnings. He walked outside and disappeared from view. So much for the theory of intermittent reinforcement.

Jack put his mouth close to Chloe's ear. "Take a look at the slot that guy was using."

She peered down into the lobby. "What about it?" she asked, equally soft. "Looks like every other slot machine I've ever seen."

"Use your other sight."

"Oh, right."

Energy swirled delicately in the atmosphere around him as she slipped into her other senses. Like some subtle, exotic perfume, it aroused him and stirred the hair on the back of his neck in a very intimate way. A man could get used to this feeling real fast.

"Oh, geez," Chloe whispered.

She shivered and stepped back quickly, coming up hard against his chest. He steadied her.

"What did you see?" he asked.

"Heavy splashes of dreamlight all over the machine. The man is definitely a talent and he was running hot, but the colors are very strange."

"Define *strange*."

"Abnormal. Sick. Wrong. I can't explain it. It reminds me of the unwholesome energy I've seen in the footsteps and handprints of some mentally unstable people on the streets. But it's not quite the same. I'm guessing the guy who was playing that slot is using some major pharmaceuticals. Judging by all those muscles, probably steroids."

He thought about that for a few seconds. "Not the kind of operative Fallon Jones would hire. Maybe there are such things as coincidences. You're sure the guy is a talent?"

"I can't tell you what kind of sensitive he is, but, hey, this is Vegas. Maybe he's a probability-talent who makes his living playing the odds here. If he's got a gambling addiction, that might explain the sickness I saw in his energy."

"I don't like it." He turned to continue down the hall, reaching for his key. "Let's go. I want us out of here as soon as possible."

She halted abruptly.

"*Jack*," she whispered, her voice strained.

He stopped. "What?"

She wasn't looking at him. Instead she was staring at the floor of the hall with an uneasy expression.

"More psi prints," she said softly. "Same bad energy."

"He was up here?"

"No. Someone else." She looked toward the far end of the corridor. "The prints came from the direction of the emergency stairwell, not the lobby stairs. But it's the same kind of sick dreamlight. This is so creepy."

"So much for the coincidence theory," he said.

They both contemplated the doors of the adjoining rooms.

"He went into number fourteen," she said quietly. "No exit footsteps. He's still inside."

29

"FALLON JONES, YOU SON OF A BITCH," JACK SAID.

He kept his voice very low, barely audible, but he felt rather than saw Chloe flinch in response. In a heartbeat he was in the zone, his senses operating at full throttle. He knew she could feel the energy that he was pushing although it was still unfocused.

"What now?" she whispered.

He looked at her. "Put your key into the lock of number fourteen and make some noise. Pretend you're having trouble opening the door."

"Jack—"

"Just do it."

He set the duffel bag and his computer case on the floor beside her and went down the hall toward the door of the adjoining room.

She took her key out of her pocket and went to fourteen. She made a production of trying to unlock the room.

"There's something wrong," she said loudly, rattling the doorknob. "The key isn't working. We'll have to go downstairs and get another one."

Jack shoved his key into the lock of the second room. He was running hot, but until he located a human target he could not use his power effectively. The laws of para-physics were hard-core when it came to using talent. To make it work you had to focus on another person or, as in the case of Chloe's talent, on the residue of psi left by that individual. You couldn't just broadcast a field of energy and use it as a shield or a weapon of mass destruction. Anyone passing him in the hall at this moment would probably have been aware of a strange, unsettling sensation in the vicinity, but that was about it.

He slammed open the door and went into the room, moving as low and fast as possible.

The bastard was in the adjoining room, gun aimed at the door. When he heard Jack he whipped around with lightning speed, aiming through the opening between the rooms.

Hunter, Jack thought. The guy was seriously bulked up on steroids like the biker downstairs.

He sensed the intruder was starting to pull the trigger, but he had a fix now. He slammed the full force of his talent at the gunman, hitting him with a river of focused energy.

The man stiffened, as though electrified. His eyes bulged as he stared into the abyss of his own nightmares. His mouth opened in a silent scream, but he was already going unconscious.

He managed to get off one shot before he fell to the floor. Jack heard a *pffft* and a thud as the bullet plowed into the bed behind him. *Silencer*. The guy had come prepared.

The intruder crumpled, unmoving, to the carpet.

Jack got to his feet and went cautiously forward. He crouched beside the gunman and started going through his pockets.

Chloe appeared in the doorway of the connecting rooms. She had her satchel in one hand, the duffel slung over her shoulder and his computer case tucked under her arm.

"Is he—?" she whispered.

"No. Unconscious." He abandoned the clothing search, picked up the gun and got to his feet. "But I don't know how long he'll be out. Now we really need to move fast."

"Okay."

She gave him the duffel and the computer case and rushed across the room to where her carry-on stood open. She started to zip it closed.

"Leave it," he said. "A suitcase will slow us down."

"But my stuff."

"Throw what you can into your satchel." He went back into the adjoining room to get his overnight kit. "We'll buy whatever you need."

She came to stand in the opening, her satchel in her hand.

"He was going to kill you," she said.

"Looks like that was the plan." He picked up the duffel, opened the door and checked the hall.

"Clear," he said. "Ready?"

"Yes." She took another look at the man on the floor as she hurried toward the door. "What about him?"

"Fallon Jones can clean up his own mess," Jack said. He headed toward the lobby stairs. "Serves him right for using sloppy talent."

She rushed after him. "Aren't we going to use the emergency exit?"

"No. Odds are the other man will be waiting for him out back with the getaway car."

"What other—?" She broke off abruptly as comprehension set in. "Right. The one we saw playing the slot in the lobby was the lookout."

"I think they were both hunters of some kind."

"Sick," she replied. "Really, really sick. I can see it in the prints."

"Jones must be desperate for agents if he's using psychos."

"I thought you said Fallon Jones wouldn't do anything drastic until this so-called experiment had run its course."

"Looks like I was wrong. He must have decided that all he cares about is getting his hands on the lamp."

"No offense, but you don't sound totally convinced."

"I'm not," he admitted. "The thing is, no matter how I come at it, my strat-talent is telling me that the whole scene just doesn't look like Fallon's work. On the other hand, I don't know if I can trust my first talent anymore. No telling what the nightmare energy is doing to it. Or to me."

30

JACK HEARD THE MUFFLED GROWL OF A MOTORCYCLE JUST
as he pushed open the lobby door. A big Harley with two men on
board shot out from the alley behind the motel, cut across the parking
lot and roared off down the street. There was no license plate visible.

He put on his dark glasses and watched the bike disappear.

"The guy we left behind in the room recovered fast," he said. "Probably his hunter reflexes."

Chloe gazed after the speeding bikes. "Low-rent muscle, all right,
but hunter muscle."

"You know, the more I think about this the more I think this just
isn't Fallon's style."

"But who else would have sent them?" Chloe demanded.

"Good question."

"Now what?" Chloe glanced around. "Something tells me there
won't be a lot of cabs cruising this neighborhood."

"We'll call one from the casino," he said.

They started back across the street. He took out his cell phone and punched in a number that he hadn't called in a very long time.

Fallon Jones answered on the first ring. "My screen says this is Jack Winters, but that can't be right. I haven't heard from him in nearly a year."

"If Chloe had gone through that door first, she would probably be dead, and I would be on my way to Scargill Cove to kill you," Jack said. "We had a deal, Jones."

Out of the corner of his eye he saw Chloe give a violent little start. Her head snapped around. Her eyes were wide and her mouth was open. He ignored her.

There was a great stillness on the other end.

"What are you talking about?" Fallon asked finally.

Jack studied the handful of vehicles in the casino parking lot, looking for anything that seemed off. "I'm still alive. What's up with that? Getting careless or just having a hard time finding good help?"

"I'm in no mood for twenty questions. Tell me what the hell is going on."

"There was a para-hunter with a silenced gun waiting for us in our room at the motel here in Vegas. Another guy downstairs acting as lookout. I've got one question: Why now? Why not wait until after we know for sure that the lamp won't work for me?"

There was a short, heavy silence.

"Let me get this straight," Fallon said. His voice was an ominous rumble emanating from a dark cavern. "Are you telling me that you've got the lamp, that you're in Vegas and that someone just tried to kill you?"

"You're good at a lot of things, Fallon, but playing the innocent isn't one of them."

"Pay attention, Winters, I've got good news and bad news." Urgency thickened the bearlike voice. "Good news is that I didn't send anyone after you. I know you're paranoid when it comes to this particular sub-ject, but I'm telling you that I have not been tracking you."

"No lies, Jones. That was part of the bargain, remember? Right up there with your guarantee that you wouldn't go after anyone connected to me. That includes my employees. Chloe Harper is working for me. She's a civilian as far as you're concerned."

"I gave you my word," Fallon said. "I've kept it."

Jack exhaled slowly. "I was afraid you were going to say that."

"Believe it or not, I've actually got better things to do with my time these days than assign a team to keep tabs on you. I haven't got that kind of manpower to spare, even if I wanted to waste it on you. Those two guys you just described weren't my people."

Some of the adrenaline was fading. Jack discovered that he was able to apply his strat-talent to something other than getting Chloe out of the motel. The first jolting thought that hit him was that Fallon sounded worried and not because his agents had screwed up.

"Okay, Fallon, for the sake of argument, say I believe you. What's the bad news?"

"I don't know who just tried to take you out, but I can think of one group that might have an interest in the lamp and also the resources to find you: Nightshade."

"I've heard about your latest conspiracy theory. But according to the scuttlebutt this Nightshade operation already has a version of the founder's formula. Why would they come after the lamp? And why now, after all this time? How could they even know about it? The Win-terses have kept that secret a lot better than the Joneses have kept the secret of the formula."

"I don't have the answers to your questions," Fallon admitted.

"Now you've got my full and undivided attention. You're the man who always has the answers."

"I sure as hell don't have any right now." There was an uncharacteristic weariness in Fallon's voice. "You said the guy waiting in your room was a hunter?"

"We didn't have much of a conversation, but I can tell you he moved like a hunter. He was also bulked up on steroids."

"Don't take this wrong," Fallon said. "I'm glad you and Chloe are okay. But how did you do it? Hunters are fast."

"I'm a strat, remember? I've got a few tricks of my own."

"Huh."

Fallon wasn't buying the explanation.

"I got lucky," Jack said. Lying came easily when you were a strat. Just part of the talent. "There was a struggle. The guy panicked and ran off, probably afraid of drawing attention. The second man was waiting in the alley out back with a Harley. No license."

"Nightshade," Fallon said. "Got to be. Listen up, Jack. You and Chloe need to ditch your phones, computers, credit cards and anything else of an electronic nature. Nightshade may be using one or all of them to track you. You both need some new ID. And I'm not talking about the papers you've been carrying around for the past year. Burn 'em."

"You knew I had some fake ID? Then you have been watching me."

"No, but I know you, Jack. We think alike in some ways. If I'd been in your shoes all these years I'd sure as hell have had some emergency ID stashed for just this kind of situation."

The black-tinted glass doors of the casino slid open with a soft hiss. Cold, stale air rushed out. Jack followed Chloe into the neon-sparked darkness.

"We're in the middle of a desert, Fallon, and you're telling me I can't use computers or phones," he said. "Just how do you expect me to come up with two new sets of ID?"

"You're in Vegas. You can buy anything in that town. But if you want top-of-the-line work I suggest you ask Chloe to introduce you to her Uncle Edward and her Cousin Dex."

Jack came to a halt near a row of gleaming, flashing, blinking slots. He took off his sunglasses and looked at Chloe. "You know that Chloe's uncle here in Vegas does fake IDs?"

Chloe's eyes widened.

"Harper work is the best," Fallon said simply. "Always has been. Family's got a talent for that kind of thing. Who do you think I use?"

He cut the connection.

31

"UNCLE EDWARD, I CAN'T BELIEVE YOU'VE BEEN WORKING for Jones & Jones since Fallon Jones took over the agency," Chloe said. She was still reeling from the news. "I don't know what to say. I'm aghast. Stunned. Shocked. Is anyone else in the family aware of this? Do Mom and Dad have any idea?"

They were sitting in Edward Harper's paneled office on the second floor above the showroom and warehouse. The address was just off Dean Martin Drive near Tropicana Avenue, a gritty, industrial neighborhood. There was a truck-stop casino next door that catered to truckers looking for a break from the long haul to California or the East Coast. Across the street was a building with blacked-out windows and a neon sign that read *Gentlemen's Club*. But here on the premises of Harper Fine Furnishings the atmosphere was classic Old World elegance.

Edward was seated behind a graceful Louis XV ormolu-mounted, veneered desk. She and Jack occupied a pair of George III mahogany chairs. The paintings on the walls were mid-eighteenth century. An expensively suited, elegantly groomed assistant had been sent for coffee. They were sipping the beverage from nineteenth-century porcelain cups. At least, Chloe thought, they looked exactly like nineteenth-century china.

Edward was a polished, patrician-faced man with silver-white hair, manicured hands and a well-cared-for body. From his tasseled loafers to his Italian jacket, trousers, tailored shirt and silk tie he was a model of the bespoke lifestyle.

"So few people appreciate quality workmanship these days," he said. He had the grace to appear mildly apologetic. "There was a time when forgery was considered an art form. But, alas, those days are long gone. Done in by desktop publishing and high-tech copiers. The business went into a general decline a few years ago—we were forced to expand our client base."

"Don't you mean you lowered your standards for clients?" Chloe said sternly. "Really, Uncle Edward. Jones & Jones?"

Edward widened his hands in a what-can-one-do gesture. "Fallon Jones pays well, and he is a connoisseur. In this day and age it is a rare pleasure to work with a client who has a truly discerning eye. And I will let you in on a little secret—this isn't the first generation of our family to make our art available to J&J."

"Oh, geez," Chloe said. "I can't believe I'm hearing this."

"I would appreciate it if you didn't mention my little arrangement with J&J to anyone else in the family, however," Edward said.

"Don't worry. Harper Investigations is big on confidentiality. It's just the shock, you know?"

"Of course. Thank you, my dear." Edward looked at Jack. "Now, then, I believe we are talking about two new complete packages. Not just the usual driver's licenses and the like but credit cards and clean phones, as well?"

"I'll also need a clean computer," Jack said.

Edward nodded. "Passports?"

Jack glanced at Chloe. "Sure, why not? We'll take the works."

"Certainly."

Edward reached under his desk and pushed a concealed button. A section of office paneling slid silently aside revealing a windowless room filled with stainless-steel workbenches and an array of gleaming, high-tech equipment. Chloe saw a familiar figure bending over a light box, a jeweler's loupe in one eye.

"Dex," she said.

She jumped out of her chair and hurried toward him through the maze of UV light viewers, cameras, laptops, printers, copiers, laminating machines and exotic lighting devices.

Dex straightened and turned. When he saw her, he grinned widely. "Hey, there, Chloe. I didn't know you were in Vegas."

Dex was about her age, tall and gangly. He had been endowed with Edward's noble features, but he lacked his parent's patina of elegance and sophistication. With his overlong, tousled hair, dark-framed glasses, rumpled shirt and jeans he looked like the brilliant artist that he was.

"It's good to see you." She hugged him warmly and stepped back. "How are Beth and little Andy?"

"Doing great." Dex glanced past her. "Who's this?"

"Jack Winters," Jack said, extending a hand.

"Mr. Winters." Dex shook briskly.

"Call me Jack."

"Sure." Dex turned back to Chloe. "What brings you here?"

Edward moved forward. "This is a J&J commission. Chloe and Jack need full packages, and they are in something of a hurry."

Dex frowned at Chloe, concern tightening his features. "You're in trouble?"

"Not me, my client." She inclined her head toward Jack. "We need to disappear for a while."

"No problem," Dex said. He still looked worried. "Are you sure you're not in danger? I know the family has had issues with J&J over the years, but Fallon Jones has been a good client. I'm sure we can convince him to supply protection if you and Jack need it. Jones owes us a few favors."

"Here's the problem," she said. "Fallon Jones has an agenda of his own in this situation, one which may or may not mesh well with my client's objective."

Edward gave Jack a cool, assessing look. "And just what is that objective, if I may ask?"

"Staying alive," Jack said.

"I see. A reasonable goal." Edward glanced at the leather duffel on the floor near Jack's right foot. "I assume your endeavor involves the Burning Lamp and my niece?"

"Yes," Jack said.

"You need my niece because you think she can work the lamp. I understand that. But if things go wrong she may be in grave danger." Edward's eyes narrowed slightly. "From you."

"No, Uncle Edward," Chloe said firmly. "That's not true. "I can handle the lamp *and* Jack's dream energy field. Trust me."

"How do you know that if you've never worked the lamp?" Dex demanded.

"We ran an experiment of sorts last night," she said quickly. "Everything went swell. Piece of cake. No problem at all."

"An experiment?" Edward did not look convinced.

Jack looked at her, brows slightly raised, but he had the good sense to keep quiet.

"I can handle this, Uncle Edward," she said, mustering what she hoped was a professional air of confidence. "Mom always told me that every Harper has a talent. Well, working this lamp turns out to be mine. But I need some time to finish the job. It's hard to concentrate with J&J and this Nightshade crowd sneaking around behind us. Forty-eight hours, okay? That's all we'll need. Please, just promise me you'll give us two days of peace and quiet."

Edward hesitated and then nodded once, decisively. "If you're quite certain that you're safe with Mr. Winters we can give you both forty-eight hours." He looked at Jack. "Our family owes your family that much."

Chloe blinked, startled. "What's this about a favor?"

Dex snapped his fingers. "Right. Winters. Old favor. I remember Mom mentioning it a couple of times. Something to do with saving Norwood Harper's life back in the Victorian era."

"Norwood Harper," Chloe repeated. "*Our* Norwood Harper? The Norwood Harper who created so many brilliant, uh, reproductions of Egyptian antiquities?"

"The one and only," Edward said reverently. "A true master. It's a long story, but suffice it to say that Norwood Harper got into a bit of a bind. Some very bad people were after him. Griffin Winters took care of the problem."

"This family always pays its debts," Chloe said proudly.

Edward inclined his head. "Indeed. Well, I suppose this means you aren't free to have dinner with us tonight."

"Another time, I promise," Chloe said. "As you can see I'm a little tied up at the moment."

Jack looked at Dex. "I don't want to be rude, but this is what you might call a rush job."

"Right." Dex crossed the crowded space to open a steel cabinet. "Where are you headed?"

"L.A." Jack said. "Or, at least, that's what I want J&J and Nightshade to think for the next forty-eight hours."

32

CHLOE WENT TO STAND AT THE TINTED WINDOWS AND STUD-
ied the neon-lit night world twenty floors below. "Okay, we are definitely moving up. From a no-tell motel downtown to a one-bedroom,
two-bath suite overlooking the Strip. I'm good with that. But why
aren't we headed toward L.A.? It would be easy to get lost there."

She heard a heavy clunk behind her. Jack had just hoisted the duffel
bag onto the table.

"Because my gut tells me that's exactly what they'll expect us to do,"
he said.

The heavy, compelling energy of the lamp was thick in the atmosphere, calling to her senses. She turned around.

"You mean Nightshade?"

"And Fallon Jones. Both sides will assume that we're hightailing it
out of town now that we know we're being hunted. It's human nature
to run in situations like this."

"So we do the opposite."

"Right."

She heightened her senses a little more and studied his prints on the leather bag. Strong, healthy dream psi, the positive results of a good night's rest, showed clearly. But she could still see faint traces of the medication he had been taking.

"Why are we worried about Fallon Jones?" she asked. "I got the impression you believed him when he claimed he wasn't gunning for you."

"I think he was telling the truth when he said that he hadn't been tracking me. But now that he knows for sure that I've got the lamp and that Nightshade is on our trail, he won't be able to resist trying to keep us under surveillance."

"For our own good, of course," she said drily.

"Probably had someone watching your uncle's store even before we got there this afternoon. The question is whether the decoy car worked."

"I'm sure it worked," she said, not without a touch of pride. "My family is very good at this kind of thing."

His mouth kicked up a little at the edges. "I noticed."

Edward Harper had arranged for an SUV with heavily tinted windows to pull away from Harper Fine Furnishings shortly before sunset that afternoon. Dex and Beth, bearing a remarkably close resemblance to Jack and herself, thanks to theatrical makeup and wigs, were inside. They had driven off quickly, headed west on I-15 toward L.A.

She and Jack had departed sometime later in the back of one of the half dozen Harper Fine Furnishings delivery vans that came and went all day long from the secure warehouse at the rear of the store. In addition to their new credit cards, ID and phones, Jack had a sparkling clean laptop. The discreet departure had been accomplished with the customary Harper efficiency.

She walked to the table and stopped, looking down at the lamp. "You sure you're ready to do this?"

He watched her from the opposite side of the table. "It's not like I have a choice. What about you?"

She knew she had to sound confident for his sake.

"Ready," she said. "First step here is to light the lamp. I think either one of us can do that, but once it's burning, you're the only one who can push up the power level."

"How do I do that?"

"I'm afraid it's going to be an intuitive thing. The process should come naturally to you because the lamp is already tuned to your wavelengths. We'll take it slow and easy, though. Whatever we do here, we definitely do not want to lose control of the power in this gadget."

"It's that dangerous?" he asked quietly.

"Yes." She paused. "But I can't tell you how or in what way it's dangerous. Power is power, though. You have to respect it."

She went around the suite, turning off the lights. The room was plunged into a darkness lit only by the cold light of neon and a desert moon. In the shadows she could see Jack silhouetted against the uncovered window.

She gave her eyes a moment to adjust to the night and then made her way back toward him. In the dim light she managed to collide with a chair.

"*Ooph.*" She was going to be bruised in the morning.

"You okay?" Jack asked.

"Yeah, sure. Fine." So much for the air of confident professionalism, she thought. She rubbed her thigh and continued on to the table. "Okay, here we go."

She heightened her senses, probing gently for the latent currents in the lamp. Energy shifted ominously in the artifact. Slowly it began to glow, giving off a weak, pale light.

"That's as far as I can take it," she said quietly. "Your turn."

Jack did not respond, but she felt the energy level rise in the room.

Psi heat stirred her senses. The skin on her arms prickled. The hair on the nape of her neck lifted. Her pulse beat faster. Excitement and anticipation revved through her.

The lamp got brighter. She went hotter and became uncomfortably aware of the residue of lust, some of it earthy and natural, some of it sick and disgusting, that stained the suite. Traces of gambling fever were everywhere in the room. The unwholesome light of other kinds of addictions glittered malevolently as well. Not even the strongest cleaning chemicals could touch dream energy. The lust on the bedding in the other room reeked.

She tuned out the extraneous energy and focused on the lamp. Fingerprints of dark, hot ultralight fluoresced on the strange metal, seething and pulsing in the shadows. Acid greens mingled with impossible shades of paranormal blues, blacks and purples. Until now she had resisted looking at the artifact with all of her senses flung wide. Now that she had looked at it, she could not turn away.

Some of the dreamlight residue on the lamp was old and glowed with a disturbing iridescence that she recognized as the hallmark of raw power. For the first time panic skittered on little rat feet across her senses. What had she gotten herself into?

She took a deep breath. She could do this. She had to do it. For Jack.

"Your ancestors left their prints on the lamp," she said. "The earliest could easily be a few hundred years old."

"Nicholas Winters." Jack's voice was low but it was freighted with the energy he was generating.

"The hues and shades and the patterns of the wavelengths are similar in some ways to your own. Psychic genetics at work. There's another set of particularly powerful prints. Newer but well over a century old."

"Griffin Winters."

She studied some of the other traces of dreamlight on the lamp.

"I can also see the prints of the women who worked the lamp. The oldest still burns with rage and despair and an overpowering need for vengeance."

"Eleanor Fleming, the first woman who worked the lamp. She's the one who bore Nicholas a son and then used the energy of the lamp to destroy Nicholas's talent."

She shivered. "Here's the really sad part: On some level, deep in her dreamscape, she loved him, or at least she was bonded to him."

"Because of the child?"

"Yes. In turn, Nicholas was obsessed with her, probably because he realized that she was the key to controlling the power of the lamp. Those two obviously had issues."

"What about Griffin Winters and Adelaide Pyne?"

She studied the second set of strong dreamprints with all of her senses. It took power to control power. Griffin and Adelaide had both possessed off-the-charts talent.

"There was a bond between them as well. It was definitely sexual in nature." She stilled. "Maybe that's the real key to controlling the lamp."

"What?"

"Some kind of psychic link between the Winters man and the dreamlight worker."

"Hold it right there," Jack said. "Don't try to tell me that the couple that works the lamp together has to be in love. Thought you said you were not a romantic?"

"Trust me, we're not talking about anything as vague and ephemeral as romantic love," she assured him. "But everyone knows that there is a lot of psi generated during sex. Maybe that's why we wound up in bed last night."

"You think the lamp made us do it? Okay, that's an original excuse."

"Think about it. We'd been near it for hours, and that sucker gives off a lot of energy. Who knows what kind of influence it exerted on our auras?"

"You definitely are not a romantic, are you?"

"Told you, I can't afford to be. Not with my talent."

"Fine. But keep one thing in mind: We were attracted to each other before we found the lamp."

"Yes." She studied the lamp. "But I wonder if that's because . . ."

"It's because we're attracted to each other," he growled. "There's no need to blame it on psychic voodoo."

"Okay, okay, take it easy."

"Let's get back to business here. Can you work this thing or not?"

"Don't worry, we're good." *Never let the client see you sweat.* "Piece of cake."

The radiation emanating from the lamp was brighter, more intense now. From the heavy base to the flared rim it pulsed with energy. She watched, fascinated, as wispy tendrils of ultralight twisted and curled. Slowly the strange metal alloy became first translucent and then transparent. The psi fire swirling within it was clearly visible.

"Jack, it's working," she whispered.

"I can feel it," he said. His voice roughened with something other than psi. "I can feel your energy, too."

He was still drenched in shadows and the icy shades of moon and neon, but the rising tide of dreamlight etched his stern features. His hard, ascetic profile was revealed in the dark hues that emanated from the far end of the spectrum.

The transformation of the lamp was complete. The artifact now appeared to be fashioned of pure, clear crystal. As Chloe watched, all but one of the stones in the rim began to change, too. Each burned with inner fire. No longer opaque, the illuminated crystals took on distinct shades of dreamlight. One shone with a dazzling silver white light. Another radiated fiery crimson energy. Currents of surreal blues and purples, greens and amber lanced from other crystals in the rim.

"The Burning Lamp," she said, enthralled.

"Yes." Jack's voice was fierce and tight.

"But why is one stone still cold?"

"It must be the last crystal forged by Nicholas, the one he called the Midnight Crystal. He wrote that it was the most dangerous of them all." Jack looked at her. "Do we need it?"

"No, I don't think so." She probed gently. "It feels blank. Like plain glass or quartz. If there is power in it, I can't sense it or work it."

"Maybe it is just ordinary glass. By all accounts, Nicholas was flat-out crazy at the end, and he was losing his talents. He was obsessed with vengeance. In that state of mind he might have convinced himself that he had infused a chunk of plain glass with great power."

Cautiously she touched the artifact, hoping intuition would guide her. A jolt of what felt like electricity slammed through her when her fingers came in contact with the transparent metal. It was like brushing up against another person's dream energy but a hundred times worse. She did not let go. She wasn't at all certain that she *could* let go, not until she had finished what had been started.

And suddenly she knew what to do next, what had to be done.

"Put one hand on the lamp," she said.

Jack did as instructed. His jaw clenched when he touched the artifact. She knew that he had gotten the same initial shock that she had received.

"Take my hand," she said.

He closed his free hand around hers. More electric psi flashed through her, stronger this time. It was all she could do to bite back a cry of pain. Jack's fingers tightened around her fingers.

She waited a moment, bracing herself for more of the disturbing shocks, but there were none.

"We're in," she whispered. "Our wavelengths are resonating with those of the lamp, thanks to you."

"Me?"

"I don't think anyone who didn't have your genetic pattern could get this far. I'm riding your currents, but I think I can control the rhythm and pattern of the lamp's energy. Sort of like riding a really big, really strong stallion."

His mouth twisted in a humorless smile. "I'm the stallion?"

"And I'm the rider. You've got the raw power, but I've got the reins."

"Under other circumstances, that could be a really interesting visual. Now what?"

"We're going to do this slow and easy," she said. "Got a feeling there could be some heavy blowback on both of us if I move too fast."

Jack did not respond. He was gazing into the heart of the lamp, riveted by whatever he saw there.

Slowly, carefully, relying entirely on her intuition, she began to work the energy of the crystal stones, stabilizing the wild currents of psi. She was already running hot psychically, but now she was starting to become physically aroused as well and not in a generic sense. She wanted to *mate*—there was no other word for it—and not with just any man. She wanted Jack and Jack alone. She *craved* him, *lusted* after him, *hungered* for him, just as she had last night when she had used her energy to shatter the trance.

"This is getting weird," she said softly.

Jack's hand was clamped around hers like a manacle, but he did not look up from the shifting energy of the lamp.

"You're a woman of power," he said, his words thick with lust and hunger.

It was all she could do not to hurl herself into his arms.

Get a grip, she thought. *It's the lamp that's doing this to us. Got a job to do here. The client needs you.*

"Open your senses to the max," she ordered quietly. "I need to be able to see the entire range of your dream spectrum."

Energy surged in the room. Hot ultralight flashed and crashed in the small space. She knew that Jack was fully, completely fired up, in the zone. The scope of his talent was breathtaking.

With an effort of will, she ignored the surges of sexual longing cascading through her. *There is a kind of freedom in celibacy. Yeah, right.*

Carefully she studied Jack's ultralight currents. What she saw stunned her. The channels between the waking state and the dreamstate were open, *even though Jack was awake and running hot.* What's more, the connection between the two states was stable. By all the laws of paraphysics, that was supposed to be impossible.

Although the channels were open and stable for the most part, there were some places on the spectrum where the currents were slightly erratic. The disturbed areas appeared to be slowly healing, but she was pretty sure she could speed up the process.

With a skill that came intuitively, she steadied the psychic radiation of the lamp and guided it so that it resonated with the wavelengths in the disturbed areas of Jack's dream channels. Within seconds the erratic areas steadied and began pulsing in a healthy fashion.

"That should take care of the nightmares and the hallucinations," she whispered. "Now I wonder if I can do something about that medication you've been taking."

The words were hardly out of her mouth when the lamp flared even higher, creating a storm of ultralight. It was as if her little mending job had turned a key in an invisible paranormal lock, releasing the final level of power within the artifact.

Jack went rigid, every muscle in his body tensing as if he'd just been shot. His head snapped back, a man in mortal agony. His mouth opened on a choked, anguished groan. He squeezed her hand with the strength of a drowning man clinging to a life preserver.

A terrible despair slammed through her. She had made a horrific error. She was killing him. Too much energy was flooding through him. No human mind could sustain such a psychic hurricane. She knew that in her bones. The lamp was not intended to work like this.

That's why it requires a dreamlight worker, she thought. *That's why you're here.*

But she sensed that it was too late to halt the process. Nothing could put this genie back into the lamp. Frantic, she tried to control the energy that had been unleashed. But she knew she could not hope to channel the full power of the raging storm of psi.

"Jack," she gasped. "You have to help me. We have to do this together."

"Yes," he said through clamped teeth. "Together."

She sensed him reaching into the heart of the storm, seizing the raw power that lay there. Only he could control it, she realized. He was the only person who could shut down the lamp. But to do so he needed her to steady the violently resonating patterns of dreamlight.

Lightly, delicately, she slipped her own energy back into the stream. In a heartbeat, maybe two, she was part of the storm. The sensation of so much heavy psi flowing through her was intoxicating, the ultimate rush. Her hair lifted, dancing around her head as though tossed by invisible winds. She almost screamed with the glorious ecstasy of it all. She really did know how to do this. Every Harper had a talent.

She forced the currents into a stable pattern. Simultaneously Jack took control of the power of the lamp. What had been a searing, surging blast of raw psi was soon reduced to a focused river of energy.

The lamp gradually darkened, going first translucent and then finally solid metal once again. The paranormal rainbow winked out. The crystals that had created it turned gray and opaque.

She looked at Jack over the top of the lamp, dazed and exultant.

"We did it," she breathed. She realized she was soaring on the thrill that accompanied the control of so much power.

Jack's eyes still burned psi green.

"*Chloe.*"

She knew that he was riding the same sensual high. He pulled her into his arms, crushing her against his chest. She could hardly breathe, but who needed oxygen? What she needed was Jack. And in that moment she knew that he needed her just as urgently, at least for now.

The kiss was hot and desperate, bordering on violent. They did not undress each other—they clawed at each other's clothes. She was vaguely aware of fabric ripping and buttons snapping. Jack unzipped her pants, grabbed the waistband in both hands and shoved the trousers along with her panties down to her ankles. Impatient, she kicked free of the clothing.

He did not bother to carry her into the bedroom. Instead, he swept out a hand. There was a heavy thud when the lamp hit the carpet. The next thing she knew she was lying flat on her back on the table, her legs dangling over the edge.

Jack got his own trousers open and moved between her thighs. He put one hand on her, testing, and she almost climaxed then and there. He probed once and then thrust heavily, deeply, into her.

Shock waves tightened everything inside her. But she was almost maxed out. The tension was unbearable—she was as taut as a bowstring awaiting the release of the arrow. All the colors of the dreamlight spectrum radiated around her, dazzling, blinding, floodlighting her senses.

Jack surged into her again. She came immediately, too breathless to cry out. The waves of energy were still sweeping through her when she heard a low, harsh growl. Jack surged into her one last time. His powerful climax rocked through both of them.

When it was over he braced himself above her, shirt hanging open, and planted his hands on the table on either side of her. His hair was damp. Sweat dripped from his shoulders onto her breasts.

"Chloe," he said again, very softly this time.

He leaned down and brushed his mouth across hers.

She touched his bare chest. His skin was slick with perspiration and very warm, as if he were running a real fever.

He straightened, freeing himself from her body with obvious reluctance. He closed his pants, scooped her off the table and carried her the short distance to the couch. He sank down onto the cushions and cradled her across his thighs. Then he leaned his head back and closed his eyes.

He was asleep within seconds.

She stirred a little and opened her senses slightly. She had burned through most of her reserves, but she had just enough energy left to look at the top of the table where Jack's hands had been a moment ago. Then she studied the carpet.

Heat and power still burned in his psi prints, but the wavelengths were stable and strong. Stray fragments of dream energy were no longer bleeding over into his other senses. There was still a taint of darkness from the medication he had been taking, but that was not the real problem.

The problem was that she was pretty sure she had failed. Clients never took failure well.

33

HE AWOKE TO THE LIGHT OF THE DESERT SUN STREAMING through the tinted windows and the sound of water running in the shower. He had a vague memory of falling asleep—going more or less unconscious—with Chloe's warm, sexy weight lying across his thighs.

It occurred to him that he felt better than he had in weeks, months. Maybe years. He was also half aroused. The morning erection felt good, too. It felt normal. Nothing much had been normal of late.

He got to his feet, stretched, yawned and wandered into the suite's second bath. When he emerged a few minutes later it occurred to him that if he moved fast he might be able to join Chloe in the shower. He'd noticed yesterday that it was a really big shower tricked out in true Vegas style with multiple showerheads and spray nozzles. A real water wonderland.

He started across the room, heading toward the master bath. Halfway to his goal he saw the lamp. It was sitting on the table.

The memory of sweeping the artifact aside so that he could get

Chloe onto the table slammed through him. He'd taken her there on the table with zero foreplay and absolutely no finesse. Last night she had saved him from becoming a psychic monster, but now she probably thought he was a Neanderthal when it came to sex. Not exactly a big step-up in status.

He went into the bedroom and opened the door of the bath. Steam rolled out in waves. Gold fixtures and marble tiles gleamed in the mist. The roar of the water was so loud he knew that Chloe must have turned on every jet, faucet and nozzle in the mini spa.

He could see her through the clouded glass walls of the shower. She was standing beneath the rushing waters, her back to him, washing her hair. He realized he was hard, fully aroused.

"In or out, take your choice but close the door," she called above the thundering waterfall. "You're letting all the heat out of the room."

He closed the bathroom door and opened the shower.

"Chloe, about last night," he began.

She straightened, opened her eyes and turned slightly toward him. "I thought we agreed that no good conversation ever started with *about last night*."

He did not know what to say. She looked so delicious standing there with water splashing and pouring everywhere, so delicate and feminine and soft. He must have crushed her on that table last night.

"I'm sorry. I don't know what I can do or say. Hell, you're bruised."

She glanced down at the mark on her thigh. "Not your fault. I bumped into a chair. You did not hurt me, so you can stop apologizing." She became very busy soaping up a washcloth. "It's not as if you attacked me. We were both in the grip of a major burn, and I think the energy of the lamp was affecting us. Things got a little energetic, that's all. Nothing to be concerned about."

She was writing off the most powerful sexual encounter he'd ever experienced as merely the result of a heavy psi burn and the effects of the damn lamp. Maybe for her that's all it had been. He realized that he didn't like that possibility.

"So, you've done it that way before?" he asked. He peeled off his shirt, dropped it on the floor and unzipped his pants. "After a burn or after working a paranormal artifact?"

"Well, no." She soaped her face. "But it's a known fact that when a person is running hot, there is a lot of adrenaline and testosterone and bio-psi chemicals flooding the bloodstream. We were both maxed out last night, and there was the added complication of the lamp, that's all. No big deal."

He kicked his pants out of the way, stepped into the shower and closed the glass door very quietly. He moved up behind her and kissed the curve of her shoulder. She froze, the washcloth covering her face.

"No big deal?" he asked. He put his hand on her hip and gently, very gently, bit her ear. "You're sure about that?"

He felt her shiver beneath his hand, but she did not pull away. He realized that he'd been braced for rejection. The relief nearly overwhelmed him.

"You know what I mean," she mumbled into the washcloth.

"No, I don't think I do." He eased her back against his heavily aroused body and moved one hand between her legs. "What happened last night was a very big deal to me. So was what happened the night before."

She lowered the washcloth and tilted her face so that the spray rinsed off the soapy lather she had just applied. Slowly she turned in his arms. She regarded him with very serious eyes.

"How do you feel?" she asked.

"Good." He considered the matter more closely and smiled slowly. "Very, very good."

She glanced at the shower door behind him. He felt energy pulse and knew that she was checking out his prints on the glass.

"Some of your dream psi was a little disturbed. That's why you were getting the hallucinations and nightmares. But I fixed the wavelengths."

"I know. The weird shit is gone." He removed the washcloth from her hands, tossed it aside and touched her nipples. "I can sense the difference."

"The weird stuff might be gone, but there are still traces of those sleeping meds. I didn't have a chance to do anything about them." She frowned intently. "They're fading, however. Shouldn't be much longer now before the last of the drug is out of your system."

He captured her face between his hands, forcing her to look at him, not the door.

"About last night," he said again.

She blinked, as though he had distracted her from whatever she had been going to say next. Her air of intense concentration slowly evaporated. She smiled. Heat and feminine mystery darkened her eyes.

"Okay," she said. "It was a big deal. So was the night before."

That was what he wanted to hear, he thought. So why wasn't he satisfied with her response? He decided he would have to think about the problem some other time. At that moment the only thing he could concentrate on was touching Chloe all over, kissing her all over. This morning he was going to do everything the way he should have last night.

Invisible energy sparked and flared in the atmosphere. Just like last night, he thought. But this time she wouldn't be able to blame it on the lamp.

A LONG TIME LATER she got out of the shower and wrapped herself in a thick white towel. He followed, reaching for one of the towels. He was feeling very good, even better than he had when he had awakened.

He smiled at her as he dried himself. "Well?"

She wrinkled her nose and turned pink, and then she laughed.

"Okay, that was a big deal, too," she said.

He grinned. "No lamp involved."

AFTERWARD HE PUT ON the new clothes the Harper family had provided. He made the call to Fallon while Chloe was getting dressed in the bedroom.

Fallon picked up halfway through the first ring. "You're not in L.A."

"Still in Vegas. Sorry about that. I wanted some privacy."

"Yeah, I started getting suspicious this morning when I saw the credit card charges. Harper running those for you?"

"Part of the full-service package. It's designed to make it look like I'm somewhere other than where I happen to be at the moment."

"You sound different. I take it the lamp worked?"

"As advertised. Chloe says my dream-psi patterns are stable again. She's right. I can sense it, too."

"So you're not going to turn into a Cerberus on me. Great. That takes one problem off my to-do list."

"You never did sound all that worried."

"Probably because I wasn't. Griffin Winters survived, so the lamp must have worked for him. Figured it would work for you, too." Fallon paused. "I'm assuming, of course, that you haven't been overcome by a compulsion to murder anyone with the last name of Jones?"

"Well, now that you mention it—"

"That was a joke, Winters."

"I knew that."

Fallon was silent for a few seconds.

"Think there's anything to the story about the Midnight Crystal that Old Nick claimed he inserted into the lamp there at the end?" he asked eventually.

"One of the rocks in the lamp stayed dark. Figure that's the one Nicholas called the Midnight Crystal. Chloe thinks it's just a chunk of glass. She couldn't sense any energy in it, and I sure as hell couldn't fire it up."

"Good news for the Jones family tree," Fallon said. "What's got me worried now is that it looks like Nightshade wants the lamp, and I can't figure out why."

"What makes you so sure that Nightshade is involved with what happened at the motel yesterday?"

"My talent," Fallon said flatly.

"Hard to argue with that. But what would they want with the lamp?"

"When I find out, you'll be the first to know. I've got a feeling that as long as you and Chloe have the lamp in your possession, though, you're both in danger."

"Why Chloe?" he asked, gut tightening.

"Because she can work the lamp," Fallon said. "If they want the lamp, they may want her, too."

"Shit."

"Harper's doing a good job. Anyone trying to follow you probably believes that you're in L.A., so I think we've got some breathing room. But we need to get the lamp into safekeeping in one of the museum vaults as quickly as possible."

"You have a plan?"

"I *had* a plan," Fallon said. "I've always got a plan. But you screwed things up when you decided to stay in Vegas. I had a couple people waiting in L.A., the kind of talents who can handle this type of work."

"Hunters?"

"*Cleared* hunters. When it comes to dealing with Nightshade, I'm not using anyone who hasn't been vetted by me, personally, unless there's no other option."

"You think Arcane has been infiltrated?"

"It's a given now that we know that the bastard who founded the organization was sitting right there on the Governing Council for decades, listening to every single one of the Society's secrets."

"Not that Arcane was ever particularly good at keeping secrets," Jack pointed out.

"The Society wasn't set up to be an intelligence agency," Fallon shot back. "We're supposed to be a group of serious academics and researchers devoted to the study of the paranormal. We publish scholarly papers, damn it. We collect artifacts for our museums. And J&J is just a small-time private investigation agency, not the CIA."

"Take it easy, Fallon. You sound a little tense."

"So sue me. I've got about a dozen irons in the fire at the moment, and they're all red-hot. Do you have any idea of how much data we collected when we took down those Nightshade labs a couple months back?"

"No."

"Neither do I because it's all locked in computers. Hard-core encryption. I don't have nearly enough crypto-talents to get the job done."

"Must be tough," Jack said, trying for soothing.

But Fallon was on a roll. "I've had to put a lot of routine cases on the back burner because I just don't have the time or the people to handle them. That means that an unknown number of sociopathic sensitives are out there right now using their talents to con little old ladies out of their life savings, picking pockets, stealing jewelry or running gangs. In some cases they're getting away with murder. Literally."

"J&J was never intended to be a police force, either," Jack reminded him.

"Who the hell is going to catch those kinds of bad guys if we don't? Regular law enforcement agencies don't even acknowledge that there is such a thing as the paranormal, let alone that some of the people they're chasing have psychic talents."

There was movement in the bedroom doorway. Jack glanced back and saw Chloe coming toward him. She looked fresh and vibrant, still a little flushed and rosy from their lovemaking and the shower.

"You need an assistant, Fallon," he said into the phone. "You should learn to delegate."

"Yeah, people keep telling me that. But I don't have time to find someone who could handle the job. And then there's the other issue."

"What other issue?"

Fallon was quiet for a couple of beats. "I've been told that I'm not the easiest person to work with."

"Hard to believe."

"I know, go figure. Thing is, even if I did find someone suitable, what are the odds that he or she would want to pull up stakes and move here to Scargill Cove?"

"What's wrong with Scargill Cove? Thought it was one of those picturesque little coastal towns like Mendocino."

"Small towns are small towns. Doesn't matter what the scenery looks like. The only movie theater here closed four years ago. The one bookstore stocks books on vegan cooking and meditation. Most of the locals can best be described as interesting characters, and the only restaurant clean enough to take a date to is the Sunshine Café, which closes at five thirty. They roll up the streets at night around here."

Jack took the phone away from his ear and looked at it. He put the phone back to his ear.

"You're thinking of inviting a woman out on a date?" he asked cautiously.

"I'm a man," Fallon muttered. "I have needs."

"Then maybe you'd better move to another town. Someplace where you have a shot at getting those needs fulfilled."

"That won't work." Fallon exhaled heavily. "I require peace and quiet. Lots of peace and quiet. Scargill Cove works for me."

"I hesitate to state the obvious, but have you considered registering with arcanematch?"

"What's the point? Everyone knows that the Society's database isn't much good at finding matches for guys like us. Look what happened when you went shopping for a wife there. You were divorced two years later."

"Just because my marriage didn't work out doesn't mean that arcanematch wouldn't work for you."

"Hell, I'm not looking for a wife. I don't have time to deal with a wife. Wives require a lot of attention."

"Maybe what you need is a wife who shares your interest in running J&J," Jack said. He wondered when he had become an expert on marriage. Fallon was right, his own had not been what anyone would call a resounding success.

"What the hell are we doing talking about my private life?" Fallon demanded. "I've got work to do. I'll get the team of hunters out to you later today. They'll be driving from L.A. Don't want to risk taking the lamp through airline security. They should reach you in about four hours, assuming I can get hold of them right away."

Fallon ended the connection, as was his custom, without bothering with the usual civilities such as *good-bye* or *see ya* or *talk to you later*. Jack lowered the phone and looked at Chloe.

"Fallon Jones is sending a team out from L.A. to collect the lamp. We've got a few hours to kill. What do you say we go downstairs and have breakfast? I'm hungry." He thought about it and smiled. This was the first time in weeks when he'd contemplated food as anything more than fuel. "Really, really hungry."

34

IT WAS IMPOSSIBLE TO GO ANYWHERE WITHIN THE SPRAWL-
ing casino-hotel complex without having to traverse the gaming floor.
Chloe lowered her senses to the minimum, but there was no way to
ignore the layers of feverish dreamprints that fluoresced everywhere in
the eternal night that enveloped the vast room.

The glowing residue of psi left by thousands of frantic, excited, and
desperate players gave the midnight realm an otherworldly lumines-
cence. Weaving a path through the glowing card tables, roulette wheels
and banks of slot machines was like swimming through a maze of boil-
ing sulfur cauldrons at the bottom of the ocean.

The hotel featured over a dozen restaurants, bars and fast-food eater-
ies, all scattered around the perimeter of the gaming floor. The large
café that catered to the breakfast and lunch crowd had a very short
line. The seating hostess showed them to a booth. Chloe ignored the
sickly psi prints that glowed all across the sparkling clean table and
opened her menu. Jack sat down across from her. He put the leather

duffel containing the lamp on one side of the seat and positioned his computer case on the other. The subtle aura of dark power emanating from the artifact misted the atmosphere of the small area.

"You're really going to give that thing to Arcane?" she asked.

Jack studied the menu. "Yeah."

"Are you serious? Do you actually trust the Society to take care of it?"

"Not one hundred percent, no." He closed his menu and looked at her. "But you rarely get a hundred percent certainty in anything. Fallon is right. The lamp will be a lot more secure locked up in an Arcane vault than sitting on an end table in my condo."

"Okay, I'll give you that," she said. "But what if one of your descendants ever needs it?"

"Same reasoning applies. Arcane has taken reasonably good care of a lot of paranormal artifacts for a few centuries. Their security is always first class these days because they've got the best crypto-talents to design it. My family managed to lose the lamp in the course of a cross-country move. Who knows? Maybe one of my great-grandchildren, assuming I ever have any, might decide to put it into a yard sale."

She got an odd little twinge when she thought about his children and great-grandchildren. His descendants would probably all be strong talents. Maybe they would have his eyes.

She forced her thoughts back to the present.

"I see what you mean." She looked at the duffel bag again. "But you're banking on a future edition of Fallon Jones or someone at his level within the Society being willing to let your descendants use the lamp if they need it. What's more, you're betting that the Society, itself, will continue to exist not just for decades but for centuries."

"It has survived since the late 1600s." He shrugged. "It's not like I've got a lot of great options. The lamp is safer with a long-standing institution like the Society, which understands the importance of paranormal artifacts, than it is with a single family."

She pursed her lips, thinking about it. "Maybe. It's just the principle of the thing. I mean, you're talking about giving the lamp to an organization run by the Joneses."

"You should talk. Your uncle and your cousin are working for J&J."

She made a face. "Wait until the rest of the family finds out."

They ordered omelets. When the food arrived Chloe shook her head, awed by the sheer size of the portions.

"Good grief. We could have split one of these," she said.

Jack forked up a large bite with obvious relish. "Speak for yourself. I told you, I'm hungry."

He gave her a wickedly sexy smile and winked. She felt her face grow warm in response. It occurred to her that she was very hungry, herself. They had both used a lot of energy last night. She dug into her eggs.

She knew she was putting off the moment when she would have to explain last night's failure. But somehow she just couldn't bring herself to shatter the warm intimacy of the morning. It had never been like this with any other man. Surely she was entitled to a little romance. Besides, maybe she was wrong. Maybe she hadn't failed.

"I couldn't help but overhear your conversation with Fallon," she said. "How long were you married?"

"Two years."

"What happened?"

"Well, according to Shannon, I was too driven, too intense. I think she used the term *control freak* a few times."

"Was she right?"

"Yes. I discovered I was good at making money. Went at it twenty-four/seven. All in all, I became pretty intense and driven and maybe something of a control freak. Guess I got stuck in that mode."

"I don't think it's a mode," she said. "It requires plenty of intensity, determination and control to handle your level of talent. Your personality and temperament would reflect those qualities, regardless of what you did for a living."

He looked up. "Nicholas Winters wrote something in his journal about the high cost of each of the three talents. *The first talent fills the mind with a rising tide of restlessness that cannot be assuaged by endless hours in the laboratory or soothed with strong drink or the milk of the poppy.*"

"Guess that explains a few of your quirks. Talent number two is accompanied by the nightmares and hallucinations problem?"

"Right."

She cleared her throat delicately. "Uh, what about number three?"

"It is supposed to be the most powerful and the most dangerous of the three talents. Nicholas wrote that *if the key is not turned properly in the lock, this last psychical ability will prove lethal, bringing on first insanity and then death.*"

Her fork froze in midair. "He specifically wrote about a key and a lock? Do you know what he was talking about?"

"No. The old alchemists were big on riddles and hidden meanings."

She thought about the feeling she'd had last night, the sensation that she had turned an invisible key in a paranormal lock. A shiver whispered through her.

"Nicholas was very explicit about the price exacted by the first two talents," she said carefully. "I wonder if he was being more literal than you think."

Jack watched her very steadily. "He also wrote that only the woman able to work the lamp could halt or reverse the transformation into a Cerberus."

Her pulse picked up, and her chest tightened. "Oh, geez. Talk about pressure. Listen, Jack, you look pretty normal to me this morning. And you said you felt good."

He smiled slightly, eyes heating. "Thanks to you."

"Yes, well—"

The burbling of her phone interrupted her. Startled, she dove into her purse and came up with the device.

"Uncle Edward? Is something wrong?"

"I got a call from your assistant, Rose, a few minutes ago. She said Drake Stone contacted her this morning. He's trying to get in touch with you. Said it was very important that he talk to you. Thought I'd better pass the message along."

A sliver of alarm sliced through her senses. "I'll call him right away. Thanks, Uncle Edward." She crossed her fingers under the table. "Oh, and the lamp worked."

"Good to know."

"Yes, it is. We don't need it anymore, so J&J is sending someone to collect it and take it to an Arcane vault."

"Best place for it," Edward said. "Arcane knows how to take care of that sort of thing."

"Thanks, again, for everything yesterday."

"No problem. Your client will receive my bill when this is all over."

She ended the call and looked at Jack. "I have to call Drake Stone. He got in touch with Rose this morning. Something about needing to talk to me immediately."

Jack lowered his fork. "What's going on?"

"I don't know yet."

She punched in the number Edward had given her. A woman answered on the second ring.

"Stone residence," a woman said.

The voice was chirpy. Different housekeeper, Chloe noticed.

"This is Chloe Harper," she said. "I'm returning a call to Mr. Stone."

"Yes, Miss Harper. Please hold."

Stone took the call immediately.

"Chloe, thanks for getting back to me." Drake sounded strained and tense.

"Is something wrong, Mr. Stone?"

"To tell you the truth, I'm not sure. I had a rather strange experience last night. Someone came to see me here at the house. I think it was about the lamp."

A sense of urgency tightened her breathing. She was aware of Jack watching her with a steady look.

"You *think* it was about the lamp?" she said carefully.

"That's the weird part," Drake said. "I can't quite remember the conversation. I admit that this was after the show and that I'd had two or three drinks to unwind before going to bed. That could explain my memory problems. But what really bothers me is that this morning I checked with the guard at the front gate."

"And?" Chloe asked.

"According to the log and the guy who was on duty last night, I had no visitors."

35

THE UNIFORMED GUARD WAVED THEM THROUGH THE GATE. Jack drove along the tree-lined drive and stopped the car in front of Stone's Mediterranean villa. Chloe grabbed her satchel, popped open the door and slid out of the front seat.

The late morning sun was bright, but the temperature was still in the low sixties. The chill she felt, however, had nothing to do with the brisk air. Her senses were fluttering the way they did whenever she walked past the entrances of dark alleys or entered a parking garage late at night. Most people try to ignore their intuition. But when you have been raised by people who accept the psychic side of their natures as natural, you learn to pay attention.

She walked with Jack along the stone path to the imposing, colon-naded entrance of the big house. As usual, Jack carried the leather duffel containing the lamp and his computer case. He pressed the doorbell.

"I still can't believe I'm actually working for J&J," Chloe said mournfully. "How the Harper family standards have fallen."

"Look at it this way," Jack said. "Jones pays well."

"Do you really think that Fallon's theory is correct?" she asked. "Do you believe that Nightshade actually sent a para-hypnotist here to interrogate Mr. Stone last night?"

"Who knows?" Jack said. "This is Fallon's conspiracy theory we're dealing with. Given his current worldview, everything is about Nightshade."

They had called Fallon Jones immediately after Chloe had ended her conversation with Stone. Fallon had been almost apoplectic with urgency. "Go see him right now. Talk to him. Get every damn detail you can out of him. Take a good look at Stone's dreamprints, Chloe. Sounds like he and the guard were given a hypnotic suggestion to encourage them to forget whoever came to see Stone. I want a full report as soon as you're finished."

"Excuse me, Mr. Jones, but are you trying to hire me to do a job for you?"

"You're a private investigator, aren't you? Not like I've got anyone else I can use on such short notice. Send me a bill later."

She opened her senses and studied the front steps. Psi light glowed faintly on the sun-washed tiles. A thrill of awareness swept through her.

"There was definitely a strong talent of some kind here recently," she said. "A woman. I can see her prints. They weren't here a couple days ago. Must be from yesterday."

Jack looked at her, his eyes unreadable behind the lenses of his dark glasses. "You're sure it was a woman?"

"Yes." She pushed her senses a little higher and concentrated harder. "But there's no evidence of instability, not like there was in the energy of the prints of the guys who tried to kill us at the motel yesterday."

"Fallon said that the psychic instability is a side effect of the drug Nightshade is using."

"Well, whoever she is, I could swear that the woman who came to see Stone is not taking the formula."

"So much for Fallon's conspiracy theory."

The door opened. A housekeeper stood in the hall. She was definitely not the same woman who had greeted them earlier. The other one had looked the part—middle-aged with work-worn hands and a polite, quietly efficient air. This woman was a lot younger and considerably more attractive. Her blond hair was in a frisky ponytail, and she was dressed in a pair of tight-fitting jeans and a snug, low-cut yellow blouse that emphasized her bust.

Chloe glanced into the hallway and studied the woman's psi prints. She'd seen the same kind of sad, sickly energy in the alleys and doorways of Pioneer Square. She wondered if Stone knew that his housekeeper was a junkie.

The blonde glanced at her without much interest before giving Jack a sexy, inviting smile.

"Mr. Stone is out by the pool," she said. "Follow me. I'll show you."

She turned and walked toward the front room, hips swaying to a silent dance beat. Chloe shot Jack a suspicious look to see if he was paying attention. He was doing an excellent job of appearing oblivious to the obvious flirtation, however. When he saw Chloe eyeing him closely he raised his brows in silent, innocent inquiry. *What?*

He had caught her. Now she was blushing again. This kind of behavior had to stop. Not only was it highly unprofessional, it was a good way to get her heart broken. Just because she could sleep with him and just because they'd had great sex on a few occasions, it did not follow that they were going to have a long, enduring relationship. Especially after she figured out how to tell him that last night had not gone so well. *Damn, damn, damn.*

She switched her attention to the view of the sparkling Roman fountains and the pool visible through the wall of windows. She was not jealous. She had no right to feel possessive. It wasn't like they were having an affair. They barely knew each other. Sure, there was physical attraction, but that was probably all there was between them unless you counted the ability to work the lamp together.

She pushed the disturbing thoughts aside. They were here to do a job. She glanced at the psi prints on the marble flooring and the richly patterned carpets. There were two more sets of fresh tracks in addition to those left by the housekeeper and the woman who had come to see Stone last night. Whoever had left them had entered the residence from the back of the big house.

The prints smoked with sick, unstable energy. She recognized the unwholesome dreamlight immediately.

She drew a sharp breath and turned toward Jack, intending to signal the danger. But he was not looking at her. He was watching the two men gliding toward them from the shadows of the hallway. The one who'd driven the getaway motorcycle had on the denim jacket he'd worn yesterday. The second man was the one who had waited for them in the motel room with the silenced gun. He had a greasy-looking scarf tied around his long hair, a biker do-rag.

"That's far enough," Do-rag snarled at Jack. He raised the gun a little and pointed it at Chloe. "I don't know what you did to me yesterday but if you try it again, I'll have time to get off at least one shot, and she's going to be the target. Got it?"

"Sure," Jack said. "Where's Stone and his housekeeper?"

"Stone and the maid aren't your problem," Denim Jacket informed him. He glanced at the blonde. "That's it, Sandy. You're done here. Get out."

"What about my money, Ike?" the blonde whined. "You said you'd pay me right after I did the job."

"Stupid junkie bitch." Ike reached into his pocket and drew out a small bundle of bills. He tossed the money on the carpet in front of Sandy. "Shut up and go out through the gardens. Same way we came in. And, remember, one word about this to anyone and you're dead."

"Don't worry." The blonde bent down, grabbed the cash and stuffed it into her shirt. "I won't talk. You know me, Ike. I'd never do anything like that."

She turned and hurried toward the glass doors. Seizing the handle, she started to pull the slider open.

Chloe felt energy shiver in the air around her. She did not need to look at Jack to see the psi fever in his eyes. And suddenly she knew what was about to happen.

Sandy started screaming, a high-pitched, keening wail of terror. She lost her grip on the door handle and began pounding frantically on the plate-glass window with her fists.

"Shut up," Ike shouted. "Stop that, you flaky bitch."

"Shit, she's gone crazy," Do-rag said. "If the guard at the front gate hears her we're gonna have real problems. He'll call in the disturbance before he comes up to the house to check it out. We gotta make her shut up right now."

"This is what we get for using a junkie." Ike swung the barrel of the silenced gun toward the screaming Sandy.

More energy flared in the atmosphere. Chloe knew that Jack had changed his focus.

Ike uttered a yelp of mortal terror but he managed to get off one shot. Not surprisingly, given his trembling fingers, the bullet missed Sandy, who collapsed, weeping. Glass cracked sharply as the small missile smacked through the window.

Ike sank to his knees, his face a Halloween mask of horror. Caught fast in the grip of some unseen terrors, he could not even scream. He fainted. The gun clattered on the marble tiles.

Do-rag leaped toward Chloe, moving with the preternatural speed of a hunter-talent. He had his arm around her throat, the nose of the gun pressed against her temple before she could take a step back.

"Don't even think about using your talent on me," Do-rag hissed at Jack. "She'll be dead before you can drop me, I swear it."

Jack halted in midstride.

Chloe reached up a hand and lightly touched Do-rag's arm. He paid no attention. He was running wide open, his entire attention focused on Jack. She pulsed a little energy into his tainted dream-psi currents. He went to sleep with shocking suddenness. The gun dropped from his hand. He crumpled soundlessly to the floor.

On her knees near the slider, Sandy wept.

Jack scooped up both guns. "We need to get these two secured before they wake up. They're hunters. We can't take any chances."

"Right." Chloe took a deep breath. Her pulse was pounding. It took a great effort to think coherently. "I saw some duct tape and wire in the pool house."

"Get both. I'll watch these three."

"Okay." She stepped around Sandy and yanked open the slider.

"And, Chloe?" Jack said.

She paused and looked back at him. "What?"

"When this is over, you can explain to me why I've still got my second talent."

36

THEY FOUND DRAKE STONE AND THE REAL HOUSEKEEPER bound and gagged in one of the bedrooms.

"Sorry about this," Drake said. He watched Chloe comfort the traumatized housekeeper. "They broke in this morning. Said they would do terrible things to her if I didn't find a way to locate you and the lamp."

Chloe shook her head. "This is our fault. I'm so sorry both of you got caught up in this."

Drake's expression was rueful. "Always knew that lamp was bad news. Never thought anyone would actually consider it valuable, though. It's so obviously a fake."

Jack went out to the pool to make the call to Fallon.

"You've got three Nightshade agents?" Fallon asked, urgency vibrating in his rough voice.

"We've got *two* confirmed Nightshade people." Jack paced alongside the sun-sparked pool, trying to assuage the postburn rush that was shivering through him. He'd used a lot of juice taking down Sandy and Ike. His reserves were badly depleted. "At least we think they're agents. They're still unconscious. The woman is awake, but it looks like she's just some poor, dumb junkie they hired to play the role of the house-keeper. I don't think she knows anything. All she cares about is getting her next fix."

"How do you know the other two are Nightshade?" Fallon asked.

"I assumed that would be your take on the situation."

"It is. Just wondered what made you buy into my theory of the crime."

"Chloe can see some weird, unstable energy in their prints. She thinks it may indicate that they're taking a heavy psychotropic drug that affects their para-senses. That would seem to support your con-spiracy theory."

"She can see signs of the drug?" Fallon asked sharply.

"That's what she told me."

"Huh. Now that's damn interesting. I've got a couple of high-level aura-talents who can see the instability in the auras of Nightshade peo-ple. Hadn't thought about using dreamlight readers to do the same thing. Makes sense, though. Any drug that can affect the para-senses is probably going to disturb dream energy as well. I should have con-sidered that angle sooner. Problem is, strong dreamlight readers are damn rare."

"There's something else." Jack walked alongside the edge of the pool. "We found another set of prints on the front steps and in the foyer of the house. Chloe says Stone actually did have a visit from a high-level talent last night. But whoever came to see him doesn't seem to be connected to what just went down. There was no bad energy in the prints."

"Have you talked to Stone about his visitor?"

"Not yet. Haven't had a chance."

"Ask him about it. I don't like coincidences, but there are some high-end sensitives in Vegas. I can think of at least two strong illusion-talents and a para-hypnotist who are headliners. A major strat owns one of the biggest casinos. And then there are always the intuitives and the probability and crypto-talents hitting town who think they can beat the odds at the tables. It's possible that Stone had a legitimate guest last night."

"One neither he nor the guard can remember? Why would a friend make them both forget the visit?"

"Stone's been around long enough to make a few enemies in that town."

"Maybe he invented the story."

Fallon was silent for a moment. "No, I don't think so. It feels like the truth."

"*Feels* like the truth?"

"It fits," Fallon said simply. "But see if he can remember any more details."

"What do we do with the bikers and the woman?"

"Behave like the fine upstanding citizen that you are. Call the cops. Tell them you walked in on a home-invasion robbery in progress. Hell, it's the truth."

"If I turn those three over to the police they'll probably all make bail before Chloe and I get back to the hotel. Either that or the two hunters will escape. The police won't have a clue that they're dealing with a couple of talents."

"Doesn't matter. Those two got caught, so they've pissed in their chili as far as Nightshade is concerned. The organization is a tough outfit. Drawing the attention of the authorities is a big no-no. Getting arrested is a death sentence."

"How does Nightshade silence its operatives?"

"Simple," Fallon said. "They just cut off the supply of the drug.

It appears that the latest version of the formula has to be taken twice a day. Skip a single dose and the senses start to deteriorate. Miss two or three doses and the result is insanity, usually followed by suicide, within a matter of two or three days. It's a very effective system for snipping off loose ends."

"I thought Arcane had some kind of antidote."

"We do," Fallon said wearily. "The team I sent out should be pulling into town soon. They'll have some with them. All my people carry a supply now when they're on a job. Feel free to make those two bikers an offer. If they tell you what they know about who they're working for, you'll let them have the antidote. Doubt if they'll take the deal, though."

"They were ready to kill Chloe and probably the housekeeper and Stone as well. I'll be damned if I'll offer them the antidote."

"Your choice." The shrug in Fallon's voice was clear. "But if it makes you feel any better, the antidote is a life sentence in and of itself."

"What do you mean?"

"It will keep someone alive and reasonably sane, but the stuff has some serious side effects: It erodes the natural psi abilities along with the formula-enhanced version. It would probably take a high-level talent like you down to a two. And there are other complications. Panic attacks. Chronic anxiety problems. Disturbing dreams. In effect, you end up with a bad case of what the Victorians called shattered nerves."

Jack contemplated the idea of two bikers with really bad nerves.

"Any chance of recovery?" he asked.

"We don't think so. For obvious reasons we haven't been able to run a lot of human experiments, and animal models don't work when it comes to psi drugs. It's probably all moot in this case. Like I said, I doubt that the two hunters you're holding would accept the antidote."

"Why not?"

"We've had some experience with Nightshade agents. They've all been thoroughly brainwashed. First, they won't believe you when you tell them that being deprived of the drug will make them crazy. Their handlers assure them otherwise."

"And second?"

"They're as paranoid about Arcane as we are about them. Odds are they won't let you administer the antidote because they'll believe that you're trying to kill them. Call me after you talk to Stone."

"Will do."

"Oh, and by the way, congratulations on your new talent."

Jack froze. "What are you talking about?"

"I could buy the fact that you got lucky yesterday and took down one hunter, but I'm not buying that you were able to take down three people today, two of whom were hunters."

"I only got the one hunter," Jack said evenly. "And the woman. No big deal. Chloe handled the other hunter."

"Whatever. Like I said, congratulations."

"You don't sound worried."

"As long as you're taking out Nightshade agents, I don't have any problem with your new talent. I need all the help I can get. Call me after you talk to Stone."

Fallon broke the connection.

PREDICTABLY, IT WAS CHLOE who insisted that they make the offer to the Nightshade agents. But Fallon Jones was right. They refused. The cops removed the duct tape and wire bindings and replaced them with standard-issue handcuffs. They stuffed both men into the back of a patrol car and drove away.

Chloe and Jack stood on the front steps and watched the vehicle disappear.

"I'm betting they both escape within twenty-four hours," Chloe said.

She shook her head. "They're hunters. They're not only preternaturally fast—they've also got para-hunting skills. The cops won't even know they're gone until it's too late."

"Fallon says they're as good as dead," Jack said. "He told me that Nightshade will drop them like live bombs now that they've been picked up by regular law enforcement. They won't get any more of the drug. First they'll go crazy. Give them twenty-four, maybe forty-eight hours at most, and then they'll commit suicide."

Chloe shuddered. "The drug is a terrible creation. Jones is right. Nightshade must be stopped."

"I'm not usually into conspiracy theories, but I'm starting to think Jones has a point about this one."

37

CHLOE GRIPPED THE COFFEE MUG EMBLAZONED WITH THE Drake Stone logo in both hands and looked at Drake. She was seriously impressed by his resilience.

"I can't believe you're going to do your show tonight after what happened to you today," she said. "A lot of folks would be gulping sedatives and worrying about post-traumatic shock."

They were sitting outside by the pool. Overhead the patio heaters spread a pleasant warmth. Drake had fixed the coffee, himself, after sending his housekeeper home to her family to recover.

"You know that old showbiz saying?" Drake asked.

"The show must go on?" she quoted.

"No," Drake said. "The *any-publicity-is-good-publicity* saying. Tonight my name is going to be all over the evening news here in town. I haven't had press like this since I was outed a few years ago. If I don't do the show tonight the rumors will really start flying."

"What rumors?" Jack asked.

"The ones that claim I'm actually dead. They've been floating around for years." Drake stretched out his legs. He studied Jack with a speculative expression. "How the hell did you get the drop on those two this afternoon and who were those guys from L.A. who took the lamp?"

"It's complicated," Jack said.

Drake nodded. "I thought it might be."

"Would you believe me if I told you that the bikers who invaded your home today were working for a secret criminal organization that uses an illicit drug that gives their agents psychic powers?"

Drake raised his eyes to the awning. "I knew it. You're with the government. What is this, really? Some kind of drug sting? Casino fraud?"

"No," Chloe said quickly. "We aren't government agents. Honest."

"Forget it." Drake held up a hand to silence her. "I don't want to know anything more about the investigation. This is Vegas after all. Around here, ignorance is, if not exactly blissful, usually a hell of a lot safer."

"Mind if I ask you a few questions?" Jack said.

Drake raised his brows. "You want to know about my visitor last night, don't you?"

"You didn't make up that story just to get us out here today, did you?" Jack asked.

"No. The irony here is that I really was planning to call you and tell you about the woman who came to see me. But I don't have any more information than what I've already told you. I just can't remember the details. Ever have a dream you can't quite recall?"

"Yes," Jack said. He looked at Chloe. "I have."

She tried to ignore him. She knew that he had a lot of questions, and it was clear that he was not in a good mood. She couldn't blame him. He had awakened thinking that he was no longer a double-talent only to discover the hard way that he could still project nightmares. As far as he was concerned he was still a psychic freak.

In addition his senses had to be close to exhausted after the way he had used them to take down Sandy and Ike. You couldn't use that much psi without paying a price. Energy was energy. When you pulled a lot of it you had to give yourself time to recover. She was feeling drained, herself. She had drawn heavily on her own talent to put the hunter to sleep.

She still had some reserves left, however.

She concentrated on Drake and opened her senses. For the most part his dreamlight looked normal, or at least as normal as ultralight could look. But there was something wrong with the hues on a few of the wavelengths. The colors were murky, and the pattern was out of sync. She'd seen that kind of trouble before.

"I think there is a possibility that whoever came to see you last night gave you a hypnotic suggestion," she said.

Drake raised his brows. "There's more than one hypnotist in this town. I know all the headliners who are any good at that kind of thing. But they're all men. And why would anyone want to put me under unless it was to rob me? Nothing was missing this morning."

"No guarantees, but I might be able to help you recall some of the details of your visitor."

"How?"

"Think of it as a relaxation technique," she said. "I promise you'll be wide awake and aware the whole time. You'll remember everything I say and do and you'll have full control of what you are telling me."

Drake contemplated her for a long moment, and then he nodded once. "I'll admit the blank spot in my memory is bothering me. If I can forget that I had a visitor last night, the next thing you know I'll start forgetting the words to 'Blue Champagne.' That would be a career killer. Let's do this."

Jack said nothing. He drank his coffee and waited.

"Stop trying to pull up the memory," Chloe said to Drake. "Let it go. You don't care about it anymore. Find the calm place inside yourself and relax."

She kept up the soothing patter while she pulsed a little dream energy at the static, murky waves. What she said was not important. The words had nothing to do with projecting energy, but she knew that if she remained silent, Drake would wonder what was happening.

She used the lightest of touches to tweak and clear the murky dream static. Within seconds the colors pulsed normally once more.

"Dark hair," Drake said. He snapped his fingers, looking very pleased. "Good cut. Expensive cut. I remember thinking she was attractive but not in a flashy Vegas way. Good clothes, too. Very stylish but very conservative suit and heels. She could have been a CEO or a lawyer."

Jack sat forward a little. "Any distinguishing features? Jewelry?"

Drake pondered the question briefly and then shook his head. "Sorry. She rang the doorbell. The guard hadn't called ahead so I assumed it was someone I knew or one of the staff. I didn't recognize her when I opened the door. Figured she was a fan who had somehow managed to get over the wall. I asked her who she was."

"What did she say?" Chloe asked.

"She said that she had come to see me. Wanted to ask me a few questions about an old antique lamp she'd heard I owned. I told her that I'd given it to another collector who had an interest in it."

"How did she respond?" Jack asked.

"She asked for your names." Drake's expression tightened. "I told her that information was confidential, and then, *damn*, in the next breath I told her your names and everything else I knew about the two of you. Why would I do that?"

"Because she hypnotized you," Chloe said.

Drake whistled softly. "She must be good."

"Yes," Jack said. "She must be very, very good."

38

CHLOE DROVE BACK TO THE HOTEL. JACK WATCHED THE ROAD ahead with a stoic expression and made another call to Fallon Jones. He told him what they had learned about Drake Stone's mystery visitor. When he was finished he closed the phone and continued to watch the road, grim faced.

"Well?" Chloe glanced at him. "Did Fallon have a theory?"

"Sure. As you might expect, it's one that fits neatly into this Nightshade conspiracy he's working on. He suspects that the woman who went to see Stone is the operative in charge of finding the lamp. He said she probably lost us yesterday when we made it look like we were headed for L.A."

"So she went back to Stone to see what she could find out?"

"She used him to locate us," Jack said. "Got lucky when it turned out that we were still in town. She set a trap, and we took the bait."

"But things went wrong. Her people not only wound up getting arrested, the lamp is now in Arcane hands."

"She screwed up." Jack leaned his head against the back of the seat. "According to Fallon that means she'll probably be dead soon."

"But she wasn't taking the drug. No traces in her dreamprints, remember? Nightshade doesn't have the option of just cutting her off."

"There are other ways of getting rid of people."

"Well, yes, but if she's with Nightshade, why wasn't she on the drug?"

"Good question. Fallon's wondering if some of the Nightshade people have decided to wait until the formula is perfected before they risk taking it."

"That would certainly be an intelligent decision. But it also means that the organization would lose its grip on its agents. The guys at the top wouldn't be able to control them without the drug."

"Well, it's Fallon's problem now," Jack said. "I've got other things to worry about. What's happening to me, Chloe?"

"I told you, you're fine. Stable as a rock."

"My second talent is back."

"And it is as stable as your first talent," she said calmly.

"That's impossible. Two high-end talents cannot coexist in the same individual without creating an inherently unstable psychic balance."

"I admit that has been a long-standing notion within Arcane."

"Probably because every time a double-talent appears, said talent becomes a psycho freak."

"You are not a freak," she said sharply. "You told me, yourself, that you felt normal again, and I can see that your dream psi is nicely balanced and absolutely stable."

"Did you know I still had my second talent?"

She sighed. "Not for sure. Not until you used it this afternoon." She hesitated. "But I did sort of wonder."

"Yeah? About what?"

"Last night when I got a good look at your dreamlight spectrum I realized that the channels between your dreamstate and your waking state are wide open and stable. That's how you're drawing the extra fire power."

"That's supposed to be impossible. If it were true I should be a full-blown Cerberus by now."

"I know," she admitted. "I'm guessing that it was the genetic twist in Nicholas's DNA that you inherited that makes it possible for you to handle the open channels."

"So what did you do with the lamp last night?"

"I think that when those channels suddenly opened a few weeks ago the abrupt change created some areas of disturbance in your dream psi. The patterns appeared to be repairing naturally. I used the energy of the lamp to speed up the process, that's all. I was going to try to clear out some of the damage done by the medication, but things got sort of complicated and I didn't have a chance to finish."

"You're telling me that you didn't try to close my dreamlight channels?"

"No," she said. "I couldn't."

"Why not?"

"Because it might have killed you," she said simply. "Or, at the very least driven you insane."

He looked at her. "Why?"

"Because what you are now is what you were genetically meant to be. This is normal for you. If I messed around with your dream-psi channels I would make you very *abnormal*. Do you understand?"

"So I'm a normal double-talent? There is no such thing."

"Well, I've been doing a lot of thinking about that."

"No kidding."

She told herself she was big enough to ignore the sarcasm. Jack was under a lot of stress, after all.

"Here's the thing," she said. "I'm not so sure that you actually are a double-talent."

He turned his attention back to the road. "Last month I was a strat.

This month I can generate nightmares. If that isn't two different talents, what is?"

"Think about it, Winters. There are a gazillion different kinds of strats, but they all have one thing in common: They possess a preternatural ability to assess and analyze a situation and then figure out how to exploit it. At its core, that is simply a survival mechanism. Probably a psychic adaptation of the primitive hunting instincts in our earliest ancestors."

"Where are you going with this?" he asked.

"I'm building my case. Stick with me. Your form of strat-talent just happens to make you very, very good at detecting people's weaknesses and vulnerabilities, right?"

"So?"

"Okay, it's a stretch from being able to assess and manipulate a person's weaknesses to being able to scare the living daylights out of that person with a blast of psi but not a big one. Once you know an individual's vulnerabilities, you have a certain amount of power and control over that person. In your case you're able to take it a step further. You can actually generate energy that zeros in on the wavelengths of a person's most elemental fears."

"I couldn't do that for the first thirty-five years of my life."

"Maybe not, but the fact that you can do it now doesn't necessarily mean that you have a whole new talent. What you've got now is just an enhanced version of your old talent."

"Enhanced as in *formula* enhanced?" His mouth hardened. "Fallon Jones might find me useful, but something tells me that the rest of the Jones family, including Zack Jones, won't be so easygoing about my new level of talent."

"Oh, yeah?" She made a rude noise. "Like anyone in the Jones family has the right to judge what's normal and what's not when it comes to talent."

"What the hell does that mean?"

"Give me a break," she said. "It's no secret that Sylvester Jones began experimenting early on in his life with various versions of his enhancement formula. Who knows what he did to his own DNA before he fathered all those little Jones boys by those three different women?"

There was a short, startled silence.

"Damn," Jack whistled softly. "I never thought of that. It might explain why that family line has always produced so many unusual and off-the-charts talents."

"Yes, it would," she said crisply.

"If my talents are normal, why the hallucinations and the blackouts? Why the disturbance to my dream psi?"

"I understand the hallucinations," she said. "That is a common problem when dream energy spills over into the other senses. As I told you, the sudden emergence of your enhanced level of talent temporarily disrupted the patterns of some of the currents of your dream psi."

"What about the blackouts and the sleepwalking?"

She tightened her hands on the steering wheel. "I suppose they could have been caused by the frayed dream channels, but, as I told you, there are still traces of what looks like heavy medication at one point on the spectrum."

"I started taking the meds *after* the blackouts and the sleepwalking episodes began."

"Were you on any other kind of medication prior to that?" she asked. "Even some over-the-counter stuff can have unpredictable effects on sensitives, especially high-level ones like you."

"Some anti-inflammatories occasionally. That's it."

"Well, if it's any consolation, the murky stuff is definitely fading," she said.

"I lost an entire day of my life, not to mention the nights when I went walkabout."

"I realize it's very unsettling," she said gently. "But things are stable now. I can sense it. Last night it felt as if we turned a key in a psychic lock. You're fine, Jack."

"I sense a *but*."

She took a deep breath. "But I'm still wondering why there is so much power locked up in that lamp."

39

THAT EVENING THEY HAD DRINKS IN ONE OF THE HOTEL BARS. Jack swallowed some of his whiskey and thought about how good it felt to be sitting there with Chloe. Like a real date, except that he could not imagine any of the other women he knew sitting there so casually across the table from a man who could plunge them into a waking nightmare in a heartbeat. Then, again, Chloe wasn't like any of the other women he knew.

"Where does J&J go from here?" she asked.

"Fallon's frustrated." He shrugged. "That is not an unusual condition for him, however."

"No luck finding the mystery woman who knocked on Stone's door?"

"No. But he seems pretty sure that's a dead end, anyway. He's convinced that now that Arcane has recovered the lamp and stashed it in one of the Society's vaults, Nightshade will terminate the project. Those responsible for the failure will be given notice in the organization's customary fashion."

"They'll be cut off the drug."

"Apparently."

"But Fallon still doesn't know why Nightshade wanted the lamp?"

"His working theory is that Nightshade went after the lamp for the same reason they wanted the formula."

She nodded. "Because it holds out the possibility of enhancing talent."

"Makes sense. But whatever the reason, we're out of it. The problem is Fallon's now."

She raised her wineglass in a small salute. "Another case closed for Harper Investigations."

For some reason he didn't like the sound of that. It sounded too final. But she was right.

"You're good," he said.

"Told you so."

He smiled. "Yes, you did. You know, I've been thinking."

"About?" she prompted. There was an aura of anticipation about her.

"According to Fallon, Nightshade is very well organized. There are several circles or cells of ascending power with some version of a corporate board of directors at the top. There seem to be no links between the circles. Each one functions independently."

The aura of warm anticipation that had enveloped her promptly faded. He was almost sure she gave a tiny, wistful sigh. He had the feeling he had screwed up. What had she expected him to say? She recovered immediately.

"In other words, J&J can take down some of the circles, but that won't help them find clues that would lead to the people at the top," she said.

"Right. But here's the thing: Regardless of how well organized it is, at its heart Nightshade has to be a for-profit business."

She raised her brows. "You mean its goal is to make money?"

"The ultimate goal for an organization like Nightshade is power. But money is the gasoline that fuels that engine. From what Fallon has told me Nightshade is, at its core, a company engaged in pharmaceutical R&D, manufacturing and distribution. High-tech labs and distribution networks, legal or otherwise, don't operate on thin air. They burn cash. Lots of it."

"Makes sense," she agreed.

"That means that those cells or circles have to make money. What's more, it's a given that each circle is kicking up a share of the profits to the guys at the top. That's how moneymaking organizations of any kind work."

"Which means?"

"Which means," he said deliberately, "that no matter how well a circle is isolated from the other circles there has to be some way for it to send money up to the top of the organization. It also has to be able to move the drug."

"Got an idea?"

"I'm wondering if Fallon Jones is paying enough attention to the oldest rule in business."

"What's that?"

"Follow the money." He drank some more whiskey and set the glass down, a sense of anticipation building inside him. "The money chain has got to be a major weak point for Nightshade, one of the places it's vulnerable."

She looked intrigued. "Have you talked to Fallon about that? Maybe he could use some help. From the sound of things he's very shorthanded."

"Maybe I'll give him a call after dinner."

She smiled a little. "You do that."

An hour later they left the casino and went out into the neon-lit fantasy world of the Strip. The night was chilly, but the sidewalks that linked the big resorts were crowded with people making their way from one glittering hotel to the next.

Along the way Las Vegas Boulevard was crammed with special effects: Full-scale pirate ships floated on man-made seas and launched cannon attacks. Flames roared from a large volcano. Gondolas drifted on a canal that looked as if it had been plucked from the heart of Venice. Fountains danced to music across a vast lake. Huge marquees emblazoned with the names of the stars and shows appearing in the big theaters glowed as bright as suns in the night.

Jack stopped on the steps of a Roman forum and made the call to Fallon.

"You got something new for me?" Fallon asked impatiently. "I'm a little busy here."

"I've been thinking about the money angle."

There was an unnatural pause on the other end.

"What about it?" Fallon asked. But now he sounded curious.

"Just wondered how far you've been able to pursue it with this Nightshade operation."

"Not far." Fallon let out a deep sigh. "On paper, at least, the labs we took down all appear to be independently owned and operated. No links to anything."

"That's impossible. There has to be a way to feed money up the chain of command to the guys at the top. There must be a way to move the drug as well."

"I agree," Fallon said. "But my people haven't been able to find any connections. When it comes to organization, these guys are good, Jack. Don't forget, it was set up by a man who spent years working undercover for a government black-ops group."

"If it's so well run, why are they using cheap, low-end muscle to do the dirty work?"

"You're talking about the two bikers who tried to grab the lamp?"

"They were hunters, but they weren't exactly top-of-the-line talents."

"Nightshade uses a lot of cheap muscle," Fallon said. "Probably because it's widely available and also expendable. You can always find more labor where that came from, if you see what I mean."

"Where?"

"What do you mean, where?"

"Where do you go to get an endless supply of expendable street muscle?" Jack asked patiently.

"Hell, try L.A. or San Francisco or Las Vegas. Guys like them are everywhere."

"But somehow you have to recruit them, get them started on the drug and then maintain control of them. Can't see a bunch of corporate suits sending people from whatever passes for Nightshade's human resources department into dark alleys to interview possible job candidates."

Fallon was silent for an uncharacteristically long moment.

"Got any ideas?" he said eventually.

"I'm thinking about it."

"Do that. Call me as soon as you come up with something solid. I could use a break here."

The phone went dead in Jack's ear. He looked at Chloe.

"I think Fallon just hired me to work for J&J," he said.

"Good move on his part." She looked back over her shoulder toward the hotel. "Well, I suppose I should go back to the room, pack and make a reservation on a morning flight to Seattle. When are you leaving?"

"Hadn't thought about it." It stunned him to realize that was the truth. Suddenly, returning to Seattle and his cold concrete-and-steel condo was the last thing he wanted to do.

It wasn't until he reached for her hand that it occurred to him that they had never done anything as simple as walking hand in hand together.

His fingers tightened around hers.

"It's been a fast few days," he said, searching for a way into the conversation. "We haven't had a lot of time to talk about other things besides the lamp."

"Such as?"

"Such as what happens now," he said.

"Now?"

He looked at her. "You're not making this any easier. I'm trying to talk about us."

"If you find it hard to talk about us maybe that's a sign that you should try another subject," she said gently.

"I'll admit I'm not good at discussions like this, but that doesn't mean I don't want to have it."

"Jack, it's okay. Really."

It didn't take a psychic to know that the conversation was going downhill fast, he thought.

"What's okay?" he asked, wary.

"You and me. You don't have to explain or apologize. I understand exactly what happened between us."

"Yeah? Then maybe you can explain it to me."

"It's the pressure of everything that's been going on." She started to wave her other hand and then evidently realized that she was clutching her heavy satchel in it. She lowered her arm. "We've both been under a lot of stress. After all, people were trying to kill us. That generates some very powerful but very temporary emotions."

"Emotions," he repeated, careful to keep his tone neutral.

"Exactly. Plus, I know you're probably feeling grateful to me at the moment because the case is now closed. That's a normal reaction. A lot of clients experience it."

"You're saying I shouldn't feel grateful?"

"I'm saying that you shouldn't confuse gratitude and physical attraction with . . . with other stuff. I'm sure there are other dreamlight readers out there who could have worked that lamp for you. You just happened to pick me, that's all."

"I was attracted to you before I knew that you would be able to find the lamp, let alone work it," he said. "And I think you were attracted to me. How do you explain that?"

"I'll admit there was definitely a strong, initial attraction between us, but it may have gotten blown out of all proportion because of the tense situation in which we found ourselves. And we can't forget the possibility that the lamp exerted some influence on our auras. We probably need some perspective here."

He pulled her out of the stream of strolling people, into the shadows cast by a large outside stairwell that led to the upper floor of a resort shopping mall. He crowded her gently, deliberately, against the stone wall and caged her there.

"Jack?"

He leaned in close, opening his senses to the subtle aura of feminine energy that was so unique to her. He put his mouth against her ear.

"You want perspective?" he asked. "I'll give you perspective." He kissed the side of her throat. "I wanted you before we found the lamp. I wanted you after we found the lamp, and I still want you now that the lamp is in Arcane hands." He brushed his mouth lightly across hers. "That's my perspective on the situation. What's yours?"

For a few seconds, she did not move. Then, with a low, throaty murmur, her arms wound slowly around his neck.

"Well, when you put it that way," she whispered.

It wasn't exactly the total capitulation he'd been going for, but he was no fool. Tonight he would take what he could get. This was Vegas, and in this town strat-talents knew when to hold 'em.

He kissed her again, feeling her soften and warm against him. The noise of the street crowds faded into the distance.

After a while they walked back to the hotel, hand in hand.

He could get used to this feeling, whatever it was. Hell, he was already addicted.

40

SHE AWOKE TO THE KNOWLEDGE THAT SHE WAS ALONE IN the bed. When she opened her eyes she saw Jack silhouetted against the window, looking down into the neon night. He had put on his trousers but not his shirt. She did not need her other senses to perceive the tension prowling through him. It was a palpable force in the atmosphere.

She sat up against the pillows and wrapped her arms around her knees. "What's wrong?" she asked.

He turned to face her, his expression unreadable in the darkness. "Could you do to me what you did to Drake Stone today?"

She frowned. "Lift a hypnotic trance? Yes, I suppose so. Assuming someone actually managed to hypnotize you."

"You don't think that's possible?"

"I think it's extremely unlikely. You're a very strong talent. High-level sensitives are notoriously difficult to hypnotize. Frankly, I doubt that anyone could put you into a deep trance, not even a strong para-hypnotist." She paused. "Not unless you cooperated."

"How would I do that?"

She wrapped her arms around her knees and considered the problem. "You'd have to deliberately open your senses like you did last night when we worked the lamp. Even then, it would be hard for anyone to put you under. And even if someone succeeded, I doubt if any hypnotic suggestion would hold for long. It would wear off quite fast."

"What if the emergence of my new talent left me vulnerable to a hypnotist?"

"We've talked about this, Jack. You don't have a new talent; you have a fully developed talent."

"Call it whatever you want. The hallucinations were a real pain in the ass, but at least I was aware of what was happening. The nightmares were bad, but I was dealing with them. It's the blackouts that have me worried. It seems logical to me that during that time my natural defenses might have been down. Who knows what I was doing or what happened to me?"

"There is no indication that you're getting your memory back yet?"

"Flickers and shadows." He looked out the window into the night. "Whispers. It's going to drive me crazy, Chloe. I need to know what happened during the blackouts and the sleepwalking episodes."

"As far as I can tell, the only thing that is still going on is the static caused by those sleeping meds you were taking. But like you said, you started those after the blackouts and the sleepwalking episodes."

"Can you get rid of the disturbance caused by the meds without the lamp?"

She thought about it. "I can calm the currents temporarily, like I did the other night, at least enough so that you can get some sleep. But I'm not sure it would be a good idea to try to do any more than that. I don't think it's necessary, either. It looks like your body is flushing out the medication on its own."

"I don't want to wait. Who knows how long it will take? I need answers now."

"I might be able to reestablish the normal rhythms of the portion of the spectrum that is affected," she said. "But if I get it wrong I might end up fraying the channels between your dreamstate and your waking state again. If I screw up, the hallucinations and nightmares will come back. If we do this, we should probably have the lamp handy, just in case we need it again."

"It would take time to get to L.A. and persuade Arcane to let me run another experiment. I don't want to wait."

"This is that important to you?" she asked.

"I have to get some answers, Chloe."

"All right," she said quietly. She pushed back the covers, got to her feet and pulled on the plush hotel bathrobe. "I'll give it a whirl but no guarantees. Understand?"

"Yes."

"And if I sense that things are going badly, I'm going to pull the plug on the experiment. Agreed?"

He did not respond right away, but finally he nodded once.

"Agreed," he said.

"Sit down," she instructed.

He lowered himself into one of the wingback chairs. She walked across the room, stopped beside the chair and took his hand in hers.

"Ready?" she said.

"Yes," he said.

"Open your senses to the max. Given your high level of talent, I need you to be all the way into the zone. Otherwise your dream spectrum isn't clear to me."

No energy pulsed.

"You don't have to be nervous about your talent," she said. "Trust me, you're in full control. You won't accidentally scare me to death.

You'd have to focus with deliberate intent to do that. Just opening your senses won't be a problem. We've been there before. Remember last night?"

His mouth crooked faintly at the corner. In spite of the seriousness of the moment there was something wickedly sexy about his smile.

"Oh, yeah," he said. "I remember last night."

She was suddenly aware of energy flaring hot in the atmosphere. She heightened her own senses and studied the heavy waves of dark dream energy that pulsed and radiated in his aura. Gingerly, she sent a little pulse of light into the section of the spectrum that was influenced by the medication.

Nothing happened.

"*Hmm*," she said. "Whatever it is, it's powerful stuff. I don't think I can reboot the currents, at least not while you're awake."

He gave her an odd look. "You want to knock me out?"

"No. I want you to go to sleep. Once you're in the dreamstate I may be able to manipulate your energy patterns more easily."

He stretched out his legs, rested his head against the back of the chair and watched her through half-closed eyes. "Now what?"

"Now you sleep," she said softly.

She took his hand again and pulsed a little energy. Jack resisted for a few seconds. She knew it was pure instinct on his part. He was not good at giving up control.

"Trust me, Jack," she told him.

He closed his eyes and went to sleep.

41

HE DREAMS . . .

He's awake again but groggy and disoriented. He's shivering, too. Same as last time. Must be running a fever.

The clang and rumble of machinery overhead reverberates through the ceiling. The noise pounds his raw, exposed senses. He opens his eyes and sees that he is in a small, windowless room. The walls are painted stark white. There is a stainless-steel counter on one side next to the door. A glary fluorescent fixture assaults his senses. He tries to lift one arm to block out the painful light, but he can't move his hand.

"Wake up, Jack."

Chloe's voice calls him out of the darkness. He wants to move toward her, but he's trapped in this fevered nightmare. The sound of the machines is relentless. His arms are bound to the side of a bed.

Rage and panic lash through him.

"Jack. You must wake up now."

Chloe's voice is stronger, more insistent this time. He struggles to free himself so that he can get to her . . .

He opened his eyes and saw her. She was still standing by the chair, her fingers wrapped tightly around his. In the neon-lit moonlight her face was shadowed with anxiety and concern.

"It's okay," he said. Adrenaline flooded through him. "I'm awake."

"Your currents look normal," she said. She did not let go of his hand. "What do you remember?"

"Everything."

It all came slamming back like a tsunami. He had to fight to control the flood tide. And then he had to fight to control his spiraling fury. He forced himself to stay focused.

He started talking, getting it all out fast while it was clear. He could not afford to risk losing even a single detail.

"Machinery on the floor above. Causing a lot of noise. All of my senses are wide open. I hurt all over. Burning up with fever. I can barely tolerate the constant clang and rumble. There is only one way to escape and that is to sink back into the dreamscape. But I'm not going down that hellhole again. No control down there. I'd rather be dead."

"Where are you?" Chloe asked gently.

"A room. Looks a little like a hospital room. Underground, I think. No windows. The fluorescent ceiling lights are on, but things are distorted. The fever is affecting my vision."

"But you can see."

"Yes. There's a stainless-steel sink and counter. An aluminum walker. A white cabinet with some medical stuff in it. A stethoscope and some kind of monitor on the wall. Also one of those little red boxes that hold used needles and syringes."

"What else do you see?"

He paused, sorting through the jumble of images and impressions. "The floor is concrete. I remember that because it reminds me of the concrete flooring the designer put into my condo. But this concrete is not smooth and polished. It's old and cracked. The kind you see in a garage."

"Or a basement?"

He considered that briefly. "Yes. A basement. I'm lying on a gurney, and I'm trying to think of my plan. I'm pretty sure I had one."

"What plan?"

"I managed to come up with it the first time I awakened. But I didn't get a chance to carry it out because they gave me another shot. I'm trying to concentrate, but the noise and the light make it almost impossible. I remind myself I'm a strat. I need to focus on priorities. I finally remember the plan. I have to get the guard into the room to make it work."

"There's a guard?"

"Outside the door. I remember seeing him the last time I woke up. I try to sit up. That's when I remember the restraints."

"You're tied to the bed?" Chloe asked, horrified.

"I'm shackled to the gurney with leather straps, the kind used in hospitals to control violent patients. There is just enough give in the bonds to allow me to pound my hands against the metal sides of the bed. The door opens, and the guard comes into the room. He looks bored with his job. I'm thinking I can work with that."

"Can you describe the guard?"

"For some reason I've labeled him Bruce. Not sure why. Probably because he's really pushing the macho biker look. Lots of denim, studded leather belt. Motorcycle boots. Tattoos. Wears his hair in a ponytail."

"Sounds like one of the guys who attacked us."

"No. A different man. But the same aura of energy. I'm pretty sure he's a talent of some kind. Given the fact that he's standing guard, I'm betting that he's a hunter. But he doesn't read like a full para-hunter."

"What do you mean?" Chloe asked.

"I can sense weaknesses and vulnerabilities, remember? My talent tells me that Bruce doesn't have the full spectrum of abilities that come with true hunter-talent. I don't know how to explain it. There's just something a little off about him."

"Like the guy who was waiting for us in the motel room?"

"Yes."

"That makes three bikers involved in this thing," Chloe said. "A lot of low-end, not-so-bright muscle. Go on."

"Bruce asks me if I need to take a leak." He cleared his throat. "Uh, use the bathroom. I tell him yes and that I really need to go bad. My voice sounds mushy, even to my own ears."

"Bruce unfastens the restraints?"

"Yeah. Tells me that if I piss in the sheets I'm going to have to clean it up, myself. Then he moves back and pushes the aluminum walker toward me. I'm sitting on the edge of the gurney. It takes almost everything I've got to stand. Feels like I'm moving through a sea of gelatin. But I take hold of the walker. That's when I realize I'm wearing a hospital gown. Going to be tough to escape from wherever I am in an outfit like that."

"What did you do next?" she asked.

"I try firing up my senses to see if that will give me some energy. I'm more than a little amazed when the room comes into sharper focus. I'm definitely stronger running hot. Not so shaky. I know I can't rely on raw psi for very long, not burning it at this rate. But for a short period of time maybe it will give me what I need."

He stopped talking for a moment, trying to process a few more memories. It was strange having them come back to him like this, as if he had just plucked them from a deep, dark hole.

"Was there a struggle?" Chloe prompted.

"No. I know I can't take Bruce in a hand-to-hand fight. Not even on a good day and this is not a good day. Bruce might not be a full hunter, but he is powerful and he will be fast. It's clear that he's not expecting trouble from me, though. Why would he? I probably look like over-cooked spaghetti to him. He lounges against the gurney and reaches for the can of chewing tobacco in his back pocket."

He stopped again, replaying his own words, trying to absorb all the new data.

"Jack, what happened next?"

"I take one step and then another with the walker. When I'm satis-fied that I can hold my own weight, I upend the aluminum frame and ram one of the legs straight toward Bruce's gut."

"Good grief. Did it work?"

"Almost. With a nonhunter I think it actually would have worked. But Bruce has the lightning-fast reactions of his talent going for him. He seizes the walker leg just before it hits him and he jerks the whole frame out of my hands. I lunge for the door, but I already know that I'm not going to make it. I can hear Bruce roaring behind me. He's in a real 'roid rage, and he's running wide open. He won't just stop me, slap me around and tie me to the gurney again. He's going to kill me. Won't be able to help himself. He's out of control."

"Oh, geez."

"And then, without even thinking about it, I know exactly how to stop Bruce."

"With your talent?"

"My *new* talent."

"Your fully developed talent," Chloe said firmly.

"I hit him with a heavy wave of psi. Bruce grunts once and drops to the floor. He doesn't move."

"Dead?"

"No." He frowned, trying to think. "Not then. But he was uncon-scious, and he must have died later because there was a report in the papers about an unidentified body found floating in Elliott Bay. The description sounded like Bruce, right down to the tattoos."

"How did you get out of that room?" she asked.

"I took Bruce's clothes. They didn't fit, but it was the middle of the night, one or two in the morning, I think. There was no one around on the street. I knew where I was. Capitol Hill. I managed to stagger the two blocks to Broadway. The bars and clubs were closing. I got a cab. I remember the driver thought I was stone drunk. I paid him with some cash I found in Bruce's wallet. I made it home and then I collapsed. When I woke up I couldn't remember anything. I ran a fever for two days. Stayed in bed. Never been so sick in my life."

"Did you talk to anyone?"

"No. When I finally recovered I told myself that the reason I couldn't remember anything was that I'd been unconscious due to a raging fever. The report of a naked, tattooed male body being pulled out of the bay appeared that same day in the papers."

"What was the cause of death?"

"Overdose, according to the press. The authorities figured he'd jumped from one of the ferries."

"But you didn't buy it," Chloe said.

He met her eyes. "It was a little tough to believe that version of events when I had a bunch of biker leathers and denims along with a pair of motorcycle boots sitting in my closet."

She pondered that for a moment. "You said the last thing you remembered before you woke up in that room was walking home after having a beer with a friend."

"Right."

"Well, that certainly explains the taint of the drugs that I saw in your dream psi. It wasn't the sleeping meds—it was whatever they gave you to knock you out and keep you under in that room where they held you prisoner for twenty-four hours. Someone kidnapped you right off the street. You're a wealthy man. I wonder if they planned to hold you for ransom."

"No," he said, very certain now. "This was all about the lamp. There has to be a connection."

"Whoever grabbed you drugged you with something strong enough to give you amnesia for that twenty-four-hour period of time. There are several heavy-duty sedatives that could do that. Also a lot of illegal stuff. Whatever they used suppressed your memories for a while, but the effects of the drug were fading because your strong talent was reasserting itself. Sooner or later you would have remembered everything. Wonder if the kidnappers realize that?"

He shoved himself up out of the chair and began to prowl the room, restless and edgy. "What about the blackouts that came afterward?"

"More side effects of the drug they used to keep you under. Meds that strong have very unpredictable effects on a lot of people, not just strong talents like you. What do you remember about the sleepwalking episodes?"

"Just that I left my condo on foot and walked all the way to a street on Capitol Hill and back each time." He stopped pacing and turned to face her. "And there's something else."

"What?"

"I did not want to be seen. I deliberately left my condo building through the rear entrance in the garage, not the lobby. I remember being paranoid about it. I was convinced that someone was watching me. And sure enough, each time there was some guy out in the alley. I didn't know who he was, but I knew that I didn't want him to see me."

"What did you do?"

"I used my talent to scare the daylights out of him. It worked. He got so frightened each time that he couldn't take the shadows in the alley. He left but he was always back in position when I returned. I worked the same trick again and slipped inside the building while he was getting over his attack of nerves."

"Sounds like whoever drugged you was having you watched."

He examined the memories again, processing details and the time frame. "Why in hell would anyone drug me and hold me prisoner for twenty-four hours and then set up a surveillance operation?"

"They didn't set you free. You escaped. Maybe they intended to keep you longer than twenty-four hours, but you got away and upset their plans."

"And why was I so sick? Do you think the fever was the result of the amnesia drug?"

"I don't know, maybe." She watched him for a moment. "You said that during the sleepwalking episodes you walked up to Capitol Hill from your condo on First Avenue."

"Right."

"Where did you go on Capitol Hill?"

"The street where I ran into the killer who tried to murder the nurse."

"What do you remember about the neighborhood?"

"It was quiet. There were a few small shops on the block, but they were all closed at night." He stopped, adrenaline kicking in as another memory slid home. "Except for the gym. Damn, that's it."

"What?"

"The sounds I heard when I woke up in that little room. Gym machines."

42

"THE LAMP," FALLON SAID. PHONE CLAMPED TO HIS EAR, HE
stood looking down at the darkened windows of the Sunshine Café.
"Somehow this has got to involve that damn artifact."

"How does that explain someone grabbing me off the street and
drugging me?" Jack asked.

"You said the room where you were held looked like a hospital room.
The first thing that comes to mind is that you were targeted for an experiment of some kind."

"Why would Nightshade want to run an experiment on me?"

"Because you're a Winters," Fallon said, impatient now. He could
feel it coming together, but some things were still too vague. He really
needed to get more sleep. "Think about it. You're a direct male descendant of Nicholas Winters. Nightshade is clearly having some problems with the formula. Maybe they're looking for an alternative. The
Burning Lamp was created for a similar purpose, to enhance naturally
occurring talent and create additional paranormal abilities. Whoever

took you may have wanted some samples of your blood for a little DNA testing and research."

"Great. So I spent twenty-four hours as a lab rat. Wonder how long they planned to keep me."

"Who knows? Maybe they didn't intend to keep you around at all after they were finished with you."

"Think they were going to kill me?" Jack asked.

"I can't say yet—I just don't have enough data. The thing is, you escaped, even though you were doped to the gills and running a high-grade fever. You managed to overpower one of their formula-hyped hunters."

"So?"

"That probably made them very nervous, but it may also have convinced them that you actually do possess more than just one talent. They would interpret that as evidence that the lamp worked all those years ago and that Old Nick's descendants are genetically enhanced."

"All right, let's play this out. I escape, and the first thing I do is go looking for a dreamlight reader and the lamp. They follow me and try to steal the lamp. Is that it?"

"I think so. Maybe."

"You don't sound like your usual ninety-eight-point-seven-percent sure self, Fallon."

"Possibly because I'm not ninety-eight-point-seven-percent certain."

"I've got some other information for you," Jack continued. "I think that Nightshade or at least the guys who drugged me and tried to take the lamp are working out of a gym in Seattle. That's where they're recruiting the cheap-ass hunter muscle."

"Huh." Fallon smiled a little. This time there was an almost audible click when lines appeared between certain points of light on the multidimensional chessboard in his mind. This time he was sure. "I like that theory. It sounds right. Tell me more."

"When I got my memories back tonight one of the things I remembered was that during my sleepwalking episodes I went back to a street on Capitol Hill where the only business open all night is a fitness club. I also remembered hearing the sound of gym machines coming through the ceiling of that little cell where they held me."

Fallon headed back to his desk and picked up a pen. "Got a name and address?"

"Sure. But before you send in a team to take the place apart and scatter the bad guys, I suggest you have someone get some deep background on it. Check out the financials, ownership, that kind of thing. Follow the money, Fallon."

"Can't think of anyone better qualified than you to handle the job."

Jack went silent on the other end for a few seconds.

"You want me to research the place for you?" he said finally.

"Why not? You're the best there is at this kind of thing. Not to mention that you've got what I like to call a vested interest in the outcome."

"I'm getting the impression that you don't have a lot of financial strats or probability-talents under contract with J&J."

"A couple but no one as strong as you."

"All right, I'll see what I can find out," Jack said. "Meanwhile, Chloe and I are going to fly back to Seattle in the morning unless you think there's any reason to remain out of sight."

"I don't think either of you is in any danger as long as that lamp is tucked away in an Arcane vault. Like I said, Nightshade will have pulled the plug on this operation by now."

"You're sure of that?"

"This is all about the lamp, Jack. And we've got the lamp under lock and key."

"Then we'll go home."

"Call me as soon as you have something on that gym."

He cut the connection and went back to the window. The Sunshine Café wouldn't open for another two and a half hours. It would be nice to be able to go down there right now, sit in a booth with a cup of coffee and let Isabella Valdez clarify his thoughts with her annoyingly positive energy field.

It would be even better to talk things over with her, but she wasn't a member of the Society, let alone a J&J employee. She probably didn't even realize that she was seriously psychic. If he tried to explain his work to her she would think he was a whacked-out conspiracy theorist who was not quite right in the head. There were enough people around already who held that opinion. He did not want her to come to the same conclusion.

43

"THE COLLEGE NOTIFIED ME THAT MY CONTRACT WON'T BE RE-
newed," Fletcher said. "But all things considered, I'm not complaining.
If you hadn't been there that night, I'd be dead. So I'm going to pay
your bill."

"Gee, thanks," Chloe said. "Because I'm certainly going to send it
to you."

He smiled ruefully. "Figured you would."

"There won't be any extra charge for Mr. Winters's services,
however."

Fletcher adjusted his glasses. "As far as I'm concerned he didn't do
me or the world any favors by dragging Madeline Gibson out of the
house. I still say he should have left her behind."

"He disarmed her, Fletcher. She shot my dog, and she was going to
shoot you next."

"The cops didn't say anything about Winters disarming her." Fletcher
scowled. "I was told that she suffered a psychotic break and collapsed."

"It was a little more complicated than that." But explanations would be even more convoluted, so she decided to stop there.

They were sitting in her office. The door to the reception area was partially ajar. Hector was stretched out on his bed, nose on his paws. He was no longer wearing the cone around his neck, and his bandage had been removed. Aside from the area on his head that had been shaved and stitched, he looked normal again. As was his custom, he paid no attention to Fletcher.

"I heard Madeline Gibson is still at Western Cove," Chloe said.

"Probably be there for a while," Fletcher said. "She confessed everything, but I hear she's still talking about the demon that came through the fire to get her. Definitely loony tunes."

"Sounds crazy, all right."

"Her lawyers will probably go for an insanity defense. The good news is that regardless of what happens she'll be locked up for a few years." He grimaced. "The way the criminal justice system works is that you can walk fairly easily on stalking and attempted murder charges, but for some reason the authorities tend to take arson seriously. Lucky me."

She heard the door of the outer office open and then Jack's low voice as he greeted Rose. Hector got to his feet and went through the partially opened door.

Chloe folded her hands on her desk and looked at Fletcher. "I'm sorry you lost your position at the college."

"I'll find another one." Fletcher lounged in his chair, cocked one ankle over his knee and studied her with a vaguely troubled expression. "Where have you been for the past few days? Every time I called, your assistant said you weren't available."

"I told you I had to go out of town on a case."

Fletcher raised his brows in faint amusement. "One of those woo-woo investigations you specialize in?"

"I never discuss my cases," she said coolly.

Fletcher switched to his serious therapist mode. "Chloe, your belief that you are psychic is directly linked to your intimacy issues. You really do need to get into therapy. I can help you."

"Funny you should mention my intimacy issues. My little problem appears to have resolved itself."

Fletcher was clearly startled. "How do you know that?"

Jack walked into the room.

"She knows it from firsthand experience," Jack said. He looked at Chloe. "Ready for lunch?"

Chloe smiled at him. "Yes, I am."

Fletcher glowered at Jack and then turned back to Chloe. "Thought he was a client."

"Not anymore," Chloe said. "Now he's my firsthand experience."

"What happened to your plans to live a celibate lifestyle?" Fletcher demanded.

"Turns out that didn't work for me."

THEY WALKED A COUPLE OF BLOCKS to a small restaurant just off First Avenue and ate fish tacos at a little round table. In the three days they had been back in Seattle they had established an intimate daily routine. They spent the nights together at her place. They ate breakfast together, and then they went their separate ways for the first part of the day. Jack showed up in her office for lunch, after which they both went back to their respective offices. They rendezvoused again at her place in the early evening. *Almost like being married*, Chloe thought. But *not quite*. Nothing was exactly like being married. Marriage was different.

"Fletcher seems to have recovered well from his ordeal," Jack offered.

"Yes. But he couldn't avoid the fallout from the gossip and rumors this time. The college is not going to renew his contract."

"Maybe he'll be more careful when he picks his next short-term girlfriend."

"Maybe, but I doubt it. Fletcher is Fletcher. He's got issues of his own. He just can't admit it to himself. How's the forensic financial-sleuthing business going?"

"There's progress, and there are dead ends," Jack said. "Lots of dead ends."

"Fallon Jones said the organization was good at covering its tracks."

"What I've got so far is a closely held corporation that owns three fitness clubs in the Northwest, including the one here in Seattle. All three gyms were independently owned and operated until last year. All three were facing bankruptcy and about to close. That's when they were acquired by a certain LLC."

"A limited liability corporation? Sounds promising."

"I think so. Something else very interesting about this particular chain of fitness clubs."

"What?" she asked, the investigator in her intrigued.

"Before they were acquired by the LLC, all three clubs catered to the Pilates and yoga crowd. But now the clientele seems to consist entirely of hard-core bodybuilders."

"Like the pair that tried to take us out?"

"Right."

She smiled. "You're thinking like a detective."

"I'm starting to realize that I always think like a detective. It's just that, until recently, the only thing I've been detecting is how to turn a profit."

"That's useful, too."

"Sure, but after a while it gets old. You know, the night they grabbed me I had been speculating to my friend Jerry about what it would be like if I woke up one morning and discovered that Winters Investments had folded."

"Wondering if you could rebuild it?"

He nodded and ate some more of his taco.

"The answer is yes," she said. "But you already knew that, didn't you?"

"Jerry said I was having a midlife crisis minus the blonde and the 'Vette."

"Instead you got me and a trip to Vegas."

Sexy laughter gleamed in his eyes. "Worked for me."

She finished her own taco and wiped her fingers on the napkin. "You like this, don't you?"

"You and Vegas? Well, you're a definite plus, but I could've skipped Vegas if I'd had to."

"I'm not talking about me and Vegas. I meant working with Fallon Jones on this conspiracy he's trying to shut down."

"It's interesting," he admitted.

"You weren't having a midlife crisis, Jack. You were just getting bored. You needed a challenge."

"I was also getting hit with the Winters Curse."

"It's not a curse," she said patiently.

He finished the taco. "I'm pretty sure that you were what I needed."

She thought about what Fletcher had said concerning her intimacy issues. "Evidently we are therapeutic for each other."

He looked amused. "Is that an academic way of saying the sex is good?"

No, she thought. It's a roundabout way of saying that I love you. But if she said the words aloud she would put him in the position of having to declare his own feelings. That could only go one of two ways: Good or bad.

It dawned on her that after all these years of trying to be honest with men, of trying to explain the serial monogamy concept and the fact that all her relationships were destined to be short-lived, she had finally found Mr. Right and now she was scared to death it wouldn't be permanent. Who would have thought that falling in love could be so terrifying?

44

CHLOE AND HECTOR WERE ON DAWN PATROL THE NEXT MORN-
ing when Mountain Man emerged from his crib in the alley where he
had spent the night. He adjusted the worn canvas duffel on his shoulder and leaned down to pat Hector.

"Hey, there, Big Guy," Mountain Man said. "How's it goin'? Looks
like that wound is healing okay."

"He's feeling much better," Chloe said. "How about you? Hector
wants to know if you're taking the meds they gave you at the clinic?"

"Yep. Right on schedule." Mountain Man reached into the pocket
of his old fatigues and produced a small bottle of tablets. "Got 'em
right here. Supposed to take 'em all week and then report back to the
clinic."

"That's great," Chloe said. "Hector wants to buy you a cup of coffee.
You got time?"

"Sure. Got nothin' but time."

They made their way to the coffeehouse on the corner. Chloe bought a cup of coffee and a breakfast pastry for Mountain Man. The barista gave Hector his usual day-old muffin. Chloe and Mountain Man sat at a table in the corner. Hector settled down beneath the table. Mountain Man liked having coffee with them, and it wasn't just the fact that the coffee and pastry were free. Chloe knew that for him it was a way of slipping back into a half-remembered dream of a time when he had lived a normal life.

"Hector wants to know if you've had any more nightmares," Chloe said.

"Last night was okay," Mountain Man said to Hector. "No dreams."

Her work was holding, Chloe thought, checking the psi prints on the coffee cup. Eventually the nightmares would return, but it looked like his dream spectrum was calm for now, or at least what passed for calm in Mountain Man's badly damaged dream psi.

Afterward they went back out onto First Avenue. A blanket of fog had settled over the city, sending it into a cold, gray twilight zone.

"Thanks for the coffee, Big Guy," Mountain Man said. He adjusted the heavy duffel that contained all his worldly possessions and gave Hector one last pat. "See ya."

Hector licked Mountain Man's hand.

"Good-bye," Chloe said. "Hector says to tell you not to forget the rest of those pills."

"I won't," Mountain Man assured Hector.

He turned and started off across the intersection, but he stopped midway and swung around. His weathered face was tightly knotted. Intelligence and a glittering urgency sparked briefly in his faded eyes.

"Hector," Mountain Man said. But his voice was different. No longer a vague mumble, it crackled with command.

Hector pricked his ears in response.

"You tell her to be careful," Mountain Man said, still speaking in that sharp, no-nonsense tone.

Chloe looked at him. "Hector wants to know why I should be careful."

"This morning feels like it did that other time," Mountain Man said. But the flicker of awareness was already fading from his eyes, and the military crispness in his voice was deteriorating back into a mumble. "At least I think it does."

"What happened the last time?" Chloe said. "Hector wants to know."

"Bastards were waitin' for us. Ambush. I could feel it. Told the lieutenant. He wouldn't listen. Said the intel was good. SOBs took him out first."

An icy shiver ruffled her senses. "I'll be careful."

Satisfied, Mountain Man continued on across the intersection.

She looked at the glowing footprints on the pavement. Beneath the layers of the unwholesome energy generated by addiction and mental as well as physical illness was the thin, wispy light of a measure of talent. It was no doubt one of the things that had kept Mountain Man alive when he and the others walked into that ambush in the desert. One of the things that kept him alive on the streets.

ROSE WAS AT HER DESK, deep into a heavy tome that bore the equally heavy title *Fundamentals of Psychology*. She looked up when Chloe and Hector came through the door.

"We need to talk, boss."

"That sounds ominous," Chloe said.

She went on into her office, sat down behind her desk and powered up her computer.

Rose slapped the book down and hurried into the inner office.

"I know you, boss," she said. "You're afraid that maybe Jack Winters is attracted to you just because you found that lamp for him, aren't you? That maybe what he feels for you is gratitude."

"Wouldn't be the first time a man went through that phase after a case was closed." She watched her calendar open. "Oh, good, I see you made a couple of appointments for me with new clients."

Rose glanced at the calendar. "The one this afternoon is Barbara Rollins. You did some work for her husband last year, remember?"

"I arranged for him to acquire some very nice Roman glass."

"Turns out Mr. Rollins died a couple of months ago. The widow is getting ready to sell his collection. She wants to talk to you about moving the pieces on the private collectors' market."

"The same way that her husband acquired them." Chloe made a note.

Rose cleared her throat. "Listen, about Jack Winters."

"What about him?"

"He may be feeling grateful to you, but that is definitely not why he is sleeping with you. By the way, speaking of sleep, do you realize that in the entire time I've known you, Jack is the only man you've allowed to stay overnight? This is huge, boss. A major breakthrough for you."

"Rose, I really do not want to talk about my private life."

"I'm just afraid you're going to screw up this relationship the way you have all the others."

"*Screw up?* I hate it when you use technical jargon. Sometimes I wish you would change majors. Ditch the psychology classes. How about accounting? We could use an accountant around here."

"You know what I'm talking about."

Chloe exhaled slowly. "I know what you're talking about, but I am not going to talk about it. Got it?"

Rose eyed her with an air of clinical speculation. "Wow. I don't believe it. You really are afraid you're going to screw up again, aren't you?"

"Terrified."

45

HIS NAME WAS LARRY BROWN, AND HE WAS THE QUINTES-
sential nerd. He was seventeen and a half years old, short, thin and
not the least bit athletic. He played chess, not football, and what
life he had he lived online. For as long as he could remember he had
been the chosen victim of every schoolyard, locker-room and classroom bully who came along. And sooner or later, a bully always came
along.

In school he had been able to avoid a lot of the traps the mean kids
set for him because he had a sort of sixth sense that warned him when
trouble was coming his way. But his keen intuition wasn't much help
against the biggest bully of them all, his father. A few months ago he
had done the only thing he could do to survive—he had left home.
Things on the streets weren't going well, however. The bad guys were
more dangerous than the classroom bullies, although none were any
worse than his dad.

But now, thanks to the online website he had stumbled across three weeks ago, his life was about to change forever. He was being offered the Holy Grail of all victims of bullying everywhere: Power.

"You've had three injections of the new version of the formula," Dr. Hulsey said. He filled a syringe from a small vial of clear liquid. "This will be the fourth. It should be more than enough to open the channels between your latent dream-psi energy and your para-senses. After that you'll be put on a maintenance dose in order to keep them open."

"I don't feel too good," Larry said.

He was sitting on the edge of a gurney in a small, white-walled room that looked unpleasantly like a medical examining room. He was shivering, and for some reason the fluorescent lights made his eyes water. The muffled clang and thud of heavy gym machines overhead was painful. Everything hurt.

"Don't worry," Dr. Hulsey said cheerfully. "The new version of the drug is very powerful and works very quickly. Your body and your senses just need some time to adjust to the rapidly rising levels of talent. You were approximately a Level Three when you came to us. Within twenty-four hours I have every expectation that not only will you be a Level Eight or Nine but you also will have an additional talent. It will be interesting to see what it is. Second talents, you understand, are quite unpredictable."

Larry watched Hulsey fill a syringe. He didn't like the doc. The guy was creepy, looked like an oversized praying mantis with glasses and a lab coat. But he was pushing past his intuition because the nice lady who had recruited him had promised that the results of the injections would be worth it. When this was all over he was going to be able to control people with psychic powers. How cool was that? No one would ever be able to bully him again.

Hulsey gave him the shot. It stung, just like last time. A flash of sick heat rolled through him. He felt nauseous.

"What happens now?" he asked.

"Now we wait," Hulsey said.

"For what?"

"For the lamp, of course."

"What lamp? Why do I need a lamp?"

Hulsey chuckled. "Well, for one thing, you'll die without it. But what really concerns me is that without the lamp, the entire experiment will be a failure."

46

SHE LEFT HECTOR ON GUARD IN THE FRONT SEAT OF THE CAR and went up the front steps of the imposing house. The residence was one of the many secluded homes on Mercer Island, an expensive chunk of land situated in the middle of Lake Washington.

Mercer Island real estate was a classic example of the oldest rule in the business: Location, location, location. The I-90 bridge linked the island directly to Seattle on the west and to the sprawling upscale suburban communities on the east side of the lake. Waterfront homes on Mercer Island were priced somewhere in the stratosphere. Large yachts were parked at the docks in front of the properties that rimmed the edge of the island.

She checked her watch and pressed the doorbell. Three o'clock.

The last time she had come here a housekeeper had opened the door, but today Barbara Rollins greeted her.

Barbara was an elegantly groomed woman in her midseventies. Her hair was silver white and cut in a short bob. Her beautifully tailored cream-colored trousers and pale blue silk shirt looked like they had come from the couture department at Nordstrom's. A small blue-and-cream scarf was knotted around her throat. There was a short stack of gold bangles on her left arm and some extraordinary rings on her fingers.

"Miss Harper," she said. Her voice was coolly polite with just the right touch of reserve that women in her position employed when dealing with salesclerks and the hired help. "Please come in."

"Thank you," Chloe said. She knew she could not achieve the same degree of refined reserve, so she went for confident and professional instead. The combination usually worked well with clients like Rollins.

She moved into the soaring, two-story foyer. A massive chandelier, in the unmistakable style of a famous Northwest glass artist, was suspended from the ceiling. It looked like an explosion of crystal flowers.

"Please come with me," Barbara said. "I want to talk to you before I show you the collection. As I'm sure you can understand, the decision to sell George's antiquities has been an extremely difficult one for me. He was quite passionate about the artifacts."

"I remember."

She followed Barbara Rollins into a glass-walled room done in classic old-school Seattle designer–style: beige-on-beige accented with wood. Beyond the windows was an extensive garden. Beyond the garden a boat dock jutted out into the lake. She was mildly surprised to see that the boat tied up at the dock was a small cabin cruiser. The last time she had called on the Rollinses there had been a large sea-going yacht sitting in the water.

Automatically she opened her senses and examined the heavy layer of psi prints in the room. Some of the tracks of dream psi were decades old. Footsteps on the carpet glowed faintly with the usual mix of human emotions—love, anger, excitement, yearning, sadness and loss. But none of the prints burned with the eerie heat that indicated powerful psychic ability. There was no sign of the disturbing acid-hued smoke that she had come to recognize as the hallmark of formula-enhanced talent.

The fact that she was even looking for evidence of Nightshade here in the home of an old client told her that her nerves and her senses were still on edge. She tried to relax and prepared to go to work.

"I don't see the yacht," she remarked.

"It went to my son and his wife," Barbara said. "But none of my children want the antiquities."

"Estate sales are often difficult," Chloe said gently. This was not the first time she had dealt with grieving spouses who felt guilty about selling off a collection of valuable objects that had been acquired by the dear departed.

"Please sit down, Miss Harper." Barbara gestured to a glass-and-beige-stone coffee table where two pots and two delicate china cups and saucers had been laid out.

Chloe sank down on one of the off-white chairs. She set her satchel on the floor at her feet.

Barbara indicated the gleaming silver pots. "Tea or coffee?"

"Tea, thank you."

Barbara picked up one of the pots. "As you know, George collected the antiquities over a number of years. I think he intended to leave them to a museum, but he never got around to making the arrangements. My son and daughter are encouraging me to sell the artifacts. But before I make any decisions I want to get some idea of the value of the various pieces. George trusted you. He said you were very reliable. Milk or sugar?"

"No, thank you."

Barbara handed her the cup and saucer. Then she poured some coffee for herself. "I suppose I shall have to think about selling the house now, as well. It's too big for one person. But I hate the thought of moving. This was our home for forty years."

"I understand," Chloe said.

She sipped some tea. In situations like this clients needed time to talk. She listened politely and tried not to glance at her watch.

Eventually, however, she set her cup down with a firm little clink of china on china.

"Shall we look at the collection, Mrs. Rollins?"

"Yes, of course. The gallery is at the back of the house."

Barbara put down her coffee cup and got to her feet. She led the way along a hall and stopped at a door that could have doubled as a bank vault. She punched in a code.

"George had this gallery built especially for the collection. State-of-the-art security all the way."

"I remember," Chloe said.

Barbara opened the heavy door and stood back graciously.

Chloe moved into the shadowed room. The space was filled with glass cases crammed with objects. A number of stone statues dotted the gallery. She set her satchel on a nearby table and started to open it. There was something wrong with the leather buckle. She could not seem to grasp it properly. A wave of dizziness hit her. She tried to focus, but the room was spinning and nothing made sense.

Tentacles of darkness reached out, wrapped around her and dragged her down into the depths.

47

"LET'S GO BACK TO THE START OF THIS THING," FALLON SAID. "How did they drug you?"

"I don't know. I went out for a couple of beers with an old friend and client," Jack said. "Jerry Bergstrom. That's all I remember."

"Eat anything?"

"No."

"Given the timing, whatever they used to knock you out had to be in the beer," Fallon said.

"I know what you're thinking. But I just can't see Jerry getting involved with Nightshade."

"The enhancement formula causes some major personality changes. None of them are good, trust me."

"He was the same old Jerry. He seemed genuinely worried about me."

"There's a para-hypnotist mixed up in this thing," Fallon reminded him. "The woman who showed up at Drake Stone's house in Vegas."

"I've been thinking about that." He went to stand at the window of the office. "It's possible that she got to Jerry. Maybe she gave him the drug and hypnotized him into using it on me. I'll have Chloe talk to him, see if she can pull up any lost memories the way she did with Stone."

"Do it," Fallon said. "Meanwhile, I think you're on to something here with this chain of gyms. The question now is, what do we do about it?"

"Shut them down?"

"Why am I always having to remind people that we're not the cops or the FBI."

"You didn't hesitate to put those five Nightshade labs out of business a while back."

"We had no choice," Fallon growled. "Zack and the Council agreed that with five labs running there was just too much of the formula being produced. We had to cut off at least some of the supply. We managed to make it look like accidental fires in all five cases. It helped that the labs were widely scattered up and down the West Coast and shared no obvious connection. But if three gyms here in the Northwest that just happen to be owned by the same private corporation go up in smoke someone will ask questions."

"Nightshade will guess it was Arcane," Jack said. "But do you care?"

"It's not Nightshade I'm worried about. They've got to know we're the folks who took down those labs. The problem with burning down the gyms would be arson investigators. We do not need that kind of attention from the authorities."

"The drawback to being a clandestine organization. Okay, so what are you going to do?"

"I'm thinking about that," Fallon said. "At this point Nightshade doesn't know that we've identified three of their recruiting centers.

They haven't even closed down the one on Capitol Hill where they held you for twenty-four hours."

"That's because they're depending on the amnesia drug they gave me to keep my memories suppressed."

"Lucky for us. I've got a couple of low-end auras watching the gym there in Seattle. We'll see what turns up."

"Are you going to try to get someone inside?"

"That's not an option," Fallon said, flat and unequivocal. "In order to do that an agent would have to subject himself to the formula. I can't allow anyone to take that risk."

"Maybe you can turn one of the Nightshade agents."

"Even if that were possible, he or she wouldn't be reliable. Like I said, there are serious personality changes with the drug. But with luck we'll get something useful from plain, old-fashioned surveillance on the gyms. The problem with surveillance is that it takes people, a lot of people. I don't have an unlimited number of agents to throw at this thing. Look, I've got to make some calls. Get back to me after you and Chloe have talked to your friend, Jerry."

"Sure." He waited for Fallon to end the connection with his customary abruptness. Instead there was silence on the other end.

"Fallon? Still there?"

"Yeah. I was just thinking."

"About?"

"About how long it's been since you and I went out for a beer. Maybe when this is over you and Chloe might want to take a little vacation. A long weekend or something."

"What does taking a vacation have to do with you and me going out for a beer?"

"You two could spend a couple of days here in Scargill Cove. Very picturesque place. You'd like it here. Weather's just like Seattle. Gray."

The phone went dead. Jack took it away from his ear and looked at it, wondering if he'd heard correctly. Had Fallon just invited him for a visit?

He shelved the question for another time and went back to contemplating the leaden sky. The tension within him was drawing tighter. He recognized it now because he'd experienced a similar sensation once before. It was the same restless, uneasy feeling that had hit him the night that Chloe had conducted the stakeout at Fletcher Monroe's house.

48

SHE AWAKENED TO THE MUFFLED CLANK AND THUD OF MA-chinery and a low moan. The latter was not a cry for help. It was the quiet anguish of a man who has given up all hope and longs only for death. The pitiful sound drew her up out of the darkness.

She opened her eyes and immediately closed them against the blinding glare of fluorescent lights.

"Ah, you're awake, Miss Harper. Excellent."

Cautiously she opened her eyes again but only partway this time. A thin, bony man in a rumpled white lab coat was leaning over her, studying her through a pair of black-framed glasses. The thick lenses gave his eyes an unpleasant, faceted look. His bald head gleamed like an exoskeleton in the harsh light.

"Who are you?" she whispered. Her voice sounded slurred, as if she'd had too much to drink.

"Doctor Humphrey Hulsey," he said. His insectoid eyes glittered with excitement. "Delighted to make your acquaintance, Miss Harper."

Squinting against the glary light she looked around the windowless room. White walls, the gleam of stainless-steel trays and counters, a guy in a lab coat and she was lying on a gurney. She knew this scene. It was straight out of Jack's memories of the place where he had been held prisoner.

Her head was clearing, but she felt uncomfortably warm. Her skin was so sensitive that the sheet that covered her was a source of pain. It dawned on her that she was running a fever. So much for the flu shot she had taken last month.

"Not a hospital," she whispered.

"No, Miss Harper," Hulsey said. "You're not in a hospital. You're in a research facility."

She wrinkled her nose. "Must be a pretty low-rent research facility. Smells like a basement."

"Yes, well, sometimes those of us on the cutting edge of science must make do with less than state-of-the-art equipment and technology. Funding is always a problem, you see."

Another weak moan rumbled through the wall behind her. The pain in the cry roiled her senses.

"Who is that?" she managed.

"His name is Larry Brown, I believe. I think of him as Subject A."

"What on earth is wrong with him?"

"I'm afraid that he's feeling some of the side effects of his treatment. I've made several modifications to the formula in recent months, but it is still quite unpredictable, especially when used in the higher doses required to induce additional talents."

"The formula." Anger surged through her, giving her strength. She pushed herself up on her elbows, vaguely surprised to discover that she was still wearing the clothes that she had worn to meet with Barbara Rollins. She was not shackled to the gurney. Evidently no one considered her potentially dangerous or likely to escape. "You've pumped him full of the founder's drug."

"It wasn't as if someone held him down and forced him to take the drug, I assure you," Hulsey said. "Subject A was a volunteer. That is the wonderful thing about my research projects. There is no lack of individuals who will do just about anything in exchange for a drug that will give them genuine psychic talents or enhance the ones they already have."

Larry Brown groaned again. She shuddered and then couldn't seem to stop shivering.

"And you call yourself a doctor," she said, disgusted. "So much for the first do-no-harm rule."

Hulsey was clearly affronted. "I am a research scientist. I come from a long line of talents endowed with a gift for science that can only be described as preternatural."

"Oh, right, that makes it okay to poison people." Her upper arm ached. Whoever had dumped her on the gurney had not been gentle.

"If it is any consolation," Hulsey said, "my interest in the formula has been peripheral until recently. I saw it, as my predecessors did, primarily as an adjunct to the main focus of my interests."

"Is that right? What are your interests?"

"Dream psi." Hulsey rocked a little on his heels and assumed a lecturing air. "Given your own talent, I'm sure you'll find what I am about to tell you quite fascinating."

"I'll bet."

He ignored the derisive tone. "Like a number of my ancestors, including the brilliant Basil Hulsey back in the Victorian era, I have long been consumed with a passion for solving the mysteries of dream energy. You see, Miss Harper, the dream-psi spectrum is still unknown territory. To this day no one can explain the act of dreaming to the satisfaction of any scientist. It is evident that the energy involved in dreaming is almost entirely paranormal in nature. Yet it remains virtually inaccessible in the waking state."

"Your goal is to tap into that energy?"

"Not only to access it but to study it and learn its secrets. The possibilities are endless." Hulsey sighed. "But one must pay the bills, eh? So, in exchange for providing me with the funding and the facilities that I require to conduct my research I have been obliged to contract with various groups and individuals over the years."

"Nightshade."

"I am currently involved with Nightshade, yes. But when I was much younger I worked for a clandestine government agency for a while. That was when I managed to re-create Sylvester Jones's formula with the help of Basil Hulsey's notebooks. After that department was closed down somewhat abruptly, I was obliged to form an alliance with William Craigmore. Does that name ring any bells?"

She struggled to concentrate. "The guy who founded Nightshade?"

"Indeed. I was his director of research. I still hold the position within the organization. Generally speaking, I begrudge the time I am forced to devote to perfecting Sylvester's drug. Nightshade cares only about enhancing certain talents. Really, it is like working for the government again. Until recently no one in the organization had exhibited any true appreciation for the science involved."

"That changed, huh?"

"A few months ago I was approached by an individual who made me an extraordinary offer, Miss Knight. She had in her possession the journal of one Adelaide Pyne."

Fighting the waves of feverish heat, she shoved herself to a sitting position and swung her legs over the edge of the gurney.

"The woman who worked the Burning Lamp for Griffin Winters back in the Victorian era," she said.

"Precisely. After I read the journal I realized that the lamp might be the key I had been searching for all these years, the device that could force open the channels between the dreamstate and the waking state and keep them open permanently in a stable fashion. I was very excited as I'm sure you can imagine. But Miss Knight informed me that there was a problem."

"The lamp had disappeared."

"Unfortunately, yes. She explained to me that she was trying to find it and that when she did locate it she would make it available to me for my research. In exchange, I agreed to run an experiment on a certain individual for her."

The incessant murmurs of pain coming through the wall were growing more anguished. She wanted to cover her ears with her palms to block out the terrible sounds, but she couldn't seem to muster the strength. She was shivering so hard now it took everything she had just to keep from falling off the gurney.

"Knight wanted you to run an experiment on that poor man in the other room?" she whispered.

"Not Subject A," Hulsey said impatiently. "Jack Winters."

She stilled. "You're the one responsible for kidnapping Jack. But why? What did you do to him?"

"Verified one of my associate's theories, of course. There was no point proceeding along that path if the first assumption proved false."

"*What* theory are you talking about?"

Hulsey frowned. "Why, that the men in the Winters line are immune to the side effects of Sylvester's formula."

She looked at him, appalled. "You injected Jack with the drug."

"Four times over the course of a twenty-four-hour period. Very high doses each time. He received more than enough of the drug to ensure a successful experiment. I had intended to keep him here another day or two to monitor the results, but he somehow managed to escape. No harm done, however. Miss Knight and I are both quite satisfied."

"You son of a bitch," she whispered. "I thought you said you only used volunteers."

"Come now, Miss Harper, we both know that it was highly unlikely

that Jack Winters would cooperate. It all had to be handled very delicately given his high profile not only within Arcane but also within the
business community. I was careful to use a strong, amnesia-inducing
sedative so that he would not remember anything of the experience. I
assured Miss Knight that if he survived, any memories that might come
back would seem no more than fragments of an unpleasant dream."

She hugged herself against the fever chills. "Bastard. You could have
killed Jack or driven him mad with that awful formula."

"I am happy to report that the experiment was, all in all, a complete
success. Winters seems to have done very well after being cut off the
drug. Miss Knight is not the only one who is pleased." Hulsey grimaced. "So is my current employer."

"What made Knight think that Jack could tolerate the formula?"

"Allow me to explain," Hulsey said, waxing enthusiastic. "The formula works by tapping into the latent power of dream energy. That's
how it enhances talents. It opens up the channels between the normal
and the paranormal, allowing access to the reserves of energy available
at the far end of the spectrum. But those channels are extremely narrow
and very fragile. Furthermore, once open, only continuous doses of the
drug can keep the channels functional. If the individual misses even a
couple of doses of the drug an irreversible instability sets in. The result
is insanity and death within a very short period of time."

"But that didn't happen with Jack."

"Miss Knight suggests, and I'm inclined to agree, that outcome is
likely the result of the genetic mutation created in Nicholas Winters all
those years ago when the lamp was first used on him. You see, the Burning Lamp accomplishes, essentially, the same thing that the formula
does. It opens up the channels between the dreamstate and the waking
state. But when the lamp was first used it evidently affected Nicholas's
DNA. Certain of his descendants, including Griffin Winters and Jack
Winters, evidently inherited a genetic ability to access the power of the

dreamstate naturally. They don't need the formula. From her reading of the Pyne journal, Miss Knight was convinced that age was a factor."

"Jack is thirty-six."

"Indeed. Miss Knight believed that if Jack had inherited the altered DNA the changes would have begun to manifest by now."

Outrage pulsed through her, as hot as the fever.

"Let me get this straight," she said. "You and this Miss Knight kidnapped Jack Winters and injected him with the formula to see if he was immune. After he escaped you sat back and waited to see what would happen to him. As far as you were concerned, he was just an experiment."

"Quite," Hulsey said cheerfully. "And a very interesting one, I must say. Following the escape we concluded that Winters was not only immune, he had, indeed, developed an additional talent. We agreed that there was no other way he could have overcome the guard. Miss Knight established a twenty-four-hour surveillance on Winters's residence. When he did not emerge for a few days, we thought that perhaps the experiment had failed. But when he finally did come out it was clear that he was in excellent shape."

"Except for the blackouts."

Hulsey frowned again. "What blackouts?"

She stopped breathing for a few seconds, trying not to show any reaction. If Hulsey did not know about the blackouts, it could only mean one thing: The watchers Jack had frightened into looking the other way when he had gone sleepwalking had never seen him. They didn't know that he had found his way back to the gym where he had been held captive.

She cleared her throat. "I just assumed that there would be blackouts, given the mix of the sedative and the formula."

Hulsey relaxed and chuckled. "Not at all. Winters is proof that the lamp can be used to stabilize the channels between the dreamstate and the waking state. It represents a huge advance over the formula. I must admit that I was very intrigued. The next step, of course, was to acquire the lamp and a strong dreamlight reader. Miss Knight was just starting to orchestrate such a search when, to our surprise, Winters himself contacted a certain private investigator who just happened to be a high-level dreamlight reader."

"That would be me."

"Indeed, Miss Harper."

"When you realized that Jack was searching for the lamp, the two of you waited to see if we would find it."

"Well, Miss Knight had not had any luck on her own, and there is that old legend, you know, the one that holds that only a strong dreamlight reader can find the lamp."

"I'm surprised to hear that you believe in myths and legends, Hulsey. Not exactly a scientific approach, is it?"

"Normally I would not give such a tale any credence, but in this case I made an exception. We are talking about a paranormal artifact, after all, one infused with a massive amount of dreamlight. It is entirely logical that a person with your unusual kind of talent would have an affinity for the lamp and, therefore, a better shot at locating it. Be that as it may, the plan worked."

"Except that your people failed in their attempt to steal the lamp. It's now in Arcane hands."

Hulsey chuckled. "Not any longer."

She gripped the edge of the gurney. "What do you mean?"

"The Burning Lamp was recovered from the Arcane vault yesterday and is now in our possession."

She was trying to wrap her brain around that disheartening news when another low moan sounded through the thin wall.

"Can't you do anything for him?" she pleaded.

"No, Miss Harper, I can't." Hulsey gave her a beatific smile. "Only you can save him."

49

"WHAT THE HELL DO YOU MEAN, IT'S GONE?" PHONE CRUSHED
in one fist, Jack used his other hand to rip open his office door. "It was
in an Arcane vault. It was supposed to be safe there."

"I told you, Zack and I have suspected for some months now that
Arcane has been infiltrated on several levels." Fallon's voice was a growl.
Tension and weariness pulsed in each word. "It's possible that one of
the Nightshade people works in the L.A. museum and has access to
the vault."

Jack went out into the hall, moving fast. "Great. You're hiring Nightshade operatives off the street to work in the Society's museums. Why
not just take out an ad in the paper? *Psychic sociopaths wanted. Excellent
benefits.*"

"In the past the Society hasn't had the time or personnel to conduct
anything more than routine background checks on low-ranking employees. I keep telling you, J&J is not some secret government agency with
unlimited funding. I'm one man trying to run the whole damn show."

Jack reached the elevator and leaned on the call button.

"I don't have time to listen to your excuses, Jones."

"What's going on? You sound like you're working out. Are you on a treadmill or something?"

"No. I'm trying to get out of the building. It's a high-rise. I'm waiting for the damned elevator."

"What's wrong?"

"Before I called you, I called Chloe's office. She never returned from her three o'clock appointment with a client. She's not answering her phone."

"Shit."

"Took the word right out of my mouth."

The elevator doors opened. He cut the connection, got inside and rode the cab down to the basement parking garage.

He made record time to the address on Mercer Island. Hector was inside Chloe's car, howling like a lost soul. When he saw Jack he ceased abruptly and waited, ears sharply pricked, every muscle taut, while Jack got the door open. Once free, he bounded out onto the pavement and charged up the walk to the entrance of the big house. He started barking wildly and clawed at the door, leaving deep grooves in the white paint.

The door opened just as Jack went up the front step. An elegant-looking woman in her early seventies appeared. Hector surged past her and disappeared into the house.

"What on earth?" The woman stared at Jack, mouth open, eyes widening with alarm.

She started to close the door. Jack got a foot in the opening.

"Mrs. Rollins?"

"I'm Barbara Rollins. Who are you?"

"Don't be afraid. I'm not going to hurt you. My name is Jack Winters. I'm a friend of Chloe Harper. She had an appointment with you at three today. She never returned to her office. I'm trying to find her."

"Miss Winters?" Barbara Rollins frowned in confusion. "Yes, I did have an appointment. Miss Harper arrived right on time. I remember now. But she left. I don't understand."

"Her car is still parked at the curb. Her dog was inside. He was howling."

"I heard a dog. I was going to call animal control." Barbara paused. Anxiety tightened her features. "But for some reason, I never got around to it. Every time I went to look for the phone number I got a headache."

"May I come in, Mrs. Rollins?"

"No, I don't know you."

Hector started barking again. He was somewhere at the rear of the house.

Barbara flinched.

"The dog," Jack said gently. "I should get him."

He used a small pulse of nightmare psi to make her nervous.

"Yes, the dog," Barbara said uneasily. "I can't have him running around my house."

Jack eased his way into the front hall. He found Hector at the sliding glass doors that overlooked the lake. When Jack opened the slider for him he rushed outside, charged across the garden and halted on the boat dock.

Once again he started to howl. Jack went out onto the dock and put his hand on the dog's head. Hector quieted. Together they looked at the empty dock.

"They took her away by boat," Jack said.

50

LARRY BROWN COULD NOT HAVE BEEN MORE THAN EIGHTEEN years old, and he was dying. A bulked-up hunter held open the door of the small room. Chloe took one step inside and halted. She thought she had been prepared, but she was, nonetheless, truly horrified. She hugged herself against the chills wracking her body.

"Dear heaven," she whispered. "How could you do this to him? He's just a kid."

Brown was lying on a gurney, leather restraints on his wrists and ankles. He was flushed with fever. His eyes were squeezed shut against the fluorescent light. The sound of her soft voice sent a shudder through him. He whimpered.

Hulsey followed her into the room and assumed a pedantic air. "Subject A has had four doses of the newest version of my formula, the same amount that was given to Jack Winters. We halted the drug last night. Dream psi is now spilling chaotically across his senses. He is not yet insane, but he soon will be unless you can save him with the lamp."

"That's impossible," she said quietly. It required everything she had to control her rage, but this was not the time to lose her temper. Hulsey might be quite mad, but he was, nevertheless, a scientist. Her only hope was that he would listen to reason. "I don't think the lamp will work on anyone else the way it did on Jack. Only someone with his level and type of talent can handle the power."

"Nonsense," Hulsey snapped. For the first time he appeared annoyed. "Power is power. Subject A was initially a Level Three on the Jones Scale but he has received enough of the formula to elevate him to a seven. That should be more than enough to handle the radiation from the lamp."

She bit back another argument. No one, including mad scientists, evidently, was immune to becoming obsessed with a theory. Hulsey was wrong, she was sure of it, but she knew that he was not going to listen to her.

Hulsey turned to the guard. "We're ready for the lamp."

"Yes, Dr. Hulsey."

Chloe went to stand beside the gurney. "Can you hear me, Larry?"

She was careful to keep her voice as low and soothing as possible. Even so, Larry Brown shivered. His senses were in such chaos now that any type of stimulation was no doubt extremely painful. He did not speak, but he opened his eyes a little and looked up at her. She saw that he was drowning in fever and terror. Very gently she touched his bound hand. He jerked in response. His lips parted in a silent scream. She maintained the light contact and cautiously opened her senses.

The shock of energy that snapped and crackled across her senses was almost more than she could stand in her feverish, weakened condition. Larry Brown's dreamlight was a dark storm of unstable psi. She managed to stay on her feet, but she had to grip the gurney rail to steady herself.

Another wave of outrage slashed through her when she saw the ravaging effects the formula had produced. Larry was well beyond being able to distinguish between his dreamscape and reality. He was living in a nightmare world.

There were voices at the door of the room. She looked up and saw two men. One of them was the hunter who had gone to fetch the lamp. He had it tucked under his thick arm.

The second man looked like a standard-issue corporate suit. He could have been an executive at an investment company. Rain dripped from his expensive coat. He wasn't bulked up like the bodybuilder hunters, but there was an air of powerful energy about him. Her senses were still open. She glanced down at his footprints. They burned with unstable, acidic fire. Whoever he was, he was taking the Nightshade drug.

"I see you were able to make it here in time for the experiment, after all, Mr. Nash," Hulsey said. He sounded sullen, even annoyed.

"There's a storm in Portland," Nash said coldly. "My plane was delayed. I told you I wanted to be on hand when you ran the test on the lamp. Why didn't you wait until you were certain I could get here?"

"There wasn't a moment to lose," Hulsey said. "Subject A is failing rapidly. Another hour or two and it might well be too late to intervene with the lamp."

There was no love lost between these two, Chloe thought, or even respect. Hulsey clearly despised Nash and, just as obviously, Nash could barely tolerate Hulsey. It was a marriage of convenience.

Nash examined Chloe for a few seconds. He did not appear impressed. She felt energy pulse and quicken in the atmosphere and knew that he had heightened his senses. She shivered again. Nash's prints were too murky and smoky to read, but it was clear that whatever the nature of his talent, it was very, very dangerous. It was equally evident that he was struggling hard to control it.

"This is the dreamlight reader you told me about?" Nash said to Hulsey.

"Yes." Hulsey did not bother to conceal his impatience. He took the lamp from the hunter and bustled across the room with it. "We were able to acquire her without incident a short time ago."

"You're certain your people weren't seen or followed?" Nash demanded.

"Absolutely, certain. Everything went like clockwork. The para-hypnotist took care of the woman on Mercer Island."

Chloe looked at Nash. "Who are you?"

"Your new boss." He paused a beat. "If you're successful here today, that is."

Fingers of crystal and ice played a staccato drumbeat down her spine.

Hulsey set the lamp on the table next to the gurney. "Time to run our little experiment, Miss Harper. And let's have no more nonsense about not being able to save Subject A. If you can't manipulate the energy of the lamp in a useful manner, we will have no more use for you, and that would be a pity, wouldn't it?"

She looked at the lamp. Power whispered in the atmosphere around it. *Jack is looking for you.* She knew that in her bones. Her only hope was to buy some time.

"Stand back," she said, trying to sound cool and authoritative, a woman of power.

"Certainly," Hulsey replied. His eyes glittered.

Nash did not move.

She put one hand on the lamp and pulsed a little psi into the waves of energy trapped inside the strange metal. Only Jack could access the full power of the artifact, but she could make it glow. That might be enough to convince Hulsey and Nash that she was activating it.

Energy stirred and shifted within the lamp. She knew everyone in the room could sense it. Larry Brown groaned and closed his eyes again.

The relic began to brighten.

"Yes," Hulsey breathed. "It's working. *It's working.*"

Nash shoved his hands into the pockets of his coat and moved a little farther into the room. His attention was fixed on the lamp.

She gave the relic a couple more pulses of power and managed to make it shine with the light of a pale moon. It did not become transparent, though. The gray gemstones remained opaque and there was no rainbow, but the transformation was dramatic nonetheless. Hulsey and Nash were clearly fascinated.

She switched her attention to Larry Brown. Carefully she probed for the currents of his dreamstate, bracing herself against the searing, disorienting waves of his drug-infused energy. The only thing that made her able to hold on was the knowledge that Larry would surely die if she retreated. Waves of dark dreamlight washed across her senses for a few seconds while she struggled to find some semblance of a normal, healthy pattern.

The taint of the formula was everywhere, distorting and disturbing Larry's natural rhythms. The chaos was growing because he lacked the strength to control the energy that the drug had released from the dream-psi end of the spectrum. The heavy, erratic waves would soon destroy his sanity and his para-senses.

But deep in the chaos there were still traces of his normal currents. She found them at last and set to work, easing calm, soothing energy into the fractured wavelengths.

There was no way to know if she was doing the right thing for Larry Brown. The experience with Jack was not applicable. His mind and body had fought off the effects of the drug and because of his genetic twist he was able to handle the currents of power unleashed from the dreamlight end of the spectrum.

But Larry Brown could not control the wild river of psi that was flooding his senses with an excess of paranormal stimulation. The only way to save him was to close down the channels that the drug had opened. It would not be the same thing as easing the disturbing currents of psi produced by her street clients' nightmares. What she was doing now would have far more profound effects on Larry Brown's senses, possibly permanent effects. She was winging it, going with her intuition, but that was all she had to work with.

Gradually she gained control. The raging, spiking currents began to respond to her careful, cautious counterpoint pattern. The wavelengths grew more stable and steady.

"It's working," Hulsey crowed softly.

Larry was visibly calmer now. His breathing slowed to a more normal rate. He opened his eyes, revealing tears of exhaustion, relief and gratitude. His fingers closed tightly around Chloe's hand.

"You're going to be fine," she said quietly.

"Thank you," he rasped.

He looked at her with something approaching adoration. She'd seen that expression before. She wondered if he would be feeling quite so grateful later when he discovered that in saving his sanity and his life she had destroyed his formula-enhanced abilities. In addition, there was no knowing if his mind would be strong enough to repair the damage done to his original talent. According to Hulsey, Larry Brown had come to Nightshade as a three on the Jones Scale. When he awakened he might not have any of his psychic senses left at all. Such a loss could be psychologically devastating.

"You need to sleep now," she said.

She gave him a little extra pulse. Larry closed his eyes and went to sleep.

With luck he would be out for a few hours. When he awoke Hulsey and Nash would realize that the experiment had failed. But she could not think of anything else to do. She needed to secure as much time as she could in order to give Jack a chance to find her.

Hulsey peered at the monitors on the wall. "Excellent, my dear. He is quite stable now. Precisely the effect I had hoped to achieve."

Not quite, she thought. She glanced at the lamp. It still glowed faintly from the initial burst of energy she had used to ignite it, but it was dimming rapidly.

"Working the lamp creates a heavy psi drain," she said. She did not have to fake the weariness in her words. "I've got to rest now. I'm ill."

Hulsey gave her an approving look. "Yes, of course, my dear. I do hope you appreciate what I have accomplished here today. I have pushed the boundaries of para-biophysics beyond even what Sylvester and Nicholas dreamed of doing."

"I'm thrilled for you." She really did need to lie down and maybe take some aspirin. The feverish sensation was getting worse.

Nash frowned. "How many doses has she had?" he said to Hulsey.

"Just one," Hulsey said absently. He was busy making notes. "But it was the new, experimental version. Quite potent. I gave it to her immediately after they brought her here. She was still unconscious. I'll give her another in two hours."

Chloe thought about the sore place on her upper arm. Panic slammed through her. "You injected me with the formula?"

"Yes, of course," Hulsey said, not looking up from his notes. "Mr. Nash, here, was afraid that you might not cooperate otherwise. I agreed with him. We wanted to make certain you were committed to the organization, as it were. From now on, you will need to take a dose twice a day. The good news is that after the first week you can switch to the tablets."

In the doorway, Nash smiled his reptilian smile. "Welcome to Nightshade, Miss Harper."

51

"YOU CAN'T GO IN ALONE," FALLON JONES SAID. "ALL I'VE GOT available are the two auras watching the gym. They're not trained for this kind of thing. Give me time to scramble some backup."

"Even if you manage to come up with a couple of hunters, it won't do any good," Jack said. "Your people would be outnumbered by the Nightshade freaks."

"I know you're something more than a strat now," Fallon said urgently. "But you're still just one man. What makes you think you can do this?"

"Power of positive thinking."

"How do you know they've got Chloe inside that gym? The auras haven't reported seeing any unusual activity in the alley or in front of the building."

"She's in there. Those bastards aren't the CIA or the FBI, either. They don't have unlimited resources any more than J&J does."

"You've got a point," Fallon said reluctantly.

"They could have smuggled her in through an underground entrance. Hell, maybe that's how they got me inside."

"It's a possibility. What exactly are you, Jack?"

"According to Chloe I'm still just a strat. But I'm a really strong strat. I'm turning off the phone now, Fallon. I don't want it ringing at the wrong time."

"No, wait, don't hang up—"

Jack cut the connection and hit the off key. He dropped the phone into his pocket, crossed the street and went down the alley behind the old brick building that housed the gym. It was only six o'clock, but at this time of the year it was already full dark.

There was a guard outside the rear entrance, but he was easily distracted by a wave of panic that had him staring, wide-eyed toward the opposite end of the ally. By the time he realized that the attack was coming from the other direction, it was too late. He swung around when he heard Jack behind him, reaching into his jacket with hunter-enhanced speed.

But there was no way even the strongest of hunters could move faster than a current of energy. Jack hit him with another sluicing wave of terror. The guard's mind could not handle the nightmare that engulfed him. He crumpled to the ground, unconscious.

Jack dragged him behind the nearby metal trash container and stripped him of his clothes, gun and keys.

Two minutes later, dressed in the guard's clothes, cap pulled down low over his eyes, he used the keys to enter the back of the gym. He generated small pulses of fear to make sure that the two burly-looking hunters he passed in the hall were distracted, unnerved and looking the other way when he went by.

There wasn't a large staff in the building. He hadn't expected to encounter a lot of people. As he had pointed out to Fallon, Nightshade was forced to work with many of the same limitations that applied to

J&J. In addition, maintaining a low profile was Job One for any self-respecting conspiracy that wanted to survive.

He found the stairwell and went down into the basement, emerging in a familiar corridor. This was the reverse of the route he had followed the night he had escaped, he thought.

He found the room where he had been held with no difficulty. Being a strat meant that you never had to stop and ask for directions.

There was a guard outside the door again, a strong indicator that Chloe was locked inside. He refused to let himself think of what the bastards might have done to her. That way lay madness. He had to stay focused, or he would be of no use to her.

52

SHE WAS LYING ON THE GURNEY, SHIVERING WITH FEVER WHEN
she heard the key in the lock. A few seconds later Jack came through
the door. He was dressed in the style of clothing worn by the guards,
right down to the cap, but she would have recognized him anywhere.
He dragged the unconscious body of the guard into the room and
closed the door.

"Are you okay?" he asked, coming toward her.

He was ablaze with psi. Energy swirled in the atmosphere around
him. The heat in his eyes could have ignited a fire. The only thing he
lacked was a flaming sword.

Avenging angel. In spite of the fever, she smiled.

"I knew you'd come for me," she whispered. She pulled some of her
own psi and used it to sit up on the edge of the gurney. "We're leaving
now, I assume?"

"Yes." He stopped in front of her, cupping her face between his
palms. "You're running a fever."

"I know. Fine time to come down with the flu, isn't it? Don't worry, I'm running a little psi to counteract the effects." This was not the moment to tell him that she had been injected with the drug. There was no knowing how he would react, and right now it was vital that he be able to focus.

"We'll talk later," he said. He took her hand and led her quickly toward the door. "We need to get out of here."

"I like a man who can prioritize."

He glanced down at her hand in his. "You're burning up."

"The psi on top of the flu. Has that effect."

"It's not the flu. They shot you up with that sedative they used on me, didn't they?"

"Something like that, but I'll be okay."

She could see that he wasn't buying her story, but she also knew that he was strat enough to realize that there was not a thing he could do about the fever.

"I'll go first," he said.

He released her hand, opened the door and moved cautiously out into the hall. She felt energy pulse a little higher around him and knew that he had just made someone out in the corridor very nervous.

"Okay," he said. "Walk ahead of me. Make it look like I'm escorting you to some other room."

She peered out into the hall. "Which way?"

"Left."

She took a deep breath and walked forward with what she hoped looked like weary reluctance. She didn't have to fake the weary part. Jack stayed close behind her.

At the intersection she stopped again.

"Right," Jack said quietly.

A door opened to her left just as she turned the corner to the right. Nash appeared. He had one hand on the knob, preparing to step out into the hall. He did not see her immediately because he was looking back into the room and speaking to someone else in low, tense tones. She could feel the disturbing energy of the lamp seeping out of the opening.

She halted and took a step back. But there was nowhere to run and no time. Nash was already swiveling toward her.

"After Brown wakes up and we've confirmed the success of the experiment, we're going back to Portland," Nash said to the other person in the room. "I want to make a few more trial runs before I let the Harper woman use that lamp on me."

"Yes, yes, I understand," Hulsey said impatiently.

Nash saw Chloe. Rage twisted his features.

"Who let you out of your room?" he snarled.

Jack came around the corner. "I did."

"Who the hell are you?"

Nash's fury was too sudden and definitely over the top, Chloe thought. It was as if he had skipped the more natural, preliminary stages of *confusion* and *annoyed authority* entirely and gone straight to *irrational loss of temper*. The Nightshade drug was affecting more than just his senses.

"Jack Winters," Jack said. "You stole a couple of things that belong to me. I'm taking both of them."

"Son of a bitch," Nash snarled. "You're not taking anything from me. You're a dead man."

A terrible blast of mind-searing energy crackled in the atmosphere of the hallway. Although Jack was the target, Chloe got caught in the backwash of power. It was as though the entire world had been set afire. White-hot psi consumed the corridor, blinding all of her senses. She reeled and fetched up hard against the wall. Consciousness started to slip away. She could not move, let alone try to flee.

She had guessed right, she thought. Nash did, indeed, possess a lethal talent. He was able to generate a killing shockwave of psychic energy.

Her vision blurred. Tears scalded her eyes. Jack was a dark figure silhouetted against the waterfall of energy. He had tried to rescue her, and he was going to die for his trouble. She had drawn him to his death, and there was nothing she could do.

The storm evaporated as suddenly as it had begun. She clawed at the wall in an attempt to stay on her feet. There was another kind of energy twisting and curling and pounding in the atmosphere now. She caught only fleeting impressions of nameless specters and heart-crushing fears, but it was enough to know that her avenging angel was exacting retribution and meting out punishment.

Someone was screaming, but it wasn't her. She did not have the strength. The screaming went on endlessly. Somewhere a man was sinking into hell.

Her badly fried senses began to clear. The screaming ceased abruptly.

She opened her eyes and saw Jack. He was still standing in the corridor, energy whipping around him. His eyes glowed like emerald coals.

"Are you all right?" he asked.

"Yes." She swallowed hard and managed to push herself away from the wall. "Yes. I'm all right. I think. You?"

"Yes. But one of them got away. There's another door at the back of the room."

She looked down and saw Nash. He lay in a dead man's sprawl on the floor of the office. His face was frozen in a mask of abject horror. His eyes stared sightlessly into nothing.

"Hulsey," she whispered. "He's the one that got away. The man on the floor is Nash. He seemed to be in charge. I think he said something about coming from Portland for the experiment."

Jack stepped over the body. He grabbed the lamp and came back to the doorway.

"Let's get out of here," he said.

Psi energy stirred within the lamp. As Chloe watched, the metal rapidly became opaque.

"Jack, you've lit the lamp," she whispered.

"We may need it."

"Why?"

"Remember you said that you were pretty sure the energy in this thing was meant to do something besides stabilize my dream psi?"

"Yes."

"I think you're right. I think I know what Nicholas created when he put the second set of crystals into the lamp. Why he went back to see Eleanor Fleming the third time."

She drew a deep, steadying breath. "Okay," she said. She pulled a little more psi to steady herself. "I assume we're going out the back way?"

"No, they'll have sealed off the alley. We'll go out the front door. They won't be expecting us to do that. Once we're outside in front of the building they can't touch us. It's only a little after six in the evening. There will still be people on the street. Too many witnesses."

"Everything has happened so fast. Maybe the guards don't know about us yet."

He glanced up. She followed his gaze and saw the security camera in the ceiling. Anyone watching would have realized by now that something odd had just gone down here in the basement. It was obvious that Nash was in a very bad way.

"Jack, I'm not sure I can do this," she whispered. "You've got a better chance on your own."

He smiled, as if genuinely amused. "Do you really think I'd leave you here?"

She almost smiled, too. "No."

"I came for you. I'm not leaving without you." He handed her the glowing lamp. "Here, hold this."

Reflexively she wrapped both hands around the heavy lamp. "I'm sorry, I don't think I can walk and carry this thing at the same time."

"You're not walking."

He picked her up in his arms and went forward, moving swiftly along the corridor. His powerful aura enveloped her. She drew some strength from him and clutched the lamp tightly. The relic was practically transparent now. The stones were heating with the colors of dreamlight.

He carried her to the stairwell. Holding the lamp in one arm, she reached down and opened the door. He climbed the two flights of stairs. She opened another door and they moved into a hallway marked *Restrooms*.

They went down the hall and into the main room of the gym.

There was a hushed, waiting stillness in the vast space. The overhead lights were off, but there was enough ambient street light filtering in through the glass doors at the front to reveal a band of heavily muscled men. They stood in a semicircle, blocking the route to the exit.

Chloe counted six bulked-up guards. Two more slithered out of the shadows behind one of the workout machines. Drug-tainted psi prints glistened evilly on the floor and fluoresced on the steel equipment.

Hunters, she thought. They would be as fast and as ruthless as a pack of wolves. Jack could not possibly have much energy left after what had happened downstairs in the basement.

"Don't hurt the woman," one of the men snapped. "She's valuable."

The hunters moved forward in a ring. Chloe watched them. If she could just make physical contact with one or two she might be of some use in the coming battle.

"Put me down," she whispered.

"No," Jack said. "We'll do this together."

"What do you mean?"

He didn't respond, but she was suddenly aware of the lamp growing warmer in her hands. Energy stirred and flashed as the alchemical metal shifted from translucent to crystal clear. The stones blazed with dreamlight.

Her feverish senses stirred. Intuitively she understood what Jack needed from her. She held the artifact aloft in both hands, summoned her waning reserves of psi and pulsed energy into the lamp, holding the currents of dreamlight steady for Jack. She understood then that he could somehow turn the lamp into a weapon, but he could not do it without her help.

All but one of the crystals ignited. Only the strange dark stone remained opaque. A rainbow of fire swept across the gym, drowning the hunters in a maelstrom of energy.

Jack's power did not crackle and pulse through the room—it *roared* silently through the space. And suddenly she understood. This was what she had done when she had worked the lamp for him in Las Vegas. She remembered the sense of a psychic key turning in a lock. She had unsealed Jack's ability to transform the lamp into a powerful weapon. In military terms the artifact was a force multiplier.

The third talent.

The hunters screamed. Their bodies jerked wildly in the intense ultralight cast by the stones in the lamp. One by one, they collapsed, unmoving.

Jack carried her through the tangle of bodies and the forest of gleaming stainless-steel machines out into the night.

"Avenging angel," she whispered. Darkness and fever started to claim her, but there was something she needed to say. "Promise me one thing."

His arms tightened around her. "Anything."

"Whatever you do, don't let Arcane give me the antidote."

"*Those bastards injected you with the formula?*"

She could hardly talk now. "Yes. But don't tell anyone."

"*Chloe.*"

"Just say I collapsed because of the heavy psi drain."

"You can't ask that of me. I won't lose you because you refuse the antidote."

"Don't worry, I'm immune. Just like you."

"What the hell are you talking about?"

"I'll explain later. All I need is a little time to fight off the effects of the drug. Just as you did. Promise me you won't let Arcane know what happened. If they give me the antidote, I might lose my para-senses for good."

"But how can you know you're immune to the formula?"

"I'm a dream-psi reader. I get my talent from the dreamlight end of the spectrum, same as you. I'm pretty sure that all of us who have an affinity for that kind of energy are naturally immune."

"*Pretty* sure."

"Okay, very sure. Makes sense when you think about it."

"How does it make sense?"

"Later." She could no longer keep her eyes open. "Right now I need you to trust me. Promise me you won't let anyone give me the antidote."

He hesitated. "Only if you promise me that you won't die."

"I'll be fine. Trust me, Jack."

"All right," he said. "No antidote."

"One more thing."

"You're real chatty for someone who is running a sky-high fever."

"I love you," she said.

She sank down into sleep. The last thing she remembered was the comforting strength of his arms and his power wrapping her close.

She thought she heard him say *I love you, too,* but maybe that was just a dream.

53

THE PHONE RANG JUST AS FALLON WAS SCOOPING AN EXTRA spoonful of Bold Roast into the filter basket of his industrial-size coffeemaker. He would have preferred to go across the street to the Sunshine Café for another cup, but the little restaurant had closed, as always, promptly at five thirty. As was his newfound custom, he had watched Isabella Valdez turn over the sign in the window. And, as was her custom, Isabella had looked up and waved cheerfully at him. Then she had walked the four blocks to the inn, where she rented a room.

He grabbed the phone midway through the first ring. "What do you have for me, Jack?"

"I've got Chloe. She's safe. We're out of the gym. If you get someone in there quickly you'll find a dead high-level Nightshade agent named Nash. We think he's from Portland. There are also a bunch of unconscious drug-hyped hunters. At least they were all unconscious when we left. Guy named Hulsey got away through what looked like an underground tunnel. That must have been how they smuggled Chloe inside without the auras noticing."

Fallon forgot about the coffee and everything else around him. He felt as if he'd been winded by a body blow.

"Hulsey?" he repeated. "Are you certain that was the name of the man who got away?"

"That's how he introduced himself to Chloe. Claimed to be the director of research for Nightshade."

"Humphrey Hulsey, Basil Hulsey's descendant." While he talked, Fallon picked up another phone and punched in a code. "We recently found out that's how Nightshade got the drug in the first place. Basil Hulsey worked on the formula for the First Cabal in the late eighteen hundreds."

"I remember the story."

"Hulsey left his notes and journals to his son, who passed them on down through the family. A couple of months ago we learned that one of those descendants, Humphrey Hulsey, was responsible for creating the new version of the drug. What did they want with Chloe?"

"It all goes back to the usual problem. The formula is inherently unstable and the results unpredictable. They figured that maybe Chloe could work the lamp to correct those issues."

"Hell. I need to talk to Chloe, but I don't have time right now. I'll call you back after I get my people into that gym."

"Don't send anyone in without plenty of backup."

"Oh, sure, like I've got plenty of backup available. Haven't you been listening? I'd send Zack in, but unfortunately he and Raine are in L.A. this week. There is one illusion-talent, who may or may not be available, in the Seattle area. He gets results, but it's usually best not to ask how."

He cut the connection to Jack and started talking urgently to the man who had answered the other phone.

The illusion-talent listened in silence.

"I'll take the job," he said. He cut the connection.

Fallon tightened his hand around the phone and took a deep breath. He did not consider himself the imaginative type, but something about the illusion-talent's ice-cold voice succeeded in chilling his senses for a couple of heartbeats. He did not like using the guy, but sometimes he had no choice when it came to agents.

He punched in Jack's number. There was no answer. He tried Chloe's cell and then her office phone.

"You have reached the office of Harper Investigations. We are unable to take your call, but if you leave a name and number we'll get back to you."

He cut the connection and sat at his desk for a while, wondering why Jack and Chloe had gone off the radar. There was only one reason that made any sense. Something had happened to Chloe while she was inside the gym. Jack was protecting her.

54

JACK'S VOICE CAME THROUGH THE DARKNESS, PULLING HER back to the surface. "Chloe, can you hear me?"

"Sure." She could feel his hand wrapped tightly around hers. She opened her eyes and looked up at a familiar ceiling. "No place like home."

"Welcome back," Jack said. His stark features were drawn hard and taut. She sensed a subtle pulse of psi.

"You're not sleeping again," she accused.

"Not for the past twenty-four hours," he said. "I'll live."

"What day is it?" she asked.

"Thursday. I carried you out of that Rollins gym the night before last."

"And he's been sitting here at your bedside ever since," Rose announced from the other side of the bed. "We all have."

At the foot of the bed, Hector got to his feet and ambled across the quilt to lick Chloe's face. She grimaced and patted him.

"Please tell me he hasn't been drinking out of the toilet bowl again," she said.

Rose looked at Jack across the width of the bed. "Definitely back to normal. I'll get her a glass of water. She needs fluids after that fever."

Memory came slamming back. Chloe clutched Jack's hand.

"Am I okay? You didn't let Arcane do anything to me, did you?"

He smiled a little. "As far as Fallon knows you're resting after your traumatic ordeal."

"What time is it now?"

Jack checked his watch. "It's just going on seven o'clock in the evening."

"That certainly explains why I have to go to the bathroom. Excuse me." She pushed the covers aside and got to her feet. Belatedly she glanced down and saw that she was wearing a nightgown. The gown and the bed were damp with sweat.

"Rose insisted on being the one to undress you," Jack said.

She felt herself grow warm, not with fever this time. "Well, it's not as if you've never seen me naked."

"No. But Rose seemed to think you would be embarrassed later. Something about your intimacy issues combined with being vulnerable because you were asleep."

"Right. Intimacy issues." She pushed herself off the bed and hurried down the short hall into the bathroom.

Hector padded after her and settled down outside the door to wait for her. *Abandonment issues*, she thought. *What the heck, we've all got issues.*

She looked into the mirror and saw a woman who had just survived a raging fever. It was not, she thought, an attractive sight. Her hair was matted with dried perspiration, her complexion was wan and dehydrated and her eyes showed clear evidence of the strain and exhaustion. She was not exactly a candidate for Miss Perky of the Month, but she was alive, reasonably sane and when she cautiously opened her senses she realized she still had her talent. *Thanks to Jack*, she thought. He had trusted her and kept his promise.

She smiled at the woman in the mirror. Suddenly she felt a lot better than she had a few minutes ago.

When she emerged from the shower she found Rose busy in the small kitchen. Jack had made a pot of herbal tea. They drank it in front of the window, looking out at the view of the old-fashioned streetlights of Pioneer Square glowing in the rainy night.

"Did you tell Fallon Jones about my theory that dreamlight talents are immune to the formula?" Chloe asked.

"Didn't know it was a theory," Jack said, his tone a little too neutral. "On the way out of the gym you said that you were sure you were immune."

She cleared her throat and reached for her mug. "Yes, well, I was almost positive. Anyhow, did you tell him?"

"No. Thought I'd leave the explanations to you."

Rose spoke from the kitchen. "Fallon Jones has called every hour on the hour since Jack brought you back here. I turned off all the phones. Doesn't that man ever sleep?"

"Not a lot, apparently," Chloe said.

There was a short silence. Chloe looked at Jack.

"So now we know the origin of the Cerberus legend," she said.

He nodded once, understanding immediately. "The third talent is the ability to use the lamp as a weapon."

"I still say it's all a single talent. And don't forget, it takes two people to work the lamp that way."

He said nothing for a moment.

"What are you thinking?" she said.

"I'm thinking that we don't tell Fallon Jones exactly what the lamp can do. Arcane doesn't need any more Winters legends."

She smiled. "Don't worry; Harper Investigations takes client confidentiality very seriously."

"Speaking of Fallon, I'm ready to give him a call. I want to find out what happened after we left the gym. There was nothing in the morning papers yesterday or today, so it looks like Arcane and Nightshade managed to keep things low profile."

"Nothing beats a couple of clandestine paranormal organizations when it comes to keeping secrets," Chloe said. "By the way, I think I know what happened to Adelaide Pyne's journal. A woman named Victoria Knight has it."

"About time you called," Fallon growled. "Chloe okay?"

"I told you that she was fine," Jack said.

"You lied. But I'm getting used to it."

"She needed rest. I didn't want you disturbing her. What happened at the gym?"

Fallon exhaled slowly. "Not much. The illusion-talent I sent in found Nash's body and a bunch of unconscious guards but not much else. Hulsey was long gone."

"What did he do with the body?"

"I didn't ask," Fallon said.

"What about computers? Hulsey's notes? Files?"

"The agent retrieved a few items of interest, but nothing that looks useful. Evidently Hulsey grabbed the essential stuff when he fled."

"Probably had it all on a computer that he took with him when he escaped through the tunnel. What about the hunters?"

"They all recovered consciousness and were offered the antidote. Four of them accepted. They're being treated now, but I doubt that we'll get anything useful out of them. Nightshade operatives at that level never know much."

"What about the ones who didn't accept the antidote?"

"The illusion-talent let them go," Fallon said wearily. "Not much else we can do. If Nightshade follows its usual pattern and cuts them loose, they'll all be dead soon. We tried to warn them, but these guys were seriously indoctrinated. It's like they'd joined a cult."

Jack thought about that. "Maybe that's how Nightshade recruits at the lower levels."

"Presents itself as a cult?" Fallon asked.

"When it comes to moneymaking businesses, nothing beats a cult except maybe the drug trade."

"I need to think about that angle," Fallon said. "We did find one guy who might be of some use. Says his name is Larry Brown. He was asleep in one of the basement rooms. Tied to a gurney. Claims a woman saved his life. The description he gave fits Chloe. Put her on."

"Later," Jack said. "She's going to eat dinner first."

"Damn it," Fallon said. But there wasn't a lot of heat in the curse.

Very gently Jack ended the connection.

55

SHE RETURNED FALLON'S CALL AFTER SHE FINISHED THE LIGHT
meal of poached eggs and salad that Rose prepared. She sat ensconced
in her big reading chair, Hector on the floor beside her, Rose fuss-
ing around her. Jack went into the kitchen to make another pot of
herbal tea.

"What the hell happened night before last?" Fallon demanded.

"Well, let's see if I can summarize," she said. "A woman named Victoria Knight somehow got hold of the journal of Adelaide Pyne. Knight
teamed up with Humphrey Hulsey to see if the lamp was the solution
to the problem of the inherent instability of the formula."

"Ninety-eight percent probability that Victoria Knight is our missing para-hypnotist," Fallon said. "It fits."

"You may be right. At any rate, Hulsey's boss, Nash, was also involved. They had me kidnapped because they wanted to see if I could
work the lamp to stabilize a very unstable talent they had created with
the formula."

"Larry Brown?"

"Right. I can light the lamp, of course, but only Jack or someone with his particular psychic genetics can access the deep power in the thing. So, to buy some time I sort of faked the whole lamp scene. I'm a Harper, remember? I can do fake. Anyway, after Larry went to sleep—"

"Hang on," Fallon cut in. "Are you telling me you saved Brown *without* using the lamp?"

"The formula, like the lamp, works by opening up channels between the dreamstate and the waking state. I have an affinity for dream psi."

"I know, but—"

"I resealed the dreamlight channels that had been opened by the drug, but I didn't have a chance to study Larry Brown's entire spectrum, so I don't know how much damage the formula did. Hulsey told me that Larry was a Level Three before they injected him. The poor kid might not have any talent left when he recovers. I'm so sorry."

"Brown was flown down to L.A. this morning," Fallon said. "He's being tested in the Arcane lab there. Early indications are that he's now a Level Two. The techs think it's possible he might recover to a Level Three. They're running around in circles like a bunch of hamsters on a wheel trying to figure out how some of Brown's para-talent survived both the heavy dose of the formula and the subsequent withdrawal. By all rights, the kid should be certifiably insane by now."

Relief washed through her. "Larry will be okay, then?"

"Looks like it, thanks to you. You're a walking antidote, Chloe Harper. Hell, you're better than the antidote we've been using because you can get rid of the effects of the drug without destroying the victim's senses. Not that I'm expecting a big rush of people looking to get off the Nightshade drug."

"Because of the cult mentality?"

"And because when the drug works, it does deliver a higher level of talent. How many people are going to want to give up real power?"

"Yes, but the long-term complications—"

"Most folks don't think long-term. Just ask the cigarette companies. I'm sure Nightshade is aware that we have an antidote but we haven't exactly had a run on it."

"In other words, they're selling the perfect drug."

"The perfect poison, as Lucinda Bromley called it in her journal."

"Bromley? Wasn't she the woman who married your ancestor, Caleb Jones?"

"Right. My multi-great grandmother. The second J in J&J. And don't say it."

"Don't say what?"

"Lately people keep telling me that I need a partner, too. But it would have to be someone I could trust completely, the same way Caleb Jones trusted Lucinda. Someone with a high level of intuitive talent so that she could almost read my mind because I can't explain everything that I do. Not a nine-to-five type who takes vacations, either. I need someone who is available twenty-four/seven. I'm not interested in a partner or a wife, but I'm starting to think that maybe an assistant might work."

She smiled. "An assistant who can read your mind, who will be available twenty-four hours a day and who never takes vacations. Good luck with that, Mr. Jones."

"Thanks," he said, oblivious. "Getting back to the antidote, do you think you could help someone who has already received it to regain her para-senses?"

"I don't know."

"A couple of months ago we used the antidote for the first time on a woman named Damaris Kemble. Long story. Let's just say we saved her life and her sanity, but she hasn't recovered her para-senses and the experts tell me that she probably never will."

"What was she before she got the antidote?"

"A Level Seven. The para-shrinks told me that, although at first she was relieved just to be alive, she's now sinking into a severe depression."

"That's not surprising. The loss of a high level of talent would be enough to cause anyone to become depressed."

"I'll have her flown up there as soon as possible. See what you can do. Send your bill to me by e-mail when you're done. By the way, I like to see *itemized* bills, not just big round numbers."

She was struck speechless for a few seconds. "You want me to work for J&J?"

"I'll start recruiting other dreamlight readers as fast as I can, but I've got a feeling that only those who are as strong as you will be able to do what you did for Larry Brown. There just aren't that many talents like you around. Arcane needs you."

"But I'm a Harper."

"I'm a Jones. What of it? I don't give a damn where I get my talents as long as I can trust them to get the job done."

She felt a strange rush of what could only be described as panic. "I live in Seattle. The nearest Arcane lab is in L.A. I really don't want to move there. This is my home. I've got family and clients here."

"The new Master of the Society lives up there near you."

"Oriana Bay. Yes, I know, but what does that have to do with it?"

"Zack and his wife, Raine, don't want to move, either. Given that Zack is now in charge of Arcane, he gets what he wants. Arcane has rented office space in the Seattle area and is getting ready to set up a lab. Meanwhile, I don't see any reason why you can't work out of your office. It's not like you're going to be overwhelmed with ex-Nightshade clients."

She took a breath. "Okay, I guess."

"I'll have Damaris Kemble in your office before noon tomorrow. Give me a complete report after you talk to her. And don't forget, I want all time and expenses itemized. Oh, and tell Jack I'm sending another team to pick up the lamp tomorrow."

The phone went dead in her ear.

She looked at Jack. "He's sending someone to pick up the lamp tomorrow."

"Is he, now?" Jack handed her a mug of tea. "Isn't that nice of him? And after Arcane did such a swell job of taking care of it last time."

She sipped some of the tea and lowered the mug. "Well, at least he doesn't know exactly what the lamp can do."

"This is Fallon Jones we're talking about. He's going to be wondering how I took down all those hunters at the gym. If he hasn't already figured out that the lamp was a factor, he will soon enough."

She studied him. "What are you thinking?"

"I'm thinking that it's probably a good idea that everyone, including Fallon Jones, the Council and Nightshade, believe that the lamp is safely back in Arcane's hands."

56

"THE FORMULA MADE ME SO GHASTLY ILL," DAMARIS KEMBLE said. She spoke in a monotone, as though just the act of talking was no longer worth the effort. "I thought anything would be better than feeling that sick. But after I recovered I began to realize what I had lost."

Fallon Jones had not wasted any time. Damaris had arrived at ten o'clock the following morning. She was not traveling alone. A J&J hunter accompanied her. Rose and Hector were presently entertaining him in the outer office.

"I think I understand," Chloe said gently. "It would be like waking up one day and discovering that you had lost one or more of your normal senses."

Damaris squeezed her eyes shut to stop the tears. "Sometimes I dream that I've recovered my sensitivity. But as soon as I open my eyes I realize that nothing has changed."

"You said that you didn't just lose your para-senses. You also lost your father and your sister at the same time. That would be a terrible blow for anyone."

"I'm seeing one of the Society's psychologists, but I don't think it's doing much good. I feel so overwhelmed. If I could just get back to feeling normal I think I could deal with the rest of it. Do you really feel you might be able to help me recover at least some of my talent?"

Chloe looked at the floor. The faint oil-on-water sheen of the antidote radiated subtly in Damaris's footprints.

"Let me see what I can do," Chloe said.

She got to her feet, walked around the desk and took Damaris's hand. Carefully, lightly, delicately, she went to work.

57

"I NEVER FOUND OUT WHY DAMARIS KEMBLE NEEDED A BODY-guard," Chloe said.

It was five o'clock. She and Jack were accompanying Hector on his evening patrol. It was that mysterious time in a Seattle winter day, the hour when the city was enveloped in the strange half light of deep twilight. The streets glistened with rain, and the streetlights glowed like crystal balls in the mist.

"Didn't Fallon tell you?" Jack asked.

"It's remarkably difficult to get information out of Mr. Jones."

"He's not much of a conversationalist," Jack agreed. "The reason Damaris Kemble needs a bodyguard is that she's the daughter of the founder of Nightshade."

"Good grief. She's Craigmore's daughter?"

"He had her on the latest version of the drug. It was making her violently ill, probably killing her. After her father died Arcane offered her the antidote. She agreed to take it. In exchange she's been telling J&J and the Council everything she knows about Nightshade."

"So the concern is that Nightshade might try to silence her."

"Right. Unfortunately, according to Fallon, she doesn't really know all that much about the upper management of the organization."

"Because her father didn't tell her much?"

"William Craigmore was a secretive bastard. When he established Nightshade, he planned the organization so that no one individual or even a handful could bring down the entire operation. It's damn brilliant when you think about it. Fallon says Arcane still knows next to nothing about the others at the top of the conspiracy."

She glanced at him. "But you said the money trail is a weak point."

"Money is always the weak point. It's the blood of any organization. Cut it off, and things start to die."

"How are you doing tracking the cash flow from the gyms?"

"Looks like the LLC that owns and operates them was, in turn, receiving funding from another privately held company located in Portland, Oregon. Cascadia Dawn. It's a regional wholesaler that distributes nutritional supplements and health food products."

She smiled at the cool satisfaction in his words.

"Sounds like a good cover for an organization that is making an illicit drug," she said.

"It's a hell of a cover. Fallon isn't rushing in this time. He's going to put Cascadia Dawn under surveillance for a while. See if he can learn anything useful. But it's probably just one more Nightshade lab like the others that J&J took down a couple of months ago. We might get some information, but I doubt that it will give us the guys at the top."

She smiled. "We? Us? As in you are now officially on J&J's payroll?"

"Are you kidding? J&J can't afford my consulting fees. This is strictly pro bono work."

"But you like it."

He shrugged. "It's a challenge."

"Which is just what you've been needing. Now what?"

"Now we have to talk."

She froze in midstep, her fingers tightening around Hector's leash. He halted and looked back politely to see why his routine had been interrupted.

Jack stopped, too, and turned to look at her. She felt energy flare.

"The other night when I carried you out of that Nightshade hellhole you told me that you loved me," he said. "Did you mean it, or was that the fever talking?"

And just like that, courage sparked inside her. Or maybe it was the realization that nothing mattered but the truth and the possibility of making a dream come true.

She let go of the leash and put her arms around Jack's neck. "With you, I always feel a little feverish. But, yes, I love you."

He framed her face with his hands. "Enough to think long term?"

"You sound like you're negotiating a business contract."

"I love you, Chloe. But I can't do the short-term, serial monogamy thing with you. It's all or nothing."

"All," she said. "Definitely all."

He pulled her close and kissed her there in the winter dreamlight.

58

FALLON JONES GAZED DEEPLY INTO THE COMPUTER, READING the report that Chloe Harper had just e-mailed to him.

. . . The problem with the antidote is that it takes a sledgehammer to do what is essentially a job for a seamstress working with fine needles and silk thread. The hammer works, but in the process creates damage of a different kind. However, I'm sure that Damaris Kemble will recover most, although probably not all, of her natural para-senses.

I'll look forward to examining more cases for J&J. Please find my itemized bill attached . . .

He filed the report and leaned back in his chair, thinking. Jack had given him some serious static about returning the lamp to Arcane, insisting that it remain in his custody in Seattle until an investigation had been conducted into the theft.

It was a reasonable request. The investigation had begun, but it was probably going to take a while, possibly a couple of weeks or more, to find the Nightshade operative who had infiltrated the museum's staff, assuming there was an infiltrator. The other possibility was that the para-hypnotist, Victoria Knight, who had drifted through the case like a ghost, had simply walked into the museum, turned a few heads with a couple of well-placed hypnotic suggestions, and walked out with the lamp.

Just as a woman named Niki Plumer had walked out of Winter Cove Psychiatric hospital after the Oriana case. A few more things went click. He watched lines appear on the multidimensional construct that existed out on the paranormal plane, connecting dots.

In two or three weeks Jack would no doubt give the L.A. museum a very interesting artifact. It would be safely locked away in the vault. Additional security measures would be put in place.

But two or three weeks was a long time, certainly long enough for a family of psychically gifted forgers to create a very good copy of the original . . .

Footsteps sounded on the stairs, interrupting his thoughts. An odd sense of anticipation whispered through him. He had not had any visitors since Grace and Luther left, and he wasn't expecting anyone. Whoever was coming upstairs was probably bringing the new computer he had ordered online. It struck him that he was in a bad way if he was actually looking forward to a visit from the delivery guy. But the regular carrier was a man. The footsteps were feminine, not masculine.

A sudden jolt of awareness snapped through him. He checked his watch. It was six o'clock. The Sunshine Café had closed half an hour ago. He had watched Isabella wave to him and walk away toward the inn, her umbrella raised against the steady rain. It couldn't be her.

She had gone home for the night. She had no reason to come here, anyway.

There was something about the pattern of those footsteps on the stairs, though. He *knew* them.

He sat very still, waiting for the knock. It came a few seconds later. He started to call out to her; to tell her to enter. The words got jumbled up in his throat. It dawned on him that a gentleman would open the door.

Galvanized, he stood and started around the desk. The door opened before he got three steps. Isabella walked into the room, rain dripping from her coat and the folded umbrella. She smiled.

"I'm here about the position," she said.

He finally found his tongue. "What position?"

"The one that's open here at Jones & Jones."

"I never advertised a job."

"No need to put an ad in the papers." She looked around the cluttered room with great interest. "It's obvious you need an assistant. You're in luck. I've always wanted to work in a detective agency, and I've been looking for something that pays a little better than the Sunshine Café. People in this town are lousy tippers. Except for you."

He suddenly knew exactly what the expression *deer in the headlights* meant.

"I hadn't gotten as far as thinking about how much the position will pay," he said, grasping at straws.

"Not a problem." She plopped her umbrella in the old Victorian umbrella stand, the one that had graced the original offices of J&J. "I'll handle the accounting and financials from now on. Get you organized. No need for you to worry about pesky details. I'm sure you have much more important things to do."

"Miss Valdez, you don't understand. This is not an ordinary investigation agency."

She took off her raincoat and hung it on the elaborately wrought cast-iron coatrack, another relic from J&J's early years in London.

"I know," she said simply.

Shock reverberated through him. "*How* do you know?"

"Because you are not an ordinary man." She gave him a brilliant smile. "It looks like we'll need to order a second desk. I'll get on that right away."

59

PHYLLIS WAS SEATED IN THE GRAND WICKER CHAIR IN THE
sunroom, her feet propped on the matching footstool. She had the morning paper in one hand and a cup of tea in the other. She looked up when
Chloe entered the room. Then she glanced at the floor behind her.

"Well, well, well," she said. Quiet satisfaction hummed in the words.
"You've fallen in love with him, haven't you?"

"I can sleep with him, Aunt Phyllis."

Phyllis laughed. "Under most circumstances that would not be much
of a testimonial. But in your case I think that says it all. And when do
I get to meet Mr. Winters?"

Jack walked into the sunroom. "How about today?" He crossed the
floor to the chair and offered his hand. "Jack Winters. It's a pleasure to
meet you, Miss Harper."

Phyllis examined him from head to toe and then she glanced at the
floor he had just crossed. She smiled and took his hand. "I am delighted
to make your acquaintance, Jack. I hope you'll stay for tea."

"Yes," Jack said. "I'd like that." He looked at Chloe and smiled.

Chloe sensed the dreamlight swirling in the sunroom. Waves of energy danced invisibly between the two of them. The light was strong and steady. She knew it would link them for the rest of their lives.

"We would both like that," she said.

60

THE OPERATION HAD NOT BEEN AN UNQUALIFIED SUCCESS.
The lamp was back in an Arcane vault, and she knew that it would not
be easy to steal it a second time. But there was no point taking that risk
again, anyway. It was clear that the experiment had failed. Larry Brown
had survived but only because of something that the dreamlight reader,
Chloe Harper, had done to him. He certainly had not come out of the
situation with a second talent or even an enhanced version of his original
ability. He had no doubt lost all of what little talent he had possessed.

Conclusion One: Her grandfather's theory was wrong. The Burning
Lamp could not take the place of the formula. It appeared to work only
on someone with the Winters psychic DNA.

Conclusion Two: The lamp could not be used to stabilize the effects
of the enhancement formula.

Conclusion Three: Judging by the fact that Jack Winters and Chloe
Harper had escaped from the gym, it appeared that there was some
truth to the legends and rumors that had always swirled around the

lamp. It was some kind of psi weapon, but it appeared extremely likely that only a Winters could access the full power of the artifact.

She'd had two major objectives when she conceived the plan. Although it was disappointing to discover that the lamp could not be used to enhance her own talent or to protect her from the effects of the formula, her second goal had been achieved. And in a spectacular fashion, if she did say so, herself.

John Stilwell Nash had been destroyed.

Her only regret was that Nash had died without ever having had a chance to appreciate the irony involved. He could not have known that the person who had set him up for the fall could trace her own family roots back to the same ancestor, John Stilwell.

The alchemists Sylvester Jones and Nicholas Winters were not the only ones who had fathered offspring after subjecting themselves and their genes to dangerous experiments designed to enhance their psychic powers. Back in the Late Victorian era, her own ancestor John Stilwell, a powerful talent enthralled by the new theories put forward by Darwin, had run a few breeding experiments of his own. Generations later, she and Nash were both the result of two of the experiments.

It was Stilwell who had stolen the secret of the enhancement drug from Arcane. Although he had never used Sylvester's formula himself, fearing its dangerous side effects, he had managed to produce some highly talented offspring, using his intuitive understanding of the laws of psychical genetics. Stilwell had died at the hands of Gabriel Jones before seeing any of his children grow to adulthood. But his bloodline had survived. She was living proof.

She walked to the window of her office and looked out over the rain-soaked city of Portland. This morning John Stilwell Nash's superior had offered her the position that Nash had recently vacated. Tomorrow she would walk into Nash's old office at Cascadia Dawn, the cover business for one of the organization's few surviving drug labs.

From there she would work her way into the Inner Circle. Her ultimate objective was now clearly in sight. In due course she would become the Mistress of Nightshade.

The knock on the door made her turn around.

"Come in," she said.

The door opened. Humphrey Hulsey skittered into the room. He removed his glasses and began polishing them furiously.

"I know that you are disappointed with the outcome of the experiment, Miss Knight," he said earnestly, "but I'm afraid that is the nature of cutting-edge science. There are always a number of failures before one makes the great breakthrough."

"I understand, Dr. Hulsey. It is unfortunate that the lamp did not work as we had hoped. However, unlike my predecessor at Cascadia Dawn, I do appreciate the nature of the scientific process, and I am prepared to accept some failures. We will now move forward together."

Hulsey stopped polishing his glasses. He blinked several times.

"Together?" he said.

"Of course. You are now my director of research. At the start of the Burning Lamp project I promised you the fully equipped lab and funding that you require for your dream work. That is what you will receive."

Hulsey glowed. "Thank you, Miss Knight. You won't be sorry."

"I'm sure I won't. You see, unlike so many before me who have been obsessed with the formula, I do understand that the secrets to enhancing talent in a stable fashion are locked in dream-psi research."

"Yes, yes," Hulsey said excitedly. "That is what I tried to explain to Mr. Nash, but he refused to listen. Both the formula and the lamp work by accessing the latent energy of the dreamstate. But dream psi is inherently unstable. That has always been the source of the problems with the drug. Until I can solve some of the riddles connected with the dreaming process I will never be able to deliver a stable, reliable version of the formula."

She smiled. "Then it is a good thing that neither you nor I have been foolish enough to take the formula ourselves, isn't it?"

He snorted derisively. "A very good thing, indeed, Miss Knight. Really, it astonishes me how otherwise seemingly intelligent people in this organization are so eager to dose themselves with such an unstable drug. Ridiculous."

The fact that neither of them was on the drug was a secret between herself and Hulsey. In an organization run by formula-dependent talents, being free of the drug gave them an edge. But it also made them vulnerable. If the higher-ups ever discovered that she and Hulsey were not using the drug, it would be a death sentence for both of them. The board of directors insisted that all members of Nightshade be on the drug. It was the ultimate form of personnel management, the ultimate form of control.

"We are a team, Dr. Hulsey," she said.

"A team," he agreed.

61

THEY DROVE DOWN TO NORTHERN CALIFORNIA AFTER THE wedding, making a honeymoon out of the road trip. They followed the old route, Highway 101, hugging the spectacular coastline. Hector rode in the backseat, his nose stuck out the window as much as possible. At night they stayed at charming windswept inns, including one aptly named Dreamscape in a little town called Eclipse Bay.

They arrived in Scargill Cove in the early evening. The lights still burned in the offices of Jones & Jones. Chloe and Jack climbed the stairs to the second floor, bags of groceries in their arms, Hector at their heels. On the landing Jack raised his hand, but the door opened before he could knock.

Fallon stood in the opening, looking out at them with a bewildered expression.

"Jack," he said. He looked at Chloe. "You're Chloe."

"And you're Fallon Jones." She smiled. "Nice to meet you in person after all we've been through together."

"What are you two doing here?" Fallon asked.

"Honeymoon," Chloe explained. "We've got a room at the inn down the street." She indicated the bags of groceries. "We heard there's no decent restaurant open after five thirty, so we picked up a few things. I'm going to cook dinner for all of us."

Fallon was beyond bewildered now. He looked poleaxed.

"Dinner?" He repeated, as if the word and the concept were new to him. "As in home cooking?"

"Right," Chloe said. "Do you mind?"

"Uh, no." Fallon frowned. "No, I don't mind."

"Where's the kitchen?" she prompted.

"It's sort of attached to my office." He glanced over his shoulder as though searching for the kitchen.

Jack held up the six-pack in his hand. "Figured you and I could have a couple of beers while Chloe's fixing dinner."

Fallon's expression cleared. He stood back, holding the door open.

"I'd like that," he said. "I'd like that a lot."

PROLOGUE FOR
DREAMLIGHT BOOK II

London, late in the reign of Queen Victoria . . .

It took Adelaide Pyne almost forty-eight hours to realize that the Rose-stead Academy was not an exclusive school for orphaned young ladies. It was a brothel. By then it was too late. She had been sold to the frightening man known only as Mr. Smith.

The Chamber of Pleasure was in deep shadow, lit only by a single candle. The flame sparked and flared on the cream-colored satin drapery that billowed down from the wrought-iron frame above the canopied bed. In the pale glow the crimson rose petals scattered across the snowy white quilt looked like small pools of blood.

Adelaide huddled in the darkened confines of the wardrobe, all her senses heightened by dread and panic. Through the crack between the doors she could see only a narrow slice of the room.

Smith entered the chamber. He barely glanced at the heavily draped bed. Locking the door immediately, he set his hat and a black satchel on the table, for all the world as though he were a doctor who had been summoned to attend a patient.

In spite of her heart-pounding fear, something about the satchel distracted Adelaide, riveting her attention. Dreamlight leaked out of the black bag. She could scarcely believe her senses. Great powerful currents of ominous energy seeped through the leather. She had the unnerving impression that it was calling to her in a thousand different ways. But that was impossible.

There was no time to contemplate the mystery. Her circumstances had just become far more desperate. Her plan, such as it was, had hinged on the assumption that she would be dealing with one of Mrs. Rosser's usual clients, an inebriated gentleman in a state of lust who possessed no significant degree of psychical talent. It had become obvious to her during the past two days that sexual desire tended to refocus the average gentleman's brain in a way that, temporarily at least, obliterated his common sense and reduced the level of his intelligence. She had intended to take advantage of that observation tonight to make her escape.

But Smith was most certainly not an average brothel client. Adelaide was horrified to see the seething energy in the dreamprints he had tracked into the room. His hot paranormal fingerprints were all over the satchel as well.

Everyone left some residue of dreamlight behind on the objects with which they came in contact. The currents seeped easily through shoe leather and gloves. Her talent allowed her to perceive the traces of such energy.

In general, dreamprints were faint and murky. But there were exceptions. Individuals in a state of intense emotion or excitement generated very distinct, very perceptible prints. So did those with strong psychical abilities. Mr. Smith fit into both categories. He was aroused and he was a powerful talent. That was a very dangerous combination.

Even more unnerving was the realization that there was something wrong with his dreamlight patterns. The oily, iridescent currents of his tracks and prints were ever so faintly warped.

Smith turned toward the wardrobe. The pale glow of the candle gleamed on the black silk mask that concealed the upper half of his face. Whatever he intended to do in this room was of such a dreadful nature that he did not wish to take the chance of being recognized by anyone on the premises.

He moved like a man in his prime. He was tall and slender. His clothes looked expensive and he carried himself with the bred-in-the-cradle arrogance of a man accustomed to the privileges of wealth and high social rank.

He stripped off his leather gloves and unfastened the metal buckles of the satchel with a feverish haste that, in another man, might have indicated lust. She had not yet had any practical experience of such matters. Mrs. Rosser, the manager of the brothel, had informed her that Smith would be her first client. But during the past two days she had seen the tracks the gentlemen left on the stairs when they followed the girls to their rooms. She now knew what desire looked like when it burned in a man.

What she saw in Smith's eerily luminous prints was different. There was most certainly a dark hunger pulsing in him, but it did not seem related to sexual excitement. The dark ultralight indicated that it was another kind of passion that consumed Smith tonight and it was a terrifying thing to behold.

Adelaide held her breath when he opened the satchel and reached inside. She did not know what to expect. Some of the girls whispered about the bizarre, unnatural games many clients savored.

But it was not a whip or a chain or leather manacles that Smith took out of the satchel. Rather, it was a strange, vase-shaped artifact. The object was made of some metal that glinted gold in the flickering candlelight. It rose about eighteen inches from a heavy base, flaring outward toward the top. Large, colorless crystals were set in a circle around the rim.

The waves of dark power whispering from the artifact stirred the hair on the nape of her neck. The object was infused with a storm of dreamlight that seemed to be trapped in a state of suspension. *Like a machine,* she thought, astonished—*a device designed to generate dreamlight.*

Even as she told herself that such a paranormal engine could not possibly exist, the memory of a tale her father had told her, an old Arcane legend, drifted, phantomlike through her thoughts.

Smith set the artifact on the table next to the candle. Then he went swiftly toward the bed.

"Let us get on with the business," he commanded. Tension and impatience thickened the words.

He yanked aside the satin hangings. For a few seconds he stared at the empty sheets, evidently baffled. An instant later, rage stiffened his body. He crushed a handful of the drapery in one fist and spun around, searching the shadows.

"Stupid girl. Where are you? I don't know what Rosser told you, but I am not one of her regular clients. I do not make a habit of sleeping with whores and I certainly did not come here tonight to play games."

His voice was low and reptilian cold now. The words slithered down her spine. At the same time, the temperature in the chamber seemed to drop several degrees. She started to shiver, not just with terror, but with the new chill in the atmosphere.

He'll check under the bed first, she thought.

He seized the candle off the table and crouched to peer into the shadows beneath the iron bed frame.

She knew that he would open the wardrobe as soon as he realized that she was not hiding under the bed. It was the only other piece of furniture in the room that was large enough to conceal a person.

"Bloody hell." Smith shot to his feet so swiftly that the candle in his hand flickered and nearly died. "Come out, you foolish girl. I'll be quick about it, I promise. Trust me when I tell you that I have no plans to linger over this aspect of the thing."

He stilled when he saw the wardrobe.

"Did you think I wouldn't find you? Brainless female."

She could not even breathe now. There was nowhere to run.

The wardrobe door opened abruptly. Candlelight spilled into the darkness. Smith's eyes glittered behind the slits in the black mask.

"Silly whore."

He seized her arm to haul her out of the wardrobe. Her talent was flaring wildly, higher than it ever had since she had come into it a year ago. The result was predictable. She reacted to the physical contact as though she had been struck by invisible lightning. The shock was such that she could not even scream.

Frantically, she dampened her talent. She hated to be touched when her senses were elevated. The experience of brushing up against the shadows and remnants of another person's dreams was horribly, gut-wrenchingly intimate and disturbing in the extreme.

Before she could catch her breath, she heard a key in a lock. The door of the chamber slammed open. Mrs. Rosser loomed in the entrance. Her bony frame was darkly silhouetted against the low glare of the gaslight that illuminated the hallway behind her. She bore a striking resemblance to the nickname that the women of the brothel had bestowed upon her: the Vulture.

"I'm afraid there's been a change of plans, sir," Rosser said. Her voice was as stern and rigid as the rest of her. "You must leave the premises immediately."

"What the devil are you talking about?" Smith demanded. He tightened his grip on Adelaide's arm. "I paid an exorbitant price for this girl."

"I just received a message informing me that this establishment is now under new ownership," Rosser said. "It is my understanding that the former owner has recently expired. Heart attack. His business enterprises have been taken over by another. Don't worry, your money will be refunded."

"I don't want a refund," Smith said. "I want this girl."

"Plenty more where she came from. I've got two downstairs right now who are younger and prettier. Never been touched. This one's fifteen if she's a day. Doubt if you'd be the first to bed her."

"Bah. Do you think I give a damn about the girl's virginity?"

Rosser was clearly startled. "But that's what you're paying for."

"Stupid woman. This concerns a vastly more important attribute. I made a bargain with your employer. I intend to hold him to it."

"I just told you, he's no longer among the living. I've got a new employer."

"The business affairs of crime lords are of no interest to me. The girl is now my property. I'm taking her out of here tonight, assuming the experiment is completed to my satisfaction."

"What's this about an experiment?" Mrs. Rosser was outraged. "I never heard of such a thing. This is a brothel, not a laboratory. In any event, you can't have the girl, and that's final."

"It appears that the test will have to be conducted elsewhere," Smith said to Adelaide. "Come along."

He jerked her out of the wardrobe. She tumbled to the floor at his feet.

"Get up." He used his grip on her arm to haul her erect. "We're leaving this place immediately. Never fear, if it transpires that you are of no use to me, you'll be quite free to return to this establishment."

"You're not taking her away." Rosser reached for the bellpull just inside the door. "I'm going to summon the guards."

"You'll do nothing of the kind," Smith said. "I've had quite enough of this nonsense."

He removed a fist-sized crystal from the pocket of his coat. The object glowed blood-red. The temperature dropped another few degrees. Adelaide sensed invisible, ice-cold energy blazing in the chamber.

Mrs. Rosser opened her mouth, but no sound emerged. She raised her arms as though she really were a great bird trying to take wing. Her head fell back. A violent spasm shot through her. She collapsed in the doorway and lay very still.

Adelaide was too stunned to speak. The Vulture was dead.

"Just as well," Smith said. "She is no great loss to anyone."

He was right, Adelaide thought. Heaven knew that she'd had no fondness for the brothel keeper, but watching Rosser die in such a fashion was a horrifying, entirely unnerving experience.

Belatedly, the full impact of what had just happened jolted through her. *Smith had used his talent and the crystal to commit murder.* She had never known that such a thing was possible.

"What did you do to her?" Adelaide whispered.

"The same thing I will do to you if you do not obey me." The ruby crystal had gone dark. He dropped it back into his pocket. "Come along. There is no time to waste. We must get out of here at once."

He drew her toward the table where he had left the artifact. She could feel the euphoric excitement flooding through him. He had just murdered a woman and he had enjoyed doing it—no, he had *rejoiced* in the experience.

She sensed something else as well. Whatever Smith had done with the crystal had required a great deal of energy. The psychical senses required time to recover when one drew heavily on them. Smith would no doubt soon regain the full force of his great power, but at that moment he was probably at least somewhat weakened.

"I'm not going anywhere with you," she said.

He did not bother to respond with words. The next thing she knew, icy-cold pain washed through her in searing waves.

She gasped, doubled over and sank to her knees beneath the weight of the chilling agony.

"Now you know what I did to Rosser," Smith said. "But in her case I used far more power. Such intense cold shatters the senses and then stops the heart. Behave yourself or you will get more of the same."

The pain stopped as abruptly as it had begun, leaving her dazed and breathless. Surely he had used the last of his reserves to punish her. She had to act quickly. Fortunately he was still gripping her arm. She required physical contact to manipulate another individual's dreamlight energy.

She raised her talent again, gritting her teeth against the dreadful sensations, and focused every ounce of energy she possessed on the currents of Smith's dreamlight. In the past two years she had occasionally manipulated the wavelengths of other people's nightmares, but she had never before attempted what she was about to try now.

For an instant Smith did not seem to realize that he was under attack. He stared at her, mouth partially open in confusion. Fury quickly tightened his expression.

"What are you doing?" he demanded. "You will pay for this. I will make you freeze in your own private hell for daring to defy me. *Stop.*"

He raised his other arm, perhaps to reach back into his pocket for the crystal. But it was too late. He was already sliding into a deep sleep. He started to crumple. At the last second, he tried to grab the edge of the table. His flailing arm knocked the candle off the stand and onto the floor.

The taper rolled across the wooden floorboards toward the bed. There was a soft whoosh when the flame caught the trailing edge of the satin drapery.

Adelaide rushed back to the wardrobe and took out the cloak and shoes that she had stashed inside earlier in preparation for her escape. By the time she was dressed, the bed skirt was fully ablaze, the flames licking at the white quilt. Smoke was drifting out into the hall. Soon someone would sound the alarm.

She pulled the hood of the cloak up over her head and went toward the door. But something made her stop. She turned reluctantly and looked back at the artifact. Smith had called it a lamp, but it did not look like any lamp that she had ever seen.

She knew then that she had to take the artifact with her. It was a foolish notion. It would only slow her down. But she could not leave it behind.

She stuffed the lamp into the black satchel, fastened the buckles and started once more toward the door. She paused a second time over Smith's motionless figure and quickly searched his pockets. There was money in one of them. The dark ruby-colored crystal was in another. She took the money but when she touched the crystal, she got an uneasy feeling. Heeding her intuition, she left it where it was.

Straightening, she stepped over Rosser's dead body and moved out into the corridor.

Behind her the white satin bed was now engulfed in crackling, snapping flames. Down the hall someone started screaming. Men and women in various stages of dress and undress burst out of nearby doorways, seeking the closest exits.

No one paid any attention to Adelaide when she joined the frantic crush on the staircase.

Minutes later, she was outside on the street. Clutching the satchel, she fled into the night, running for her life.